# HER BEST KEPT ROYAL SECRET

## LYNNE GRAHAM

# SHY INNOCENT IN THE SPOTLIGHT

## MELANIE MILBURNE

MILLS & BOON

First Published in Great Britain 2021
by Mills & Boon, an imprint of HarperCollins*Publishers* Ltd,
1 London Bridge Street, London, SE1 9GF

www.harpercollins.co.uk

HarperCollins*Publishers*
1st Floor, Watermarque Building,
Ringsend Road, Dublin 4, Ireland

Her Best Kept Royal Secret © 2021 Lynne Graham

Shy Innocent in the Spotlight © 2021 Melanie Milburne

ISBN: 978-0-263-28261-0

09/21

MIX
Paper from
responsible sources
FSC™ C007454

This book is produced from independently certified FSC™ paper
to ensure responsible forest management.
For more information visit www.harpercollins.co.uk/green.

Printed and bound in Spain
by CPI, Barcelona

# HER BEST KEPT ROYAL SECRET

## LYNNE GRAHAM

MILLS & BOON

# CHAPTER ONE

'WHEN AM *I* going to marry?' Angelino Diamandis rolled his dark heavily lashed eyes with slumbrous amusement in receipt of his brother's question.

Christened Angel by his friends, it being an in-joke that he was anything but angelic, the ruling Prince of Themos sprawled back on the upholstered ottoman in an untidy but indisputably graceful tangle of long lean limbs and simply smiled over his cup of coffee. The movie-star good looks that had long made him a favourite of the paparazzi had rarely been more breathtakingly obvious.

Prince Saif of Alharia, clad in the traditional silk finery of a bridegroom, studied his younger half-brother with an unimpressed frown. 'Why are you smiling? As though I had asked you something foolish? You are a head of state and one day, just like me, you must marry. Neither of us has a choice.'

That last statement was voiced without resentment or self-pity, Angel acknowledged, wryly amused by his brother's heartfelt sense of duty and honour. Saif still rejoiced in a streak of naivety that Angel had never had. Saif had been surrounded from birth by all the safety

barriers a devoted elderly father considered necessary
to conserve his only son's happiness and security.

Angel, in comparison, had never known either parental love or parental protectiveness although he had
never admitted that to a living soul. He had been raised
by servants and sent to boarding school, his parents
much craved but distant figures on his horizon…until
he'd gained the maturity to see what they were *really*
like. Catching his mother in bed with his best friend at
the age of fifteen had been a cruel wake-up call to reality, and being exposed to his father's equally grubby
activities had been crushing. He had learned that all the
money, privilege and status in the world couldn't com-
pensate for an essential lack of decency and good taste.

Angel had, however, left his brother with his innocent illusions intact about the mother who had abandoned him and her first husband, the Emir of Alharia,
to run off with Angel's father. Queen Nabila and her
equally self-indulgent second husband, King Achilles,
had, after all, died in a helicopter crash when Angel
was sixteen. There was no good reason now to tell Saif
the ugly truth about the mother he had never known.

'Not much choice when it comes to marrying,' Angel
conceded ruefully. 'But I still wouldn't have agreed to
go into an arranged marriage with a bride I haven't met,
as you have done.'

'You *know* the precarious state of my father's health.'

'I do, but I also think you will eventually have to
stop tiptoeing around him.'

Saif stiffened defensively. 'You say that because I
have not yet had the courage to tell my father about my
relationship with you…and I've hidden you away here

in a forgotten part of the palace to conceal your presence in Alharia on my wedding day.'

Angel nodded gently. 'We are not children who need to hide wrongdoing,' he murmured wryly. 'Our mother grievously betrayed your father, but our blood tie should not be denied because of her behaviour.'

Saif looked troubled, too honest a man to deny that fact. 'In time I will tell him that we have a sibling relationship.'

Annoyed that he had taken his bad mood out on his serious older brother by reproaching him, Angel changed the subject. 'I will not be entering an arranged marriage as such when I wed but I have already chosen my bride.'

'You are in love?' Saif flashed him a sudden smile of mingled surprise and approval. 'I had not thought you would even recognise that possibility.'

'And you were right,' Angel interposed. 'I'm not in love and neither would Cassia be. She is simply the most suitable woman I know to take on the role of Queen, although to be frank I have not yet discussed the subject with her. It is merely that I know her practical views on marriage. Status and wealth appeal most to her.'

'Cassia!' Saif sliced in, his consternation unhidden because he had clearly been taken by surprise by that familiar name. 'That *frozen* blonde?' Breaking off midsentence, Saif reddened at his lack of tact and compressed his lips shut again before concluding, 'Forgive me... I was—'

Angel shifted a dismissive hand and laughed with genuine appreciation. 'No, Cassia and the iceberg that sank the *Titanic* do have much in common,' he responded equably. 'But that's the type of wife I would prefer. I don't want an emotionally incontinent bride or a demanding one or one likely to be unfaithful or careless of appearances. Cassia will suit me and my needs as the ruler of Themos very well indeed. Our sole challenge would be the production of an heir because I don't think she is a very physical woman, but no doubt we would deal with that requirement when the time arrives…and neither of us would be in any hurry to get to the altar. I am only twenty-eight and she is twenty-five. According to our constitution, I cannot be crowned King until I marry or produce an heir.'

Saif dealt him a remarkably sombre look. 'Such a bloodless arrangement won't work for you, Angel. You have much more heart than you are prepared to admit. Even if Cassia seems the perfect candidate now, at some stage of your life you will want *more*,' he declared.

Angel simply laughed again, utterly unconvinced by that sentimental forecast, indeed, only his respect for his brother killing the scornful rebuttal ready to leap to his tongue. He had never been in love in his life, and he didn't believe he was capable of that kind of self-delusion. It was his belief that love was more often the excuse for the dreadful things that people did. His mother had told him that it had been her love for his father that had made her desert her first husband. Of course, she hadn't even mentioned the infant son she had left behind at the same time, he recalled in disgust, or the fact that she had already been pregnant with Angel by Prince Achilles. Too often, Angel had seen friends treat each other badly and employ love as a justification for cheating, lying and betraying the trusting or the innocent. He was a realist. He knew exactly what sort of marriage he would be getting if he wed a woman like Cassia and that brand of icy detachment would suit him to perfection.

'I must return to the reception.' Saif sighed with regret. 'I am very sorry that you are unable to join the festivities.'

Setting his cup aside, Angel vaulted fluidly upright. 'No, you were right to hide me,' he said softly. 'I was, as I often can be, impulsive in flying out here the instant you told me you were getting married. For sure, someone would have recognised me at the party.'

His brother gave him a discomfited look and Angel suppressed a sigh but there was nothing he could do to change the situation. He, the child of their mother's scandalous second marriage, could not expect to be a welcome guest in the Emir's family circle. Some day, of course, that would change when nature took its course and the elderly Emir passed, but it was unlikely to change any sooner. Angel rejected the faint sense of resentment afflicting him as he accompanied his brother out to the open galleried corridor beyond the suite of rooms where he had been placed. The palace of Alharia was a vast building, built over many centuries and capable of hiding an army should there be that necessity, he thought wryly, glancing over the wall into the courtyard beneath and catching a glimpse of red hair that spun his head back.

'Who's that?' he heard himself ask of the woman below, playing with a ball and a couple of young children.

'Haven't a clue,' Saif admitted. 'By the look of that starchy uniform, someone's nanny...she probably belongs to one of our wedding guests.'

*Belongs?* Just as if the woman were a stray dog,

Angel savoured with amusement. Was he quite as remote from the domestic staff as his elder brother appeared to be? He didn't think so. His childhood had put
paid to that lofty royal distance. The only affection he
had ever received had come from his parents' employees and he had learned to think of them and see them
as individuals rather than mere servants there to ensure his comfort.

'It was the red hair. It always catches my eye,' Angel
confided truthfully, still looking down into the courtyard while censuring himself for doing so.

Obviously, it wasn't *her*! As bright as she had been
at Cambridge when he met her, there was no way she
would now, five years on, be as humbly employed as a
nanny in service. And why hadn't he long since forgotten about that wretched girl? With her combat boots,
stroppy attitude and blue eyes deeper and truer in colour than even the legendary Diamandis sapphires? He
gritted his teeth in annoyance at the vagaries of his persistent memories. Was it because she had been the one
who, in popular parlance, had got away? Was he still
that basic? That male and predictable?

'Yes…that's very noticeable,' Saif remarked with a
hint of amusement. 'You are an unrepentant womaniser, Angel. Everything the global tabloids say about
you is true but at least you have enjoyed the freedom
to be yourself.'

'And so will you some day.' Angel gave his brother's
shoulder a quick consoling pat even while he knew that
he was voicing a white lie intended to comfort. As an
obedient son, most probably a *very* faithful husband
and the future emir of a traditional country, Saif was
unlikely to ever have the liberty to do as he liked, but

there was little point in reminding him of that hard fact, Angel reasoned with sympathy.

Luckily for Angel, his subjects didn't expect moral perfection from their monarch. The island of Themos in the Mediterranean Sea was a liberal and independent nation. Although it was a small country, Themos was also incredibly rich because it was a tax haven, beloved of the wealthy and famous for many affluent generations. The royal family of Diamandis was of Greek origin and had ruled Themos since the fifteenth century. Throughout history Angel's wily family had retained the throne through judicious alliances with more powerful nations and, while their army might be small, their formidable financial holdings ensured that Themos would always box above its weight.

Angel studied what he could see of the nanny, the gleam of that fiery hair displayed in a simple long braid visible beneath the woven sun hat she wore. In the sunlight that braid glittered like polished copper, summoning up further uninvited echoes from the past. Squaring his wide shoulders as he separated from his brother, Angel turned away and returned to the suite that had been put at his disposal, a glossy concealment of the truth that he was under virtual house arrest until he flew out of Alharia again because his brother didn't want him to be seen and recognised.

Regrettably, Angel hadn't realised that *that* would be a problem. He had assumed that the wedding ceremony would be a hugely crowded public event, not a strictly private affair with only the Emir and the bride's parents in attendance. He had arrived for the wedding with the comforting belief that there would be so many people present that he would easily escape detection.

The discovery that he could not attend either ceremony or reception had exasperated him. As an adult, Angel had little experience of disappointment and certainly not the boredom of hiding out alone in Victorian surroundings, far removed from the comforts he took for granted. He wasn't a 'kick back and watch television' kind of person, he reasoned irritably, but it *was* only for a few hours. He reached for his phone as it vibrated.

It was the pilot of his private jet. A fault had been discovered in the landing-gear hydraulics. Angel winced even as he was assured that the mechanics team that had already flown in would be working on the problem through the night in an effort to get him airborne and back home again as soon as possible. He swore under his breath and paced the Persian carpet below his feet, wondering what he could possibly do to pass the time…

Gabriella flicked through the television channels again in search of entertainment, but it was no use. Even though she spoke the language, nothing she had so far seen could capture her attention.

In an effort to dispel her bleak mood, she stood up, stretching in the light white cotton sundress she had donned once the sun went down, and her official workday was over. Not that she had had the opportunity to do any *real* work during her brief stay in Alharia, she reflected wryly. Having registered her services with an international nanny agency the month before, Gaby was only accepting short-term placements. A couple of bad experiences in more permanent positions had made her wary and she intended to be far more cautious when choosing her next live-in employer. Providing childcare cover for wedding guests in the Alharian royal palace had sounded like a ridiculously exciting, glamorous and *safe* job. Only in actuality the experience, while certainly safe, had proved to be anything but exciting and glamorous. Tired of sitting around doing nothing, she was counting the hours until her flight home the following day.

Aside from an hour in the afternoon spent supervising two six-year-olds, she hadn't *had* any children to look after because most of the guests had either left their kids at home or had brought their own staff with them. Someone had overlooked that likelihood when hiring her and she had been surplus to requirements. So, what else is new? she asked herself with faint bitterness. Being an unwanted extra was a painfully familiar sensation for Gabriella.

Her parents and her little brother had died in a motorway pile-up when she was fourteen years old and recalling the sudden savagery of that shattering loss could still make her skin turn cold and clammy. Grief had shot her straight from awkward adolescence into scary adulthood long before she was ready for the challenge. Her mother's kid sister, Janine, had become Gaby's reluctant guardian and virtually all the money that her parents had left had been used to pay for the fancy boarding school that had kept her out of Janine's hair. She had received a terrific education at the cost of the love, security and healing that she had needed so much more. Barely a year after losing her parents and brother she had decided that she would concentrate on becoming a top-flight nanny, after graduating from university. In her innocence, she had assumed that living in a family situation would ease her heartache for the family she had lost.

Only, Gaby reflected with deep sadness, she had been far too young and ignorant of the world when she had made that decision. Unhappily, the job hadn't worked out the way she had hoped and now she was wondering whether she should be looking at a different career option. Thankfully, she did have the qualifications required to seek an alternative. Gifted from birth, Gaby spoke six languages fluently and had a working knowledge of several more along with a first-class degree in Modern Languages from Cambridge University. The prospect of looking for a starter job in another field held little appeal for her, however, when she was able to earn an excellent salary in the job she was in. Sadly, though, her recent experiences as a nanny had sapped her confidence and left her feeling more alone than ever. Should she fight through that feeling? she asked herself as she lifted her soft drink and wandered out to the courtyard outside her room.

Colourful glass lanterns burned below the loggia that ringed all four sides. Tall fluffy palm trees cast giant shadows across the terracotta floor tiles and the fountain gently spraying water down into a circular pond. The warm still air was infused with the fragrance of exotic flowers, and the sound of the falling water was soothing. There was nothing glamorous about the old-fashioned nursery she had spent her day in, the few people she had met or her small unadorned bedroom, but the courtyard was a truly beautiful place.

She sat down on a stone bench, determined to appreciate her surroundings because tomorrow she would be returning to London and searching for somewhere to live again. She didn't want to overstay in her aunt's spare room. She and Janine had never been close. A fresh live-in position would make practical sense, but she could only grimace at the prospect and as she lifted her head and straightened her tense shoulders in denial of that awful surge of anxiety her long loose hair shimmied round her in rippling waves. Nobody was ever going to scare her like that again, she promised herself fiercely, but the fear that someone might try to do so still lingered...

Angel saw her from the walkway above, but she was seated in the shadow of the trees. Only a pale gleaming pair of shapely lower legs was visible from his vantage point. A confident half-smile tilting his wide sensual mouth, he strode down the corner staircase and saw her in the light shed by the lanterns, her metallic copper hair shimmering in a glorious tumble of bright splendour. Angel stopped dead. He had a 'thing' for redheads because of a young student who had had hair exactly like that and he was immediately gripped by an intense sense of familiarity.

But it could not be Gabriella Knox, it wasn't possible, he reasoned with a frown of disbelief, his keen dark gaze narrowing as he stared across the courtyard at her, and instantly fierce recognition fired inside him. That nanny he had glimpsed earlier? It *had* been her. It *was* her! His focus now considerably more intent, he appraised her in search of change and found little evidence of the years that had passed.

Possibly that oval face of hers was a little finer now that she had reached her twenties, he reasoned, but, if anything, she was even more of a beauty than she had been at nineteen. Her hair was spectacular, and the delicate cast of her features was only accentuated by her fair, flawless skin. She was a little on the small side, indeed barely five feet two inches in height, but that did not dim Angel's appreciation of her other charms. The average man might first notice Gaby's hair and her face, but her highly feminine curvaceous figure commanded equal attention. Five years earlier those wondrous curves of hers had infiltrated his every fantasy.

Back then, he had quantified Gabriella's appeal, pigeonholed her and rationalised his attraction to her because right from the start she had been trouble and Angel had never in his life before or since chased trouble in his sex life. He didn't take risks; he didn't *need* to take risks. Women were invariably all too willing to agree to his smallest wish…only *not* Gabriella. Gabriella had stood firm, defying him to the last.

Yet in his opinion what he had asked for had not been unreasonable. Other women hadn't argued, most certainly hadn't accused him of trying to steal their freedom or control them. He had an understandable need for discretion in the women he took as lovers. But Gabriella had been too outspoken, volatile and independent to agree to his rules. Encounters with women who only wanted to bed him to sell a story to the paparazzi had educated Angel the hard way and, while the great and good of Themos couldn't care less that their ruling prince might have remarkable staying power between the sheets, Angel held himself accountable to a higher standard than either of his parents had observed. He believed that revelations in print about his sex life were seedy and undignified.

'Gabriella…' Angel murmured tautly.

Gaby was frozen in fear when she glimpsed a dark male silhouette at the edge of the courtyard, but then fear turned into incredulous recognition. Shock kept her locked to the stone bench. Initially she was unable to credit that it could be Angel, but being forced to accept that it *was* him could only horrify her. Meeting Angel again plunged her into a nightmare of mortification, forcing her back into the painful insecurities of her younger self.

For the space of a crazy few weeks, she had once been madly in love with Angel Diamandis, but he had made unreasonable demands and torn her tender heart to pieces. Subsequently, he had shown neither remorse nor regret. After a massive fight in which she had screamed at him and thrown things, it had all been over, her pride's sole consolation being that she had dumped him and refused to listen to his excuses. They had certainly not parted as friends and she had been grateful when he had finished his degree and returned home to Themos, so that she need not continue seeing him around.

'Angel...' Her strained voice emerged somewhere between a whisper and a croak.

He was so very tall, at least six feet three inches and built with all the classic muscular power of an athlete, broad shoulders and strong chest tapering down to a narrow waist and long, powerful legs. When had she forgotten just how tall he was? In a dark, exquisitely cut designer suit, he was as elegant and classy as he had always been. With every breath that he drew, Angel exuded sophistication, royal pedigree and immeasurable wealth. Even casually clad in jeans he had been an arresting sight, she conceded as he stalked closer, his striking grace of movement holding her attention more than she liked. She hated him, she reminded herself, so why was she staring at him like a rabbit mesmerised by headlights? Of course, five long years on, she didn't want to *still* be showing hostility, she reflected in dismay, her cheeks warming, because wouldn't that kind of oversensitivity only encourage his voracious ego? Be calm, be cool, be polite, she urged herself in desperation.

He moved closer and the lights edging the path illuminated him to gleam lovingly over hard slashed cheekbones set high beneath olive skin, and shadow deep-set dark-as-coal eyes before glimmering across the sculpted lines of his wide, sensual mouth. He was still beautiful in a way she had never known a man could be and he still inexorably took her breath away. The very first time she had seen him she had been unable to *stop* looking at him and she had tripped over her own feet and fallen down a step, bruising and cutting her knees. Blood had seeped from the wounds as she'd fought the angry tears stinging her eyes for the pain she had inflicted on herself from clumsy inattention. It had not occurred to her in that moment, or to anyone else, that Angel would simply stride across the courtyard, scoop her up into his arms and take her away for coffee and a clean-up as if such care from a stranger were the most normal thing in the world. But then, that Samaritan act had been pure Angel, reacting to a stray impulse and utterly unpredictable.

'I suppose you are one of the wedding guests,' Gaby surmised, dredging herself up out of the depth of memories that threatened to drown her. She was rather pleased at the level tone of her voice, which suggested that his sudden appearance was not fazing her at all.

'Something like that.' Angel shrugged as only he

could do, a graceful shift of a broad shoulder that was continental, eloquent and highly sophisticated in its dismissal. 'But what are *you* doing in the Alharian palace?'

'It would be lovely to sit here and catch up,' Gaby declared with a fake smile pinned to her lips as she rose hurriedly to her feet. 'But I'm tired and I was just about to return to my room for an early night.'

'You can't *still* be that angry with me!' Angel shot at her in sheer wonderment.

Gaby stiffened and lifted her chin, denying the hot colour of embarrassment she could feel flooding into her cheeks. 'Of course not.'

'Then be normal and join me for a drink.'

'I don't think that would be appropriate,' Gaby parried uncomfortably.

'Since when did I do appropriate?' Angel mocked. 'Don't be a killjoy. Seeing you again here after so many years is a hell of a coincidence and, since we both seem to be at a loose end, why shouldn't we catch up?'

Gaby gritted her teeth on an acerbic retort, which would be all too revealing to a guy as shrewd as Angel. What he didn't know about women hadn't yet been written. He was the biggest playboy in Europe, a living legend of a womaniser. She had her pride, of course she had, and the last thing she wanted him to suspect was that she was still prickly about what had happened between them when they were both students... For goodness' sake, how juvenile would that be? she scolded herself frantically, desperate to take control of the encounter. It was not even as though they had had an actual relationship back then. They had shared a couple of dates and it had been over before it even properly began between them.

'Why not?' she agreed without looking at him, belatedly recalling that he was a prince and that even when he was a student his circle of friends had made a point of always addressing him with the very proper title 'Your Highness' or 'sir', and that they had visibly winced for her every time she'd neglected to employ the same honorific. It hadn't been a deliberate omission, though. The reminders of his true status had always come as a surprise to her because, when they were alone together, he had told her to call him Angel and she would always forget who he really was.

She had forgotten because she needed to forget who he was to be with him in *any* way. A royal prince when she was ordinary. A very rich young man when she lived from hand to mouth, a perennially broke student. A sexual sophisticate when she was still a virgin. But she had closed her eyes to reality because she had wanted desperately to *be* with him, only she had not been quite desperate enough to sign away her legal rights at his request! And when she had told him *no*, a word Angel had had very little experience of hearing and no prayer of ever accepting, he had gone off in search of a more accessible and accommodating woman, keen to do whatever it took to be with him, even if the resulting fling would only last a couple of weeks. The longevity of Angel's interest in a woman lasted about as long as a snowflake falling in summer.

Quieting those turbulent memories while struggling to recover her composure, Gaby accompanied Angel up the stairs in the corner. 'Where are you taking me?' she asked.

'My suite is on the floor above.'

A *suite*, well, that was only to be expected given his

status in comparison to her own. 'I'm surprised we're in the same wing,' she confided. 'This seems to be a rather out-of-the-way corner of the palace and I understand why *I* was put here because children can be noisy.'

'I was a last-minute guest and a late arrival,' Angel slotted in, his explanation smooth as glass.

He was lying. Gaby didn't know why he was lying about something so trivial, but five years earlier she had worked out that Angel was at his most smooth and lazy in tone when he wasn't telling the whole truth, when he was probably bending it for her benefit or his own. He was coldly logical, manipulative, indeed far too clever for his own good, and yet his flaws had inexplicably fascinated her far more than they had repelled her. He had tried to run rings around her and impress her with his wealth and she had stood back watching, involuntarily intrigued by that Machiavellian intellect of his as he tried to discover her weakness and use it against her.

'What do children have to do with your presence here in Alharia?' Angel enquired, pressing open a door that mercifully led not into a bedroom as she had feared, but into a spacious sitting room.

'I work as a nanny. This was a short booking.'

'You surprise me.'

'I'm extremely well paid and I enjoy the travel,' she said lightly, determined to reveal nothing private. 'Where are your bodyguards? I thought you never travelled without them.'

'I have no need of bodyguards in a palace as well guarded as this one.' Angel had left his security team behind in a city hotel because an entourage would only have drawn more attention to him. 'What would you like to drink?'

'I thought alcohol was forbidden here?'

'No, it's not. The Emir merely disapproves but he doesn't limit his guests. There are chilled wines available,' Angel murmured, studying her with narrowed eyes of appreciation, well aware that she would slap him if she knew that he was looking at her when her thin cotton dress was transparent against the light.

She wasn't wearing a bra and he could see everything from the colour of her white panties to the lush swell of small full breasts crowned with prominent pink nipples. He very much enjoyed that view. As a dulled throb pulsed at his groin he dragged his attention from her again, mocking himself for being so very easily aroused. As a man accustomed to topless-bathing beauties, why was he getting hard as a rock at the shadowy glimpse of a nipple? He marvelled at his lack of discipline and wondered if he could put it down to the complete shock of seeing Gabriella again. She unsettled him and he didn't like that.

'Rosé…or white wine. Either will do,' Gaby declared, walking across the room because she felt very self-conscious standing there like a statue. She settled down on a satin-covered gilded sofa that was not conducive to relaxation and lifted her chin, striving to appear composed and uninterested at the same time. 'So, catching up?'

Keen to avoid the pitfalls of a too-personal conversation with Gabriella, Angel rolled his memory back several years. 'Whatever happened to those two best friends of yours? The blonde twins?'

It was a winning question, marvellously uncontroversial, he registered as a sudden smile of surprise chased the tension from her plump pink lips. Most women he knew became competitive and curt if he enquired after any other female, convinced that only they should have his attention, but Gabriella was remarkably generous in that line. 'Liz and Laurie?' she queried. 'They both trained as teachers and now they're married.'

*'Married?'* Angel stressed in astonishment. 'At your age?'

'And Liz has already had her first child,' Gaby completed calmly. 'A little boy. He's so cute.'

Angel winced as if such fond talk of children were in some way embarrassing. 'You always liked kids, so I suppose I shouldn't be surprised that you decided to work with them, but there is so much more in the world.'

'Wine, men and song aren't really my style,' Gaby said drily, her attention locked to him in spite of her efforts to look away.

But there Angel stood, a living, breathing magnet for female attention. It was as if he sucked all the oxygen out of a room when she looked at him because she could barely swallow, and her mouth was dry. She still struggled to credit that a man could be as breathtakingly handsome as he was without being excessively vain or making the smallest effort to impress. She remembered the extraordinary efforts other women had made to grab his attention at university and reminded herself that she had not been one of them.

Angel flashed a sizzling smile at her as he uncorked a bottle of wine and poured it. 'I wondered how long it would take you to make an insulting remark about my reputation.'

Gaby went pink and lifted her chin as he crossed the room to extend a wine glass to her. 'You're reading something into my response that wasn't intended.'

Angel grinned as if she was hugely amusing him. 'You're so full of prejudice that you don't even see it. Instead of acknowledging the attraction between us, you look for an excuse to write me off. It was always like that. You never gave me a fair chance.'

Infuriated by that condemnation, Gaby leapt upright. 'I—'

'And now you're going to shout loudly at me and throw things to make sure that you can't *hear* anything that you don't want to hear,' Angel forecast, smooth as glass.

Gaby could feel temper mushrooming up inside her like an explosion and she swallowed it back while her hands closed into tight fists of restraint. Angel gazed back at her, dark eyes flaming like golden torches of challenge, and she sat down again abruptly, refusing to fulfil his low expectations of her.

'I think I've grown up a little more than that,' Gaby murmured stiffly, her spine rigid, her chest still heaving as she battled to get her temper back under control. No man had ever driven her to such immediate rage as Angel did. He had a special knack in that department. They were oil and water or hay and a lit match, she conceded heavily.

'Prove it,' Angel invited, striving not to let his attention be drawn by the shimmying swell of her sumptuous breasts below the cotton. 'Enjoy your wine. Talk to me.'

# CHAPTER TWO

'WHAT DO YOU want to talk about?' Gaby asked very drily and sipped at her wine.

'Tell me what it is like being a nanny,' Angel invited, folding down into an armchair in a graceful sprawl that signified a level of relaxation that could only make her envious.

Gaby sighed and attempted to mirror his laid-back vibe. 'My first couple of placements were great and I got to travel and use my linguistic abilities. That's what gets me the best jobs—keen parents who want bilingual children or tutoring.'

Angel angled his darkly handsome head to one side. 'Yet I hear a jaded note in your voice.'

Gaby grimaced. 'Because my last two jobs were *too* challenging. First, I landed an employer who wanted to turn me into a maid of all work round the clock to justify my excellent salary.'

'Were you living in the household?' Angel queried.

'I usually do.'

'That makes you an easy target.'

Gaby winced and gazed down into her wine glass. 'My duties are listed on my employment contract, but I had to resign to enforce them and, as always, I hated leaving the kids because I had become attached to them. It was the job I took after that one, though, that was the *real* problem...'

The silence hummed. Angel studied her, admiring the copper shine of her hair in the lamplight, the pale perfection of her dainty profile, the long feathery lashes momentarily veiling the dark blue depths of her eyes.

'And the problem *was*...?' Angel prompted, watching as she glanced up through her lashes and bit at her full pink lower lip, sending a roar of arousal coursing through him that tightened every defensive muscle in his lean, hard body.

Gaby tensed. 'The husband. The wife and the children were lovely but he...he was scary.'

Angel stiffened and sat forward, brilliant dark golden eyes now intent. 'How...scary?'

'He was a banker. He asked me to join him for a drink once when his wife was abroad and I said no and he didn't make anything of it, but he began to hang around when I was looking after his kids...and of course I couldn't object to that,' she pointed out ruefully. 'I was careful to act very much like an employee to keep the boundaries up. Unfortunately, it didn't stop him. There were little admiring remarks, little touches, never anything I could make a fuss about though, and he would stand too close, getting right into my space. It was intimidating. He was a big guy.'

Becoming increasingly restless as he listened, Angel sprang upright, his anger stirred by the thought of her being frightened by another man. 'And *then*?'

'My room was in the basement and he began to come down there at night and walk up and down the corridor. I went out once and he said he was reorganising the wine cellar, and maybe he was, but it went on for weeks. It got to the stage that every time I looked up, he was close by, watching me. I got nervous and tried to avoid him, but it was hopeless. I felt like I was being stalked. I was scared of him, scared of what he might try to do if he got the opportunity,' she admitted, her eyes stinging with guilty tears.

'Of course you were scared.' Angel sank down on the sofa beside her, startling her, and she lifted her head to look at him. 'Any woman would have felt threatened by that kind of behaviour…and presumably there were times when you were alone in the house with him?'

'Yes,' Gaby conceded, relieved by his understanding and grateful for it as well because it was not a story she had shared with anyone else, fearful that they might suspect she had been flirtatious and had somehow invited the man's unwelcome interest. 'And I hated those times when his wife was away. I went out those evenings if I could…but then he would be hanging around when I came back, acting creepily friendly.'

Angel appraised her pale, anxious face and the teardrop inching its way down over a delicate cheekbone and something cracked inside him, unleashing a tangled flood of emotions that powered right through and straight past his innate reserve and distrust of women. It was a gut response to curve a supportive arm around her taut, trembling spine. 'Why on earth are you crying and sounding so apologetic about what must have been a ghastly experience?'

Setting her glass down, Gaby sucked in a shuddering breath and coiled helplessly into the comforting heat of him. 'The whole thing made me feel so weak and I didn't feel safe, yet all the time I was worrying that maybe I was being silly, too imaginative and making a fuss about nothing…or that at some stage, without even realising it, I might have done or said something that encouraged him.'

Angel frowned, his censorious golden eyes in a direct collision with her strained gaze. 'No, you didn't. I know you. You're blameless in this. It was your job to keep yourself safe and he was a threat. He was probably getting off on your fear. It was a power trip for him and sooner or later I believe he would have assaulted you,' he forecast.

Gaby shivered. 'I thought that too. I hated myself for giving way, but I was so scared of him I handed in my notice and warned the agency about him. Unfortunately it's put me off taking another live-in position.'

'Of course it has. Is that why you're here in Alharia in a temporary job that you are vastly overqualified for?'

'Yes…and I needed a breathing space before I decided what to do next.'

'You have to be the least weak woman I have ever met,' Angel intoned in a fierce undertone.

And her tummy flipped an entire somersault in receipt of the glow of appreciation in his stunning gaze. She felt warm, reassured, championed for the first time in her adult life. She had never had anyone behind her before. When she had been bullied at boarding school, her aunt had told her that it was her own fault for winning prizes every year and that being less of a 'brain-box' would make her more friends.

'I never thought that you would admire strength in a woman,' Gaby confided, looking up at him without bothering to hide her surprise.

'I'm no saint…and I *didn't* admire it when you were using that strength of will against me,' Angel told her bluntly.

A helpless gurgle of laughter was wrenched from Gaby at that admission. Sometimes Angel was so honest that he made her toes curl. Embarrassed by an amusement that struck her as less than generous, she buried her hot face in his jacket. If she was as honest with herself, that strength of hers five years ago had only been staged for his benefit and her pride. Never had she wanted so badly to have an excuse to give in and settle for a casual fling with a man who only wanted her body and nothing else from her. But Angel hadn't given her that excuse because he didn't lie, and he didn't pretend. He had been quite upfront about his desire only for sex. The recollection still pained her and in response she pushed her troubled face harder into his lean, muscular shoulder.

The warm, achingly familiar scent of him engulfed her in an intoxicating wave. He smelt good enough to eat. There was a hint of his usual cologne with an undertone of clean, spicy masculinity that made her nipples tighten and her thighs press together. That fast, that naturally, her body reacted to Angel with the off-the-charts sizzling chemistry that had almost destroyed her the last time they were together. That craving had almost torn her apart. Shaken by the surge of reaction gripping her, Gaby lifted her head and tried to will herself into backing away.

'You're a snuggler,' Angel condemned, his extraordinary dark golden eyes locked to her flushed face.

'Guilty as charged,' Gaby conceded.

His dark head angled down, and she literally stopped

breathing. He looked as though he were on the brink of kissing her and she wanted him to kiss her so badly but, if it hadn't happened five years ago, what were the chances of it happening now? Back then Angel had thought far in advance of his every move, foreseeing every possible betrayal and complication in his relationships. He had wanted the reassurance of a signed non-disclosure agreement before he became intimate with a woman. And Gaby had *refused* to sign and that had been that, the end of the road before she even got walking down it, because Angel would not take the risk of trusting her to that extent.

'You smell of…roses, is it?' Angel murmured, staring down at her, dark eyes glowing, gleaming gold, exotically fringed by a luxuriant ring of dense black curling lashes. His tawny eyes were so gorgeous it was hard to look away from him.

'Yes…er…fancy skincare creams in my en suite,' Gaby mumbled, and it was as if time was slowing down for her as the tension between them thrummed like a warning drumbeat. 'We shouldn't be this close.'

'If you were a fire, no matter how many warnings I was given I would still get burned. It was always like that,' Angel told her sibilantly, his breath ghosting across her cheek as he brought his lips down to the level of hers and kissed her.

His acknowledgement that he still wanted her as much as he had years earlier lifted Gaby's self-esteem to giddy heights and made her feel more secure. What she was feeling was *not* one-sided; it was mutual. His mouth on hers wasn't just a kiss, though, or indeed anything like any kiss she had had before. Her hands travelled up slowly over his broad chest to his strong shoulders and into his hair, because a kiss from Angel shot her onto another plane entirely.

Her fingertips toyed with the thick black silky hair at his nape, shaping the base of his skull. His tongue traced the seam of her lips and then delved between, ignited a lightning storm inside her that sent sensual sensation arrowing along every nerve ending she possessed. A violent shiver rattled through her, a piercing sweetness rising as his tongue duelled with her own. It was electrifying as her nipples swelled and pinched taut and she pressed instinctively closer to him, squirming as a pool of liquid heat gathered in her pelvis.

'That was worth waiting for,' she gasped inanely as he released her lips to drag in a shuddering breath.

Laughter rippled through Angel as he stared down into her flushed face, revelling in the blueness of her eyes. 'I don't want to stop...' he confessed in a driven undertone.

'I'm not signing anything!' Gaby exclaimed as though he had flipped a switch on her, and as more colour flooded her anxious face at that embarrassing exclamation she reached up a hand and gently framed a high sculpted cheekbone. 'Can't you trust me that far?'

'I don't carry round non-disclosure agreements in my back pocket,' Angel countered with sardonic bite. 'And there's no personal insult in the provisions I take to protect myself. I have never fully trusted any woman.'

'I think that's sad,' Gaby told him truthfully while at the same time a tiny bit of panic was gripping her, because she had just given him the green light to go ahead without even properly thinking about what she was doing.

Yet choosing to be with Angel felt seductively like

following a natural instinct and surrendering to the inevitable. Fighting the desire to be with him five years earlier had been a serious challenge. Back then she had still suffered from the illusion that Mr Perfect was probably waiting to meet her round the next corner in her life and she had been content to have faith and wait, had naively assumed that some day soon another man would make her feel exactly what Angel made her feel.

Only it hadn't happened, and, goodness knew, she had tried hard to recapture that sizzling connection with someone else. In Angel's wake, however, real life had proved a downer. She had met men who groped, men who demanded, even men who made passes at her friends. Indeed, she had met every combination of bad in the male sex and several men who were perfectly decent and acceptable but not one of whom had inspired the insane craving that Angel could incite with one wickedly sensual smile. It had taught her a lesson. It had taught her to look back with regret at the experience she had missed out on, although she had never regretted refusing to sign that non-disclosure agreement. That had been a line she refused to cross even for his benefit.

'Maybe it is sad but that's how it is for me,' Angel parried without apology, swooping down to capture her mouth again. 'Am I moving too fast for you? I plead guilty... I am insanely impatient, and the first time there'll probably be more speed and passion than finesse, but I promise to make it up to you the next time...'

He was so outspoken that Gaby didn't know where to look. She had never been open about sex. She had had to fake knowledge she didn't have to fit in when she was younger but as she'd matured she had simply sought friends who slept around less and didn't judge her for her more old-fashioned outlook.

Gaby trembled as his lips caressed hers, every sense on a high of exhilaration at the taste and the scent and the feel of him against her. The strap of her dress loosened and slid off her shoulder and she tensed, gasping into his mouth as he unbuttoned its twin.

'Time we moved this to a more private place,' Angel told her, springing upright and bending down to lift her clean off the sofa before she had even guessed what he was planning to do.

He carried her into the bedroom next door and settled her down on a huge ornately carved wooden bed in a far grander room than the one she had been allotted. It reminded her of the differences between them, the fact that she was staff and that he was usually the boss in every scenario. Only not *her* boss, she reminded herself as she lay back, striving to seem calm, only she wasn't calm with her brain running riot. She didn't want him to know that he would be her first lover. Angel would see significance in that and possibly even think she was a little bit weird for still being so inexperienced at her age. No way was she willing to give him that satisfaction!

Angel shed his jacket, his tie and kicked off his shoes with a haste that was unlike him. He stared at the woman on the bed, the embodiment and fulfilment of a dream and a long-held fantasy, he conceded abstractedly. Possibly there was some excuse for that uncool haste of his. She looked amazing, her hair tumbling across the pillow in a silken cloud of colourful waves, blue eyes with the depth of gemstones luminous against her porcelain skin.

He unbuttoned his shirt, unzipped his trousers, the eager throb at his groin growing in intensity as she watched him.

As his lean bronzed physique emerged from his discarded clothing, Gaby was mesmerised. He was all hard contours and strength, from the ripple of muscles across his abdomen as he moved to the breadth of his hair-roughened chest. A dark furrow of hair dissected his flat stomach and ran down out of sight into his boxers and there her gaze lingered, warmth blooming in her cheeks because the fine fabric accentuated his jutting arousal.

He dropped down on the bed beside her, lifting her up and reaching for her unstrapped dress to slide it up over her head. As her breasts were bared Angel expelled his breath in a rush. 'Beautiful,' he husked, his hands rising to cup the full swells, his thumbs grazing across the swollen nipples, making her shiver because she was incredibly sensitive there. He lowered her down to the pillows again and whisked off her last garment without her even properly being aware of it.

Shifting against her lazily, he angled back his hips to remove the boxers, and for several heart-stopping seconds as he came back to her she felt him rubbing against her lower stomach, and then he rose up on his elbows and crushed her parted lips hungrily beneath his again, rolling her over and stroking her breasts. He trailed his mouth down the slope of her shoulder and caught a straining nipple between his fingers, closing his lips round the swollen tip and tugging on it. A tiny moan escaped her, her hips rising at the ache forming between her legs.

Kneading the soft swells, he utilised the edge of his

teeth and flicked his tongue across the rosy buds, creating a chain reaction to the heart of her that made her clench her inner muscles tight. When he directed his attention to her damp core and circled her clitoris, it was too much stimulation for her overexcited body and a climax engulfed her at shattering speed. Her body convulsing, she was insensible to everything for some moments and then she blinked up at him in surprise and faint mortification as though that lack of control had shamed her.

'I like that you're as ready for this as I am,' Angel growled appreciatively, shifting down the bed, long fingers trailing down a still-trembling thigh.

And Gaby closed her eyes tight as he parted her legs because she had always wondered about *that* practice and she wasn't going to let shyness and embarrassment come between her and the chance of enjoyment. He ran his tongue over her tender core and, from that first teasing caress, she was electrified, reduced to a quivering bundle of thrumming impatience and anticipation, so intense she could barely dwell on the pleasure because her body was screaming for the finishing line. And when it came in a flood of convulsive blistering pleasure she cried out in wonder because she had never felt anything that powerful before, and in the aftermath she felt boneless.

But Angel didn't allow her to rest back and relax, he gathered her up again and ravished her swollen mouth with his own, his lean, powerful body hard and hungry against her as they strained together and she felt him glide between her legs, both smooth and something slightly colder and more abrasive brushing against her. *Cold?* A faint furrow of confusion indented her brow as his movements ensured he partially entered her wet channel and her every sense screamed with anticipation.

'I should have a condom on,' Angel breathed, and he abruptly withdrew from her again, pulling back from her to reach for protection.

It was only once he leant back to deftly don a contraceptive that she realised that he was pierced, and before she had even thought about it she was reaching out to brush a fingertip over one of the steel beads that had touched her. 'I wondered; I didn't realise—'

'It's called a Jacob's Ladder. I had it done when I was eighteen and aching to be the coolest kid ever. It hurt like hell, and took for ever to heal, but women like it and some believe it adds to their pleasure,' he imparted with wry amusement.

Gaby reddened, out of her depth and feeling it at that moment. Angel came back to her, dark golden eyes ablaze with hunger. 'I don't usually spend the whole night with a woman, but I think I'll break that rule for you. Prepare to be ravaged within an inch of your life,' he teased.

'What will the ravaging consist of?'

'As much down-and-dirty sex as we have the energy to enjoy,' Angel asserted with a flashing smile of scorching confidence.

And she envied him. Oh, how she envied him in that instant for his sheer sexual confidence when she was striving to conceal her inexperience. She was terrified of him noticing that she was a virgin, terrified of doing something that gave that embarrassing little secret away. 'It's been a while for me,' she remarked carefully.

'How long?'

'Months,' she told him tightly without meeting his eyes. 'I've had to move around a lot this year.'

Angel bent down to nibble at her full lower lip while he stroked her quivering body, firing up responses that had momentarily gone into abeyance. A spiralling heat warmed her lower body, desire sparking afresh, blurring her insecurities. 'I imagine you're very choosy,' he murmured huskily. 'I'm lucky to have made the cut.'

Gaby laughed. 'I can't take you being humble seriously.'

'Enjoy it while it lasts, *kardoula mou*,' Angel advised, shifting over her, and settling between her thighs before tipping her up and surging forward.

Gaby buried her face in his shoulder, drinking in the evocative scent of his skin, striving not to tense, not to give way to nerves, not to expose herself in any way. He entered her in one deep thrust and pain and pleasure warred together, her heart rate speeding up until it seemed to be thundering inside her chest. She unclenched her teeth, hoping that that single jolt of pain meant that the worst of her initiation was over. She felt stretched, invaded, alarmingly sensitive as he moved and a strong wave of powerful pleasure traversed her lower body, much more satisfying than she had expected. He plunged deeper still, and elation tugged at her, backed by a renewed need that clawed at her with the most wicked impatience.

Feverish excitement claimed her, and she arched up to him, writhing in pleasure as he moved faster and harder, her lips parting on a moan of mingled delight and surprise. Feeling freed from her physical self, she surrendered to the hot drowning pleasure pounding through her. Release came in a great wave of sensation and he loosed an uninhibited shout of satisfaction as he reached the same conclusion.

Gaby blinked back the strangest moisture flooding her eyes. It had been *that* good that it had knocked her emotionally off balance, she told herself uneasily. Well, hadn't she chosen well when she decided that she would go ahead and take a chance on him? But enough was enough. If he didn't usually spend the whole night with a woman, she wasn't going to be the woman who urged him to break his rules.

'I should go back to my own room,' she whispered shakily.

An offer that would usually have relieved Angel only made him tighten his hold on her. 'I want you to stay. Let's make the most of being together here.'

And Gaby thought about it and reckoned that it could probably seem a bit nervy on her part to flee the instant the deed had been done. She knew that what he was really saying was that she would never see him again, that their intimacy was a one-off event and not to be repeated. Well, she wasn't naive enough to have expected any other denouement. From what she knew of his reputation, 'one and done', as she had once heard a guy quip, was Angel's normal modus operandi.

'Gabriella…' he pressed in the silence.

'I'm thinking about it. I think it would be better if I left now.'

'Only if you take me with you for the rest of the night.'

Gaby laughed at that idea. 'I only have a single bed and a little slot of a room. It wouldn't be quite your style.'

'Let's stay where we're comfortable, then…you were spectacular, *glykia mou*. I can't let you go yet.'

He hadn't noticed that he was her first, Gaby savoured, relaxing a little on that thought. Not losing face with Angel was of paramount importance to her. He slid out of bed and strode into the adjoining bathroom. Light framed his tousled black hair and tall powerful back view and not a smidgeon of regret assailed her.

It was perfect, she told herself happily. There were no witnesses, no cameras, nobody at all to remark on their brief intimacy. It was casual and private. By the time morning came, she supposed it would get a little awkward, but her flight was mid-morning.

'I can't afford to sleep in,' she warned him.

'I won't let you. I routinely wake up at dawn,' Angel murmured, sliding into the bed beside her again and pulling her inexorably back to him.

Standing at the foot of the bed in the dawn light filtering through the curtains, Angel viewed the sleeping woman. Copper hair as vibrant as Gabriella was in spirit spilled across the pillow, a delicate flush on her cheeks, a peaceful curve to her intoxicating pink lips. The night had been unforgettable…but now it was over.

Angel didn't do complicated with women and anything with Gabriella was destined to get messy. Without a signed NDA, he had taken a major risk with her, choosing to trust her this *one* time. Now he needed to walk away. He *had* to walk away. Intelligence told him that he had no alternative because he would not have a future with any woman until he took a wife. Gabriella was under his skin but, unlike his weak father, he was *not* in thrall to Gabriella, and he was strong enough to walk away. He would leave Gabriella a note. His private phone number? He winced and decided that encouraging any kind of ongoing contact with a woman who contravened his rules would be inadvisable. So what if she labelled him a four-letter word of a guy? He would never see her again—*never, ever*, he swore to himself grimly.

# CHAPTER THREE

'YOU HAVE OPTIONS,' Gaby's friend Liz reminded Gaby ruefully, several weeks after that night in Alharia.

Gaby grimaced. Yes, she knew the options. There was termination and there was adoption, both of which were terrifyingly final. She couldn't face either choice and, in fact, that part of her that had long dreamt of having a family again actually wanted to *celebrate* the pleasure of becoming a mother. Stark terror, however, threatened to drown that guilty seedling of joy. The prospect of single parenthood was decidedly scary. Somehow, she would manage, she told herself urgently, although she suspected that her job as a nanny would become too physically demanding when she reached late pregnancy. She would have to find less taxing work by that stage, and she didn't have much time left because she was already more than three months along.

How had the unthinkable happened? That one night in Alharia still haunted her. She would never forget waking up alone in that palace bedroom, feeling very much like a meaningless one-night stand. A servant had wakened her with breakfast in bed. Presumably, Angel had organised that before his slick and silent departure. Gaby had felt too sick with angry mortifica-

tion to eat and had fled back to her own room to pack.
Angel hadn't even left her his phone number. No matter what lens she used to look back on that night, her
perspective didn't change: Angel had treated her like
dirt, disposable dirt. The least he could have done was
wake her to say goodbye before he left but, instead, he
had settled for the easier option.

'If you're planning to keep the baby, you'll need the
father's support to make that possible,' Liz pointed out
sensibly. 'It's hard and very expensive to raise a child
alone.'

Gaby gritted her teeth at the concept of Angel being
supportive in such circumstances. He would do what
the law demanded for a child he didn't want but she was
quite certain that he would not wish to be an active parent. He would be angry, bitter and hostile and there was
nothing she could do to change that reality. As a man
who proudly conserved his royal dignity, determined
not to even have his name linked with a woman's in the
press, he would scarcely welcome an illegitimate child.

'I'll tell him in a few months' time,' she remarked
stiffly.

'You shouldn't leave it that long,' her friend contended.
'Give him time to adjust to the idea before the birth.'

Gaby shrugged. She knew what she had to do but
she was in no hurry to do it. 'I could have a miscar-
riage...or something, so I should wait. And if I leave
telling him a bit longer, there'll be no room for him to
suggest a termination.'

Liz frowned. 'Would he do that?'

'I really don't know but I'm not willing to put myself
in that position,' Gaby admitted quietly. 'It'll be enough
if he knows before the baby is born.'

'I still can't believe you had the bad luck to run into Angel Diamandis abroad where you'd be all alone with him,' the blonde lamented. 'I mean, what were the odds that you would meet your first love again like that?'

Gaby wrinkled her nose. 'He wasn't my first love, well, not in the way you mean.'

'Gaby, you were besotted with him, and Laurie and I hated him because he was such a player and he *knew* what he was doing to you when he demanded that stupid agreement from you! You would've got badly hurt if you had got any closer to him,' Liz said feelingly. 'And now look what's happened!'

'I'm a big girl and I got tempted. I didn't expect *this* development.' Gaby sighed, reflecting that Angel had used contraception throughout the night, although he had possibly been a little careless in not taking precautions sooner the first time. 'If I'd been on contraception myself, I suppose I would have been safe from this happening…but I swear Angel is the only man alive who could make me behave the way I did.'

'You and how many other women? Yes, he's incredibly hot, but he is also very much a bad boy and dangerous.' Liz groaned, vaulting upright as a baby's cry sounded upstairs in the small terraced house. 'I'd better get Robbie, and don't forget that he arrived even though George and I were *careful*. Only abstinence is a foolproof method of birth control.'

Chastened by the reminder, Gaby thought about the baby she had conceived. She had seen her child on the ultrasound screen and that viewing had stolen her heart at first glance, wiping out every sensible thought.

But her pregnancy had still come as a huge surprise. Her menstrual cycle had not stopped completely until the second month and she had been so busy working short-term placements and finding a flat share that she hadn't noticed. Her breasts had got bigger, but she had simply thought she was putting on weight. Only the final cessation of her cycle had warned her that something was wrong. Liz and her sister, Laurie, had been stunned when she had finally told them about her night with Angel in Alharia, and although her friends had then persuaded her to do a pregnancy test, she had still been genuinely shocked by the result.

Even so, she refused to let herself panic. In due course, she would make a discreet approach to Angel, although she was in no hurry to do so. After all, he had made his lack of interest in her clear by not contacting her again. Had he wished to seek her out he could've easily discovered where she worked, but he clearly had not wished to see her again. And that was fine. A one-night stand didn't make a relationship, only it was more than a little disheartening to appreciate that a guy who had once flooded her flat with flowers to impress her had walked away from their night of passion with such ease, consigning their brief intimacy to history.

Her thoughts pulled her back into the past and she remembered how Angel had ferried her back to his elegant Cambridge town house after she fell down the steps in front of him. He had put plasters on her cut knees, making her feel like a child again. His friends had sat around being polite but staring, visibly unable to comprehend his interest in her. Inevitably, Angel had been part of the student elite, beautifully dressed and wealthy young people, several who also enjoyed titles or famous parents and who, even though they attended the same university, lived an entirely different and more glamorous life than more ordinary students.

Gaby had been mesmerised by those dark golden eyes fringed by inky black lashes. Breathing that close to Angel had been a challenge and when he had asked her out to dinner, she had loosed an uncomfortable laugh and had said that she was too busy studying to go out in the evenings. Realising that he was a prince, as everyone else treated him with near reverence, had turned her off rather than *on* and his surprise at her rejection had embarrassed her even more.

'I'll change your mind,' he had told her confidently and that afternoon the flowers had arrived, ridiculously extravagant, gorgeous baskets overflowing with exotic blooms that had so cluttered her small living space that she'd had to give most of them away to neighbours and friends.

Naively, she had associated the giving of flowers with romance. The next time she had run into Angel had been at the library. Over coffee she had thanked him for the flowers, and she had been ready to say yes to dinner should he have asked her again, only Angel had told her instead that he was flying home for three weeks. Regrettably, his disappearance had only fuelled her infatuation.

'Angel plays with girls like you, that's all. Don't start building fantasy castles in the air just because he's interested in you at the moment…a moment is as long as Angel's interest lasts,' Cassia Romano had told her bitchily, going out of her way to *bump* into Gaby after a lecture and deliver that unnecessary warning.

Cassia, a blonde with the looks of a supermodel and reputedly the holder of a defunct Italian aristocratic title, had never strayed far from Angel's side. He had treated Cassia like a friend, but Gaby had recognised that possessive Cassia was ambitious to be rather more than that.

Gaby had run into Angel his first day back in the UK and had agreed to dine out with him that evening with her emotions running on high.

'We've got absolutely nothing in common,' she had told him uneasily.

'What does that matter?' Angel had asked lazily. 'We only get one chance to make the most of being young and single. I'm not ashamed to admit that I'm not in the market for anything more serious.'

And that candour of his had acted on her that night like the warning jolt of lightning, blowing her romantic hopes sky-high with the truth that Angel, the ruling Prince of Themos, did not see their relationship progressing beyond the level of a fling. She should have backed off then, she reflected, five years older and wiser, but in those days she had been very much into excusing or glamorising Angel's every flaw. She had told herself that his honesty was refreshing and that she should not condemn him for it. After all, she was still a teenager and wasn't looking to settle down either. And that night she had decided that he would become her first lover. Never in her life had she even imagined the sheer strength of the physical attraction that Angel exuded for her.

'You'll only be another notch on his bedpost,' her friends had warned her.

'But he'll be the first notch on mine,' Gaby had parried, lifting her chin.

'That's not enough when you're already obsessed with him. You'll want more.'

But Gaby had already known that 'more' was not on offer and rather than walk away from a fling that refused to be a fantasy at that stage she had decided that she would settle for what she could get. Only it hadn't turned out like that because, after a couple of more casual meetings, when Angel still studiously refrained from touching her in any way, she had asked him why that was so. And he had explained that he didn't risk getting involved or being alone with a woman unless she had signed a non-disclosure agreement promising never to take photos or talk about him to anybody. He had presented the concept as being protective for both of them because it would have barred him from ever discussing her with anyone either. But the idea of signing a legal agreement to get any closer to Angel had chilled Gaby to the marrow as well as insulted her integrity.

For a start she hadn't liked it being almost taken for granted that they would become lovers when whether she would or not was for her to decide in the moment. She had been repulsed by his lack of trust in her sex and disturbed that he didn't already realise that she wasn't a social climber, a gold-digger or a woman keen to attract publicity. She had told him that she couldn't possibly sign such a document. He had done his own case no favours when he'd pointed out that every other woman he had been with in recent years had agreed to the measure. He had, admittedly, endeavoured to explain himself and had assured her that he would ensure that she had her own legal advice, but it had all been too much and simultaneously too *little* for Gaby when set beside her own foolish romantic hopes.

She had had a mini meltdown and had told him that she would never sign the document and that they were done. Angel had come over all blue-blooded royalty and had reacted with icy dignity, a response that had given her wounded feelings absolutely no satisfaction. Her only consolation in the final row that had followed the day afterwards was that Angel had lost his temper as well.

The next evening, her friends had accused her of moping and had dragged her out to a party. Angel had been there. He had acknowledged her with a casual inclination of his handsome dark head but had made no attempt to speak to her. An hour later she had seen him kiss another woman out on the terrace, a woman she had seen him with before, and shock and possessive rage had assailed her. While she had told herself that it was over between them, in the back of her mind she had expected him to return to her. When he had reappeared back inside, she had breezed past him and hissed in an undertone that he was a dirty, rotten cheater.

Enraged by that condemnation, Angel had called at the flat she had shared with the twins an hour later.

'We are over. You don't own me,' he had told her.

And she had flung a teddy bear at him, the only thing within reach. Mortification still seized her whenever she remembered that moment.

Angel, however, had reacted as seriously as though she had thrown a brick at him. 'You refused to sign an NDA,' he had reminded her doggedly.

'What sort of a man in today's world asks a woman to sign an NDA?' she had slammed back at him, punctuating her demand with a rather more solid pottery mug.

Angel had ducked and the window behind him had been smashed and as shards of glass went flying in all directions he had closed a hand round her arm and furiously demanded, 'Are you crazy?' His tawny eyes had blazed gold as the heart of a fire.

Shaken by the damage she had caused and embarrassed when her friends came rushing in to check on them, she had backed away. 'I'm not saying sorry,' she had told him childishly. 'I wish I'd hit you!'

And those had been her very last words to Angel five years earlier. And that was what bothered her most about Angel. The feelings he triggered inside her were too powerful and he made her too needy. It took her back to the savage loss of her family at fourteen when she had first learned how much it hurt to lose anyone you loved. She could neither afford nor wish to develop such feelings for Angel.

Angel studied the email and gritted his teeth. He had been ignoring it in his inbox, reluctant to open it, to be forced to handle the conflicting reactions assailing him at the sight of her name. Only now was he finally reading it, only to be taken aback by its very brevity.

I need to meet with you in person concerning an urgent personal matter.

He was conscious of a savage sense of disappointment. He really had believed in his heart of hearts that Gabriella Knox differed from his previous lovers, but that she should contact him months after their Alharian encounter was revealing, he reflected with angry scepticism. Obviously, she wanted something from him, as so many of her predecessors had, and his wide experience of such approaches suggested that what she wanted was most probably money. Or another night with him?

That would have been Angel's preferred option, but even that was controversial because he knew he could not afford to surrender to temptation again. Memories of that night had plagued him ever since and unnerved a man who considered himself stable as a rock in that line. He didn't repeat his sexual encounters, considering it far simpler and safer to simply move on to a fresh conquest. Such recollections didn't usually linger, nor did they have the weird effect of making him ridiculously critical of the other women he met, while just thinking about Gabriella still made him hard. So, no, he definitely didn't want to see *her* again, but innate caution warned him that he had to check out *why* Gabriella had got in touch. And he would guard against any inappropriate further familiarity by bringing legal counsel with him, he decided with a forbidding smile. *That* would impose a barrier and would also ensure that he stuck strictly to business.

Three weeks later, Gaby climbed laboriously off the bus and walked towards the hotel at which Angel had agreed to meet her. So much cloak-and-dagger nonsense, she reflected ruefully. Did he really see that as still necessary? Still, she could concede that, given the choice, he would not want to be seen in public with a pregnant woman lest he was exposed as the father, but, barring anyone looking *very* carefully at her, she had done her very best to conceal her condition.

She wore a voluminous winter coat over a loose black knit sweater dress and long boots. She was more than eight months pregnant and had not intended to leave telling Angel quite so late, but it had taken a month for her to get a response to her email and then another few weeks to set up the appointment and regrettably she had not factored in that time lag. Perhaps she should consider herself lucky that Angel was willing to agree to an actual meeting, she thought irritably, but really approaching the Queen would have been easier than gaining access to the ruling Prince of Themos.

It was only fair that she tell him that she was having a child…a little boy. Angel had a right to know he was soon to become a father. It didn't mean that she was expecting anything from him, she reasoned soothingly, bolstering her proud independence.

'Are you Miss Knox?' A man in a suit with a security bud in his ear approached her the instant she entered the hotel foyer.

Gaby stilled in surprise. 'Yes.'

'Please come this way,' the man urged quietly.

She was swiftly ushered into a lift by the man, much as though she were engaging in espionage, and her mouth quirked, her sense of humour tickled. Certainly, it would be the only thing she had to smile about on this particular day, she reflected unhappily, because she was not looking forward to telling Angel news that he would not want to hear. Angel would not be familiar with being put in that invidious position, particularly when he had no control over the situation. One of the first things she had noticed about Angel was that he liked and even expected to control everything happening around and to him. He fervently guarded himself from the unexpected. And what could be more unexpected and unwelcome than an unplanned pregnancy?

Pale at that knowledge, Gaby accompanied the security man out of the lift and straight to the door, which opened ahead of them. An unfamiliar brunette in her thirties appeared in the doorway and gave her a frosty appraisal. 'Miss Knox? Gabriella Knox?' she queried.

'Who's asking?' Gaby countered quietly.

'I'm here, Gabriella,' Angel's dark deep drawl sounded from deeper in the room, cold and audibly edged with impatience.

Gaby crossed the threshold, conscious of the woman closing the door behind her and remaining with them. 'I didn't realise that I would have to ask to see you alone,' she said flatly.

'This is one of my lawyers, Petronella Casey,' Angel informed her calmly.

Gaby lifted her head high and squared her shoulders. 'I'm not prepared to talk to you with a third party present,' she told him, scanning him with veiled eyes, taking in the superbly tailored grey designer suit, the wine-red shirt, a gold playing card cufflink visible at one wrist. Tall, dark, breathtakingly handsome and sophisticated, but still flawed and imperfect when he could greet a brief email with such cynical distrust and distaste.

She marvelled that he could still look so beautiful and yet act as remote as the Andes from her, as if that night in Alharia had never happened, as if she were an absolute stranger. It hurt, of course it did, but she rammed that hurt down deep inside her and strove to rise above it, trying not to dwell on the lowering awareness that any kind of involvement with Angel had always caused her pain. It was a little too late to be reminding herself now of that sobering reality, she conceded wretchedly.

The brunette stepped forward. 'I assure you that whatever is said in this room will remain completely confidential,' she declared, with a cool smile that might have been intended as reassuring but which missed its mark when she had 'legal shark' written all over her.

Gaby had no intention of being humiliated by the presence of another woman in the room while she staged a deeply personal and private conversation with Angel. 'I'm afraid it's a question of you leaving…or *me* leaving,' she explained with quiet dignity.

'Be reasonable, Gabriella,' Angel intoned in the most forbidding tone she had ever heard from him.

Angel studied her in frustration, absently wondering if she had come direct from a funeral, because the long all-black outfit seemed like overkill otherwise and, what was worse, swallowed her tiny stature alive, literally covering her from head to toe. But simultaneously the colour black also threw the splendour of her shining copper hair, dark blue eyes and faultless porcelain skin into prominence, lending her the luminous quality of a star against the night sky, a poetic thought so unlike his usual thought processes that Angel almost winced for himself.

'Why should I be reasonable when you're being so unreasonable?' Gaby asked sharply, flinching as her baby boy tumbled inside her and kicked hard against her bladder. He was a very active baby and a large one. A date for her C-section delivery was already set. 'I came here to speak to you in private but if you can't even grant me that courtesy, I'll leave.'

The lawyer, Petronella, stepped forward without warning. 'If you're in agreement, I'll wait outside, sir. You can call me back in at any stage.'

Colliding with Petronella's intent gaze, Gaby reddened as she grasped that the lawyer had recognised the reason behind her desire for privacy. Of course, another woman *would* notice that she had dressed to hide her body faster than the average man and have worked out why.

Angel shifted a hand in a gesture of agreement but settled angry dark golden eyes on Gaby. Such stunning eyes, she thought with regret at the prospect of what was coming, tawny brown with the glow of honey in sunlight and ringed by lush black spiky lashes.

As the door snapped shut on the lawyer's exit, Angel stared at her. 'Right…just get to the point quickly and we'll wrap this up,' he urged harshly.

'What did I ever do to you to deserve such a lack of good manners?' Gaby asked in helpless condemnation.

A faint rise of red over his high cheekbones told her that she had made a direct hit and the bad side of Gaby rejoiced while the more sensible side of her winced, because riling Angel was scarcely in her best interests in her current predicament.

'I apologise if I've been curt,' Angel breathed between gritted teeth. 'But it has been many months since our last meeting in Alharia and naturally I am curious as to why you have demanded this meeting.'

'It wasn't a demand, Angel. I believe it was a polite request,' Gaby protested, struggling to keep her hot temper under control. 'But since you urged me to get to the point, I'll do that and free us both from this unpleasant confrontation.'

'It is *not* a confrontation!' Angel bit back at her in a seriously rattled undertone.

'Oh, I think it *is* when you greet me with a lawyer by your side,' Gaby contradicted with confidence, an icy flash lightening her blue eyes. 'Relax, Angel. I'm only here as a courtesy and I have no intention of approaching the press in any shape or form. However, you do have the right to know that I'm…' she hesitated '…pregnant.'

And the word fell like a giant rock dropped into a still pond. That imaginary resounding splash was as loud as the shattering silence.

Later she thought that she would never, as long as she lived, forget the look of pure naked antipathy and contempt that flared in Angel's lean, hard-boned features as he intoned very drily, 'Well, if you *are*, it can't possibly be mine!'

# CHAPTER FOUR

STATED RIGHT UP FRONT, before she even got the chance to speak in her own defence, Angel's explicit rebuttal was a daunting challenge.

'You seem very sure of that,' Gaby responded without any expression at all, although her small figure was stiff and her face pale. His icy expression and the rigid tension spliced into his lean powerful frame were totally unfamiliar to her. It was as if something had flipped in Angel, something she hadn't met with in him before.

'I am. Have you any idea how often I've been through this scenario with other women?' Angel derided with a curled lip. '*Four* times at the last count! I know exactly what happens next. You will threaten me with legal action and take it to court for a DNA test and only then will your claim be exposed for the lie that it is. As I'm sure you know you can make a great deal of money out of the publicity that any paternity case against me will give you.'

'I've already told you that I don't want publicity and the only claim I would make would be support for our child.'

'Don't say "our"!' Angel incised. 'It's offensive! If you are carrying a child, it is *not mine*.'

Gaby breathed in slow and deep, tamping down her ire with difficulty. But, if Angel had already been falsely accused on several occasions of having fathered a child, she could at least understand his distrust even if she resented it. 'I am not those other women, Angel,' she began. 'And—'

'But you've just proved that you *are* by forcing me to meet up with you and trying to pass off some other man's child as mine!' Angel condemned, nostrils flared on his classic straight nose, his strong masculine jaw at an aggressive angle. His eyes shimmered gold, narrowed, dagger-sharp and angry.

'Why are you so convinced that this is not your child? Aside from your outrage that I should *dare* to confront you with this development, please explain,' Gaby urged thinly. 'Are you infertile? Specially blessed not to reproduce by your throne? There is no such thing as one hundred per cent efficiency with any form of contraception!'

'But it's remarkable how often it *allegedly* fails for me,' Angel intoned very drily.

'Let me get this straight…you think that you have the right to insult and punish me for your experiences with other women, who lied and plotted to try and entrap you or make money out of their connection with you?' Gaby slammed back at him wrathfully. 'How fair is that?'

'You forced me into this meeting,' Angel derided, his stunning eyes awash with anger. 'What else am I supposed to think?'

Gaby inclined her chin. 'I didn't force anything. I asked politely,' she reminded him curtly. 'This child is *your* child. Nor am I apologising for that when you must know as well as I do that no contraceptive method is totally safe. Let's at least behave like adults here.'

'I am dealing with this like an adult,' Angel sliced in icily.

'No, you're not. You're *ignoring* the situation by making the assumption that I'm lying,' Gaby censured. 'But, in only a few weeks I will give birth to your son.'

'At which time you will doubtless contact a lawyer and make a legal claim, which will eventually go to court and a DNA test,' Angel cut in drily. 'Why would I waste my energy on the issue now?'

When he put it like that, Gaby could see his point when he was so utterly convinced that the child she carried could not possibly be *his* child. Even so, she loathed him for his attitude and knew she would never forgive him for it or for treating her like a con woman, meeting with him to scam and fleece him. 'Well, I've done my duty by informing you of the situation and, considering your mindset, I have absolutely nothing more to say to you. Have a nice life, Angel. You'd have to be dying in a ditch for me to cross your path again!'

With that proud declamation, Gaby stalked out of the room with her head held high and moved back to the lift. When Petronella Casey walked back into the hotel suite, Angel was preoccupied with his thoughts, his lean, darkly handsome features shuttered. He was recalling his mother's infidelity and his father's weak inability to deal with her behaviour. Angel had vowed that he would never allow himself to be put in such a position, and as time had moved on, and he'd learned for himself how dishonest and untrustworthy women could be, his attitudes had only hardened.

'Evidently you do not believe a word that that young woman said,' Petronella remarked quietly. 'Whereas I suspect that it might be wise to pay a little more attention to her.'

'Of course Gabriella's lying,' Angel asserted with ringing confidence, doubt or insecurity rarely featuring in his decisive nature. But it was also only now occurring to Angel in that same moment that, if she was *not* lying, he had burned his boats with a vengeance. 'She has to be lying, just like her predecessors. Hire a private investigation agency to look into her. I should take every precaution.'

'Bear in mind that in spite of the barrage of paternity claims that you have endured,' Petronella murmured in a diplomatic undertone, 'sooner or later and by the law of averages there will possibly be a woman telling the truth.'

'With respect, I hope you are mistaken,' Angel breathed tautly. 'The first male child born to me is automatically the heir to the throne. That is in our constitution and not something I can change.'

But the question had been raised and he could not ignore it, even if the prospect shot naked alarm through him. What if he were to become a father? How the hell could he ever handle that? He was the product of no parenting, who only knew what to avoid rather than what a father should do.

Gaby walked back into Liz's home with tears walled up in a dam behind her scratchy eyes. She had never been so grateful that her friend was on maternity leave and still accessible rather than back at work. The blonde took one look at Gaby's tight, pale face and immediately gave her a hug. 'It was *that* bad?' she whispered in dismay.

'Yes. Plan A was a major fail, so I will move immediately to plan B,' Gaby quipped a little chokily. 'Angel is not planning to be supportive or involved in any way. He refuses even to recognise that this *could* be his child, so that's that, then.'

'He still has to pay child support, whether he likes it or not,' Liz argued vehemently.

'*If* I can't survive without his help,' Gaby qualified. 'But if I *can* get by, he will never lay eyes again on me or his child in this lifetime.'

Just as Gabriella had spent troubled weeks striving to work out her future with a young child to raise, Angel had, possibly for the very first time in his life, been required to work through months of stress, inconvenience and ultimate disappointment. Why? Gabriella Knox had, to all intents and purposes, disappeared off the face of the earth and, with her, the child Angel now suspected was *his* child as well.

On his monthly trip to London to ensure that the investigation agency he had hired were still making the search for Gabriella a top priority, he learned that there had finally been a breakthrough and intense satisfaction gripped him, the frustration of the past nine months draining away to be replaced by a powerful need for action instead. Now all he had to do was seal the deal and he saw refusal on her part as so unlikely as to be virtually impossible...

Gaby smiled as the early-summer sunshine engulfed her in the garden. It wasn't hot but it was infinitely preferable to another grey wet day. She tossed the clothes pegs and sheets into a basket to carry back indoors. The long winter at the isolated farm had provided a wonderfully therapeutic time out for her, calming wounded and tangled emotions, soothing the painful regrets and showing her the way forward.

And her way forward, she reflected fondly, was definitely through her son, Alexios. She set down the laundry basket for sorting later and padded into the cosy living area, which comprised kitchen, dining and sitting room. An elderly woman sat there in an armchair. Clara Paterson, her friend Liz's godmother, was a widow in her seventies and recovering from recent minor surgery. Clara was currently waiting to move into a more compact property in town and Gaby was staying with her as a temporary housekeeper. Living in the Scottish borders while looking after Clara had given Gaby a comfortable peaceful home while she adjusted to being a new mother.

Not that Alexios, beaming at her from the rug at Clara's feet, looked like much of a challenge, she conceded proudly. He didn't bear much resemblance to her or, for that matter, Angel. Nobody in her family had had bright green eyes or black curls, but then, neither did Angel, so she had no idea whose ancestor had donated those genes. It didn't much matter either, she reflected cheerfully. What *did* matter was that Alexios was a happy, healthy eight-month-old baby, already crawling and trying to talk to her. He had his father's brash confidence and fearless approach to life, but he was infinitely more loving in nature. And Gaby had discovered that not since the death of her family when she was fourteen had she ever loved anyone or anything as much as she loved her baby.

The earth-shattering racket of a helicopter passing

overhead barely made her blink because the house was only a few miles from a military base. A frown line pleated her brow, though, when the noise not only failed to recede but also increased and she moved to the front window, disconcerted to see a craft landing in the field beyond the wall surrounding the garden.

Clara peered out of the window beside her. 'That's *not* an army helicopter,' the older woman commented knowledgeably. 'And what's that flag on the bodywork? I don't recognise it...'

But Gaby *did*. The stripes of colour and the dragon logo featured on the flag of Themos. Her slim body froze inside her jeans and sweater, her pale aghast face suddenly washing with colour. 'It's Alexios's father... he's found us.'

'About time too,' Clara remarked calmly. 'You can't hide for ever with a child.'

'But he didn't *want* to know about Alexios!' Gaby protested.

'He's a very stubborn young man but he's had time to see the light. An alpha male can react badly when you plunge him into a situation out of his control,' Clara commented.

'Clara!' Gaby exclaimed in surprise. 'What do you know about alpha males?'

'Probably more than you do,' Clara quipped with a smile. 'I was married to one for almost half a century and there's not a day goes by when I don't miss his bossy, bullheaded ways.'

Gaby patted the old lady's thin hand comfortingly. 'I know...'

'So, go and deal with yours...*sensibly*,' Clara stressed.

'I'll watch Alexios until you're ready to introduce him to his father.'

Gaby was too respectful to tell the older lady just how far removed she was from the point of introducing her son to his very reluctant parent. Instead, she nodded as she watched a tall, frighteningly familiar figure clad in a winter coat and dark suit literally step over the low garden wall and head across the lawn to the rarely used farmhouse front door. She felt sick with stress, but her tummy was twisting with a fury she could not suppress. How dared Angel track her down after the way he had treated her at their last meeting? *How dared he?* There was nothing even slightly sensible about Gaby's attitude to such an incursion into her much-cherished privacy.

As the front doorbell wheezed from long disuse, Gaby glimpsed her reflection in the hall mirror, her mass of copper hair tamed and anchored somewhat messily to the back of her head, her flushed face bare of cosmetics. So, she wasn't exactly looking her best and why would she even think about something as trivial as her appearance at such a moment?

Her rage at Angel's characteristic chutzpah simply boiled over. In the back of her mind were all the times she could have done with the support of her child's father in recent months, not least when she had struggled to cope with a newborn's demands just after her C-section or during the many disrupted and sleepless nights that had followed before Alexios had eased into a routine. There had been the rather frightening knowledge that, while friends might help, she was essentially alone and had to handle her own emergencies. Becoming a single parent with that awareness was very stressful and in the early days she had had nightmares about what would happen to Alexios if anything were to happen to her.

Gaby jerked open the front door without unhooking the security chain that allowed it to open only a few inches. Through the gap, though, she saw Angel, with his smoulderingly beautiful face that could make angels weep and poets sigh. Silky black hair flopped above his brow and striking tawny eyes set off flawless cheekbones and a full sensual mouth. Once one glance at him had sent wanton shimmers of excitement travelling through her, but this time around seeing Angel was like having an ice cube trail down her rigid spine as she deliberately chose to remember the humiliation he had doled out to her that day in the London hotel.

'I realise that you're probably surprised by my arrival.'

'*Gobsmacked!*' Gaby shot back at him with deliberate vulgarity.

'May I come in?' Angel dealt her a gleaming narrow-eyed appraisal, the kind of rapier look royalty wore like a blazing shield of confidence, warning her that he was not expecting to meet with any opposition. His audacity only inflamed her more.

'*No!*' Gaby snapped caustically and she slammed the door shut again. Spinning in a rapid arc, she folded her arms and paced the narrow hall.

Angel pressed the bell again. 'I'm not leaving,' he announced from outside, that perfect diction of his enunciating every syllable with clarity.

Gaby gritted her teeth and only just resisted the childish urge to drag the door open again and scream at him. Nobody could unleash her temper more easily than Angel.

'Is this what you call adult behaviour?' Angel enquired sibilantly from behind the glass door.

Her hands clenched into fierce fists. Had she had a brick in her hand she would have thrown it at him. Instead, she paced up and down the hall, battling to get her tempestuous emotions in check. He was so cool and calm, and it inflamed her when she thought of what he had made *her* endure.

Yet she also knew that what she was feeling wasn't *all* Angel's fault. Time had made her more honest with herself. She had been madly in love with Angel at university and he had hurt her badly. It had not been a girlish infatuation that she could quickly put behind her, it had been full-blown over-the-top love, bordering on obsession. And, sadly for her, some lingering shard of those soft, sappy feelings had made her succumb to that one-night stand in Alharia because the attraction had been as strong as ever. Even so, she couldn't blame him for walking away afterwards when she had been well aware of his womanising reputation.

But she *did* very much blame Angel for his attitude when she had confronted him with her pregnancy. She didn't care that he had been taken by surprise. She had no sympathy for him on that score and much more sympathy for herself, walking round the size of a barrel for months on end while agonising about how she was to cope and survive as a single parent. And then the father of her baby had flatly refused to accept *his* share of the responsibility and had shot her down in mortifying flames. It would be a cold day in hell before she forgave Angel for that crushing rejection!

'Gaby?' Clara murmured from behind her. 'I've put

Alexios up for his nap and I'm heading out to the green-house.'

Gaby whirled round, taken aback to see Clara now clad in her outdoor jacket and boots. 'OK…'

Angel appeared behind the older woman and Gaby's jaw simply dropped at the sight of him indoors rather than outside where he should still have been.

'I brought your visitor in through the back,' her employer and friend informed her quietly. 'You need to talk…and not through a closed door.'

Angel surveyed her with hidden fascination, unable to forget how long it had taken and how hard it had been to find her again. He could feel untamed emotion buzzing through him and that annoyed him when he needed to be in cool control of himself, unlike his parents, who had never been in control or even accepted that they ought to be.

Flags of embarrassed colour had flown into Gabriella's already flushed face, Angel noted appreciatively. He didn't think there could be a woman alive who could look as beautiful as she did without making the smallest effort to do so. There she stood, blue eyes burning bright, utterly enraged by him, in a shabby old pastel-pink sweater and faded jeans, both of which clung to her mesmerising curves like a second skin. For a split second, Angel forgot why he was there, forgot their audience, forgot everything and almost reached for her like a hot, thirsty man tempted by a drink of water. In terms of sexual need, he reasoned grimly, he was both hotly aroused and *very* thirsty. Annoyance at his masculine predictability chilled his overheated blood and he tilted his arrogant dark head back to study Gabriella with an assessing look. Was she the mother of his son…*or not*?

'Well, I won't say that that wasn't embarrassing,' Gaby breathed tightly as she marched past him back into the living area.

'Since the lady appears to know who I am, will she be discreet?' Angel enquired.

And that fast, Gaby wanted to thump him again. 'Of course she will be. Clara isn't remotely interested in you or in publicity,' she pronounced curtly. 'What are you doing here? What do you want from me?'

'I would like to see the child,' Angel intoned without any expression at all. Gaby interpreted that as Angel, *unusually*, watching his every word.

'You said that child was nothing to do with you!' Gaby reminded him.

'May we sit down and discuss this important matter?'

'You're asking me to be reasonable when you were not remotely reasonable with me nine months ago?' Gaby launched at him incredulously. 'I can't believe your nerve!'

The smooth, hard planes of his lean bronzed features were impassive, infuriatingly uninformative. 'You've said that to me before.'

'Yes...' Gaby compressed her lips on the reminder.

'It could be...' Angel breathed in deep and slow '... that I was a little hasty at our last meeting.'

A spasm of intense satisfaction arrowed through Gaby at that unexpected admission from Angel. 'A little hasty? Is that so?'

Picking up on her pleasure at his discomfiture, Angel gritted his even white teeth. 'Yes, that is so. As you pointed out at the time, there is always risk attached to sexual intimacy.'

'I do not view the conception of my son as a risk.'

Angel shrugged a cashmere-clad broad shoulder, seemingly indifferent to her sensitivity, his hard, handsome face unyielding. 'I should have acknowledged at the time that there was a chance that I could be responsible, but I had already been through this scenario with one too many of your predecessors with the result that I was too angry to be logical. My background has made it a challenge for me to trust women.'

Gaby did not like being included in the category of 'predecessors' but her curiosity was piqued by his admission that he found it difficult to trust her sex. 'It was one night,' she conceded with a careless shrug that in no way mirrored how she felt about it. 'Now that you're apologising, I suppose I can follow your feelings to some degree.'

'I was not aware that I was apologising,' Angel framed grittily.

'If you're not prepared to apologise for the way you treated me that day at the hotel, I have nothing more to say to you,' she told him truthfully. 'Nobody treats me like that and gets away with it!'

Angel ground his teeth together again.

'You see, I understand that you're rude because you're used to people tiptoeing around your royal person, but your birth and your wealth do not mean that you are better than I am,' Gaby spelt out succinctly. 'Or that I will let you get away with behaving as though you are.'

Angel's brilliant dark golden eyes smouldered as though she had lit a fire behind them. 'Message received,' Angel murmured dulcetly, disconcerting her with that easy switch. 'I apologise for treating you unfairly.'

Gaby hadn't believed that he would or even could

climb down off his high horse and the shock of that accomplishment knocked her off balance. 'All right…so let's move on. Why do you want to see Alexios? Surely you would want DNA testing before doing so?'

'Is it true that he has green eyes?' Angel demanded, startling her with that apparently random question.

'Yes, it is…but what does that have to do with anything? And how did you track me down here anyway?' Gaby pressed in a ruffled tone.

'Let me give you a hint…you've been too active on social media with your friends. I've been searching for you for months,' Angel revealed. 'There were no leads until I was able to establish a link between Laurie Bannister, your friend Liz's twin, and you. From that point it was possible to check out their connections to find out where you might be.'

'What do you mean by searching?' Gaby prompted in dismay at what he had revealed. It was true that she had often chatted to Liz's twin, Laurie, online, mentioning meetings because Laurie lived only forty miles away with her husband.

'If your son is also *my* son, we have a situation which I cannot ignore. He would not be an ordinary child—he would be a *royal* child. It was imperative that I locate you and check it out. I used a private detective agency to trace you.'

'Through my friends,' she repeated in horror. 'You had someone snoop into *their* lives to track *me* down? That's appalling.'

'If you had left a forwarding address or told your friend Liz that it was acceptable to tell me where you were, we wouldn't be in this position now and I wouldn't have had to have anyone investigated,' Angel countered without hesitation.

Gaby studied a scratched area of the pine kitchen table, mastering her resentment. It was done and too late to complain about anyone's privacy being invaded, she conceded grudgingly. Perhaps telling Liz not to share her address, should Angel enquire, had been a step too far in mistrust…and he had enquired through staff. But then, she recognised ruefully, she had wanted to *punish* him, an urge which Clara's intervention had reminded her that she needed to suppress.

'Look,' she said stiffly. 'Come into the…er…sitting room…' Walking back across the hall, she pushed open the door of the room that was hardly ever used, crossing to the window to lift the blind and let in the sunlight. 'Do you still drink black coffee with one sugar?'

Angel released his pent-up breath, registering that Gabriella wasn't going to shout or throw things at him again. The strangest sense of disappointment instantly afflicted him and took him aback. No woman had ever argued with him or criticised him the way that Gabriella did and why the hell would he miss that?

'Yes, thank you,' he murmured with scrupulous politeness.

Angel sounded smooth as glass and Gaby shot him a suspicious glance, wondering what manipulative thoughts were currently operating behind that wickedly attractive façade of his. As she had learned in the past, he was clever, *very* clever, and well able to play the long game to conceal his true purpose. But just then she had more on her mind than working out Angel's motivation and she bent to light the gas fire in the chilly room before speeding off to check on Clara and make the coffee.

She could have taken Angel up to the small apartment above the extension where she lived but that would take him too close to her son and she wasn't ready for that step yet. So, instead of that she put on the kettle and hurried out to the greenhouse to see Clara.

'We're in the sitting room, so you don't need to stay out here if you don't want to,' she told the older woman gently. 'Sorry about the shouting. I'm afraid Angel tends to send my temper sky-high.'

'I reckon his temper is every bit as bad as yours but he's too reserved to let it fly,' Clara surmised as she worked at her bench, potting up seedlings. 'He's much too handsome for his own good, and he'll be a truckload of trouble, but I suspect he might be worth it. Only you can decide if he is.'

'He's only here because he is finally accepting that Alexios could be his,' Gaby muttered unhappily.

'Whatever happens, you mustn't get into a hostile relationship with him.'

'How could it be anything other than hostile?' Gaby's lovely face was strained as she hovered in the greenhouse doorway.

'It *has* to be something else for your son's sake. Boys need a father,' Clara informed her.

Paling, Gaby walked back indoors to make the coffee. Be polite, be civilised, she instructed herself, stop making it all so personal and emotional. Wasn't that a dead giveaway of how Angel made her feel? Getting all riled up and shouting? She was making it far too obvious that she was emotionally involved and had been wounded by the fallout of that night in Alharia. Gaby flinched at the thought and reminded herself that she had been a consenting adult, who had believed that she knew exactly what she was doing. It was a little late now to acknowledge that she had fooled herself into reaching for what she thought she wanted only to discover afterwards that she had secretly wanted much more than a brief sexual encounter...

Angel was cold and he stood by the fire, which put out a miserable amount of heat. He checked his watch, regretting that he had to be back on Themos by morning to attend an important event. He needed time to deal with Gabriella and he didn't have time to spare. In any case, he was naturally impatient, he conceded, a muscle tightening at his strong jaw as he struggled to clamp down on the volatile mix of anger, frustration and desire that Gabriella always evoked.

Her reappearance with a tray almost made him laugh. Gabriella serving him graciously with coffee was not a vision that rose easily to his imagination. He grasped the cup.

'Months ago, you joked on social media about having a child with green eyes and curly hair,' Angel remarked tautly.

Gaby lifted a brow. 'And the significance of that... is?'

'My mother had green eyes and curls. She was a legendary beauty. Queen Nabila. Look her up online,' Angel urged forbiddingly, as though the subject were distasteful to him.

And, of course, on his terms it *had* to be distasteful to contemplate the likelihood of his first child having been accidentally born to an ordinary woman not of his choosing. Both his parents had been born into royal families and he knew nothing else.

'But that could just be coincidence,' Gaby heard herself declare because, when push came to shove, she was realising that she was not eager to share her little boy with Angel. No doubt that was selfish but that was how she felt. Alexios was her family now and, having lost her family when she was fourteen, she was particularly keen now to hold her son close.

'Do you have reason to believe that your son could have been fathered by someone else?' Angel queried curtly. 'Were you with any other man shortly before or soon after me?'

A tide of angry red flooded up her throat into her cheeks. 'There was no other man. You were my first...' and her voice ran out of angry steam on that admission because she had not meant to tell him that much.

Angel's ebony brows pleated in consternation. 'Your...*first*? Are you serious?'

'Wish I wasn't but *yes*,' Gaby confirmed with bitter force.

'I wouldn't have taken you to bed had I known that,' Angel breathed in a driven undertone, swinging away from her to stand by the window and stare out, his strong profile taut and set. 'I don't mess around with virgins. It's too inequal, too open to misinterpretation.'

'Not in my case,' Gaby said dulcetly. 'I knew what I was getting and I got it.'

Angel flipped back to her, sizzling dark golden eyes bright as the sun. 'And what's that supposed to mean?' he flared back at her, sensing that he was being insulted.

'A guy who wouldn't even wake me up to say goodbye.'

Angel visibly ground his even white teeth together

and then froze to say, '*No*, we're not doing this! You're not going to derail me from the reason I'm here by making me angry again,' he told her harshly. 'And I'm here to ask if you will agree to a private DNA test being done.'

Gaby recalled how he had thrown it in her face that *she* would drag *him* to court to demand a DNA test. 'No.'

Angel's gaze narrowed, hardened. 'Then we go through the courts.'

Gaby paled at that immediate rejoinder. 'No, there's no good reason to take it that far.'

'Yes, there is. If your child is mine, then I will have to marry you!' Angel bit out rawly.

Gaby's dark blue eyes widened to their fullest extent and she stared back at him in disbelief. 'Now it's my turn to a-ask if you are serious,' she stammered unevenly.

'Serious as a heart attack,' Angel qualified without a shade of amusement.

# CHAPTER FIVE

THE MUG OF coffee in Gaby's hand trembled and she sank down into an armchair. 'You'd have to *marry* me?'

Angel swallowed hard. He would have to marry her to ensure his child was properly protected from damaging influences. After his own childhood experiences, he would *have* to be directly involved in the raising of his own child because the alternative would be, to his mind, a sin. He accepted that bringing up his child was his duty, but he also knew that, thanks to his own dysfunctional background, he had not a clue how to be a good husband or father, which was rather daunting. He studied Gabriella, striving to read her reaction to what he had said, but her jewel-blue eyes were unrevealing and she looked more shocked than anything else.

'We're jumping the gun,' he acknowledged. 'First, will you agree to the DNA test and will you allow me to see him?'

Gaby swallowed so hard she hurt her throat. 'Explain why you said that you would *have* to marry me,' she prompted tightly.

'My firstborn son is the heir to the throne.'

'But we're not married!' she protested.

'We don't have to be according to the constitution

of Themos in which the firstborn son inherits. In the seventeenth century one of my ancestors was unable to have children with his wife but he already had a son by his mistress and his son took the throne after him. His father changed the rules to keep the Diamandis family in power. Married or not, if your son is mine, he will be my heir,' Angel explained flatly. 'And if I marry you, you will eventually be the Queen of Themos, ruling by my side.'

'For goodness' sake…' Gaby set down her coffee and released a deep sigh. 'I had no idea. I didn't even think Alexios could ever be the heir to anything that belonged to you,' she framed truthfully.

'If you're telling me the truth and I was your only lover, he won't be illegitimate for very long because our marriage would legitimise his birth,' Angel breathed tautly. 'So, the DNA test?'

'I suppose I don't have much choice on that score because it wouldn't be fair to you or my son to refuse. On that basis I'll go along with it,' Gaby muttered uneasily.

'I'll make the arrangements,' Angel told her as he pulled out his phone, speaking in fast idiomatic Italian to whoever was at the other end of the line, an employee, she decided, because Angel was reeling off instructions. Someone was to come to the house to perform the DNA test and fast-track the results back to him.

He dug his phone back into the pocket of his cashmere coat and raked long brown fingers through the luxuriant ebony hair brushing his brow, tousling it. Her breath snarled up in her throat as he glanced back at her through a fringe of inky spiky lashes, his eyes a simmering slash of gold as hot as the heart of a fire, his lean, strong jaw framed and enhanced by black stubble.

Her body came to life as though he had flipped a switch, her breasts tightening inside her bra, a tugging sensation clenching the heart of her. She shifted uncomfortably in her seat, her colour heightening.

*I will have to marry you?* Not words she had ever expected Angel to say to her personally, not even in some crazy fantasy. Even as a teenaged student she had never dreamt big enough to imagine herself marrying a royal prince. But why would he *have* to marry her? Because Alexios was his heir? Surely if legitimacy were not demanded, marriage would be unnecessary? She could not, even in the wildest reaches of her imagination, picture being married to Angel, whose lifestyle was so far removed from her own. Themos was a very glamorous place, packed with the rich, famous and powerful. The island teemed with yachts, luxury hotels and casinos and staged world-class fashion, sport and charity events. Nobody would match someone as ordinary as she was to someone like Angel, the ruler of his own little country.

'May I see him?' Angel pressed.

Gaby's lips parted to utter a negative but then she thought about it. She already knew that Alexios was Angel's flesh and blood and soon *he* would know as well. What good reason did she now have to refuse him access to a mere glimpse of his sleeping son?

'OK, but you'll have to be very quiet. He's cross as tacks if you wake him in the middle of a nap,' Gaby warned, leaving him to follow her back across the hall into the kitchen, where a small corner staircase led up to her little apartment.

'What are you doing living here?' Angel asked.

'Clara had knee surgery and needed someone around

to help until she was mobile again. Alexios was a newborn. This arrangement suits us both because we both still have our privacy. In a few weeks, Clara will be moving into a smaller house in town, which will suit her better, and Alexios and I will be moving on.'

'To where?'

'I haven't decided because Clara doesn't have an actual moving date yet.' Gaby opened the door of her accommodation at the top of the stairs. 'Her son lived here until he emigrated.'

Angel thought the large room with its shabby furniture and small kitchen area at the far end was a dump. He paused by the one connecting door. 'Is the child in here?' he prompted.

Her face taut, Gaby stepped past him to open the door quietly and step into her bedroom, which she shared with her son. As luck would have it, Alexios was already awake, sitting up in one corner of his crib, hugging his rabbit blankie. A huge welcoming grin lit up his little face when he saw her. Behind her, she heard Angel release his breath in a sudden hiss.

'He has my mother's eyes,' Angel whispered hoarsely. 'And he looks very like baby pictures of me.'

'Surprise, surprise,' Gaby said drily as she bent down to lift the child already holding his arms up in anticipation. 'I did tell you he was yours.'

Angel tensed as she spun back round to face him. He wasn't comfortable with young children. None of his friends had had kids yet. Nobody handed him a baby and expected him to know what to do with it...but Gaby *did*. She plonked the child into Angel's arms as though he were a parental veteran.

Angel stared into those vivid green eyes that reminded him so disturbingly of his late mother. His son smiled and planted a chubby little hand against the stubble surrounding Angel's mouth, fingers exploring that interesting roughness. The baby giggled.

'He's not used to men, so you'll be a novelty,' Gaby remarked, feeling that in the circumstances she was being remarkably generous in sharing her son.

That innocent chuckle released Angel's tension. A smile flashed across his wide sensual mouth and Gaby's heart stuttered in receipt of that powerful flare of raw masculine charisma. Illuminated by that smile, his lean, darkly handsome features were incredibly appealing.

'He seems to be a happy baby.'

'He is. Why wouldn't he be? There are no problems in his little world.' Gaby moved back out of the bedroom. 'Do you want to play with him?'

Angel winced. 'I wouldn't know how to. You called him Alexios?'

'It's Greek.' Gaby coloured with self-consciousness.

'My great-grandfather was also called Alexios,' Angel remarked.

'Was he?' Gaby lifted and dropped a shoulder, refusing to be drawn as she reclaimed her son. She settled down on the rug with him and pulled over a plastic basket of toys. 'Come on,' she murmured ruefully. 'You have to learn how to play with him some time.'

Angel, the picture of elegance in his designer silk-and-wool-blend charcoal-grey suit worn beneath his coat, froze and gave her a startled glance. 'Right now?'

Gaby settled sapphire-blue eyes that gleamed on him. 'Now would be a good time. It's the easiest way to make him relax with you.'

Angel shed his coat and dropped down into the nearest armchair with the air of a condemned man.

Gaby disregarded his absence of enthusiasm. Angel did not like to be ignorant in any field. Anything that made him vulnerable seemed to put him on edge, but she wanted to see if he could make an effort and unbend for Alexios's benefit. She piled up bricks and Alexios sent them flying with exuberance. She settled a toy lorry into his lap, which he lifted to chew.

'Shouldn't you take that off him?' Angel enquired.

'No. Everything goes in his mouth at present. He's teething,' Gaby told him, trying not to stare as Angel inched forward off the chair much as though he were approaching a snapping shark and settled a plastic car on the rug in front of her son.

Angel made what she deemed to be 'boy' noises with the car and Alexios was delighted. From that point on she might as well have not been there for all the attention she received from her two companions and Gaby quietly left them to it, busying herself by making her son's lunch.


'He's falling asleep,' Angel complained.

'He will…he didn't have his usual nap,' Gaby reminded him, amused by his tone of disappointment. Alexios was a novelty for Angel and it worked both ways, Gaby conceded wryly. Men often played in a different way with babies than women did and Alexios had enjoyed Angel's more physical, noisy approach. She wasn't jealous of the bond she had seen developing between father and son because she could see how beneficial it would be for her child. 'But try to keep him awake. I still have to feed him.'

'And then perhaps we could talk...'

'There's not a lot to talk about... I mean, that reference to marriage was just pure insanity,' Gaby told him irritably as she busied herself in the little kitchen area. 'We'd probably kill each other by the end of the first month!'

'But what a way to go...' Angel husked, disconcerting her with that purred sensual response.

Sidestepping that inappropriate comment, Gaby picked up Alexios and slotted him into his high chair, attaching a bib and lifting the feeding dish. 'Let's stick to basics here. If you want a relationship with Alexios, I'm not planning to stand in the way.'

'It was premature to refer to marriage. I shouldn't have opened with the subject,' Angel cut in smoothly.

And that interruption convinced Gaby that he had never meant to mention marriage in the first place, which made much better sense to her. In the heat of the moment, he had got carried away. Her tense shoulders relaxed a little as she fed Alexios, making aeroplane noises and gestures with the spoon to keep him awake.

'I don't have any lunch to offer you,' she told Angel awkwardly. 'Clara and I usually have a snack rather than a meal.'

'Not a problem. I have to leave soon. I have an event to attend at home first thing tomorrow morning.'

Instead of feeling relieved by the reference to his departure, Gaby felt a sense of loss and hated herself. All right, Angel had been a colourful addition to her day, but she shouldn't have any personal reaction to him. The drama was over, a DNA test would be done, presumably fences would be mended for the sake of peace and Angel would become an occasional visitor in his son's life, she reasoned, censuring herself for getting more than superficially involved in his arrival.

Angel watched her tuck her sleepy son back into his cot. His proximity unnerved her. The room seemed to shrink around her as she brushed past him and closed the door. The faint tang of his cologne assailed her, firing memories of that night in Alharia, and she jerked back another step, accidentally knocking her hip against the wall.

'You're so jumpy around me,' Angel remarked.

Unwarily, Gaby glanced up and was immediately ensnared by dark golden eyes that burned through her defences like hot lava. 'Do you blame me? I mean, after what happened between us in Alharia?' she extended uncomfortably.

'No regrets this side of the fence, *glykia mou*,' Angel husked, staring down at her, the luxuriant black tangle of his lashes intensifying his stunning gaze. 'I'm no hypocrite. It was an extraordinary night.'

'Oh, *please*, like I believe that after the number of such encounters that you must have had!' Gaby riposted helplessly, breathless and taut in spite of every effort to remain unaffected by him.

'Extraordinary and unforgettable,' Angel repeated in defiance of that charge as he backed her into the wall, suddenly dangerously close and as dangerously intent on her as a tiger that had been provoked.

A ripple of awareness that was so highly charged that it almost *hurt* travelled through her slender frame. Her breasts felt constrained by her bra, the sensitive tips pushing to prominence against the scratchy lace while a clenching sensation tugged in her pelvis. Hot colour flooded her cheeks at that wholly primitive response that had nothing to do with logic and she trembled.

Angel scored a gentle fingertip across her cheekbone, his gaze molten gold with hunger, and it was too much for her in the mood she was in, all the emotional distress his appearance had evoked fusing with a desire she could not suppress. Stretching up on tiptoe, she claimed his wide sensual mouth for herself. He tasted of mint and fresh air and sunshine and a raw need that reverberated through her like a lightning strike. His mouth crushed hers and she felt as though she was collapsing into him until he edged her back against the wall for support. His tongue delved and liquid fire stabbed through her and that fast she wanted to rip his clothes off...

Her fingers dug into his shoulders, laced into his thick black hair. The fine fabric of his trousers couldn't conceal the bold thrust of his erection against her midriff and her hand travelled down over his chest to trace the throbbing evidence of his arousal. He groaned under his breath, pushing against her, tugging at the waistband of her jeans, pushing down the zip.

Their mutual hunger was frantic, uncontrolled. There was nothing seemly about it, she would later concede when she thought back to that moment and shuddered with embarrassment. But right then the allure of the forbidden sucked her right in and swallowed her alive. The brush of his fingers against her stomach was familiar, the less innocent slide of his hand beneath her knickers desperately desired and his carnal touch there, where she ached most of all, unbearably exciting. She pushed against him and quivered, helplessly enthralled by the demands of her own body, her heart racing and her blood thrumming with a wild insistent beat in her veins. Desire had caught her in a steely, unbreakable hold and with every plunge of his wicked tongue and every stroke of his hand her defences splintered and weakened. Her sensation-starved body surged to a feverish peak at his command alone. In climax, she jerked and gasped and then gasped again, pleasure claiming her in long, tingling waves.

'You drive me...*insane*,' Angel groaned just as her jeans began to slide down her thighs.

In that same instant a mobile phone buzzed loudly and he looked at her and she looked at him and just when she believed that he would ignore his phone, he glanced down at his watch instead and suddenly swore in ragged Greek. 'If I don't leave now, the jet will miss our flight slot!' he bit out in raw frustration.

Gaby turned crimson and yanked up her jeans, her feminine core still pulsing and her nipples as hard as bullets. She had craved sex with Angel as much as though he were an addictive drug. She couldn't believe what she had almost done, and her sole consolation was that a glance at Angel's unconcealed tension and discomfiture confirmed that he too was full of incomprehension at what had almost transpired. Up against the wall as well, she reflected sickly, like a wanton desperate hussy.

'Throw me out before I do something worse,' he urged in a driven undertone, brilliant eyes shielded by his lashes to glittering stars in darkness. 'You destroy my self-discipline...'

And she had no discipline whatsoever around him either, Gaby acknowledged with sudden shamed bitterness as she led the way back downstairs to the separate front door she rarely utilised to speed his departure. This time, however, he took her phone number.

'The test will be done within forty-eight hours,' he promised her before he stepped back over the wall and climbed back into the helicopter. 'I'll be in touch.'

And that was that, but she was shell-shocked, deeply shaken by that encounter. Angel had played with Alexios and had warmed up to their son in a way she had not known he was capable of achieving. Angel was so shuttered, so locked up in himself most of the time, and that arrogant, bold surface gloss of his usually hid the fact from the world. It was a challenge for him to loosen up, to relax his guard and yet he had done it for a baby's benefit. He had done silly things to amuse Alexios and that had touched Gaby in the most unexpected way. Would that willingness to get down to a child's level last? Would her son truly become Angel's heir? For good? Or just until Angel married and had another male child with a carefully chosen royal wife?

Those were questions and concerns that were still troubling Gaby while she walked up the gentle hill behind the farm on an afternoon six days later. She was taking a break because Alexios was having his nap and Clara had friends in for lunch.

Within twenty-four hours of Angel's visit, a technician had arrived to perform the DNA test and in due course Angel had texted Gaby to confirm that Alexios was *his* son…as if she had ever been in any doubt of that fact! She had to wonder why he had bothered to send that text without sending an unreserved apology with it because the year before, when she had approached him with her pregnancy, he had treated her like a gold-digging, publicity-seeking fraudster. Did he regret that now? Did he wish he had listened, *believed* her? Or did the ruling Prince of Themos not concern himself with such trivia as his past mistakes?

As she reached the top of the hill and stood looking out at the view, a helicopter swooped down to land in the field fronting the farmhouse. A tall man sprang out and her nervous tension rocketed as high as the skyline as she began to move back towards the house. Within minutes, the same figure reappeared and passed through the gate behind the farm to start moving in her direction. Her breath shortened in her throat and her pace slowed as she recognised that the visitor striding through the rough field grass towards her was indeed Angel. Why on earth was he here again so soon after his last visit?

'Gabriella…' Angel hailed her long before he reached her, black hair tousled by the breeze above his lean bronzed face, dark eyes narrowed to focus on her with noticeable intensity. Shockingly spectacular, shockingly sexy. He stopped several feet away, an incongruous picture in his designer suit against the backdrop of a windblown field.

'I was coming back to the house,' Gaby muttered uncomfortably, feeling rumpled and messy in the face of his habitually immaculate presentation.

'We can walk back together.'

Gaby shot him a fleeting look of frustration. 'What are you doing here again?'

With sheer force of will, Angel held that darting evasive glance of hers, dark golden eyes flaring bright. 'You should know why I'm here. I did warn you. Alexios is my son, and we will have to get married. The sooner we do the deed, the sooner life can settle down again and the less chance there will be for the press to make a spectacle of us and our child,' he concluded grimly.

'But you *can't* be serious about us getting married?' Gaby argued, her steps faltering as she turned round to face him.

'I'm deadly serious,' Angel contradicted.

'But why?'

'Your son's future is in Themos and I will not allow you to deprive him of his birthright and heritage,' Angel countered without hesitation.

An angry flush mantling her cheeks, Gaby flung her head back, copper strands sliding back from her face to accentuate her fine bone structure. 'I have no intention of depriving my son of anything that he *needs*!' she stressed.

'That's good, because he needs his father just as much as he needs his mother,' Angel slotted in glibly.

'What a shame you didn't feel that way last year when I approached you!' Gaby framed furiously. 'If you had *listened* to me then, you would have had much more time to decide how *we* should move forward as parents, and I very much doubt that you would have come up with anything as crazy as marriage being the solution!'

'Leave the past where it belongs and concentrate on our child for the moment,' Angel urged with a rapier-sharp edge to his intonation. 'Right now, Alexios is our most important concern. Let me tell you, I am determined that my son will have a far better and happier start to life than I ever had!'

'That's all very well,' Gaby muttered, taken aback by that sudden shadowy revelation about his own childhood and tucking it away for later examination. 'But marriage between us is *not* the solution.'

'I will be straight. It is either marriage or a custody case because I will fight you through the courts before I risk allowing my son to grow up without daily access to the country which is his!' Angel sliced back at her, stealing the breath from her lungs and freezing her in place while he strode back towards the farmhouse.

In fear, Gaby shook off her nervous paralysis and chased after him. 'You don't mean that, you *can't*!' she protested. 'Would you really try to take Alexios away from me? Are you really that cruel?'

'I would do it with great regret because a loving mother is a huge gift and I have no desire to separate you from each other. On the other hand, Alexios belongs with his father as well and if we cannot agree a compromise, I would have no choice but to fight you.'

'And...the only available compromise is *marriage*?' Gaby almost whispered, pale as death now.

'Yes. That way he has both of us and we share him, and he grows up in the country which he will one day rule,' Angel conceded, the harsher edge to his deep dark drawl easing a little. 'He will be my priority in life... I promise you that. I will be a parent in every way possible to him. There is *nothing* that he will lack...'

Wholly taken aback now by that passionate declaration of his parental intentions from a man whom she had once naively assumed couldn't care less about such matters, Gaby swallowed hard and said nothing, which of course turned out to be a mistake when Angel continued speaking.

'Perhaps it would be easier for you to give him up altogether and get on with your life, unrestricted by our son's status,' he intoned, shocking her even more with that suggestion. 'A royal life is full of restrictions and

I believe you have less interest in such a lifestyle than many women I've known.'

Gaby blinked while she tried to think fast about the horrible options he was putting before her. 'All these years and that's the very first compliment you have ever given me that didn't relate to my looks.'

Angel frowned. 'No, I'm not that superficial.'

'With me, you were, but maybe you're always like that with women,' Gaby remarked with a dismissive shrug. 'I'm afraid I'm not prepared to walk away from Alexios even though I suspect that that option might suit you the best.'

'Even though his mother walking away would *break* my son's heart?' Angel breathed with incredulous bite. 'You don't think much of me, do you? I would never wish such hurt on my son as abandonment by a parent would bring. It happened in my own family and the pain of it resonates even in adulthood.'

Gaby felt as though she had been thoroughly scolded. Her pallor was chased off by a guilty flush while she wondered who had been abandoned in childhood in his family circle. 'Who in your family did that happen to?'

Angel's lean dark features tensed. 'That is a private family matter I cannot discuss with you.'

Gaby reddened and looked away again. 'Let me sum up what you've said. According to you my choices are pretty basic. Marriage or a court battle? Not much room to negotiate there.'

'Yes,' Angel confirmed. 'But there is no viable alternative.'

Gaby chewed her lip to ensure that she didn't erupt into a flood of exasperated disagreement. In a world where single parents were commonplace, of course there were alternatives, only he was not prepared to consider them. And she didn't feel that she was in a strong enough or safe enough position to risk angering Angel by fighting bitterly with him. Angel would make a terrifying enemy, and not only because of his stubborn, arrogant and implacable character, but also because of his standing in the world. He was incredibly rich, and he enjoyed diplomatic status. He also had many friends in high places. In a court case centred on a child with a royal birthright, a child who was undeniably important to the country he would one day rule, how could she be sure how such a judgement would go? Mothers did not automatically retain custody of their children in all circumstances. Mothers could and indeed did lose their children if the father were deemed to be the more suitable parent to have custody. Angel might well fit that category when, one day, Alexios would become King.

'If it's a choice between a custody battle and marriage, I'll go for marriage,' Gaby murmured tightly, resisting the urge to point out that, in her opinion, he was not actually giving her a choice that she could reasonably be expected to think about.

Angel flashed her a sudden brilliant smile, relief lightening his unusually expressive dark golden eyes. 'It's the right decision,' he assured her.

'But that still leaves us a lot of stuff to talk about,' Gaby pointed out.

'No, it doesn't,' Angel stated with his usual confidence. 'Once we're married, everything will fall naturally into place.'

'Yes, what about…the other hundred and one things that matter in a marriage?' Gaby pressed urgently.

'We will be a normal couple…*and* we will be a family like other normal families.' Angel had difficulty putting into words exactly what he wanted for his son, but the word 'normal' kept on cropping up along with his highest hopes, reminding him that nothing about his own childhood had been remotely normal…at least, only normal for a severely dysfunctional family.

Angel knew that he was struggling to find words because on many levels he was in turmoil. He had only just discovered that he was a father and to some degree that was terrifying when he looked back at how much his own parents had let *him* down as a child. He knew that he would have to make a lot of sacrifices to be a decent parent. He would have to be there for the big things like birthdays and the little things like learning to swim. He would have to be there when life was good, but he would have to be there even more for his child when his life was difficult. Too often, proud independence had forced Angel as a child to hide his problems and struggle to deal with them alone.

Guilt pierced him when he remembered how he had rejected Gabriella when she was pregnant, when his care for his child and his child's mother *should* have begun. He had already failed them once, he could not, would not, do it ever again. He wanted Gabriella, but control with a woman was everything, he reasoned. As long as that sexual desire didn't get out of hand or threaten to turn into anything that would put him at risk of foolishness, it would be fine, he assured himself.

Gaby studied him in shock at that announcement he had made. 'But there's nothing normal about the life you lead.'

'That life of self-indulgence is over,' Angel told her

almost harshly. 'Alexios will come first in all things. I want him to be happy in a family setting.'

'Yes, of course, but what about all the women you currently run about with?' Gaby vented between clenched teeth as they reached the farmhouse.

'For once in your life, could you practise optimism?' Angel cut in reprovingly. 'Could you expect the best from me instead of only the worst? I can do faithful if I have to.'

Gaby was in absolute shock at the awareness that she had agreed to become Angel's wife, even while she knew that she would sooner not have been the catalyst for Angel saying that he could do faithful if he *had* to. There was nothing normal about that constraint and she wondered how to tell him that creating a normal family would not be easy for a man from his very different background unless he was willing to make enormous sacrifices. Why? Angel had never in his life had to respect limits. As far as she knew he had always done exactly as he liked, and he had done so from a terrifyingly early age. How on earth did he imagine that he would give up the freedom and variety of his very active sex life with uber-glamorous women?

And how on earth could someone who, by the sounds of it, had never known normal in his own childhood declare that he would provide it for Alexios? It was annoying not to know more about his background and troubling that he was so secretive on that topic. The inner conflict he was so determined to conceal only increased her curiosity while his willingness to change his life to best accommodate their son's needs could only impress her.

# CHAPTER SIX

'*THIS* IS THE LIFE!' Liz declared with a wicked grin as she nestled back in an opulent leather seat on the Diamandis private jet and saluted her sister, Laurie, and Gaby with a cocktail glass in her hand. 'I give you a toast—to the woman that broke the mould and exceeded all possible expectations, who is about to become a *royal* princess!'

'Pretty sure you just set feminism back by a century or two!' Laurie groaned for her twin. 'No, but I will toast Gaby for her power in getting a commitment-phobic prince to the altar! I think that's the real achievement here.'

'Alexios…' Gaby reminded her friend gently.

'Your prince isn't so slow that he couldn't have wriggled out of marriage if he had wanted to,' Liz opined. 'You set far too low a value on your own worth.'

'Gaby, *nobody* was immune to Angel's attraction at university and loads of women chased him. You're the only one *he* had to chase that I know of and the only one who ditched him!' Laurie told her with unhidden pride.

Gaby smiled with as much affectionate amusement as she could muster, full of regret that she could no longer be as frank as she had once been with her friends. She bent down to secure Alexios into his seat because the jet was about to land on Themos. It was not that she didn't trust her friends not to betray her, more that she felt that her son's privacy had to be protected and family secrets fell under that same label. The true background to the royal wedding due to take place in forty-eight hours would go to the grave with her, she decided morbidly. She hoped she would never be bitter enough to expose Alexios to the reality of his father's ruthlessness. When it had come down to marriage or running the risk that she might, at the very least, lose full-time custody of her son, Gaby had crumbled, and the matrimonial option had won. Angel had subjected her to his version of a shotgun marriage...

Unfortunately, exposure to Angel generally made her feel that she was weaker than she should be. He was blackmailing her, but she was still fiercely attracted to him and fascinated by him. She suspected that she would always want more than Angel would give her: feelings as opposed to orgasms. Although the latter were wonderful, she craved a stronger connection with him.

Only three weeks had flown by since that final epic meeting with him in Scotland. Everything that had happened during those weeks had exceeded Gaby's wildest expectations. Angel had phoned her every day, but generally only to ask random questions about Alexios or advance information she needed to know about the wedding arrangements.

A lawyer had arrived with a pre-nuptial contract for her to peruse and had advised her to obtain her own independent advice. Gaby had instead read it cover to cover. Aside from Angel's conviction that he should keep her in the lap of luxury for the rest of her

days regardless of how she behaved, and his desire for
Alexios and therefore Gaby, as his mother, to remain
on Themos, even in the wake of divorce, she had found
nothing untoward in the conditions. It had proved to be
a practical, businesslike document and she had signed
without further ado.

A woman from a famous fashion studio had flown
from Paris to Clara's house to measure Gaby up for a
wedding gown and to give her a preview of exclusive
models and accessories. As her matrons of honour, Laurie and Liz had also been included in that procedure at
their own homes. The extravagance of such an approach
to staging a wedding within so short a time space had
stunned all of them.

Clara had received an invitation but had opted not
to attend, insisting that she would enjoy her goddaugh-
ters' photos and descriptions of the event more. With
her husband currently working abroad, Laurie would
be replacing Gaby and helping Clara move into her new
home. Gaby's fiercely ambitious aunt, Janine, who was
working towards a partnership in her legal firm, had
decided that she couldn't afford to take time off to see
her niece married, and Gaby had not been surprised by
that unsentimental decision. Janine's driving force had
always been her career.

'Oh, my word, look at those beaches!' Laurie proclaimed and Gaby peered out of the nearest window to
see a disorientating blur of tree-lined coves with shimmering golden sands meeting a turquoise sea before the
jet swung over land again and she glimpsed buildings
and trees. Anticipation blossomed inside her.

The unbelievable opulence of Angel's private jet,
where the three women had been waited on hand and

foot from the instant they boarded, had startled Gaby, who wasn't accustomed to frills or even treats. She had gone from being a teenager always short of cash, and trying to conceal the fact, to an adult who saved constantly for a rainy day…and her rainy day had been pregnancy and motherhood, which had emptied her savings account.

The jet landed at Leveus, the capital city of Themos. An official came on board to check their documentation and then ushered them out into a limousine waiting right beside the jet to pick them up. The hot sun enveloped her, golden and warm on her skin, and Gaby soaked it up.

'Yes, definitely the dream life,' Liz proclaimed with a grin. 'Glorious sunshine. No queues, no baggage worries, no waiting for transport. All the hassle has been smoothed away for your benefit.'

'And there's no chance of paparazzi stealing a first view of the bride-to-be and the heir,' Laurie completed with satisfaction.

'The paps aren't allowed to operate on Themos,' Gaby explained, turning pink when her companions looked at her in surprise that she should know such a fact. 'They've been banned on the island because there are so many famous residents here, keen to protect their privacy.'

'Someone's been doing their homework,' Laurie teased.

'Of course I have,' Gaby confirmed as the limo filtered into a traffic stream that featured the very expensive cars utilised by an overwhelmingly rich populace. The crowded streets were lined with elegant exclusive stores. Even at first glance the Mediterranean city seemed glossier and brighter than others because there was no litter and the buildings all appeared to be in excellent repair.

'Oh, there's the cathedral where we'll be enjoying your big day!' Liz commented excitedly as the limo passed through a large, charming square dominated by the tall trees that framed the weathered cathedral, which was centuries old.

Gaby had indeed done her homework on the history of Themos and the ruling family, her retentive brain having absorbed every fact she'd dug up on the Internet. She had also studied numerous photos of Angel's parents. She had been startled by how much Alexios and Angel both resembled Angel's mother. Alexios had her distinctive black curls and green eyes while Angel had inherited her movie-star perfect features.

Angel came from an exotic background of almost unimaginable wealth, privilege and antiquity. Over the centuries, many larger than life personalities had graced the Diamandis family tree. Womanisers, warriors and adventurers featured heavily in Angel's ancestry. For goodness' sake, she thought ruefully, his mother had been an Arabian princess, a woman so flawlessly beautiful that Gaby had found herself studying her photos in fascination. The story recounted on the official royal website had gently hinted that family opposition had forced the Princess and Angel's father to run away together, and it had all sounded terribly romantic, which did nothing whatsoever to explain Angel's deep cynicism about women and life in general. When Angel had pressed her to marry him, he had, possibly without meaning to, revealed that his own childhood might have been less than perfect, and Gaby was very curious to know that story.

The Aikaterina palace was on the coast outside Leveus. It sat at the centre of a fabulous country estate comprising hundreds of acres of historic gardens and woods that were open to the public on certain days of the year. The woods ran all the way down to a private beach. Gaby had studied pictures online, reading about the original medieval fortress at the core of the building, the Renaissance wings and the Versailles-influenced extension that housed public rooms with a spectacular décor. Money, it seemed, had never been in short supply in the royal family.

'My word…' Liz sighed in wonder as the car swept between giant gilded gates and proceeded at a stately pace along a gravelled driveway lined with graceful cypress trees. Swathes of lush green grass rejoiced in the sun-dappled shade. 'This is some place.'

'It's really beautiful… I'm seeing my dream woodland garden,' Gaby remarked shakily, her nervous tension beginning to climb.

'Dream house, dream life, dream—'

'Angel may be rich as Midas and *look* like a dream, but he's a darned sight more complicated than that!' Liz reminded her twin wryly.

Very sexually driven though, Gaby was thinking helplessly, recalling that heart-stopping clinch against the wall, her body involuntarily tightening deep down inside. She was remembering Angel's assurance that they would have a normal marriage and she marvelled at the concept, convinced as she was that Angel had never enjoyed a normal relationship with a woman in his entire adult life. Women were merely the entertainment in

Angel's high-powered unscrupulous world, not equals, never partners. How would he adapt to living with a normal woman with ideas and opinions of her own? Particularly a woman whom he had ruthlessly blackmailed and intimidated into marrying him and who was still as angry as hell over the fact? Well, he would just have to learn, she reasoned with a spirited toss of her bright head as she climbed out of the limo inside the imposing porticoed shelter of the palace entrance and turned back to detach her son from his car seat.

No sooner had she released Alexios's belt than a hand touched her shoulder and she turned round to find Angel impossibly close. 'Let me...' he urged.

Colliding with hawklike dark golden eyes sent the butterflies tumbling through her and an intoxicating wave of awareness claimed her simultaneously, muscles tightening, heart accelerating, nerve endings awakening. On weak legs she stepped back and watched as Angel scooped Alexios out. Her son recognised him and laughed, delighted to see his father again because Angel, who had played with him, signified fun.

'Welcome to your new home,' Angel husked, radiating satisfaction and triumph in one fierce charismatic smile as she accompanied him into a vast marble and gilded entrance hall where several small groups of people awaited them. 'Allow me to introduce you to everyone...'

The first candidate was Marina, a smiling older woman introduced as 'Head of the Nursery'.

Taken aback and not in a good way, Gaby turned to Angel. 'I don't think—'

'Naturally you will be our son's primary carer but there will be occasions, such as the wedding and various events, when we will not be available, and we need a good support system. The nursery staff under Marina's steady hand will step in to fill the gaps.'

Gaby swallowed hard at that blunt appraisal of the near future. She also felt horribly like kicking Angel as though she were a cross and frustrated child. Why did he never discuss things in advance with her? Why did he never warn her? She was *not* unreasonable. He thought of everything but neglected to share his thoughts with her. That was unnerving. She smiled and shook hands with the older woman.

'You needn't worry about the quality of our son's care. Marina was a nursery maid when I was boy. She's kind and affectionate,' Angel murmured in her ear as he led her forward to meet the older man, Dmitri, who ran the household. He brought forward various advisors and administrative staff and, in the midst of those introductions, Gaby was unpleasantly surprised to spot Cassia Romano standing to one side chatting to Liz and Laurie. The slender blonde beauty, who rarely revealed any sort of emotion, wore a surprisingly bright smile. Gaby could see that her friends were disconcerted by that transformation because at university Cassia had not deigned to acknowledge either twin, even though both women had shared classes with her.

'Cassia has volunteered to show you the ropes around here,' Angel informed her calmly. 'She knows how everything works and I believe she has entertainment organised for you and your friends this evening.'

'Does she work for you?' Gaby enquired stiffly.

'Yes. Her father is a senior courtier and I've known her since we were children. It's not easy to define her position because she falls somewhere between an em-

ployee and a friend,' Angel advanced. 'And she may
not have been very approachable when you first met
her, but that will have changed because you are now
the future consort.'

'I see.' Gaby did see and she didn't like the news that
Cassia still held the status of a trusted friend.

Her reading of Cassia in the past had been that, in
spite of constantly playing the 'good friend' card, Cassia
would do and say anything to frighten off other women
and catch Angel for herself. Even so, Gaby had never
seen the smallest sign of intimacy on his part with the
beautiful blonde and back then Angel had been very
much prone to treating Cassia like the wallpaper, pleasant to have in the room but worthy of no particular notice. And nobody knew better than Gaby that when
Angel wanted a woman, he smouldered and burned
like the heart of a fire around her, she acknowledged as
she encountered a scorching glance from his stunning
dark golden eyes and her entire skin surface prickled.

Cassia moved forward. 'I hope your flight wasn't too
tiring, Miss Knox,' she murmured with a pleasant smile.

'Gabriella, please. How are you, Cassia?' Gaby asked
politely.

'I can't address you by your first name. It would
break protocol,' Cassia informed her with deadly seri-
ousness, as if the bending of one little rule would in-
voke a lightning strike. 'Let me show you to your suite.'

'Thank you, Cassia. I'll take care of that,' Angel interposed, still hugging Alexios to his broad chest like a
solid little comforter. Her son was resting his head down
sleepily on his father's shoulder, eyelashes drooping.

Angel showed her into a lift tucked in below the

sweeping staircase. 'The nursery is on the top floor. I think we'll go there first.'

'Yes, Alexios is tired. He gets all excited about new places and new people and he hasn't slept today.'

Her breath locked in her throat as she looked at him, ensnared by black-lashed tawny eyes that she could not withstand, and it was like standing too close to a fire, getting burned but still craving the pain.

*'Theos mou...'* Angel growled in a roughened undertone. 'I want you.'

Every nerve ending in Gaby's body melted into liquidity and overheated her. She was frozen there, her brain momentarily in stasis from the sheer rush of excitement. Angel closed the distance between them, pressing her back against the wall of the lift while his mouth hungrily crashed down on hers. His tongue delved between her parted lips and she was electrified, desire like a roaring wave engulfing her trembling body. Her hand flew up, fingers splaying to spear into his hair and hold him to her. He ravished her mouth with feverish urgency, his passion unleashed, and she was utterly lost in the sensation and excitement of the moment when a little squeak of protest alerted her to the reality that Alexios was being squashed between their bodies.

She jerked sideways and back from Angel as though she had been burned by a live wire and, in a way, she felt as though she had been.

Angel stared down at her in consternation. He had not intended to touch her, but no woman made him feel what Gabriella made him feel: that agonising, clawing need to physically connect. He didn't want that kind of incendiary bond with *any* woman, he never had because he knew the pitfalls all too well. Hadn't he watched his father sink into the gutter in his attempt to hold his own with the woman he had married, the woman he'd loved beyond reason?

'I don't think that was a very good idea,' Gaby quipped, controlling her anger at both him and herself with difficulty as she lifted her complaining son out of his arms.

'It was exactly what I wanted. Celibacy doesn't agree with me,' Angel imparted as they stepped out of the lift. 'I'll be in your room when you return from your evening out.'

Gaby flushed to the roots of her hair, thinking guiltily that he could hardly be blamed for the assumption that he would be welcome in her bed, and she squashed the instant leap of excitement at that idea. She was annoyed that she had not pushed him away. Why did she always let herself down around Angel? Why could she never deny the irresistible pull he exerted over her? Just for once, couldn't she have stepped back and told him tartly to keep his distance?

'No, please don't bother,' she warned him. 'I think you're forgetting how low you had to sink to get me to agree to this marriage.'

'No, that *wasn't* me sinking low. I believe that I was aiming *high*! Admittedly I put you under pressure, but I was thinking of the future and taking a unilateral decision as to what was best for the three of us as a family,' Angel shot back at her without apology. In fact, he had the nerve to give her a questioning look as though astonished that she had not yet recognised the higher purpose behind his intimidation tactics.

Gaby gritted her teeth, reckoning that he was shrewd enough to have justified anything short of murder. 'I should've known you'd behave as though you did us all a favour!' she snapped.

'So, you're pulling a Lysistrata to punish me…you're on a sex strike,' Angel clarified very drily, referring to the ancient Greek comedy by Aristophanes. 'And how good a start do you think that will give our marriage?'

'Right at this moment, I don't really care!' Gaby told him truthfully as he led the way into a very grand nursery that was startlingly contemporary.

'I had it updated for Alexios. It hadn't been used since I was a little boy,' he explained when he saw her staring at the very fancy train-shaped cot and the purpose-built storage for toys and books, every shelf already packed in readiness with items calculated to appeal to a toddler.

Marina appeared with Alexios's shabby baby bag in tow, and Gaby's rigid stance eased and she smiled in relief. In a matter of minutes, Alexios was changed and tucked into the cot. Angel closed a hand over her stiff fingers and led her away again. 'Cassia has some kind of hen party organised for you tonight, but I imagine that it will be a very *proper* event, shorn of phallic symbols and any silliness. She's invited my uncle, Prince Timon's two daughters.'

'Your cousins, who are acting as bridesmaids for us?' Gaby broke in.

'Yes, and some other young relatives whom you should meet before the wedding.'

Gaby nodded. 'Where are you heading tonight?'

'To a business investment dinner,' Angel told her, urging her down another flight of stairs. 'Generally, I have a pretty packed calendar, but I've pushed as much as I can to later in the season to enable me to spend time with you and Alexios.'

'We shall be honoured,' Gaby responded deadpan, only to still as Cassia emerged from a room just ahead of them.

'Forgive me for interrupting you but the Crown council meeting is about to begin downstairs, sir,' she announced. 'I can show your fiancée to her room.'

'If you will excuse me,' Angel murmured, stepping away from Gaby.

'Come this way, Miss Knox,' Cassia directed with confidence.

Gaby compressed her lips because she had wanted to tackle Angel about the nursery being a ten-minute hike from her room and Cassia's company was unlikely to ever be welcome. On the other hand, had she stayed with Angel in the mood she was in, they would probably have had another argument, she acknowledged ruefully. Perhaps she should be grateful for a breathing space.

'These are your rooms,' Cassia announced, throwing wide the door of a large sitting room and standing back for Gaby to precede her over the threshold. 'Last occupied by the Prince's mother and freshly decorated for you.'

The décor was very grand in airy shades of white, pale blue and green. Delicate panels painted with classic flowers ornamented the walls, providing the perfect backdrop for the beautifully crafted modern furniture. A huge bunch of artistically arranged flowers in a crystal vase scented the air. Cassia opened doors to show her the bedroom, the adjoining bathroom and the dressing room, saying, 'I hope you like the clothes…'

'Clothes?' Gaby queried with a frown.

Cassia slid back some doors to display a multitude of garments hung in zipped bags and entire shelves of folded clothing. 'The Prince ordered a new wardrobe for you.'

'That was very generous of him but I shan't *need* all this,' Gaby said.

'Living on Themos, you will need all of it. Wearing designer apparel is part of your public image as the ruler's wife,' Cassia informed her. 'I would suggest you choose a cocktail dress for dining out tonight. I hired a maid with the experience to do your hair and advise you on outfits.'

Gaby pushed a polite smile onto her lips. 'How thoughtful of you,' she said quietly.

'In the circumstances, I'm being very generous,' the blonde told her disquietingly.

'Which circumstances would those be?' Gaby asked.

Cassia folded her rather thin lips. 'Your bridegroom was originally planning to marry me… Oh, the Prince never said so, but I *knew* that he saw me as an ideal match.'

'Good heavens…' Gaby muttered in a shaken undertone. 'I had no idea.'

'Why should you have?' Cassia responded dismissively. 'That's water under the bridge now…forget I mentioned it.'

'Yes,' Gaby agreed, grateful to move on from an awkward subject but thoroughly needled by the blonde's coy little announcement. It stung, made her feel like a usurper in the position that Angel had given her. Cassia just oozed smugness and conceit. But was her contention true? How could the blonde beauty make such a claim when even she admitted that Angel had never discussed the subject with her? Of course, Cassia enjoyed unlimited confidence.

And Gaby could quite see that, as a local, accustomed to the royal lifestyle by her father's standing, Cassia Romano, with her icy aristocratic elegance and perfect diction, would have been an excellent choice of bride for Angel. Only the fact that Angel had never actually got around to mentioning marriage to Cassia or even reviewing the idea with her struck Gaby as revealing, much more revealing than Cassia was willing to accept. In reality, Angel had been in no hurry to marry anyone and only their son's accidental arrival had changed that.

'Your friends are in the suite opposite,' Cassia told her as she departed. 'We'll be leaving for dinner at seven.'

Liz, who was a real fashion buff, had a ball trawling through Gaby's new collection of clothing. Both women were shell-shocked when she shared Cassia's announcement.

'I know,' Gaby groaned. 'I didn't know how to feel about her saying that either.'

'Perhaps she's simply a very honest person and preferred to put the fact out there,' Liz opined with a wince.

'Maybe it was all in her head, this idea that Angel was planning to marry her, and she just likes to play the victim.' Laurie was less charitable. 'I can see no good reason for her to share her personal belief that she was to be his wife with anyone...particularly with the woman he's about to marry.'

'I think possibly Cassia may just be a little strange.' Gaby sighed, fingering a silky blue dress that appealed to her and tugging out a strappy pair of blue pearlised sandals that she couldn't wait to try on. She would not complain to Angel about the new clothes he had provided because her own wardrobe contained very few fancy outfits and none at all that could have qualified as designer. 'I think I'll wear this…it's smart without being over the top.'

'Do you think we'll be heading to a nightclub after the meal?' Laurie asked wistfully.

Gaby grimaced. 'I doubt it. Cassia doesn't strike me as the type, but look on the bright side…eating out is infinitely preferable to a formal reception staged simply for people to meet the bride.'

An hour later, fully dressed and ready to join her friends, Gaby emerged from her bedroom and came to a halt when she found Angel awaiting her in the sitting room. He was poised by the window, sunshine gleaming over his black hair, accentuating his hard, bronzed features and the sharp edges and hollows that made him so strikingly handsome.

'I forgot to give you this,' he murmured, stalking forward and reaching for her hand. Without hesitation he threaded a giant square-cut sapphire and diamond ring on her wedding finger. 'Everyone will be expecting to see a ring…why disappoint them?'

Gabriella looked fabulous in an understated dress that made the most of her feminine curves and slender shapely legs. The colour brought out the blueness of her eyes, the porcelain fairness of her skin and intensified the copper vibrance of her tumbling hair.

'Oh, I don't know…' Gaby stretched out a hand to watch the gorgeous jewels glitter in the sunlight. The sapphire was a deep velvety blue, surrounded by tapered baguette diamonds in a ballerina setting. She was shaken by its sheer *presence* on her finger. It was the sort of a ring that would stop traffic in the street, and she struggled to act as though she were accustomed to such magnificence. 'Is it really necessary to fake an engagement?'

Angel frowned, black brows pleating. There were times when Gabriella frustrated him beyond belief, and this was one of them. He didn't understand her in the way he had long understood other women. She didn't go into ecstasies over expensive jewellery, and she hadn't even mentioned the clothes. The gestures that usually smoothed feminine pride and other sensitivities didn't work for him with her.

'I meant well,' he breathed tautly. 'It's hardly fake when we're getting married the day after tomorrow, is it? But we skipped the conventional steps.'

'We skipped a lot of stuff,' Gaby told him tightly.

Intoxicating dark golden eyes framed by lush black lashes held hers. 'But this is a fresh start.'

'No, it's another chapter. We didn't *have* a proper start so we can scarcely have a fresh one,' Gaby contradicted, her tension easing only when her friends appeared in the doorway. 'Sorry, I have to go.'

All the way down to the entrance hall where Cassia awaited their arrival, Gaby castigated herself for her ungracious behaviour with Angel. She dug out her phone and texted him straight away, telling him how much she loved the ring and she thanked him very much for the new clothes. Sometimes in an effort to play it cool with Angel, she got things badly wrong and slid into sulky ingratitude, she acknowledged uneasily as her friends exclaimed in wonderment over the glittering sapphire and Cassia's lips flattened to a thin line on her words of congratulation.

The restaurant was very large and imposing and frantically busy. Gaby thought it was a surprising venue in which to stage a small, supposedly discreet dinner party. They were met at the door and conveyed straight to a central circular table. Several other young women were already seated there. In the flurry of bright introductions that followed and the serving of drinks, Gaby's tension began to lift. She sipped the glass of champagne that was served to her first, noticing that Cassia seemed to intimidate the other women present, giving her the impression that the blonde was not widely liked.

Not long after she had ordered her meal, she began to feel very hot. 'Are you warm?' she asked Liz.

'No, I'm fine. The food looks amazing,' her friend confided. 'But I'm surprised Cassia decided to stage this somewhere so public. Every diner here is frantically trying to work out which of us is Angel's bride and I've seen people taking covert photos on their phones.'

Gaby struggled to focus on Liz's amused face. Her mouth was very dry, and the room felt airless. As her tummy gave a nauseous lurch that terrified her, she flew upright. 'I'm off to the cloakroom.'

'Want company?'

'No, no, thanks.' Gaby didn't want an audience if she was about to be ill, nor did she wish to cast a dampener on the evening out. As she straightened, she felt dizzy and she wondered if she had picked up some ghastly bug travelling. Well, she would just have to get over it and fast, she thought worriedly as she followed the sign into a plush cloakroom. Her legs felt weak. Her breath rattled in her chest and something akin to panic assailed her at the rapidity with which she was falling ill. She dug out her phone and, without even thinking about it, pressed Angel's number.

'I'm not well,' she whispered. 'I'm feeling really ill, Angel...don't want to wreck the party—'

'Where are you?'

'Don't know name of restaurant...in the cloakroom,' she slurred as she slumped down on a padded chair.

The claustrophobic room was swirling round her, and the phone slid from her fingers as her head fell back, too heavy for her to hold upright. A moment later, she knew no more.

# CHAPTER SEVEN

GABY WAKENED GROGGILY in a darkened room, snatches of foggy recollection tugging at her woozy brain. Her lashes fluttered in confusion as she slowly breathed in and out, relieved to discover that she could catch her breath easily again. She shifted her arm, and something tugged painfully at her skin, causing a sound of discomfort to escape her.

A hand settled over hers. 'Relax. You have an IV line in...you were dehydrated,' Angel explained.

And the instant she heard his voice, Gaby felt the panic recede and she was soothed. She remembered the tightness in her chest, the difficulty in breathing and the way she had slumped in the cloakroom. 'I'm sorry,' she mumbled, taking in her surroundings and realising that hours must have passed because it was dark beyond the window. 'What time is it?'

'It's the middle of the night. You weren't fully unconscious when I found you, but this is the first time you've come round enough to speak,' Angel told her grimly.

'I'm in hospital?'

'Yes, but I'm taking you out of here the minute the doctor tells me I can,' Angel announced as he paced at the foot of the bed.

He looked ruffled, black hair tousled, his tie loosened, dark stubble outlining his strong jaw line. He still looked gorgeous though, just a little less immaculate than usual. 'I felt ill… I phoned you,' she recalled thickly, trying to regroup and compose herself.

'And I thank God that you did,' Angel breathed with raw sincerity. 'You were roofied…in a public restaurant. It is beyond belief that such a thing could happen to my bride! I could not believe that you could be at risk of any kind on such an outing. Believe me, I will not be so careless of your safety again!'

'Roofied?' Gaby gasped in disbelief. 'I was drugged? How is that possible?'

'We will find out,' Angel intoned wrathfully, smouldering golden eyes welded to the pale drawn triangle of her face. 'I assure you that we will find out who is responsible for this outrage. But it makes no sense. It is not as though you were in a club where someone might hope to steal you away from your companions. Nowhere could have been more public, more apparently safe… the police want you to make a statement.'

Gaby was reeling from what he had told her. 'Of course—'

'Like me, they are very much taken aback by this assault and are determined to find the culprit,' Angel breathed heavily. 'I would never have forgiven myself had anything happened to you. Why on earth did you leave the table?'

'I wasn't feeling well, and I didn't want to spoil the evening for everybody. I thought if I got away I would get some air and start feeling better…but when I think about it, that was foolish.'

'Yes. It was dangerous, less safe for you to do that…

but in a crowded restaurant and with you the guest of honour, who could have hoped to have removed you from the premises without it being noticed?'

'Maybe that wasn't the intent, maybe someone just wanted to make me ill,' Gaby muttered uncertainly. 'I only had one glass of champagne and nothing to eat. We had only just ordered. The only people who came close to me were the sommelier and the waiter.'

'Unless the drug was administered by one of your companions at the table,' Angel slotted in darkly. 'We cannot ignore that possibility, unpleasant though it is to suspect friends and family members of such an offence.'

'*Not* Liz and Laurie,' Gaby affirmed her complete trust in her friends.

A doctor arrived to check her over. Angel hovered, his anxiety a revelation to her because she had never seen Angel less than cool and collected or so concerned about anything. She was shaken too by the acceptance that when she had begun to panic as her body had failed to cooperate with her, she had instinctively turned to him for help. Without a moment's hesitation she had known that she could depend on him in a crisis and that revealed a level of basic trust in Angel that she had not known she had.

'Liz and Laurie are waiting outside to see you. They couldn't be persuaded to continue the evening and they followed me to the hospital in a taxi,' he told her with faint amusement. 'Despite my discouragement.'

'Never try to come between a woman and her best friends,' Gaby teased with a sudden smile.

A wicked grin of amusement chased the gravity from Angel's firm, sensual mouth and his dark golden eyes smouldered a lighter shade. Her mouth ran dry as her nipples pinched taut and an almost unbearable ache stirred between her thighs. Hunger clawed at her and she gritted her teeth in an effort to restrain that fierce surge of sexual awareness. As colour washed her cheeks, she turned her head away in embarrassment. 'I still can't believe that someone gave me a drug... I suppose I don't *want* to believe it.'

'None of us do but you arrived here quickly enough for the hospital to administer a blood test and we have the proof.' Angel sank down on the edge of the bed, dangerously close, frustratingly far, the faint scent of his cologne assailing her, achingly familiar. 'From this moment on you will enjoy a steel ring of protection around you...*nothing* like this will ever happen to you on my watch again,' he swore emphatically.

'It's not your fault. There are people who do bad stuff everywhere,' Gaby whispered soothingly, touched by his desire to make her feel safe again and ashamed of her own responses.

She had wanted to drag him down into the bed with her and the intensity of that desire shocked her. Attraction was one thing, ferocious craving an unbalanced and obsessive response, and Gaby admired restraint and sense much more. She could not admire the needy woman whom Angel was turning her into. It took her back to university and the pain of severance when Angel had finished his exams and returned to Themos. She had believed that she would never see him again and while in one way it had been a relief, in another it had hurt intolerably. Not for anyone was she revisiting those feelings, she assured herself bracingly.

She gave a statement to a police inspector who was very nervous at being in Angel's presence. Gaby had nothing much to tell the officer. She had not noticed anyone paying particular attention to her in the restaurant and did not feel that she made a very good witness. Liz and Laurie came in to visit her and Liz admitted that she had suspected something was wrong and had followed her to the cloakroom, only to find her passed out.

'And then Angel arrived when I was trying to revive you and it was all high drama then. He was very upset, and he grabbed you up and carried you out of the rear entrance of the restaurant with all his security men trying to take you off him and he wasn't having that. He didn't want anyone else touching you.'

'You know, I've never been his biggest fan,' Laurie chipped in ruefully. 'But he *is* brilliant in an emergency. I saw another side to him. He's very protective and he was in a rage that you had been harmed but his temper didn't get in the way of ensuring that you received immediate attention.'

At some stage of their visit, Gaby drifted into a doze and when she wakened again, Angel was back with her and a golden dawn was lifting the light levels in the room. 'Have you been here all night?' she asked, noting that the stubble surrounding his wide, sensual mouth was much darker and heavier.

'Yes. The doctors are happy for you to leave now and your maid has sent a change of clothes for you. If you feel up to it, we'll head back to the palace for breakfast.'

Uncomfortable because she felt such a mess, Gaby sat up and pushed back the sheet to swing her legs experimentally off the side of the bed.

'Careful,' Angel warned, cupping her elbow to keep her steady. 'You could still be dizzy.'

Gaby grasped the bag he handed her and entered

the bathroom, keen to remove her make-up and have a shower. Her reflection made her groan out loud. Her eye make-up had smudged, and she looked like a racoon. The shower refreshed her, but she still felt uncharacteristically weak. Not the way a woman wanted to feel the day before her wedding, she reflected ruefully, wondering who on earth had put that drug in her drink. Or even had it been meant for someone else at the table? Mulling over every possible permutation of what had happened, she put on the tailored trousers and top packed for her use and brushed her messy hair before bundling it up in a bun.

'I think I'll need another nap,' she confided in the limousine wafting them back to the palace. 'But Alexios will be wondering where I am.'

'When we get back, I'll spend some time with him. You need to rest. The wedding will be tiring,' Angel warned her. 'And I have some jewellery for you to examine.'

Back at the palace, Gaby took a nap. When she was up again, Angel brought a collection of jewellery to her suite and encouraged her to look at the pieces. 'I am hoping that you will choose to wear the sapphire set with your wedding dress. They are family heirlooms.'

Shock having seized hold of her lungs, Gaby stared down in disbelief at the jewellery on display for her benefit. It comprised a magnificent sapphire and diamond tiara, a pendant and earrings. 'Wow,' she framed limply, for she had no words to describe such glittering theatrical opulence. 'Did this superb set belong to your mother?'

'No, my mother preferred contemporary pieces. The sapphire set belonged to my father's mother. They are of Russian origin and design and she brought them with her when she married my grandfather. The choice of whether or not you wear them tomorrow is, of course, yours.' Angel paused. 'I believe you have a dress fitting now...your maid reminded me.'

Gaby winced. 'I forgot about that!'

'They're waiting for you in the room across the corridor,' Angel told her helpfully.

The afternoon bled away in a welter of wedding business, from how she was to wear her hair to which door she was to use entering the cathedral. A miniature map of the floorplan was laid in front of her. Not having realised until that point quite how elaborate the arrangements had to be for so large and important a wedding, Gaby began feeling increasingly nervous. What would Angel expect of her in her role as his consort? Would she be able to cope? As anxious as she was, it was a relief to head up to the nursery where she planned to spend some time with her son.

Alexios, however, was in the bath and when she peered in, she was taken aback by the sight of Angel in his shirtsleeves getting thoroughly wet as he dive-bombed their son's plastic ducks from on high. Water splashed everywhere as Alexios squealed with pleasure and smacked the water in excitement.

Marina, hovering at the back of the room holding Angel's jacket, beamed and stepped back into the nursery to join Gaby. 'They are having so much fun together,' she said happily.

'Yes,' Gaby agreed. 'I won't disturb them. I'll come back to feed Alexios in half an hour.'

In truth she was fascinated to see Angel more relaxed than she had ever seen him, his luxuriant black hair tousled, dense black lashes low over glittering dark eyes narrowed with mirth and appreciation, his damp shirt plastered to the sculpted lines of his muscular chest.

And she thought then, *this* is what he meant about being a 'normal' family, this is what Angel wants for our son and what he will actively strive to create. For the very first time, Gaby fully accepted that Alexios was Angel's son as well and she was grateful for their connection. In fact, she was impressed that Angel was putting in the effort and not simply going through the motions or relying on his wealth and what he could buy for his son's entertainment to do that bonding for him. Alexios was acquiring a father with an old-fashioned hands-on approach and she could not have been happier for her son. If only she didn't have to wonder if she would receive the same keen attention as Angel's wife...but she didn't want to be a duty in Angel's life or an extension of her son in his eyes. She was winding herself up, agonising about what he felt, and she felt, she told herself irritably. Where was the profit in that?

'So, nerves eating you alive yet?' Liz teased when the three women gathered for a relaxed spa evening in Gaby's sitting room.

'They will be by tomorrow but right now...' Gaby lifted her hands and dropped them again '... I have no regrets and I'm convinced that I've made the right decision.'

# CHAPTER EIGHT

GABY TOOK A final spin in front of the cheval mirror and the silk crepe skirt overlaid with Italian silk studded with crystals and mother-of-pearl teardrops flared out with the sleek weight of a luxury finish round her legs.

The off-the-shoulder design and skilled shaping at waist and hip flattered her curves while the narrow column of the skirt and her high heels gave her extra height. With the fabulous tiara anchored like a coronet of diamond fire in her mass of upswept copper hair, and the sapphire earrings and matching pendant, she knew that she had never looked better, and that knowledge gave her much-needed confidence.

'Absolutely fantastic,' Liz sighed fondly, snapping yet another photo with her phone.

'Are you ready, ladies?' Cassia asked brightly from the doorway. 'Could I have a private word with the bride before we leave for the ceremony?'

Liz walked straight out but Laurie walked across to the dressing table and fluffed her hair, taking her time over departing. Cassia, sheathed in a stylish cinnamon-coloured dress looked as glossy and bandbox fresh as if she had stepped straight off a magazine cover. She closed the door to ensure the conversation could not be overheard and Gaby's brow furrowed, her tension suddenly increasing.

'Cassia?' she questioned uneasily.

'I've agonised long and hard over whether or not to tell you about my personal relationship with Angel,' the blonde told her calmly. 'But, going forward, I prefer to be honest and open…'

'I haven't a clue what you're talking about,' Gaby admitted in a strained undertone.

'Angel and I have been lovers for years and I don't expect that to change after the wedding,' Cassia murmured, her face flushed, her pale eyes cast modestly down. 'We have a long-term, convenient connection. You will have to accept that if you want your marriage to work. Angel expects to do as he likes when he likes and that will not change.'

Gaby's chin lifted, her eyes cool as Cassia's drawling tone of self-satisfaction sent ice splinters travelling through her tummy. 'I don't believe you,' she retorted flatly.

She knew Angel better than she had years earlier and she recognised his essential streak of honour and decency, which was also laced with honesty. She doubted very much that Angel was indulging in some grubby sexual relationship with an employee behind closed doors.

That bold proclamation of disbelief seemed to disconcert the other woman. Cassia straightened her shoulders, her pale blue eyes sharp and glassy with the sheer loathing she had previously worked so hard to hide but which now shone like a beacon in her gaze. 'I assure you that I am telling you the truth. For goodness' sake, why on earth would I lie to you about such a thing?'

Gaby resisted a powerful urge to enlighten Cassia

about the effects of jealousy, rage and resentment on the female psyche. Cassia had patiently waited for her moment backstage for years while Angel entertained himself with an endless variety of women. Possibly, Cassia had assumed that age and boredom would make Angel switch his focus to matrimony and finally acknowledge that his reliable friend and right-hand woman, Cassia, would make the perfect wife. But, sadly for her, it hadn't happened. Not only had Angel failed to demonstrate any pressing need to settle down, but he had also fathered a son who could not be ignored with another woman. And all of a sudden, Cassia had found herself out in the cold, serving a rival whom she viewed as vastly inferior to her superior self.

'You're lying,' Gaby stated with quiet conviction. 'I understand why and I'm sorry that you feel the way that you obviously do, but there is nothing anyone can do to change the situation and I fully intend to marry Angel today.'

'You'll regret this!' Cassia hissed in a seething undertone. 'Believe me, you'll regret it! I'll make your life hell and don't doubt that I have the power to do it!'

All that Gaby regretted at that moment was the knowledge that she would have to share their conversation with Angel. How could she possibly work with or accept advice from a woman who hated her? She wasn't looking forward to having to explain why that was so to Angel, who would not be happy because he had long regarded Cassia as a dependable friend.

'And you really don't think that there's a shred of truth to her story?' Laurie prompted her friend worriedly fifteen minutes later during their drive to the cathedral.

Gaby's dark blue eyes were calm. 'I don't. I'm a good observer and I've never seen even a hint of physical familiarity or sexual awareness between them. It was Cassia's last-ditch attempt to wreck the wedding but, unfortunately for her, it didn't work.'

Liz was frowning. 'I can't see Angel having an affair with a member of his staff…and why would he want to anyway? He's never been short of female attention. You'll have to tell him what she said.'

Gaby winced. 'Some time obviously but not today. I'm not going to let Cassia get to me.'

Laurie smiled. 'That's the right attitude to have. But just the same, I'll send you the recording.'

Gaby's eyes widened. '*Recording?* What recording?'

'I don't trust Cassia. I left my phone on the dressing table in the bedroom to record your conversation before I left you alone with her,' she confided.

'My word, my sister, the consummate spy!' Liz gasped in delight.

'You recorded us?' Gaby prompted in astonishment as her friend simply nodded and grimaced.

'Sorry, I just didn't trust her at all…'

Walking down the aisle in the echoing grandeur of the cathedral with its soaring ceilings and packed pews demanded every bit of Gaby's confidence. She worked at keeping her head high, looking neither left nor right even as she felt the rustle of turning heads and heard the low murmur of comment that accompanied her passage. Angel wanted her to be his wife. That knowledge lifted her. It was only that the packed cathedral and her new status were a little intimidating. At the altar she saw Angel with another equally tall black-haired man by his side and she saw Angel swing round to openly stare as she approached, and colour flared like a burning banner in her cheeks.

One look at his bride and Angel was riveted to the spot. Gabriella's dress clung lovingly to her shapely curves and yet exposed only her creamy shoulders. Her glorious hair was piled in a vibrant copper mass on top of her head, providing a wonderful setting for the superb tiara glittering below the lights. The priceless sapphires merely enhanced her bright blue eyes and the luminosity of her skin.

'I'm impressed, little brother,' Crown Prince Saif of Alharia murmured softly from behind him. 'You did better than well.'

Angel's calm soothed Gaby's galloping nerves. They might have been alone in the room for all the attention he paid to their surroundings and their audience. She supposed that level of sangfroid only came with practice and experience. During the ceremony, he lifted her hand to slide on the platinum wedding ring and she glanced up, ensnared by his stunning tigerish eyes, and her heart started to race in spite of the acid reminders she was pushing quite deliberately through her brain.

This was the guy who had blackmailed her to the altar and trapped her between a rock and a hard place by using her precious son as a weapon against her. And he might have tried to wrap up his behaviour in clean linen by insisting that he was only thinking of what was best for all three of them but, in truth, Angel had merely utilised his power to get what he wanted at speed and with minimal personal effort. And he hadn't given her any time at all to adjust to the new status quo. Worse still, his demand for 'normal' in such an abnormal marriage was even less reasonable.

Desperately stoking up her anger in self-defence, she listened while the priest spoke timeless words over their bent heads. She looked at the ring on her hand and contemplated a truth she had long avoided. She had been in love with Angel at university, but she had refused to admit it to herself. In those days, unhappily, she had underestimated Angel's stubborn, wilful streak. She had assumed that he would compromise over the NDA she had refused to sign. She had failed to recognise just how ruthless Angel was at heart, not to mention how swiftly he would move on from her. The hurt inflicted by that rejection had taught her not to assume that a man would react the same way she did to obstacles. Angel hadn't cared enough about her to reconsider his boundaries or his rules. Indeed, when she had coincidentally seen him kissing that other woman at the party, he had been demonstrating his indifference to her...and hitting back. Don't forget that, she reminded herself doggedly. Angel was a vengeful soul.

Indeed, so fiercely and efficiently did Gaby revive her every worst thought and feeling about Angel that her profile might have been chipped out of pure ice as they walked back down the aisle again, his arm resting lightly at the base of her rigid spine. Only at that point did she register that she was reviving her negative outlook as a defence against the other powerful emotions flooding her. Angel and what he might do and what he thought meant so much to her *because* she still *loved* him.

It was a moment of revelation that shook and stunned Gaby in the wake of that anxious flood of critical recollections. Fear of allowing Angel to have that power over her again had made her throw up every possible barrier because naturally she didn't want to get hurt again. Only, sadly, her emotions and the world in general were not under her control.

'You look stunning,' Angel murmured softly. 'But you can smile now.'

'To do that I would have to have something to smile about,' Gaby countered in a dry joke, her mouth quirking as they walked out onto the steps, and dismay gripped her when she realised that television cameras awaited them.

Angel caught both her hands in his and tugged her round to face at him. 'We did it for Alexios but that doesn't mean that we can't enjoy being together,' he told her softly, his dark drawl roughening as he gazed down at her. 'Or that we can't make a huge success of this marriage.'

His striking dark golden eyes held hers with savage intensity, as though he were demanding that she concede those points. A flush of heat and awareness enveloped her entire body, slowly sliding over her prickling skin like a silken caress, awakening every nerve ending and causing a tightening at her feminine core. The sensation was so strong that it almost hurt, and the tip of her tongue slid out to wet her taut lower lip.

'Don't do that when we're in public,' Angel warned her in a roughened sensual undertone. 'It turns me on way too much.'

Gaby's eyes widened and the butterflies tumbled in her stomach and for the space of ten seconds there was nothing and nobody else in the world for her. He linked his fingers with hers and walked her down the steps past the flashing cameras and shouted congratulations. She was still trying to catch her breath as he tucked her into the waiting limousine.

'I'm looking forward to introducing you to my brother, Saif, and his wife, Tatiana, at the reception,' Angel volunteered with a shimmering smile.

'You have a brother?' Gaby exclaimed with incredulity, still struggling to shake herself free of the sensual spell that he could cast. 'Since when did *you* have a brother?'

'A half-brother from my mother's first marriage,' he explained. 'My brother is the Crown Prince of Alharia. Our mother was married to his father, the Emir, first. She deserted the Emir and my baby brother to run off with my father. The divorce was very discreet. I was born only weeks after my parents married.'

'Why was your relationship with your brother kept a secret?' Gaby prompted in curiosity.

'Saif's father is old and ill and still sensitive to that ancient scandal. Saif knew the Emir would be upset if he admitted that he had sought me out, but he finally bit the bullet and owned up. Today he just turned up and told me that he intended to be my best man. I was shocked,' Angel confided with a softened light in his gaze. 'But I was very pleased to have him by my side.'

'I can see you were,' Gaby admitted, jolted by the emotion unhidden in his expressive eyes. 'Oh, my goodness, now I know what you were doing in Alharia when we met again! Obviously, I guessed you were a wedding guest but—'

'Yes, I flew in for Saif's wedding only to discover that I couldn't show my face at the event in case I was recognised. He hadn't told his father about our friend-

ship at that stage,' Angel told her heavily. 'That was a
sobering experience…'

Gaby wondered how much experiencing that disappointment that same day, over his brother's reluctance to
acknowledge their familial bond, had influenced Angel
in his attitude towards her that night when Alexios had
been conceived. 'I expect it was…and Saif must have
felt it too. I'm sure he must've felt that he was letting
you down,' she remarked thoughtfully. 'That's why he
was so determined to show up for *your* wedding and
show the world that he is your brother and proud of it.'

Angel glanced at her with veiled appreciation, impressed by her understanding. 'He's sensitive that way,
more so than me. I did understand how difficult a position he was in, with the Emir having a weak heart.
That's why Saif being here today with his wife and son
means a great deal to me. Their son, Amir, is almost
the same age as Alexios…'

'And our sons will totally ignore each other,' Gaby
forecast with a chuckle. 'They're too young to be play-
mates yet.'

Much of the tension that had gripped her in the cathedral had drained away again. 'So, your mother left
Saif behind in Alharia as a baby when she met your
father. That must've been a very difficult decision for
her to make.'

Angel shot her a wry shuttered glance. 'I doubt it.
She didn't like children much. She never saw Saif again
and she didn't *try* to see him either. Saif swears that his
father would have allowed her access to him, but she
never asked for it. Instead, she acted as though he had
never been born.'

In receipt of that rather astonishing information,

Gaby widened her eyes, and her lips parted in a sound-less 'oh' of surprise. Saying that she *didn't like children much* was a very revealing admission to make about one's mother, she reflected on a surge of frustrated curiosity, but, as the limousine was drawing up at the palace, she clamped her tongue between her teeth and said nothing before gathering herself to walk back into public view.

A photo session had been set up in one of the grand ground-floor reception rooms. The wedding party was the main feature of those photos. She was briefly introduced to Prince Saif, who grinned at her and waved at a small blonde carrying a baby. 'My wife, Tatiana. She's dying to meet you.'

'I shall look forward to it,' Gaby said warmly as Marina appeared in the background with Alexios.

'Do you have any objection to Alexios joining us for the photos?' Angel murmured covertly. 'I thought it would be a pleasant, unfussy way of introducing him to our country.'

'No, I think it's a good idea,' Gaby agreed, flushing as the photographer sent her a reproachful look as he tried to keep everyone engaged with the session. 'But I'd agree to anything right now to get my paws on my son again. I've hardly seen Alexios since we arrived.'

'It looks as though he feels much the same way,' Angel remarked, watching his son squirm frantically in Marina's hold and stretch out desperate arms in his mother's direction.

Gaby clasped her son and endeavoured to restrain him from bouncing on her lap. Angel grabbed him and occupied him for a few minutes. The photo session came to an end. Alexios returned sleepily to Marina, and

Angel and Gaby greeted their guests in the ballroom where the meal was being served. She met Saif's wife, Tatiana, and took to her immediately. Her warmth and friendliness were very welcome, and it was no time before the two women and Liz and Laurie were discussing babies and laughing while Alexios and Amir sat on a rug side by side, only noticing each other when the more mobile Alexios moved to snatch at a toy that Amir also had his eye on.

Laurie approached her when they were taking their seats for the meal. 'Have you told Angel yet about Cassia?' she asked covertly. 'I've sent you the recording.'

'Thanks…no, not yet. I'll choose a quieter moment,' Gaby declared, reluctant to admit that she really didn't want to tackle the topic or make use of the recording. It seemed underhand.

In addition, Gaby didn't like attacking or confronting people. Perhaps resentment had sent Cassia recklessly over the edge and she would regret her wild claim and the subject would never be mentioned again. Did she really want to be responsible for Cassia being disgraced and losing her job? Gaby didn't believe that Cassia was Angel's occasional mistress, she really *didn't*…but she supposed there was always the chance that she was being foolishly blind and naive, and she had to share that little scene with Angel.

'So,' Gaby whispered under cover of the music during the meal. 'Are we going anywhere after this ends?'

'Into the mountains to my grandparents' hideaway,' Angel murmured. 'Although we have many other more glamorous options. I have a yacht and property in several major cities, but I thought that right now we would both enjoy time to decompress in a peaceful setting. Alexios and Marina will join us there tomorrow.'

'Oh…'

'You can tuck him in for the night before we leave,' Angel told her teasingly.

Angel's uncle, Prince Timon, and his wife took charge of the reception late afternoon and urged the bride and groom to make a quiet getaway.

'Don't take off the dress,' Angel urged as Gaby walked towards the stairs, intending to do just that.

She spun back, soft pink warming her cheeks. 'I was planning to put on something comfy.'

'That doesn't sound very sexy,' Angel husked. 'And the dress and the sapphires are a dynamite combo.'

'I *can't* travel to a mountain hideaway in a tiara and a wedding dress!' she hissed back half under her breath.

'We have one wedding day, one wedding night…this is a special occasion,' Angel persisted, his dazzling dark golden eyes gripping her. 'Let's for once leave the sensible and the comfortable for another day, *hara mou*.'

'I'm *not* always sensible!' Gaby bit out in a mortified undertone.

His brilliant eyes gleamed. 'If you're not, *prove* it.'

It was true and she wanted to kick him for knowing the fact. She had always been sensible. Her parents had raised her that way, teaching her to set a good example for her little brother. After the death of her family and the pained awareness that her aunt really didn't want the stress of raising a teenager and had only taken her on out of a sense of duty, Gaby had known that she could not afford to make any waves and she had focussed on being even *more* sensible. In denial of the obvious, she climbed into the SUV that awaited them outside the palace still in her dress and the sapphires. With incredulity, she watched Angel swing into the driving seat, sleek and assured in faded jeans and an open shirt.

'*You*…changed,' she enunciated grittily.

'Yes…why? Were you just gasping for the opportunity to strip me out of my morning suit…or were you hoping I would do a lap dance for you and make the encounter a little more stimulating?' Angel purred with rapier-sharp amusement.

Gaby tipped her head back, thinking that Angel in all his bronzed muscular glory was quite exciting enough without a lap dance included. 'Well, we all have our fantasies,' she countered, refusing to rise to the bait.

'Care to share?' he prompted.

'Not right now,' Gaby replied unevenly, keen to change the subject because when Angel mentioned intimacy, however obliquely, he threw her into a quandary because she had still to decide whether or not she intended to share a bed with him again. She liked to think things through but around Angel such straight thinking was a challenge. When she tried to weigh pros and cons into the equation it made her feel petty and appreciate that she needed to simply go with the flow.

'I like your uncle, Prince Timon, very much,' she remarked quietly.

'A less than deft change of topic,' Angel mocked. 'Yes, Timon is a good guy and I was very lucky he agreed to accept the Regency and take charge after my father died. He had a life of his own as a business mogul in New York and he put it aside for several years for my benefit. For a younger brother, who never wanted the throne and barely knew his nephew, it was a big sacrifice. I couldn't have managed without him though, and he taught me a great deal, particularly about business.'

'Yes, you were only sixteen. Losing both parents together must've been devastating for you,' she muttered ruefully. 'I know I've never really got over losing my parents and my kid brother and I was only a couple of years younger at the time.'

Angel reached for her hand and squeezed it. 'I know you were devastated. When you told me years ago, there were tears in your eyes and the way you talked about your parents and little brother made it obvious that you were a happy foursome. Your loss was tragic...'

'Yes,' she whispered unevenly.

'The death of my parents was probably easier for me,' Angel conceded tautly after a long stretch of silence had prompted her to turn her head and look at him enquiringly. 'We weren't a close family. They had their lives and I had mine and, aside from photo opportunities to sell the cosy family concept to the public, I only saw them occasionally when I was home from boarding school.'

Gaby was frowning. 'It sounds pretty cold and artificial.'

'It was.'

'So why did they have you?'

'Don't be naive. My father needed an heir for the throne and once I was born he could relax, duty done.'

'And your mother...you said she didn't like children much?'

'She didn't but I'm not sure my father would have married her if she hadn't got pregnant, so my conception was probably planned every step of the way,' Angel said cynically. 'Her family had married her off to a man old enough to be her grandfather and she wanted out of Alharia…look, I really don't want to talk about this.'

Disconcerted by that blunt admission, Gaby swallowed hard. 'Er… I—'

'You seem to have an incessant curiosity where my family is concerned. I should warn you that there's a lot of murky messy material in my background, not the sort of stuff you would enjoy hearing about,' he assured her pointedly.

Gaby had paled, recognising that she had pushed too hard too fast for him to talk about his troubled background. He wasn't ready yet to talk, to share with her, but time, she reflected, would make him more comfortable with her. Naturally, her curiosity had increased when she'd learned through his half-brother's existence that there was another whole layer to his family circle.

'I'm not a prude,' Gaby murmured tightly, referring to his assumption that she would be upset in some way by what he called 'murky material' in his background. 'Sensible doesn't mean stuffy.'

'A virgin at twenty-four? That speaks for itself. Look in a dictionary and under P for prude you will find an image of someone who looks remarkably like you!' Angel riposted.

'If you weren't driving, I'd thump you!' Gaby told him tartly.

'See…*sensible*,' Angel murmured, soft and smooth as silk, reaching for her hand and bringing it down on a lean, powerful thigh, the strong muscles below the taut denim flexing beneath her palm. 'You can't change what you are at the core.'

'I seriously hope you're wrong in that conviction,'

Gaby contended. 'After all, you're a womaniser and I don't want to be married to a womaniser.'

'I made the most of my freedom while I was a single man, nothing wrong with that,' Angel asserted with unblemished cool. 'Now I'm in a different phase of life and I want a successful marriage.'

'That all sounds very good on paper but it's not easy for a leopard to change his spots over the long haul,' Gaby opined, not so easily convinced that he could be a changed man.

'You cherish such low expectations of me, and do try not to refer to our brand-new marriage as "the long haul". That's downright disheartening,' he censured while electric gates swept back to allow the SUV access to a steep track lined with trees that arched overhead in a living canopy.

The track became rough and stony and passed along the edge of a large lake, also surrounded by woodland. A sprawling stone and wood building that looked remarkably like a large Tuscan farmhouse came into view. It was very picturesque and not at all what she had expected of their destination.

'This place hasn't been used much since my grandfather passed away half a century ago. My parents weren't into country life. I did think about tearing it down and replacing it with something more contemporary.'

'Oh, no, look at those roses!' Gaby exclaimed, already climbing out of the car to get a closer look at the superb many-petalled ivory blooms trained to frame the veranda. 'It would be a sin to disturb them.'

She likes roses, Angel registered, watching in fascination as his bride lifted an almost reverent fingertip to stroke a velvety soft cream petal. He wondered if she would ever touch him with the same appreciation and wondered why he would even want that from her, why the sight of her hair gleaming in the sunshine, her delicate profile and the glitter of the dress sheathing those wondrous curves almost dazzled him. Sexual deprivation, he reckoned wryly. He'd be seeing unicorns in the woods next. After all, women *never* dazzled him.

He was not easily impressed by her sex. He knew that very few women could be trusted, for women had let him down time and time again, not least the one who had given birth to him. No, keep it all in proportion, he urged himself. Gabriella was a rare beauty, clever and entertaining and in a decidedly different style from his previous lovers, but she was also completely infuriating on a regular basis.

'There's a rose garden somewhere around,' he proffered vaguely, feeling oddly guilty for that last critical thought as he thrust open the door and urged her inside. 'I used to fish in the lake when I was a boy.'

Gaby stared at the rustic wooden stairs several feet ahead of her and shone her inquisitive gaze round the roomy hall, with its old-fashioned black-and-white photos on the walls and the cosy fireplace adorned with a basket of greenery and a vase of roses. 'It's charming,' she said softly.

A little woman emerged from an ultra-modern kitchen that looked new and bobbed a curtsey. 'This is Viola, Gabriella. She looks after the house while her husband and sons tend the vines. She's a wonderful cook,' he murmured in a low voice, switching to Italian as he told the older woman that she was free to finish for the day. 'Let me show you the rest of the house…'

Upstairs he showed her into a big airy room with ancient floorboards and a high beamed ceiling but while the surroundings were old, the furnishings were modern. Pale green and white drapes fluttered in the cooling breeze emanating from the open French windows. Gaby walked through them out onto a large balcony that literally seemed to be hung on the edge of a cliff to give a fabulous view of the wooded mountain range and the agricultural land spread out in the valley below. 'I feel as though I'm standing at the top of the world,' Gaby murmured appreciatively.

'Apparently, my grandparents stumbled on this place soon after they married. The house was derelict, and they rebuilt it and extended it several times. I imagine the lake sold itself because my grandfather was, apparently, a keen fisherman.'

'But you didn't know them personally,' she gathered, by the way he was talking.

'No, they had my father later in life and had passed by the time I was born. It's a shame. By all accounts, my grandfather had the stability that my father lacked.'

Gaby tensed as Angel drew her back into the shelter of his body and slowly turned her round. 'There are upwards of sixty hooks on the back of that dress,' he informed her with glittering dark golden eyes.

'I know,' Gaby admitted with a rueful grin as she collided with those beautiful, black-fringed eyes of his. 'But sometimes you have to work harder for what you want...'

'Is that so? You married a guy who likes shortcuts,' Angel told her, sweeping her up into his arms and striding back into the bedroom.

'People who take shortcuts often pay poor attention to detail,' Gaby warned him with dancing eyes as she gazed up at him. 'And you *are* the party who chose the sixty-plus hooks for me to travel in.'

'But I excel at detail,' Angel swore, setting her down beside the bed and embarking on the hooks that followed her taut spine.

All of her was rigid, she registered uneasily, and not with antipathy. In fact, her whole body was tense with a wicked, almost joyful anticipation.

'Am I allowed to take off my shoes, because they're pinching my toes?' Gaby whispered. 'Or would that spoil the fantasy?'

Angel laughed and lifted her up onto the side of the bed, lifting her skirt to expose her feet. Lean brown hands curved to her slender thighs as she kicked off her heels with a wince, but she was infinitely more aware of his fingers almost absently stroking her skin. He bent to close a hand round one slender ankle and the same talented digits gently massaged her sore toes, slowly and carefully. A soft sigh of relief escaped Gaby and she leant back on her elbows to extend her foot for more of the same treatment.

Smouldering dark golden eyes gripped hers and her tummy somersaulted, heat surging at the heart of her. Her breath caught in her throat as she gazed back at him, mesmerised by the glittering intensity of his eyes set in his lean dark features. That fast she knew she had been kidding herself about having to make a decision about whether or not she would share a bed with him again. She looked at him and she craved him. It was that simple, *that* basic, like the tingling prickling of awareness engulfing her and the surge of blood rushing through her veins, making her agonisingly conscious of certain parts of her body.

'*Theos mou*… I want you,' Angel growled, hauling her up to him to snatch a raw, hungry kiss awash with so much passion that it sizzled. 'I was burning for you the instant I saw you in the cathedral. You looked ravishing… I couldn't believe you were mine.'

Her lips pink and lush from the onslaught of his, she pulled him down to her and tasted his sensual mouth again for herself, rejoicing in the hard strength and weight of him over her, desperate for that connection. The plunge of his tongue lit her up inside like a firework display and she squirmed, trembling as his fingertips brushed her bare thigh, eased beneath the lace edge of her knickers and stroked the swollen folds between her legs. She jerked, wildly oversensitive to the smallest touch.

'Angel, please…' she hissed, needing more, wanting more with every fibre of her body.

'Detail at which I excel…' Angel reminded her raggedly, tugging her back upright again, turning her around and attacking the hooks afresh. 'I must demonstrate a little finesse.'

He spread back the fabric from her spine and pressed his lips to a quivering shoulder blade. Her breath hitched low in her throat and hung suspended as he released the hooks one by one while trailing his mouth very lightly over the most sensitive span of skin on her back. It was sensual, rawly sexual, everything Angel could promise with one burning look and her body behaved accordingly, her breasts feeling constricted inside her fancy bridal corset, her nipples peaking into tight buds, the dampness of response pooling between her thighs.

As the last hook released he tugged on the sleeves and her wedding dress tumbled round her toes. The faintly cooler air from the open windows cooled her overheated skin. Angel closed a hand round a slender shoulder and urged her back to face him.

'How am I supposed to stay in control when you look like every guy's fantasy?' Angel enquired, a faint flush scoring his high cheekbones as he scanned the delicate palest blue beribboned mini corset, the diaphanous knickers and the suspenders anchored to the silk stockings.

That he could not hide how impressed he was sent a shot of pure adrenalin powering through Gaby's lack of confidence. With one bedazzled appraisal, in that moment Angel made her feel like the most seductive, gorgeous woman alive. 'You don't need to...er...stay in control,' she murmured.

'I didn't the last time,' Angel muttered in a haunted undertone.

A fractured memory of that night crept back into Gaby's brain, the sort of recollection she had rigorously suppressed for almost eighteen months. But just then she was remembering that wild, seething passion that had gripped them both throughout that night, incomprehensibly rising again and again even when she ached in every limb, even while she marvelled at how utterly compulsive, how driven sex was with him and not at all the less involved, more casual activity that she had once vaguely imagined it would be in her ignorance.

'Yes...but it was...amazing,' she almost whispered, colour warming her cheeks.

His dark golden eyes smouldered like molten honey. 'And for me,' he confessed grittily, as though it pained him to admit the fact.

He disconcerted her then by dropping to his knees to tug down the filmy knickers. Stiff with self-consciousness, she stepped out of them. That night in Alharia, she had not had to deal with the embarrassment of her nakedness, but here it was broad daylight and her body had changed from what it had been eighteen months earlier. Her hips had widened, her breasts were larger, her tummy was no longer perfectly flat and taut while silvery stretch marks and a C-section scar marred skin that had once been smooth.

His long fingers holding her steady, he used his mouth on her heated flesh. A ripple of raw arousal shimmied through her like an intoxicating drug. She told herself she would stop him, because standing there in the sunshine with that happening to her seemed totally shameless, but instead of stopping him her fingers sank into his luxuriant black hair and little gasps of sheer bliss were wrenched from her.

And then, right when she was on the very edge of satisfaction, Angel vaulted upright and lifted her back onto the side of the bed. *'Angel—'* she began.

'I don't want you to come until I'm inside you, *hara mou*,' Angel husked, unzipping his jeans at speed and ripping open a foil packet with his teeth like a man on a mission to win a marathon.

'I'm on the pill now!' she heard herself exclaim as if that were relevant, when really, she thought a second later, it wasn't in the same way because they were married.

For a split second, Angel paused, a frown line dividing his black brows, and then he flashed her a brilliant smile. 'Good to know...' he muttered thickly.

There was a moment when he stood over her, fully erect and ready for action, and her heart thumped so hard she was afraid that he would hear it. The urgency in his every movement only reflected the crazy pent-up need clawing at her. He tipped her back with ruthless hands and sank into her hard and fast and she cried out at the intensity of the sensation, the ripple of response clenching her as his piercings increased her sensitivity.

'Did I hurt you?' he exclaimed, suddenly freezing.

*'No!'* she gasped frantically. 'Don't stop!'

Angel grinned wickedly down at her, black hair tousled by her fingers. He shifted his lean hips with expert precision, sending delicious feelings tumbling back through her again, answering the hunger controlling her with his own. Excitement laced her pleasure, her heart pounding, her body quivering with surging response. Need was a tight knot deep in her pelvis, pushing her ever on towards fulfilment. As he set a hard rhythm, pounding into her, sensation piled on sensation. Angel had incredible stamina and within minutes an explosive climax took hold of her. With pleasure roaring through every fibre of her body, she cried out and flopped back on the bed, weak in the aftermath.

Angel tugged her up into a sitting position and released her from the corset, rolling down the stockings with quiet efficiency. Then he removed the tiara and the rest of her jewellery and set it aside. 'Are you hungry?' he asked her.

'My goodness, no,' she mumbled, smothering a yawn.

He pulled back the bedding and gently rolled her unresisting body below the sheet. 'Get some sleep.'

'It's our wedding night,' she reminded him guiltily.

'And you've already surpassed my every expectation,' he murmured softly, smoothing her tangled hair back from her brow. 'I'm going for a shower and then I'm coming to bed too. It has been a very long week.'

'Yes,' she agreed drowsily. 'I have to talk to you about Cassia soon.'

Unseen, Angel grimaced, although he could not say that declaration had been unexpected. Cassia had been hostile to Gabriella even at university and possibly it had been unreasonable of him to assume that Cassia's cool assistance would be welcome to his bride. Sadly, there was nobody more efficient or informed on his staff, he reasoned wryly, but that was life. Unlike him, other people let personal feelings get involved and that always caused trouble.

Yet he couldn't be sorry that he had married Gaby, instead of Cassia, who had once looked so perfect on paper. Now he recognised how Gaby's warmth, both as a personality and as a parent, drew him, how stupendous their sexual connection was proving to be and how intriguing he found that lively outspoken independence of hers.

# CHAPTER NINE

GABY WAKENED WITH a sense of well-being that was rare for her. It took a minute or two for her to recognise the lovely sun-drenched bedroom and reorientate herself again after all the excitement of the wedding...*and* the night that had just passed.

A dreamy smile curved her relaxed face, and she shook her head, thinking of that middle-of-the-night passionate encounter and suppressing a sigh. It was only sex, she reminded herself doggedly, and Angel had always excelled in that field. It didn't mean anything either and she needed to remember that the same man had blackmailed her into marriage. It didn't matter that he had had good intentions when he had utilised such pressure and intimidation.

Feeling a little less relaxed and forgiving, indeed annoyed that Angel could so easily make her forget what was truly important, Gaby sat up.

'Oh, good, you're awake,' Angel remarked from the doorway, startling her.

'What time is it?'

'Half-ten...you've slept twelve hours...aside from the occasional waking moment,' Angel rephrased with an utterly mesmerising sensual smile.

Staring at his lean, darkly handsome features just a heartbeat too long, Gaby turned her head away as she scolded herself for being such a pushover. But there he stood, her new husband, and he was strikingly, rivetingly spectacular, lounging there in the doorway without a care in the world, casually clad in a black open shirt and tailored chinos that accentuated every sculpted line of his lean, powerful physique. If she was a pushover in his radius now and again, she thought ruefully, at least she had some excuse.

'Alexios?' she queried anxiously. 'Is he here yet?'

'Marina's bringing him this afternoon. Right now, all you have to worry about is coming downstairs to eat. Since we skipped dinner last night, Viola has made a banquet for breakfast,' Angel explained. 'And it will be served on the terrace behind the house.'

Gaby scrambled out of bed and streaked into the adjoining bathroom and then streaked out again, still naked, to grab a suitcase in search of clothes.

Angel swept it out of her hand and planted it down on the luggage rack by the wall. 'Viola will unpack everything for you. We may not have a full staff here, but you don't need to do everything.'

'I'm used to doing everything,' Gaby muttered, suddenly alarmingly aware of her nudity and wondering how she had contrived to forget that reality for even a minute. She rummaged through the case, located a sundress and vanished into the bathroom, taking in a deep breath only once she was alone again. Then she thought of that 'P for prude' crack and pulled a face at her own reflection. In time she would get more comfortable with that kind of intimacy, she reasoned ruefully.

When she emerged again, the bedroom was empty,

and she went downstairs where Viola was waiting, her smile widening in delight when Gaby addressed her in Italian. The older woman showed her out through a door onto what Angel had referred to as a terrace, a misnomer if ever she had heard one, Gaby reflected in wonderment as she scanned her surroundings. Stone pillars ran along the rear of the house, marble stretched below her feet and fabulous classical frescoes adorned what had once been the back wall of the house. It was incredibly theatrical and unexpected and Gaby grinned.

'I can see that, in spite of appearances at the front of the house, your grandparents brought the palace here with them,' she remarked with a smile as Angel rose from a low wall to greet her arrival.

'Viola told me that while my grandfather was in his library, my grandmother spent her time out here painting and working on garden projects.'

'Viola's worked here for a long time, then,' Gaby commented. 'Did you visit this house as a child?'

'Marina brought me here to go fishing and run wild in a way that I couldn't at the palace. Even when I was a kid, I was expected to behave like an adult there,' Angel admitted, pulling out a chair for her at the table that was swiftly becoming laden with the variety of options Viola was wheeling out for their delectation.

'Weren't your parents here as well?' she asked in surprise.

'No, but I often brought schoolfriends here with me.'

As his lean, darkly handsome features tightened and shadowed, Gaby's brows pleated. 'And what was that like?'

'Usually good fun with little adult intervention. It was different once I was older.' Angel fell silent and looked out to the garden as though an unlucky memory had stopped him dead in his tracks. She wondered what that memory was and what had triggered it, wondering if it might explain Angel's lack of trust in women, wondering if one of the schoolfriends had actually been a youthful *girl*friend. Sooner rather than later Gaby intended to find out, but she would take one small step at a time.

Like the 'terrace', the garden was much more elaborate than one would have expected from the farmhouse setting. A riot of roses grew round a central fountain while box-edged beds were planted with herbs and perennials and paved paths ran between. Across to one side and screened off by a hedge, she saw the pale watery gleam of a swimming pool.

'It's really beautiful here,' she said, keen to move on from the family and schoolfriends topic, which had silenced him. She knew enough to surmise now because, clearly, Angel hadn't enjoyed a family life with his parents or a happy childhood. Either his parents had been too detached in nature or too busy as the sovereigns of Themos to spend much time with him.

Angel smiled again and she knew that changing the subject had been a tactful move, even if curiosity needled her more every time she had to do it. She had not known that Angel could smile at her as much as he did, and she liked that change. Angel had always struck her as rather dark and reserved at his core, rather than open and smiley.

She ate with appetite, helping herself to tasters from various plates and giving him a running commentary on her preferences while he ate only fruit, finally admitting that he had breakfasted around dawn, being an inveterate early riser, no matter how tired he was or where he was in the world. Seated dreamily in a rocking chair in the shade, Gaby sipped her coffee, pleasantly replete from the meal.

'So,' Angel murmured softly. 'Cassia?'

And Gaby almost choked on her coffee. 'Yes, that topic's likely to be pretty difficult to tackle,' she mumbled in an awkward recovery.

'Why should it be? Cassia is not good with other women, but she is exceptionally good at what she does at the palace,' Angel opined.

Gaby stiffened at his supportive, approving intonation when referring to the blonde. 'Did you ever think of marrying her?' she heard herself ask rather abruptly.

Taken aback in turn by that sudden question, Angel frowned. 'In these circumstances I would like to say no, but it would be a lie. For a couple of months before I met you again, I did consider Cassia as a bride because I've never wanted an emotional connection with a woman,' he explained curtly. 'I don't feel anything for her and I'm not particularly attracted to her, but I did think she would be a suitable choice for the role of future queen…and then you came along.'

'And Alexios came along,' Gaby filled in, striving to conceal her dismay at what he had told her, which meant that on that score, at least, Cassia had not been lying. At some stage, the blonde *had* been in the running to be Angel's wife and she had been astute enough to guess that fact without him ever voicing the idea.

'It *was* merely a thought,' Angel extended as if he sensed her unease. 'I didn't mention the idea to her or indeed ever let our relationship become close. Once one crosses those boundaries with a member of staff it is impossible to step back.'

Some of Gaby's healthy colour had returned to her cheeks and, indeed, she even contrived to smile at him. 'So, you've never had sex with Cassia?' she double-checked.

His frown darkened. 'Of course not. What is this all about, Gabriella? I'm beginning to feel as though I'm on trial for something.'

Gaby raised an anxious hand. 'No, no, absolutely not! But this topic and your explanation does lead into what I had to discuss with you relating to Cassia,' she framed uncomfortably. 'Yesterday, on the very day of our wedding, Cassia told me that you and she were lovers on an…er…casual basis and that that would be continuing *after* our marriage…'

Angel sprang upright, golden eyes gleaming dark and hard as jet with astonishment. 'She's an old friend. Are you sure you understood her correctly?' he shot at her.

Gaby was knocked off balance by that immediate expression of doubt and his grim change of mood. 'Yes, I understood her perfectly. Maybe you don't *want* to believe me, Angel, but she *did* make that claim before the wedding. I'm sorry, but I don't lie about stuff of that nature.'

'I didn't accuse you of lying,' Angel countered tautly. 'But in my experience, women often do tell lies about each other.'

'And now you're just showing your prejudice,' Gaby told him, a chill running down her spine even if, unusually for her with Angel, she retained her calm. And she knew why: she was in shock at his flat refusal to credit *her* side of the story.

Angel spread two lean hands in an expressive arc of disagreement and dismissal. 'I can accept that you don't like her and that you don't want to work with her. However, I've known Cassia since childhood, and I have never known her to be less than truthful.'

'So, I'm the liar.' Gaby framed that obvious deduction with gritted teeth.

Angel shrugged an unapologetic shoulder and turned on his heel. 'Let's not go there. I'm going out before I say anything that I will regret,' he bit out. 'I'm disappointed in you, Gabriella!'

'Not half as much as I'm disappointed in you,' she riposted, and for a split second she simply sat there before she plunged to her feet and grabbed up her phone.

*'Angel!'* she called, racing after him because he was already halfway out of the heavy wooden front door.

His arrogant dark head turned, and he shot her a winging glance as though incredulous at her audacity in daring to approach him again after what he had said.

'I want you to listen to this…' she murmured quietly as she opened her phone and extended it to him. 'But, in the mood that you are in, *not* while you're driving.'

'I am *not* in a mood,' Angel bit out from between white even teeth.

He was struggling not to lose his temper. It was written all over him from the flush on his exotic cheekbones to his fiery gaze right down to his knotted fists. He had ridiculously expressive body language and she wondered why it was that, even when she was mad as hell with him and reeling with the hurt that he had caused, she still just wanted to soothe him much as if he were Alexios.

'What is...*this*?' he questioned rawly, grudgingly accepting the mobile phone.

'It's a recording of the conversation that I had with Cassia. No, *I* didn't record it... I'm not that quick off the mark or suspicious. It was Laurie who recorded it. When Cassia asked to speak to me alone Laurie didn't trust her and she left her phone recording in the bedroom with us,' Gaby advanced stiffly.

'How sordid,' Angel pronounced with slashing distaste.

'You know what?' Gaby elevated a dark coppery brow. 'Sordid or not, I'm belatedly very glad to have the proof of that conversation when evidently I married a guy yesterday who doesn't believe a word I say,' she condemned as she walked away again.

'Gabriella—?'

Gaby spun back, blue eyes flashing as bright as the sapphires she had worn the day before. 'I've said all I want to say for now. But when you return, I will be getting some things out in the open for your benefit,' she warned him curtly before she walked back outside again.

She was shaking like a leaf from the amount of emotion she was holding inside herself. She reached for her coffee again, but it was cold. Viola appeared with a fresh pot and began to clear the table, occasionally shooting troubled glances at Gaby's pale set visage.

'He was a very unhappy little boy, ignored and neglected by his mother,' Viola whispered in Italian. 'And a temper like...like a firework display!'

'I can imagine that,' Gaby commented, striving to relax sufficiently to smile reassuringly at the older woman while tucking away those nuggets of information. He must have been so hurt and damaged by that maternal negative response, she thought unhappily. The same woman who had abandoned Saif as a baby had been no warmer a mother to Angel and yet she had had every opportunity to be a parent to Angel. The first woman who should have loved and nurtured him had refused to do so. Was that why he found it so hard to trust people?

Even *her*? His new bride? Angel had blindsided Gaby and plunged her into shock. He didn't trust her. He might have married her, but he didn't have any more faith in her word than he might have had in a stranger passing him on the street and that *hurt*. In addition, he only trusted Cassia more because he had known the woman for years.

That was a moment of revelation for Gaby. She thought about that non-disclosure agreement she had refused to sign at university even though it had meant that she'd lost any chance of being with Angel. Why hadn't she recognised then just how deep Angel's distrust went? There it had been, a blatant signpost, and yet she hadn't seen his fatal flaw. How stupid and naive was she?

He trusted Cassia more because he had known her from childhood and had presumably never witnessed Cassia's less attractive flipside. For that reason, when he heard that recording, he would be abashed, she reflected without pleasure. But regrettably for Angel it would only figure as one more piece of proof that *no* woman in his life could be trusted...

Angel drove up to the mountaintop viewpoint and parked. He was in a rage because he had believed that

Gabriella was superior to the other women he had known, too honest to malign an employee who had once offended her, too decent to use her newly acquired status against someone who could not fight back. When would he learn? he asked himself angrily as he climbed out of the car with the phone, ignoring the bodyguards spreading round the car park to protect him. He had worked out when he was very young that the only person he could fully rely on and trust was himself.

He hit the play button on the phone, lean dark features tense and dark and brooding. He listened and the angry flush on his cheekbones slowly drained away. His lush black lashes hit his cheekbones as his lips parted on an unspoken but vicious curse. The whole truth and nothing but the truth...even if it was an *ugly* truth? He knew he had dug himself into a very deep hole. A taxi hummed at the entrance to the car park, doubtless eying the flag on the SUV that signalled Angel's presence. He sprang upright and swung back into the SUV to drive down the mountain again.

Back at the house, he strode into his grandfather's library, needing the familiar warmth of its seclusion and the aged whiskey in the crystal decanter. He poured himself a drink and knocked it back with unusual enthusiasm. It still didn't wipe out the image he kept on seeing of the dead look in Gabriella's beautiful eyes and her pallor. He breathed in slow and deep while the heat of the alcohol burned the chill from his chest. He had screwed up. Why did he always, absolutely *always* screw up with Gabriella?

And as he paced the floor, it seemed so obvious to him why things went continually wrong with Gabriella. His childhood had screwed him up. In any relationship with a woman, he would always be waiting for the axe to fall, and so he had avoided relationships altogether once he'd left his teens behind. All because his mother had been a cold creature, more interested in her latest lover and the beautiful face that met her in her mirror than in her own flesh and blood?

Angel knew right then and there that he didn't want to go through life refusing to have faith in others. What sort of an example would that set his son, Alexios? Alexios, in his innocence, had offered his father instant love and trust. And if he wanted to be the father and the husband that his wife and child deserved, he had to open up and share his past to give his trust as well.

Gaby sat down to lunch alone. She had no appetite, but Viola had been so attentive that she felt that she had to eat lest she hurt the older woman's feelings. Mostly she had sipped her wine, relieved to feel a little bubbly boost from the alcohol when the rest of her felt as flat as a pancake. She wandered round the paved garden with her glass, enjoying the sunshine warming her skin and settling down on a stone seat with beautiful roses blooming all around her.

She heard the crunch of Angel's footsteps on the gravel before he moved onto the paved path and her slim shoulders squared.

'Will you come into the house so that we can talk?' Angel enquired quietly.

'I really don't think that we have anything to talk about,' Gaby parried, fixedly studying the rose bed directly ahead of her.

'Please…' Angel planted his big strong body in front of her view.

It was a word he rarely employed and he got points
for it. In any case, she knew they had to talk even if she
didn't see what exactly they could discuss. 'There's not
very much to say about your prejudice against women,'
she murmured flatly.

'I have my reasons.'

'Reasons you won't share,' Gaby cut in.

'I will. I will talk freely,' Angel asserted, crouching
down in front of her, endeavouring to enforce eye contact. He reached for her hand, but she yanked it back
and he sighed. 'I haven't been in what you would call a
relationship before, not a proper one. I *will* make mistakes because I haven't got that experience.'

'You've been with more women than…probably Ca-
sanova!' Gaby condemned wildly, wrongfooted by a
humble approach that she could never ever have expected from Prince Angel Diamandis. 'Don't try to
make a lack of experience an excuse!'

Accidentally, she connected with tawny black-
fringed eyes that were the purest gold in the sunshine
and her mouth ran dry.

'That was sex and only sex, *not* relationships,' Angel
specified tightly.

Gaby flushed with pleasure at that admission and
slid upright. 'OK.'

He walked her silently indoors to the library she
had heard about and not seen, and it was as much of an
anomaly in such a house as the classic frescoes painted
on the rear terrace. It was two storeys tall with a spi-
ral staircase in one corner. Customised carved wooden
bookshelves covered every wall, and the shelves were
packed, upstairs and on the mezzanine above. Sumptuous sofas, armchairs and a large desk completed an

ambience that would have been more at home in a Victorian mansion. And yet that very unexpectedness made her like the house even more and wish that his grandparents had survived for her to know them, because she was beginning to understand that the farmhouse had been their escape from the Aikaterina palace, a private place where they could be themselves and indulge their interests like private citizens rather than royals.

'It's very comfortable in here,' she remarked, sinking down on an opulent sofa covered with striped pale green velvet and liberally fringed and tasselled.

'I find it very hard to trust people.' Angel leant back against the desk, visibly striving to look relaxed but taut as a bowstring to her more discerning gaze, every line of his lean, powerful physique tense. 'It probably started when I was a kid. My mother didn't have time for me or interest in me. She lacked the maternal gene, if there is such a thing.'

'I'm sorry,' Gaby almost whispered, reluctant to interrupt but needing to express sympathy.

'But possibly the most damaging event for me happened when I was fifteen…' Angel's voice trailed off and he compressed his wide, sensual mouth. 'It is hard for me to tell you something I have never shared before with anyone.'

Gaby sat in the suffocating silence waiting while Angel collected himself like a male about to climb a challenging mountain.

'I brought my best friend back to the palace for the summer vacation and she…she seduced him—'

'She…*what*? How old was he?' Gaby broke in, utterly taken back.

'He was fifteen too. I found them in bed together and

afterwards when I tried to confront her, she said, *What did you expect when you brought home such a beautiful boy?* She had neither regret nor shame.'

Gaby had paled as he'd spoken, and she didn't know what to say. It was too shocking and disgraceful for her to label or contrive some trite remark, because nothing could soothe such a betrayal for an adolescent boy, or the adult son who still cringed recalling that distasteful experience.

'I shouldn't have been surprised. I was aware of her many lovers. She was a great beauty, but she was a heartless mother,' he proffered stiffly. 'I have not shared these facts with Saif…and would like your promise that this will remain a secret, because I see no reason to distress him now with the truth about our mother.'

Gaby gave a vigorous nod and muttered, 'Of course. I won't ever mention it to anyone.'

'That is probably where what you see as my lack of trust began,' Angel continued tautly.

'Probably,' Gaby conceded uncomfortably.

'Then the very first woman I slept with sold the story of our encounter to an international tabloid newspaper, and several after her did the same. That was when I began to look for signed non-disclosure agreements to protect myself,' Angel framed grimly. 'My parents were surrounded by sleazy rumours and conjecture for the whole of their reign. There was a lot of truth in the sleaze, but I wish to create a different image for Themos. I did not want that smut and sleaze and gossip to damage the kingdom's reputation.'

A knock sounded on the door and Angel stalked impatiently across the room to answer it. While she could have suspected some irritation on his part as Viola bus-

tled in carting a massive tray, he, instead, took the tray
from her and thanked her warmly. He settled the tray
on the desk and sighed. 'She knows I missed lunch so
she *has* to feed me.'

'She seems very fond of you.'

'Yes, the older staff who work for the family were
the parents that my own parents couldn't be bothered
to be,' Angel explained wryly. 'I was very fortunate to
have them and I am equally fond of them. They went
beyond their jobs to show me interest and kindness.'

Gaby got up to pour the coffee and pile sandwiches
on a plate, which she extended to him. 'Yes, I'm helping feed you!' she said tartly. 'I haven't forgiven you
yet, but I am starting to understand where and why you
started thinking the way that you do. The real problem,
though, is that you keep on making me pay for your past
experiences and, regardless of what a bad time you've
had with other women, I'm not prepared to accept that
*I* have to pay for *their* sins.'

'And I don't expect you to,' Angel assured her. 'I
have to change my outlook.'

'It's not that easy to change your basic nature,' Gaby
cut in, unimpressed.

'It's lot easier if you can see that you have continually *wronged* someone else, particularly someone who
has never given me cause for such distrust,' Angel dis-
agreed, giving the words emphatic weight.

Disconcerted by that frank little speech, Gaby sank
back down on the sofa. 'Continually?' she queried that
use of the word.

'I may make mistakes but I'm not stupid, *hara mou*,'
Angel contended. 'We didn't get together when we were
students because of my lack of trust, but I'm a little

more mature now, although looking back on the way I behaved when you tried to tell me that you were pregnant, that maturity wasn't on view.'

Gaby suppressed a deep sigh of relief that he had truly begun to examine the way he had always treated her as though she were as untrustworthy as some of her predecessors.

'So, you see, you *can* teach an old dog new tricks,' Angel murmured with wry self-mockery. 'I can change. I can see when I'm being unreasonable now...because it's you.'

'And Cassia...?' she prompted uncertainly.

Angel munched through a sandwich in reflective silence. 'She'll have to leave our employ. I was really shocked by that conversation. Thank Laurie for recording it. I would never have dreamt that Cassia would tell lies like that. I did have total faith in her as an employee, but what she said... I'm sorry that I gave you the impression that I trusted her more than I trust you, because that is untrue. I simply had to think it through.'

'But the recording helped and hit home like a sledgehammer,' Gaby gathered with hidden amusement as he wolfed down another sandwich and she refreshed his coffee.

Her earlier sense of despair was gone. Angel was more emotionally intelligent and stable than she had believed he was, but her heart ached for the betrayal his mother had visited on him. He was damaged by the indifference and betrayal of a nasty mother and a succession of lovers, who had wanted him for his status and wealth and had then used him as a publicity tool to enrich themselves.

'What I regret most...is that day you came to the

hotel to tell me that you were pregnant, and I refused to listen,' he confided heavily. 'That mistake cost us both so much. All that was on my mind was the number of other women who had claimed to have conceived by me and had lied. In the following weeks I did become more rational and appreciate that I had reacted that way because I assumed you were lying as others had before you and that that belief upset me...and in some way prevented me from taking a more logical approach.'

'I do understand that,' Gaby murmured ruefully. 'Even at the time I understood that, but I also assumed that you wouldn't want anything to do with our child anyway.'

'I'm a possessive tyke when it comes to anything belonging to me,' Angel confided with a gleam in his beautiful eyes. 'I was searching for you within days of that blasted meeting that went so wrong. I was so angry with you. I still don't understand *why* I was angry with you.'

'Surprises are a challenge for you?'

'No. Is it possible for us to start again with a fresh page?' Angel asked, lacing his long fingers with her shorter ones.

'I don't see why not,' Gaby conceded unevenly, emotion surging as she looked at him, another revelation infiltrating her awareness. She still loved him and the more he told her, the more he talked, the better she understood why she loved him. He had his faults, just as she had, but they were working through them. They were both older and wiser and Angel was being forced to share a lot more of himself with her, but she wasn't about to tell him that she loved him when he had told her that he didn't seek an emotional connection with a woman. She desperately wanted to ask him why he had said that, but she reckoned that he had already had quite enough of such stuff to discuss that day, without her choosing to add another complication that he had to explain.

'I want to kiss you...' Angel told her huskily, feeling as though a great weight had fallen from him, relief and a sense of peace assailing him and a whole rush of other feelings he couldn't label following in their wake. 'But I don't know if—'

Gaby took the cup of coffee out of his hand and set it aside with confidence. 'You're a miracle worker. A couple of hours ago, I wanted to run away or push you off a cliff and now... I want to kiss you back.'

'If I'm honest, I want a hell of a lot more than a kiss,' Angel confided raggedly, his smouldering golden gaze telegraphing a hunger she understood right down to the marrow of her bones.

'Kind of guessed that.' Gaby laughed, recognising that they had moved a major obstacle in the path of their relationship and were already moving on in a better direction. And for Angel, she realised, renewing physical intimacy after all that emotional intensity was a much-needed release.

'A sex strike would be very effective on me,' Angel confessed with sudden appreciation.

Her nose wrinkled. 'Kind of guessed that too.'

Angel vaulted upright and pulled her with him across to the staircase in the corner. 'Takes us straight upstairs,' he told her with a wickedly sexy grin.

# CHAPTER TEN

ALMOST TWO WEEKS LATER, Gaby traced idle fingers across Angel's bronzed chest. 'So, this not seeking an emotional connection with women,' she mused as lightly as she could in tone. 'What's that all about? You made it sound like some sort of mission statement.'

Gaby wanted to know if she could ever be honest with him about how she felt about him. Or would her feelings always have to be a secret?

'It was. It came from seeing how my father was affected by my mother. She ruined him. I think he loved her, but she wasn't the sort of woman who made a man better and stronger for caring for her...and he was rather a weak man.' Angel rested his head back on her lap, black lashes almost hitting his cheekbones as his long lean body stretched in relaxation. 'I was told by a reliable source that his lifestyle only became as debauched as hers once he realised that she would never be faithful to him. Just think of how much better a man he might have been had he fallen for a classier woman.'

'Yes, but that was him and you said he was weak. Nobody would call you weak,' Gaby assured him with shamelessly seductive intent, slender fingers smoothing down over his bare abdomen, hearing the responsive hitch in his breath, fingertips teasing through his happy trail along the waistband of his low-slung denim shorts. 'So, why can't you have an emotional connection?'

'Could be because I'm too busy handling the sexual connection!' Angel teased with a wicked grin, rolling over and back to tumble her down flat on the rug below the trees at the edge of the woodland. It was one of the few places in the grounds of the house that they were safe from any kind of surveillance, although Gaby had heard Angel having an earnest discussion with his head of security about the risk of drones. The chances of anyone catching a snap of her in a bikini or, worse, rolling about half naked with her husband outdoors, were slim to none, she thought fondly.

The days they had spent together since the wedding had flown past at unbelievable speed, packed with outings, time spent with Alexios, nights of passion and more happiness than Gaby had even known she could feel.

He had taken them out to show them his country and they had travelled back and forth across the island, visiting the the most gorgeous beach, where Angel had built Alexios his first sandcastle and then smashed it flat to make his son laugh. They had dined at a trendy bar above the beach where everybody had watched them covertly, but they had been left in peace, neither photographed nor approached. As Alexios had dozed off in his high chair, she had realised that Angel could go nowhere on Themos without being recognised. They had spent the previous weekend sailing on his yacht with Marina in tow, so that they could go clubbing at the southern tip of the island where there was a very exclusive resort. She had swum, snorkelled, danced, slept for hours both day and night after yielding to Angel's seemingly insatiable appetite for her, and one day had slipped so smoothly into the next that she could not now imagine a life without him.

'You've got to stop trying to play games with me, *hara mou*,' Angel husked, hungrily claiming her pink lips and sending her heartbeat to a racing pitch. He lifted his tousled dark head and, tawny, black-lashed eyes glittering over her, he smiled again. 'I'm a master gameplayer and I will trump you every time. Of *course* I have an emotional connection with you.'

Her face was burning but her discomfiture was not sufficient to prevent her from saying uncertainly, 'You…*have*?'

Angel grinned, pure devilment dancing in his eyes as he coiled back from her and started to gather up the picnic stuff. 'Naturally. You're my wife and the mother of my child. You belong in an entirely separate category.'

Gaby's teeth gritted. It was one of those regular occasions when she still wanted to throw something at him for being the clever clogs he was always going to be. She didn't want to be in a category all on her own, she only wanted to know exactly how he felt about her. She wanted to know his every thought and feeling too, she conceded ruefully, and neither desire was likely to be met.

They walked along the path by the lake until the house came into view again.

'It really enraged me when you accused me of cheating on you all those years ago,' Angel remarked without warning.

Gaby sighed. 'I know that technically we had broken up and you were free to do as you liked, but I was upset. Who was she?'

'An ex. It went no further than what you saw. I *wanted* to upset you,' Angel admitted, startling her. 'An unpleasant urge to follow, I'm afraid. We were both very young, Gabriella. You, in particular, at nineteen were far too young for me. I may only be a few years older, but I was many years older in terms of sexual experience. You were just a baby in comparison, and you were right to say no to me. I reckon you had more emotional experience then than I had, though.'

'Sometimes you surprise me.'

'In what way?'

'In a *good* way,' Gaby stressed helplessly because she admired his honesty as they walked back to the house by the side of the lake.

Marina was in front of the house, sitting on the grass with Alexios, and Gaby's son lifted his arms and loosed a baby shout when he saw his parents.

'I *love* being appreciated,' Angel admitted, closing an arm to her spine. 'Can I tempt you into having a second child with me yet?'

Shock stilled Gaby in her tracks. 'Why?'

'I missed out on so much the first time around.'

'And it was all your own fault—an *own goal*, I think you could call it,' Gaby pointed out gently. 'And no, it's too soon for me to consider another pregnancy... maybe next year.'

Just thinking about the concept blew her mind. Was she really that secure that she could even consider another baby? She couldn't demand love from him as though it were some kind of right written into the marriage vows, could she? Self-evidently, Angel wanted their marriage to work, and he wanted it to last. He had put in the effort, baring his soul of his worst secret to explain why he suffered from such distrust. With that one act he had blown a huge hole in her defences.

Gaby believed that Angel had been more sinned against than he had sinned. The mother who should have loved him had instead withheld her love and attention and had then let him down unforgivably by succumbing to lust rather than considering or even respecting her son's needs. He was ashamed of both his parents, ashamed and filled with distaste and regret for the different experiences other adults had with their closest relatives. At least she had warm loving memories of her parents, she reflected ruefully. Until Angel had told her about his childhood, she had not fully appreciated how lucky she was to have had fourteen years with a caring family.

They had only just stepped indoors when his mobile phone began ringing. As she carried Alexios upstairs for his bath, she heard his voice take on a clipped cold edge that was unfamiliar to her and she wondered if something had gone wrong back at the palace. Angel had made several trips back to meet obligations that could not be cancelled, and although she had offered to accompany him he had always refused, telling her that she would have her own schedule and duties to fulfil soon enough.

'The Crown council want the Coronation held within three months and that will keep us busy for weeks,' he had pointed out. 'When we get time off, we take it, and I don't want you feeling like you have to spend less time with our son.'

There was a terrible irony to the reality that she now understood exactly *why* Angel had insisted on marrying her. Sadly, that truth hurt. His childhood had been quite miserable. Materially he had had everything, but emotionally he had lived in a wasteland where only his parents' employees had brought warmth into his life. As a result, Angel was determined that Alexios would have a much more positive experience, which he believed entailed two caring parents and stability. Angel set a very high value on a mother's love. So, he had married her for their son's sake, and he would *stay* married to her for their son's sake, so naturally he was inclined to look on her a little as though she could be a baby dispenser. Having discovered to his surprise that he adored his son, he was now keen to encourage Gaby to give him another child.

With Martina's efficient assistance, Gaby bathed Alexios and got him tucked into his sleepsuit, ready for his supper. When she walked back into her bedroom, she was surprised to find Viola already packing for her, for they had not planned to return to the palace until the following evening.

She went downstairs and discovered that Angel was still on the phone. Suppressing a groan, she grabbed a coffee from the machine in the kitchen and walked out to the terrace. Clearly there was some sort of crisis and they were leaving sooner than they had expected.

'What's happening?' she asked as Angel strode out to join her.

'An almighty mess,' he told her grimly, his beautiful mouth compressing. 'We'll discuss it on the drive back to Aikaterina.'

Within twenty minutes they were on the road. Gaby cleared her throat and shot a bemused glance at Angel's tense profile.

'Cassia is in a cell at police headquarters,' Angel revealed, staggering her with that news.

'But what on earth—?'

'The waiter serving you at that restaurant the night you were drugged went missing and, when the police tracked him down, he confessed that he had been given the pill and paid to drop it into your glass of champagne,' Angel explained tautly. 'His bank account contained a substantial sum of money and when the police "followed the money", as they say, it led straight to Cassia. She was arrested. Supposedly she intended you no real harm. She expected you to collapse under the influence of the drug, and look like a drunk or behave in some foolish way that would embarrass you, and therefore me as well, in public…'

Gaby's eyes were huge. 'Good heavens…' she whispered in shock. 'And what was she hoping to achieve with that? That you would cancel the wedding? Turn your back on your son? I don't think so.'

'Whatever Cassia's intentions, I now have to find a way to deal with this problem, and without blowing apart the rest of my household staff. Until I've had more time to think, Gabriella, I can't discuss this further with you.' Angel abruptly drew their conversation to a close and resumed his brooding demeanour as he stared out of the window.

Gaby felt stung that he'd shut her down so decisively. This involved her. She was the one who'd suffered at Cassia's vindictive hands. She had every right to demand that Angel share his plans for dealing with Cassia with her. How could she ever believe that they could have anything approaching a real marriage if, even after baring his soul and seemingly accepting that she would never hurt him, Angel was still shutting her out? After all their talks over the last couple of weeks she'd felt so sure that they were starting to really connect, that maybe he could fall in love with her as she had fallen so deeply in love with him. But the moment something like this happened—something big—Angel was reverting to type.

And as angry and shocked as she was at Cassia's actions, a tiny part of her felt some sympathy for the woman—after all, hadn't she thrown all of her usual caution to the wind as she'd allowed herself to be swept up in the whirlwind that was Angel? Who could better understand Angel's powerful draw than herself? Look at the lengths she had gone to to experience even a slither of his attention. She'd married the man—and not because she'd had to, but, she freely admitted now, because she was in love with him. She knew all too well the pain of loving a man who would ultimately never let himself love her back. Cassia had very obviously had deeper and more enduring feelings for Angel than anyone had realised in order to have gone as far as to drug his fiancée two days before her wedding!

They passed the remainder of the journey in stony silence, and, with Alexios sleeping peacefully in his car seat, Gaby didn't even have the comfort of her son to distract her from her increasingly despairing thoughts. She now saw that she had a decision to make. Stay in her marriage to Angel and break her heart over him, or leave and break her heart anyway…

The moment they pulled up at the palace, Angel leapt from the car, his mobile phone pressed firmly to his ear as he marched inside and disappeared, leaving Gaby to get herself and their son out.

* * *

Gaby had spent what felt like hours holed up in the nursery with Alexios and Marina, struggling to distract herself from her spiralling thoughts concerning Angel and the future of their marriage. She wondered what was being discussed, what decisions were being made on her behalf. Would he ever tell her just what went on behind those closed doors?

The door to the nursery opened and Angel appeared.

He asked her to join him in his wing of the palace.

'*Your* wing?' she questioned, it not having occurred to her before to have wondered where his bedroom was. 'I assumed we'd be sharing.'

'Which I was about to suggest,' Angel volunteered as he walked her along the wide, high-ceilinged, hugely imposing picture gallery that connected the two different sections of the palace. 'My parents occupied separate wings.'

'And you were on the top floor, all of you nicely separated,' she commented.

'That's how they lived but it's not how I want to live,' Angel admitted bluntly.

His crest would have risen in her eyes had it not been for his brooding silence in the car, and the spiralling, panicked thoughts it had triggered in her. How was she supposed to know how Angel wanted to live when he never properly opened up to her? But dared she hope that was about to change? Nervous beyond belief, feeling her future happiness at stake, she couldn't help but notice that the wing that he inhabited was much more formal and traditional with oil paintings on the walls and grand antique furniture. 'You'll have to give me a tour of this place. I had no idea that this side was so different from mine. I've seen the public rooms down-stairs, of course.'

'We only use the ground-floor reception area for major events and, since times have changed and people have become more egalitarian, I don't use them half as much as my parents did.'

He showed her a room off a long wide marble-floored corridor. 'I thought the nursery could move in here and we could have Alexios closer to us…there's rooms for the staff as well.

'This is the sitting room,' he told her, standing back to allow her to admire a giant expanse ornamented with formal drapes and a massive marble fireplace. 'It should be dragged into this century, like a lot of the accommodation in this wing. But I'm not interested in the décor, so I'm hoping you will step in…'

'It's possible,' Gaby commented, not wishing to give a definitive answer as yet and commit to a move within the palace. She'd not even decided if she could stay in the marriage yet. What had been decided about Cassia?

'This is the master bedroom…and it connects with another bedroom, which you could use as a dressing room or whatever.' Angel studied her fixedly, a frown line starting to pleat his brows. 'You're very quiet.'

'You've obviously done a lot of thinking about this rearrangement, but right now I'd prefer to talk about Cassia and why you went so broody and quiet on me in the car after telling me she was the one who drugged me,' Gaby confessed ruefully, wandering across the huge gilded room with its ridiculously majestic bed on a low dais, which was surrounded by gilt pillars. It was a level of splendour and magnificence so far removed from her experience that she felt intimidated. Slowly, she turned back round to face him.

'Seriously?' Angel grimaced. 'I've spent half the day having to talk about Cassia, with her parents, her friends, her colleagues—it's been endless. I've had to be polite, tolerant and compassionate when only a couple of centuries ago I would more happily have stuck her in a dungeon in the basement and had her executed... and, to be quite frank, *that's* the endgame I would've preferred!'

Astonished by that shattering declaration, Gaby gaped at him, blue eyes very wide.

'Well, how do you expect me to feel?' Angel demanded. 'You could have had an allergic reaction to the drug, could have been seriously harmed by it, but Cassia didn't care,' Angel bit out. 'I think she simply wanted to hurt you because you were marrying me. I am stunned that I failed to appreciate, in all the years I have known her, what a scheming, vindictive woman I had working for me!' Angel exclaimed harshly. 'How did I *not* know? How could I have been so blind to her real nature?'

'She wasn't family or your girlfriend,' Gaby proffered. The depths of the turmoil Angel was finally sharing had her instinctively looking to comfort him. 'I suspect that you never looked that closely at her. She's poisonous but I don't think men find that trait as easy to spot as women do. So what *will* happen to her now?'

'I want to keep a lid on this whole toxic mess. I want to ban her from Themos, which, believe me, will be punishment enough.'

'You don't want her charged?' Gaby countered in surprise.

'Ultimately, as the injured party, the decision is yours. If you want her in court, you must make that choice.'

Gaby breathed in deep and slow. 'But you would prefer to brush the whole thing under the carpet?'

'I wouldn't have put it in those words but, yes, that is the preferable option in my opinion. If we prosecute her, it will hit the press. I don't want to treat the world to the story of my bride being roofied before our wedding. Regrettably, in our circumstances and with my reputation, nine out of ten people will assume that I was having an affair with Cassia and that sordid interpretation will accompany us all to our graves. Clearly, Cassia was violently jealous of you.'

'And very possessive of you,' Gaby filled in. 'I think she truly believed that she would end up as your wife. Had believed that for many years.'

'Unfortunately, most people will believe that she had cause to be jealous even though she didn't. I do want her punished, but in a manner that also respects her family's service to the throne and removes her from Themos and your radius,' he extended gravely. 'Her father, Piero, is a long-standing family friend and a very decent man. He and his wife are in pieces over their daughter's treachery, but your safety must come first. If Cassia went to prison she would be out again within a few years. As it is, in return for her confessional statement, I will remove her citizenship and she will not be able to get back onto the island.'

Gaby nodded comprehension.

'That is my preferred solution because I never want to lay eyes on her again in this lifetime,' Angel continued with grim intensity. 'It protects her parents' reputation and residence here as well. They are wealthy and can maintain contact with their daughter however they wish in the future. I could never forgive her, though, for what she did to you...*that* could have had a tragic conclusion!'

His dark deep drawl roughened as he finished speaking and she gazed across the room at him, momentarily entranced by the volatile liquid gold of his gaze, sensing the powerful emotions he was restraining.

'I'll go with whatever you choose,' Gaby responded with a sigh. 'A scandal would be embarrassing, and *if* she went to prison—'

'Oh, she would *definitely* go to prison on Themos,' Angel incised. 'Buying a banned drug and using it to assault my bride? She has broken several laws and the charges are serious, not inconsequential.'

Angel fell silent then and Gaby could feel the despair in him, which made her wonder if something else was wrong. 'Angel, is there something else I need to know?'

'You were targeted *because of me*. Your life was put at risk *because of me*.'

'That's not how you should view her unbalanced behaviour.'

'No, but it's the bald, unlovely truth!' Angel sliced back harshly. 'I had a dangerous employee, and I didn't realise it. Not only didn't I realise it, while I was refusing to give you my trust, I was giving *her* my trust and regarded her as a friend! Cassia could have *killed* you with that drug!'

'Luckily, she only gave me a headache,' she said soothingly.

'Luck doesn't count when it comes to your safety,' Angel informed her. 'You mean the world to our son and to me, *hara mou*. Anyone who wishes you even the smallest ill is unwelcome on Themos.'

Surprise filled Gaby, swiftly followed by pleasure.

'I let you down with Cassia and I feel so guilty about that,' Angel exclaimed abruptly, disconcerting her. 'I let myself trust her rather than you…you, who have never done a single thing to inspire distrust!

'I couldn't have survived you being hurt,' Angel confided, stalking closer, his brilliant gaze intent. 'I need you to be happy and content here in the palace, living on Themos with me…'

Gaby could feel her heart beating very, very fast, as if she were on the point of starting a race. 'Why?'

'You know why,' Angel told her confidently. 'You own me body and soul. Why else were you asking me about why I had never wanted an emotional connection with a woman? I'm in love with you. I've probably been in love with you since you were a student, only I couldn't feel safe with you then without an NDA and I turned my back on you…but I never forgot you for so much as a week at a time. I tried to find you in other women, and I couldn't…'

'Oh, my word,' Gaby whispered, in so much shock that she actually felt dizzy.

'Is that *all* you've got to say?' Angel exclaimed.

'I had no idea that you loved me,' she muttered unevenly. 'No idea at all. I had hoped that you might come to fall in love with me, because I've been in love with you again since the wedding… I don't know how, though—it's not like you deserved love after forcing me into marrying you in the first place. But I do love you, flaws and all.'

'That was a kind of backhanded declaration,' Angel complained with his usual arrogance. 'You wouldn't have married me if you hadn't secretly wanted to. You're a tough cookie. You would have fought me to the last gasp if you didn't want me as well.'

Gaby looked reflective and then nodded grudgingly, because there was a certain amount of truth in that accusation.

'*Theos mou*…we're almost fighting about it!' Angel carolled in disbelief as he grabbed her up in his arms. 'You crazy, wonderful woman! I love you to hell and back.'

'It's to the moon and back,' she corrected.

'No, it *was* hell when we were apart. We had those few weeks and I felt so alive and impossibly happy when you were around, and then it all vanished as though it had been a dream,' he confessed in a fracturing tone of regret, his dark golden eyes full of turmoil as he remembered that period. 'I was miserable without you in my life.'

'That NDA,' she reminded him gently, but she was not as unhappy as she should have been to hear that he had been miserable without her. 'You broke my heart.'

'Broke my own too, but I don't think I was ready to commit to our future back then,' Angel told her ruefully. 'And you were too young and naive to handle me, but it's not like that any more.'

'No, it's not.' Gaby could barely credit what he was telling her, but a ball of warmth was expanding inside her chest and it was happiness, joy, all the things she had assumed she would never be able to feel with Angel except in fleeting moments. But what he was offering her now was so much more. Love would keep them together through the tougher times. Love would embrace Alexios in a cocoon of security as well. She smiled.

'You don't throw things now, you talk, you clarify,' Angel pointed out lethally.

'Keep quiet or you'll put me in a bad mood,' Gaby warned, trailing off his tie, embarking on his shirt with even more enthusiasm.

'Does this mean you're planning to move into my bedroom?' Angel husked.

'It's under consideration,' Gaby countered, not wanting to give away her every advantage at once.

'How hard do I have to work to get what I want?'

'I should think you'll be very busy persuading me tonight that having you in the same bed has benefits,' Gaby told him impishly, her sapphire eyes full of tender amusement.

Long fingers framed her vibrant face and he looked down at her with an adoration he couldn't hide, which lit her up inside like a torch. 'I love you so much, *asteri mou*...'

'My star?' Gaby translated. 'Good grief, you can be romantic.'

'Wasn't it romantic when I asked you to keep on the wedding gown and the sapphires?' Angel complained.

'No, that was you living out a fantasy, but I was still underestimating you then. You were trying and I didn't see it. You were right. My expectations *were* too low,' Gaby confided, wrenching him out of his shirt with a huge smile, struggling to come to terms with the concept that Angel Diamandis was, finally, absolutely hers. 'I will never stop loving you.'

'I won't let you stop. You have a lifetime ahead, which you will share with me and our family. For the first time ever, I have a family and I will do whatever it takes to keep it,' Angel swore fiercely, and then he gathered her into his arms and passionately kissed her breathless. 'Right now, we're going to celebrate.'

'Bossy...much?' Gaby asked.

'Secretly you like it,' Angel told her, his lean dark devastating features illuminated by a charismatic smile.

'Just you keep on telling yourself that. I love you *in spite* of your bossy taking-charge ways,' Gaby informed him.

'I just love you because you're beautiful, fierce, clever and sexy,' Angel murmured thickly as he tugged her down onto his opulent four-poster bed with sensual urgency. 'Note that I'm not criticising anything.'

'Hush,' Gaby urged, resting a fingertip against his parted lips as she gazed lovingly down at him. 'You make me incredibly happy...'

'We have a whole lifetime ahead of being together, *kardia mou*,' Angel savoured, tugging her inexorably down to him, stretching sinuously over her, all hot, sexy masculinity and unafraid to show his arousal.

Gaby emerged flushed and breathless from a passionate kiss. 'What about dinner? Won't the staff—?'

'They'll wait until we call...perks of royalty.'

'Or being a ruthless operator,' Gaby slotted in before he kissed her again and her worries about being more polite and considerate with the staff melted away, because when she was with Angel, nothing, absolutely nothing else, mattered and she too wanted to celebrate their new happy togetherness.

# EPILOGUE

*Six years later*

'THEY'RE ALL DOWN?' Angel murmured quietly from the doorway. 'Even Castor?'

Gaby grinned at him from the side of the cot where their youngest child slumbered. Even at ten months old, Castor was very different from his older, more tolerant brother. Castor had a shocking temper when life didn't go his way and he only slept when it suited him. He didn't like strange faces, unfamiliar places or different food. Keeping their baby boy content entailed effort.

'Fresh air works magic,' she said, and the King and Queen of Themos, both dressed down for their stay at the lake house in the mountains, walked to the door of the bedroom next door, where four-year-old Eliana slumbered, her shock of copper hair as bright as her mother's, her lively blue eyes shut, fast asleep after a day racing through the woods in her big brother's wake.

Alexios was dead to the world, sprawled out across his bed as though he had been felled there. Gaby lifted the tablet that had fallen from his hand and set it aside. He was her firstborn and she couldn't credit now that he had ever been a baby because he was so big and likely to be even taller than his father when he reached maturity. He looked like his father, but he had the temperament of neither parent. He was intelligent and thoughtful, an energetic boy but slow to anger and very patient.

'He really enjoyed you taking him fishing this morning,' Gaby told him as she closed the door.

'No more about the kids,' Angel growled, nipping at the skin between nape and shoulder and sending a thrilling pulse of desire thrumming through her. 'Saif and Tati will be here soon with their crew and they'll be jet-lagged and they won't settle for hours.'

'Stop complaining,' she scolded. 'You love seeing your brother and his brood.'

'It's our wedding anniversary. Remind me why we wanted to entertain other people?' Angel urged, guiding her into their bedroom with single-minded intent.

'Because Saif and Tati are the only company we have that we can totally relax with,' she reminded him softly, because it was true. They could say whatever they liked in company with family, for there was no fear of saying anything that might offend or be controversial or appear in the press, and that was probably one of the reasons that the two couples had become such close friends. It didn't hurt that they were all young and had children in the same age group either. In addition, Gaby had become very fond of Saif's down-to-earth wife, Tati.

'You're right. I'm being selfish because when I finally get you all to myself, I don't want to share you with anybody, even... *Theos mou*...my own kids.' He groaned as he pressed kisses across her bare shoulders, tugging her shirred sundress down to expose her unbound breasts, cupping that soft weight with another sound of masculine appreciation. 'This is my favourite dress—'

'Because it comes off quickly. Sometimes you are very basic,' Gaby teased, even as she arched her spine and pushed her taut nipples into his hands, quivering as that touch of abrasion sent a hot dart speeding into her pelvis.

'And you don't like it?' Angel growled, grazing his teeth across her sensitised skin as he backed her down on the bed, shimmying off her remaining garments with sure hands.

'You know I love it...' Gaby looked up at him, her heart in her eyes, an ache stirring at her core as he stood over her, swiftly shedding his clothes, revealing that long, lean, muscular bronzed body that she never tired of appreciating.

'As I love you, *Vasilessa mou*,' he husked, coming down over her, taut and ready for action.

*My Queen.* Literally and figuratively, that was how Angel treated her. She revelled in the sense of security he gave her every time he looked at her. She had the family she had always wanted, and the wonder was that he had wanted the exact same thing. She saw the tenderness, the appreciation, the unquestioning loyalty that he gave her. And the nights with him were out of the world as well, she reflected, her neck arching with her spine as he sank into her with hot, driving impatience and the excitement took her by storm.

Afterwards, listening to Angel in the shower when she felt too lazy to as much as shift a toe, she thought about how lucky she was.

Angel was a terrific father, always involved with the children, encouraging as much as he disciplined, understanding when the kids got it wrong, as children so frequently did. He had also been a wonderful supportive guide while she learned how to deal with being a royal consort. Her language skills had proved very useful, and she had been warmly conscious of Angel's pride in her ability. Tati's advice had proved good as well, although the Emir of Alharia lived in a much more formal manner than his younger brother did. Angel had dismantled much of the pomp and ceremony at the palace and embraced a more contemporary style, but Saif didn't have the same freedom because his country was more conservative.

Her friends Liz and Laurie were regular visitors with their families. The previous month they had invited them all to Paris to spend the weekend with them in Angel's fabulous town house there. Saif and Tati had joined them as well and the weekend had turned into a terrific party.

But as a rule, Gaby and Angel found their relaxation as a family unit by spending weekends alone at the house in the mountains. Free of the formality of the palace and the many staff, they got to be themselves and it kept the children grounded because nobody waited on them at the lake house. That was a much better preparation for the real world than the palace was and taught them some independence. And to her chagrin, when Viola was away on a break, Gaby had discovered that Angel was a much better cook than she was. But then, one of the joys of being married to Angel, she thought fondly, was the number of surprises he could still give her.

'Almost forgot,' Angel remarked as he walked back through the bedroom, showered and fully clad with that leaping energy he never lost. 'For our wedding anniversary…'

'You already bought me that necklace!' Gaby exclaimed, sitting up in bed.

'This is a ring…' Angel informed her somewhat smugly, lifting her hand to thread a diamond eternity ring on beside her wedding ring. 'For ever and ever, you are mine and I am yours…it's engraved on the inside.'

Minutes later, she realised what time it was and fled into the shower to get dressed because Saif and Tati were due to arrive. They were both downstairs as the helicopter came in to land at the front of the house.

'You finally cracked the mould,' she told Angel tenderly. 'That engraving is truly romantic…'

\* \* \* \* \*

# SHY INNOCENT IN THE SPOTLIGHT

## MELANIE MILBURNE

MILLS & BOON

To all the nut allergy sufferers out there.

Your daily battle to stay safe is such a challenge
and often goes unrecognised.

And a special thank-you to Emily Payne,
for describing what it feels like to
experience both anaphylaxis and its treatment.

And here I was, thinking being gluten intolerant
was bad! xxxx

# CHAPTER ONE

ELSPETH STARED AT her twin sister in heart-stopping, skin-prickling, I-can't-believe-what-I'm-hearing alarm. 'You want me to do *what*?'

Elodie rolled her eyes as if it were a competitive sport she was trying to win a gold medal in. 'It's not like you've never been a bridesmaid before. This will be—'

'The one and only time I was a bridesmaid, the bride didn't show up,' Elspeth said with a speaking look. 'Or have you completely erased jilting Lincoln Lancaster from your memory?'

Elodie gave a dismissive wave of her hand. 'Oh, that was years and years ago. Everyone's forgotten about that now.' She leaned forward on the sofa with a beseeching puppy-dog look in her blue eyes. 'So, will you do it? Will you stand in for me, just for the wedding rehearsal, in the Highlands of Scotland? You've always said you'd like to see where our ancestors came from. I'll be back in time for the wedding and we'll do a quick switch and you can leave by a back door and no one will ever know a thing.'

'But why can't you be there yourself? What's so

important that you can't be there for your friend the whole weekend?'

'Sabine is not actually a close friend as such,' Elodie said with a side note of cynicism in her tone. 'I know for a fact I've only been invited to be her bridesmaid because of my fame as a lingerie model. She likes to surround herself with influencer types and apparently she sees me as one. I've only met her a handful of times, which is why you and I switching places will work so well.'

Elspeth cast her gaze over her twin's beautifully made-up face, her professionally styled hair and perfectly manicured hands. They might be identical twins but they lived in entirely different worlds. Elodie's world was exotic and expansive and exciting. Elspeth's world was small and secure and safe…well, as safe as anyone could be who lived with a life-threatening peanut allergy. Elspeth wanted to help her sister, they were close and had always had each other's back, but they hadn't switched places since they were kids. But a society wedding was a big deal. She wasn't great at mingling, hated small talk and was painfully shy when out of her natural environment.

But then, the chance to visit Scotland, the birthplace of their ancestors, was tempting—especially without her overprotective mother tagging along as she did the last time Elspeth tried to have a weekend away. Talk about embarrassing.

*But…*

Her life to date had been a series of 'buts' and 'what ifs'. She had missed out on so many activities her peers took for granted. Her world had shrunk while her sister's had expanded. Their mother's fear for Elspeth's survival since infancy had become pathological. But, to be fair, there had been a few horrendous moments during her childhood and adolescence when she had accidentally come into contact with peanuts. Her first proper date being particularly notable. One kiss and she had to be rushed to hospital in a sirens-screaming, lights-flashing ambulance. Not fun. Travelling anywhere outside her safety zone was fraught with potential danger. What if she ran out of EpiPens or couldn't get to a hospital in time? What if she made a complete and utter fool of herself? 'I don't know…'

Elodie bounced off the sofa and placed her hands on her hips, her expression etched in stern lines of reproof only an older sister by ten minutes could pull off. 'See? You *always* do that.'

Elspeth looked at her in puzzlement. 'Do what?'

'You limit yourself. You say no when deep down you really want to say yes.' Elodie ran a hand through her long curly mane of red-gold hair. 'You do it because of Mum always being so overprotective of you. But you need to get out more, Els. You have to prove to Mum you can do stuff on your own and this is a perfect chance to do it. You have no life other than working at the library. You haven't been on a date since you were eighteen, for God's sake. And apart from work, you spend most of your time alone. Don't you want to see how the other half lives for a change? Have some fun? Be daring and spontaneous?'

Elspeth knew there was an element of truth in her twin's observation—a truth she had been avoiding facing for quite some time. Her world was small, too small, and lately she had been feeling the walls of her tiny world closing in on her even more. But that didn't mean stepping into her twin's sky-high party-girl shoes for twenty-four hours in the Highlands of Scotland was a wise or sensible thing to do. 'But you haven't answered my question. What's so important that you can't be at the wedding rehearsal yourself? Why the need for the crazy subterfuge?'

Elodie lowered her hands from her hips and sat back on the sofa opposite Elspeth. She clasped her hands between her bent knees, her eyes sparkling with barely contained excitement. 'Because I have a top-secret meeting in London about possible financial backing for my own designs. You know how desperately I want to launch my own label? Well, this could be my big chance to do it.' Her expression suddenly became as sombre as an undercover operative talking to a fellow agent. 'My *only* chance to do it. But I don't want to compromise my current contract if word got out that I was thinking of leaving. I want the finances done and dusted before I hand in my resignation.'

Elspeth could understand her twin's desire to leave the world of lingerie modelling behind. She, personally, as an introvert, could not think of anything more terrifying than strutting down a catwalk in just knickers and a bra or a bikini. But her extroverted twin had up until recently seemingly enjoyed the limelight, lapping up the fame and regular travel to exotic locations for photo shoots. When Elodie uploaded a new bikini on her Instagram account, the sales went through the stratosphere. Elspeth, on the other hand, didn't have any social-media platforms, nor did she have any bikinis. She was a one-piece, keep-her-life-private type of girl.

Would it hurt to step out of her comfort zone for

twenty-four hours? To switch places with her twin just long enough to see what life was like on the other side? It wasn't as if she were going on a photo shoot for her twin. It wasn't even for the actual wedding, just the rehearsal. 'Is there anyone else you know who's going to the wedding? I mean, more intimately than the bride?'

Elodie reached for her drink on the coffee table, her eyes not quite meeting Elspeth's. 'One or two casual acquaintances maybe.'

Elspeth sat up a little straighter in her seat, a chill running down her spine as if a blast of cold wind had blown through the window straight off the top of the Cairngorms. 'But what if someone realises it's not you?'

'How will anyone know it's not me?' Elodie asked. 'You were the one who insisted I never mention I had an identical twin when I started modelling. The most I've ever said in an interview is I have a younger sister, but I didn't say how much younger. Your privacy will remain intact because everyone will think it's me, not you. And because you're not on social media, and you were home-schooled, there are no photos of us together, no one is likely to make the connection. Our secret will be safe. Trust me.'

'But what about your wedding?' Elspeth said. 'Some photos of the wedding party were leaked online, remember? And everyone at the wedding had a go at me because they thought I must have known you were going to pull the plug on Lincoln. I'm sure I was referred to as your twin in at least a couple of press releases.'

Elodie chewed at her lower lip for a brief moment, her smooth brow furrowing slightly. But then her expression went back to its I've-got-this-covered mode. 'That was so early in my career, no one will remember it. Lincoln was far more famous than me back then.'

'But that's exactly my point. What if someone did a little research? Once online, always online, remember?'

'You're worrying too much.'

Elspeth had good reasons for not wanting any media exposure as a result of her sister's career. Elodie had always played on her looks, always loved being the centre of attention, always loved working the room. Elspeth had done the opposite—always downplaying her physical assets so as to avoid the attention her twin craved. Elspeth could not bear the thought of dozens of paparazzi chasing her down the street, thrusting numerous camera lenses in her face, potentially mistaking her for her twin. Could not bear the thought of her private life being made fodder for gossip magazines.

Could not bear to be compared to her vivacious twin and found lacking.

Elspeth wasn't charming and vivacious, she wasn't a social butterfly, she was a moth.

But...the prospect of twenty-four hours pretending to be her twin did trigger a strange sense of excitement in her blood. It was a chance to step out of her cocoon of cotton wool. The cocoon their mother had wrapped her in since her first anaphylactic reaction as a two-year-old. She wasn't two any more. She was twenty-eight and tired of being mollycoddled by her mum. Moving into her own flat a month ago had been the first step towards greater autonomy. Maybe this would be another chance to prove to her mother she could move about in the world without putting herself in mortal danger.

'Okay…' Elspeth mentally crossed her fingers. 'Let's do it.'

'Yay!' Elodie flung her arms around her and almost lifted her off the floor in a bone-crushing hug. 'Thank you. Thank you. Thank you. I'll never be able to thank you enough for doing this.' She planted a smacking kiss to Elspeth's cheek. *'Mwhah.'*

Elspeth grimaced and peeled her twin's octopus-like arms from around her body. 'You'd better save your thanks until the gig is over. I don't want you to jinx me.'

'You'll be brilliant. Remember that time we switched on one of our access visits to Dad when we were ten? He never guessed the whole weekend.'

'Yes, well, that says more about Dad than it does our acting ability, even if you did do rather a fantastic job of pretending to be a bookworm.' It was an amazing feat on her twin's part, given Elodie had dyslexia and avoided reading whenever she could. Elspeth, on the other hand, had been reading since she was four and, as she'd been home-schooled by her mother due to her allergy, her life had always revolved around books and reading. And now, her work as a library archivist was a dream career, one where she was paid to do what she loved.

Elodie laughed. 'I was bored out of my brain and I nearly went cross-eyed trying to make sense of the words. Give me a juicy gossip mag any day.'

'Even when you're in one?'

Elodie's eyes sparkled like fairy lights. 'Especially when I'm in one.'

Now it was Elspeth's turn to roll her eyes and she suppressed a shudder. 'Eek. I can think of nothing worse.'

* * *

Mack MacDiarmid surveyed the wedding preparations taking place on his country estate, Crannoch-brae, with a critical eye. Weddings weren't his thing but his younger brother, Fraser, wanted to be married at home, so no expense was being spared to make it a wedding to remember. The fact his troubled brother was finally settling down was definitely something to celebrate. Mack had spent way too many years worrying about Fraser's tendency to act impulsively and irresponsibly, but Fraser's fiancée, Sabine, had come along at the right time and Mack hoped her stable influence over time would be the making of his brother. It had certainly worked miracles so far, but Mack's inner cynic was holding its breath.

The garden where the service was to take place had never looked better. The wisteria walk was in full bloom, the sweet fragrance filling the air. The castle had been cleaned from top to bottom—everything sparkled, everything shone, everything glowed. The guests' rooms had been aired and made up and the kitchen was full of catering staff busily preparing the food for the weekend. Even the notoriously capricious summer weather had decided to cooperate. It was cloudy today, but tomorrow's forecast looked promising—bright and sunny. There was a storm predicted for later in the evening, but the wedding ceremony would be well and truly over by then.

Sabine was darting here and there, double-checking everything was going according to plan, which was supposed to be the highly paid wedding planner's job, but Sabine wasn't the sort of person to relinquish control to someone else. Not that Mack could talk—he had triple-checked everything too. He wanted his brother's wedding to go smoothly, which meant he was issued with the job of keeping an eye on Elodie Campbell, one of the bridesmaids, in case she caused trouble. Exactly what trouble she might cause was anyone's guess. Fraser had been a little cagey about his connection with Elodie but Mack had checked her out online and drawn his own conclusions. She was a stunning lingerie model with more followers on social media than had some Hollywood celebrities. She had jilted her fiancé at the altar seven years ago and had developed a reputation as a party girl ever since. He knew from experience party girls were notoriously unpredictable but he was well prepared.

Mack had made it his life's work to be well prepared. Losing his father to suicide at the age of sixteen had forced him to never leave things to chance, to always be vigilant, to tick all the boxes, to do what needed to be done, to say what needed to be said, when it needed to be said.

To *always* be in control.

Mack turned to look back at the house and caught sight of a red-gold cloud of hair and a pale oval face looking down at him from one of the guest rooms upstairs. He had never met her in person but he had seen enough photos of her in the press to recognise Elodie Campbell. An understated version, that was. She was wearing a cream silk wrap and, with her wildly curly hair pulled up in a makeshift knot on her head, she had an old-world air that was utterly captivating. She could easily have been one of his ancestors travelling through time to pay a ghostly visit. He lifted a hand in a wave but she darted away from the window so

quickly he blinked a couple of times, wondering if he
had indeed imagined her standing there. He shrugged
and continued on his way. Perhaps the stunningly beautiful Elodie Campbell didn't like being seen without
her make-up on.

Elspeth leaned back against the wall of her bedroom
and clutched a hand to her chest where her heart was
bouncing up and down like a yo-yo on an elastic string.
She was in no doubt the man she had seen just now was
Mack MacDiarmid. Elodie had shown her a photo on
her phone of Fraser and Sabine, and had briefed her
about a number of other guests, but told her zilch about
Mack MacDiarmid other than he was wealthy and had
a reputation as a love-them-and-leave-them playboy.

She had done her own research and found a couple
of articles about Mack online. Named after his father
Robert but going by the nickname of Mack, he was
a successful businessman and entrepreneur who had
made millions in various property developments both
in the UK and abroad. Crannochbrae was his ancestral
home and he had restored it, managed and developed
it since his father's death when he was a teenager. But
the photos of him in the articles hadn't prepared her
for seeing him in the flesh, even if it was from three
storeys above. Tall and lean with a rangy build, Mack
MacDiarmid had an aura of command and authority
that was unmistakable…and a little unnerving to say
the least. Would he see through her act? Why had she
thought she could pull this off? She wasn't used to
being around men like Mack MacDiarmid. Powerful,
dynamic men who had made their fortune from being
whip smart and intuitive.

As Fraser MacDiarmid's older brother, Mack was part of the wedding party, which meant there would be no way of avoiding coming into contact with him. Although, since she would only be in her sister's shoes for the rehearsal, the contact would hopefully be limited. But had Mack ever met her twin before?

Elspeth grabbed her phone off the bed where she'd left it earlier, and, pointedly ignoring the ten text messages and five missed calls from her mother, quickly fired off a text to her twin.

Have you ever met Mack MacDiarmid in person?

The three little dots appeared to signal Elodie was texting back. And then the message came through.

No.

What about Fraser, the groom?

The phone indicated her message had been read but there was no answer, which either meant Elodie was called away to her important meeting or didn't want to answer. Elspeth had a feeling it was the latter. She smoothed a hand down over her churning stomach. Why had she agreed to do this? She took a calming breath and pushed away from the wall. She agreed to do this because she wanted her sister to succeed in her new venture. Elodie was tired of modelling and wanted to express her creativity. It was up to Elspeth to pull this off for the next twenty-four hours. She knew her twin almost as well as she knew herself. She stared at her twin's face every day in the mirror. It was simply a matter of putting on her twin's make-up and clothes and adopting her twin's friendly and chatty, outgoing and super-confident personality and no one would be the wiser.

How hard could it be?

# CHAPTER TWO

ELSPETH MADE HER way down to one of the main reception rooms in the castle, where the bridal party was gathered for welcome drinks. In spite of her you-can-do-this pep talk earlier, a colony of razor-winged butterflies was attacking the lining of her stomach. She was dressed in one of her twin's designer outfits—an electric-blue satin sheath of a dress that clung to her body like a long, silky evening glove. The blue made her eyes pop, so too did the smoky make-up she had put on. The dress was way more revealing than any she would normally wear, but, hey, Cinderella had to get used to wearing a sparkly ball gown and glass slippers, right? Her twin's shoes weren't made of glass but they were higher than any Elspeth had ever worn before. And they cost more than a month's wages. She'd had to practise wearing them by doing laps of her bedroom before she ventured downstairs. She had only stumbled once, so she was quite pleased with herself.

Years of watching Elodie get ready for a photo shoot had certainly paid off. Elspeth's skin was flawless, her eyes highlighted by eyeshadow and eyeliner and lash-lengthening mascara. Her lips were shiny with straw-berry-flavoured lip gloss and her pulse points sprayed with a heady musky perfume that had only made her sneeze once. So far.

But, make-up and beautiful clothes notwithstanding, Elspeth knew she was walking a fine line and, at any moment, one misstep could blow her cover. How on earth did undercover agents do this sort of thing day in and day out? It was enough to give you a stomach ulcer.

Elspeth was still a little wide-eyed about spending the weekend in an actual castle. How many people outside royalty owned their very own castle? But that was the sort of wealth Mack MacDiarmid possessed. His ancestry went back centuries and she couldn't help feeling a little impressed by her surroundings. There were so many rooms, so many stairs, so many turrets it was as if she had stepped inside a fairy tale. The grounds were extensive with both formal and wild gardens, rolling fields and dense woods backdropped by the craggy Highlands. Situated on the shore of a small loch, the estate was picturesque and private, the perfect setting for a wedding. Everything was in tip-top shape. No crumbling walls or sagging ceilings, no draughty corridors with inadequate lighting or heating, no dust sheets draped over furniture or cobwebs hanging from the cornices or the crystal chandeliers. There was even a shiny suit of armour in the gallery, along with huge portraits of previous generations of MacDiarmids. Huge whimsical flower arrangements adorned every room, her own room included. Only the wedding party was staying at the castle but, since she was one of six bridesmaids, she hoped she would be lost in the crowd.

But as soon as she walked into the reception room, Sabine, the bride, rushed over to her.

'Elodie! You look amazing as always.' Sabine did the air-kiss thing and stood back to run her gaze over Elspeth's outfit...well, her twin's outfit, that was. 'That blue is so stunning on you. And your make-up is so professional and we haven't even had the make-up artist, Maggie, do her magic on you yet.'

'Oh, this old thing?' Elspeth waved a hand in front of her twin's outfit in exactly the same dismissive manner Elodie would have used. 'You look lovely too. I'm sure you'll be the most gorgeous bride ever.' Okay, well, maybe her twin wouldn't have laid on the compliments quite so enthusiastically but Elspeth thought Sabine was a very pretty girl-next-door type who was positively glowing with happiness. It made her wonder if falling in love with the man of her dreams could work the same magic on her. As if. Who was going to fall in love with a girl who couldn't walk past a bowl of nuts without having a panic attack?

'I'm so honoured you could find time in your busy schedule to be my bridesmaid,' Sabine said. 'It means the world to me. You're such a fantastic role model at how to look fabulous without even trying.'

*Without even trying?* Elspeth had to hold back a spluttering laugh. She had been trying to turn herself into a glamour queen for the last two hours. Sheesh. How did her twin do this every day? It was positively exhausting.

'It's a privilege to be here,' Elspeth said with a smile. 'It's such a beautiful place to hold a wedding.'

'I know, right? Mack, Fraser's brother, was so generous to let us use it,' Sabine said. 'Have you had something to eat?' She beckoned over a waiter who was carrying an array of delicious-looking finger food on a silver tray. 'These are scrumptious. I've had three of them already.'

Elspeth studied the tray of food for a brief moment, deciding against taking anything off it. She had two EpiPens in her clutch purse but the last thing she wanted to do was blow her cover in the first hour by triggering her allergy. She had considered quietly alerting the catering staff to her dietary issue but decided against it. It would draw far more attention to herself than she wanted, especially as there was no record of her twin ever having an allergy. Who knew if a paparazzo was lurking about ready to leak something to the press? It was easier to avoid eating. Besides, she had fresh fruit and nut-free cookies in her suitcase. There was a lot she would do for her twin but starving herself was not one of them. 'Thank you but I'm not hungry.'

'No wonder you're so slim,' Sabine said with a rueful grimace. 'I could never be as disciplined as you are. I love my food too much.' She looked past Elspeth's shoulder and smiled a broad smile. 'Let me introduce you to your host and bridal-party partner for the weekend.' She took Elspeth by the arm and led her to the other side of the room. 'Mack, this is Elodie Campbell, the famous lingerie model I was telling you about.'

Mack MacDiarmid turned around and met her gaze for the second time that day. A frisson passed over her flesh, her heart rate sped up and her mouth went dry. He was taller than she had calculated—at least six foot four—with broad shoulders and piercing grey-blue eyes framed by prominent eyebrows. His hair was dark brown with one or two threads of silver at the temples giving him a distinguished, old-before-his-years aura.

His hair was slightly wavy and casually styled with one
or two curls kinked over his forehead, lending him a
rakish look that made her heart flutter. His square jaw
hadn't seen a razor in a day or two, which should have
made him look unkempt but somehow did the opposite. The designer stubble was rich and dark with a light
sprinkling of silver throughout that, if anything, made
him even more heart-stoppingly attractive.

'How do you do?' Mack held out his hand and she
slipped hers into its firm clasp. If his Scottish accent
and whisky-rough voice weren't enough to dazzle her
senses, his touch more than completed the job. His
skin was dry and warm, his fingers long and tanned,
and a zap of electricity shot from his hand to hers with
lightning-fast speed.

'Pleased to meet you.' Elspeth couldn't get her voice
above more than a scratchy whisper and was aware of
scorching heat pooling in her cheeks. Eek. Her twin
hadn't blushed since she was twelve. How convincing
was she going to be if her cheeks fired up every time
Mack MacDiarmid glanced her way?

Mack released her hand but his gaze remained teth-
ered to hers with an unnerving intensity. 'Welcome to
Crannochbrae.'

'Thank you. It's been ages since I've been to Scotland. It's such a beautiful place, especially here in the
Highlands. You have a gorgeous home. The gardens
are spectacular. You must have millions of bees in total
raptures with all those flowers.' She knew she was talking too much but something about Mack's commanding
presence and unwavering gaze deeply unsettled her.
She got the sense he was not easily fooled, not easily
deceived, not easily manipulated. She started to ques-

tion her sanity in agreeing to switch places with her twin. Why had she thought she could do this convincingly? It had been easy to fool their father all those years ago—he had never been able to tell them apart even when they were babies and toddlers, even before he left their mother for another woman when they were five.

But Elspeth got the feeling Mack MacDiarmid was a man who never let anything escape his notice. Every little detail was noted, documented, filed away for reference, for clarification. For close investigative study.

Mack's gaze narrowed ever so slightly. 'Didn't you have a photo shoot on the island of Skye a couple of months ago?'

'I—I did?' Elspeth looked at him blankly for a moment, her heart skipping a beat. 'Oh, yes, I forgot about that, silly me. I do so much travelling I can't remember where I've been or how long ago it was. Yes, of course, Skye was stunningly beautiful.' Double eek. This was proving to be harder than she had first thought. Her twin was always dashing off to yet another shoot in an exotic location, so it was hard to keep up with her movements. Elspeth vaguely remembered Elodie mentioning something about freezing to death on a Scottish beach modelling next summer's swimwear range. She tucked a strand of hair back behind her ear and beamed up at him as her twin would have done.

Mack's smile didn't make the full distance to his penetrating eyes. 'You enjoy travelling for work?'

'Love it. So many places to see, so many people to meet. Of course, it's not always glamourous. There's a lot of waiting around on shoots, a lot of time in hair and make-up and living out of a suitcase and so on.'

Elspeth was repeating all the things her twin had told her over the years but even to her own ears, it sounded inauthentic. As if she was playing a part, which she was. Would he see through it? He didn't seem the type of man to be easily taken in. He was too suave and sophisticated and street smart. Never had she felt more out of her depth. Like a teensy-weensy goldfish flung out of her tiny bowl into a vast ocean of whale sharks.

'Can I get you something to drink? A cocktail? Champagne? G and T? Wine?' Mack asked.

Unlike her twin, Elspeth rarely drank alcohol. She had never really developed a taste for it because she so rarely socialised. But she figured it would look odd if she didn't have what her sister would normally have. Besides, a little Dutch courage might come in handy right now. 'Champagne would be lovely, thank you.'

Mack moved away to fetch a drink for her and Elspeth took a moment to try and calm her racing pulse. She couldn't stop following Mack with her gaze, drawn to him in a way she couldn't explain. He was so…so dynamic. So potently, breath-snatchingly attractive. It was as if every other man she had ever met paled in comparison. Not that she had met a lot of men in a dating sense. After her last date when she was eighteen, she had ended up in hospital with anaphylactic shock. Her mother had almost had a breakdown over it and Elspeth hadn't dated since. But that was why she had moved out of home a month ago, so she could live without her mother hovering and fussing over her as if she were still a child. She wasn't a child. She was a fully grown adult and could take care of herself. And this weekend was a good chance to prove it, to herself if not her mother.

'So you've finally met my big brother,' a male voice said in an undertone from close behind her.

Elspeth turned and encountered Fraser MacDiarmid. She recognised him from the photo Elodie had shown her. He was good-looking but not in the same category as his older brother. He was an inch or two shorter and carried a bit more weight around his middle. His jaw wasn't as strong, his gaze not as direct, his aura not as dynamic. Fraser was bland and boring where his brother, Mack, was compelling and captivating.

'Oh, hello...' Elspeth was at a loss to know what else to say. She couldn't remember if her twin had met Fraser or not and mentally rewound her conversation and text messages with her. Surely it was just the bride Elodie knew? But there was a familiarity about Fraser's manner towards her—the way he was standing so close, for instance—that suggested he considered her twin far more than a passing acquaintance.

Fraser gave her a smile that wasn't really a smile. 'I know what you're up to, you know.' His voice was still pitched low, as if he didn't want others to overhear.

Elspeth straightened her shoulders and willed her knees not to tremble. 'I have no idea what you're talking about.' At least *that* wasn't a lie.

His smile became vicious, like a stray dog baring its teeth. A don't-mess-with-me-I'm-dangerous-if-provoked warning. He leaned a little closer, his beer-scented breath wafting over her face. 'You think you're so clever wangling an invitation to my wedding just to watch me squirm.'

Why would he feel the need to squirm? What exactly had gone on between Fraser MacDiarmid and her twin? A fling? An affair? Elodie hadn't mentioned anything about a fling with the groom. She had casually dated on and off in the seven years since jilting her fiancé, Lincoln Lancaster, but never for longer than a week or two. She claimed she didn't want to be tied down. She insisted she wasn't looking for Mr Right and the white picket fence and a pram parked in the hallway. But something clearly had gone on between Fraser and Elodie. But what?

'I was flattered to be invited to be one of Sabine's bridesmaids,' Elspeth said, desperately trying to stay as cool and collected as her twin would have done.

'I bet you were.' Fraser raked her with his gaze. 'But if you so much as whisper one word of what happened between us that night in London, I'll deny everything and make you look like the troublemaking fool you are.'

Her heart banged against her ribcage and a cold shiver scuttled down her back. *What had happened between them?* As much as it shocked her to be threatened by a man who was clearly a bit of a bully, Elspeth stayed in her twin's character with renewed vigour, even with a little more confidence. After all, Fraser MacDiarmid clearly didn't suspect she was a stand-in—he was treating her as if she were indeed her twin. Someone with whom he had had some sort of encounter that he was now desperate to keep secret on the eve of his wedding.

Elspeth inched up her chin, her gaze pointed. 'But will your fiancée believe you?' She was proud of how sassy and defiant she sounded. So like Elodie it was kind of spooky. Not that she could ever be as confident and in charge as her twin, more was the pity. But it sure was rather thrilling to pretend.

But then she noticed Mack coming back with her glass of champagne, his intelligent gaze taking in the tense little tableau between her and his brother.

'Ooh, lovely,' Elspeth said, taking the glass off Mack with a smile bright enough to outshine the crystal chandeliers above. 'My favourite. Cheers.' She took a generous sip of the champagne and was pleasantly surprised to find she liked the taste. But maybe that was because it was the best champagne money could buy. No doubt Mack MacDiarmid would not serve cheap imported sparkling wine from the local off-licence at his brother's wedding. Or maybe it was because, right then, she needed all the help she could get to get through this ridiculous charade.

But *was* it so ridiculous?

The realisation drifted into her mind that, right now, a part of her was actually enjoying herself. She was a little out of her comfort zone, sure, but no one so far had guessed she wasn't Elodie, even Fraser, who apparently had had some sort of illicit tryst with her twin. *Go me*, she thought. Who knew she could act so convincingly? But—even more exciting—she was getting a buzz from being in the company of Mack MacDiarmid. Every time he came within a metre of her, every cell in her body tingled with awareness.

'Excuse me, I have to mingle with the other guests,' Fraser said, and strode away with a deep frown carved between his eyes.

Mack looked down at her with an unreadable expression on his face. 'Everything all right?'

Elspeth blinked up at him guilelessly. 'Sure. I'm having a marvellous time. Just super. Everything is just wonderful.'

His gaze drifted to her mouth, lingered there for a pulse-racing moment. 'Liar.' His voice was deep and rumbly and it did strange things to the base of her spine, making it all tingly and loose.

Elspeth had to remind herself she was pretending to be her twin. Elodie would not stand there with her heart pounding and her senses on high alert. She would not be intimidated by the most handsome man she had ever met. She would stand her ground and give as good as she got. 'You don't look like you're having a wonderful time either.'

'What makes you say that?'

She gave her version of one of her twin's classic insouciant one-shoulder shrugs. 'All these people you don't know or even particularly like traipsing all over your home all weekend, getting drunk and up to who knows what else.'

One side of his mouth tipped up in a cynical half-smile. 'Is that your plan? To get drunk and get up to who knows what else?'

Elspeth took another sip of her champagne, deciding it was as addictive as verbal sparring with the Laird of Crannochbrae. His eyes continued to hold hers in a challenging lock, his mouth still tilted in an enigmatic smile. 'I don't have a plan. I like to live moment to moment. It's way more fun.' She beamed another smile at him. 'You should try it some time, Mr Control Freak.' She drained her glass and set it down on a nearby table. *Mr Control Freak?* Eek. What had made her call him that? It sounded as though she was actually flirting

with him. She had never flirted with anyone. She had
missed out on the flirting gene…or so she'd thought.

His eyes went back to her mouth and she had to fight
the impulse to lick her lips. What was it about this man
that made her feel so reckless and excited? Was it the
champagne going to her head? Or was it Mack Mac-
Diarmid's disturbingly attractive presence?

A flinty light came into his eyes. 'I would advise
you, Miss Campbell, against doing anything that would
jeopardise my brother's wedding this weekend. Do I
make myself one hundred per cent crystal clear?' His
tone was commanding, so commanding and dictato-
rial it made her bristle on her twin's behalf. What the
hell did he think Elodie would do? Her twin might be
a little wild at times but she would not wilfully sabotage someone's wedding day. She had sabotaged her
own, sure, but that was another story. One Elodie had
not yet told anyone the full details of, not even her.
Elodie refused to talk about why she jilted her fiancé
and Elspeth knew better than to keep pressing her to
do so. Elodie could pout and stonewall for weeks on
end if pushed too hard. She was so stubborn she could
have made a career out of conducting training work-
shops for mules.

Elspeth moved a step closer to Mack, close enough
to smell the citrus and woodsy notes of his aftershave.
She had to fully extend her neck to maintain eye contact. Had to resist the sudden urge to stroke her hand
down the peppery stubble on his lantern jaw to see if it
felt as sexy as it looked. Had to stop herself from staring at his sensually contoured mouth and wondering
what it would feel like against her own. 'You're not the
boss of me but I bet you'd like to be.'

*Oh. My. God. Listen to me. I am so nailing imper-
sonating Elodie right now.*

A line of tension rippled across his jaw and his gaze
hardened another notch. 'You're way out of your league
playing with me.'

Elspeth suspected even her outgoing don't-mess-
with-me twin would be way out of her league playing
with Mack, let alone her quiet and shy and socially
inexperienced self. She lowered her gaze to the firm
line of his mouth, her stomach bottoming out. 'What
makes you think I want to play with you?'

He held her gaze for a long throbbing moment. 'I
know your type.'

'And what type is that, pray tell?'

'The type of woman who likes to be the centre of
attention.'

Elspeth lifted her eyebrows in an exaggerated manner. 'My, oh, my, what an appalling opinion you have of
me—someone you've only just met. But don't worry,
Mr MacDiarmid. It's not my intention to outshine the
bride. This is her wedding weekend, not mine.'

'I heard about your ill-fated wedding day. Tell me—
how did your fiancé feel about being left standing at
the altar? Are you still on speaking terms?' There was
a note of censure in his tone that, in all honesty, Elspeth had heard in her own voice when asking her twin
about why she had done such a thing. That awful day
was still etched in her mind. Seeing the look of bewil-
derment and then thunderous fury on Elodie's fiancé's
face. The shocked embarrassment of the guests, the
horror on their mother's face. Everyone turning to her
and insisting she must have known something as Elodie's identical twin and why hadn't she let them know,

blah blah blah. It had been beyond upsetting and embarrassing to admit she had known nothing. She had been just as blindsided as everyone else.

'It was seven years ago,' Elspeth said with a parody of her twin's nonchalance. 'He's forgotten all about me now.' That wasn't a lie either. Lincoln Lancaster had only ever had eyes for Elodie and would have probably forgotten the existence of her shy twin after all this time. And hopefully everyone else at the wedding that day. But whether Lincoln had forgotten Elodie was another matter.

'How well do you know Sabine?'

'Clearly well enough for her to want me to be one of her bridesmaids.' Elspeth gave him another plastic smile straight out of the party girl's playbook.

'And my brother, Fraser?'

Elspeth was aware of heat pooling in her cheeks and her smile fell away. 'Wh-what about him?' Her voice didn't sound as steady as she would have liked. And nor was her heart rate.

Mack's eyes became diamond hard. 'Describe your relationship with him.'

Elspeth pinched her lips together and held his gaze with a defiant glare. 'What are you implying?'

He gave a low deep grunt of cynical laughter that made her bristle from head to foot. 'You know exactly what I'm talking about.'

If only she did know. Elspeth was furious with her twin for putting her in such a compromising situation without giving her the full picture. How was she supposed to do a convincing job of pretending to be her twin when she didn't know what her twin had been up to? 'I hardly think it is any business of yours, Mr Mac-

Diarmid.' Her voice was so tart it could have done a lemon out of a job.

Mack stepped a little closer and her breath caught in her throat and her cheeks heated up another notch. But it wasn't just her cheeks that were hot—her whole body was on fire, as if he had triggered an inferno in her flesh. 'I'm making it my business.' His tone had a gravelly edge that sent tingles down her spine, so too did the smoky grey-blue of his eyes.

'If you're so keen on finding out, why don't you ask your brother?'

'I'm asking you.'

'I refuse to discuss this while there are people about.' Elspeth began to move away before she got too far in over her head but one of his hands captured her slim wrist on the way past. She stopped dead, not because his grip was forceful—it wasn't. But because his touch was electrifying and it sent tingling shock waves through her entire body.

Elspeth looked down at his long, tanned fingers curled around her wrist, her heart slipping from its moorings in her chest. She hadn't been touched by a man in a decade. His touch set fire to her skin, every whorl of his fingers searing her flesh like a scorching brand. She brought her gaze back up to his and injected icy disdain in her voice. 'If you're so keen to avoid making a scene at your brother's wedding rehearsal, I suggest you take your hand off me this instant.'

The air was charged with a strange energy like a tight invisible wire stretching, stretching, stretching almost to snapping point.

Elspeth held his gaze with a strength of willpower she hadn't known she possessed. She would *not* be intimidated by him. She would not scuttle away like a scared little rabbit in front of a big bad wolf. She would stand up to him and enjoy every heart-stopping moment. Never had she felt so exhilarated, so alive and aware of her body. Flickers of lust stirred between her thighs, her breasts tingled and tightened, her blood rocketed through her veins at breakneck speed.

But as exciting as it was to stand up to Mack MacDiarmid, she couldn't quite forget she was playing a role. She was *pretending* to be Elodie. And as empowering as it felt to interact with such a dashingly handsome man, she had to remember it was a charade. She could never be part of the world her twin lived in. She could do a walk-on part for twenty-four hours but that was all. It was crazy to think otherwise.

Mack's fingers loosened a fraction but only enough to reposition so his thumb could measure her racing-off-the-charts pulse. 'Why do you I make you so nervous?' His tone was silky, his gaze penetrating.

Elspeth hoisted her chin. 'I'm not intimidated by you.' Or at least, she was pretending she wasn't intimidated. Pretending she wasn't rattled, unnerved, intrigued and bewitched by him.

He gave an indolent smile and stroked his thumb across her blue-veined wrist, her sensitive skin tingling, fizzing in delight. 'Meet me in the library in half an hour. We'll continue our discussion in private.' He released her wrist and turned and walked away before she could think of an answer. Or a reason not to meet him.

Elspeth let out a long wobbly breath like someone squeezing the last bit of air out of a set of bagpipes. Meet him in private? To discuss what? Things she had absolutely no clue about? Being anywhere alone with

Mack MacDiarmid was asking for trouble. He only had to look at her to send her heart racing and her blood pumping. She looked down at her wrist where his fingers had touched her and a frisson passed through her body. Her skin felt as if it had been permanently branded—it was still tingling, all the nerves rioting beneath her skin.

At least her twin would be here first thing in the morning, so she could get out of this farce before she made a complete and utter fool of herself. If only Elodie had prepared her a little more. Why hadn't her twin told her what had occurred between her and Mack's younger brother, Fraser? For something had gone on, of that she was sure. She picked up another glass of champagne off a passing waiter and took a sip to moisten her powder-dry mouth. The last hour had given her a taste for top-shelf French champagne and a brooding Scotsman.

And she didn't know which one would do the most damage—the demon drink or the devilishly handsome Mack MacDiarmid.

Mack cornered his brother a short time later in what used to be the music room. It was now a spare sitting room but it wasn't used that often. He had sold his beloved piano years ago and had never got around to replacing it. He had given up his dreams of a musical career and concentrated on salvaging the family's estate instead. Mack closed the door with a resounding click and eyeballed his brother. 'Tell me what's going on between you and Elodie Campbell.'

Fraser's gaze darted away from his as he walked to the other side of the room to pick up an ornament off a side table. 'Nothing's going on.' He put the ornament down again and then straightened a photo of their mother.

'But something did go on between you.' Mack framed it as a statement because he knew when his brother was lying. 'I thought you were worried Elodie Campbell might dance on the tables or drink too much and act a little inappropriately with the father of the bride or something. But *this*?'

Fraser loosened his tie with one hand as if it were choking him. Beads of perspiration dotted his forehead. 'It was nothing.' He clenched his fists and added with greater emphasis, 'It meant nothing. *She* meant nothing.'

Mack drew in a breath and slowly released it. 'I'm the last person to judge someone for having a one-night stand but were you engaged to Sabine at the time?'

His brother's cheeks developed twin flags of colour high on his cheekbones. 'I'm not going to answer that because it's none of your damn business.'

Mack frowned. 'Because it's too confronting to openly admit you've been a prize jerk?'

Fraser gave him a glowering look. 'It was only the once. No damage has been done. Sabine doesn't know and I'd like it to stay that way.'

Mack let out a curse in Gaelic. 'Damage *has* been done. Sabine thinks the man she's marrying tomorrow is loyal and faithful. How many other women have you been with since you've been engaged to her?'

'It's none of your business, Mack. You're not my father.'

'No, but you're turning into ours,' Mack shot back. 'Dad didn't have the guts to be honest about the mistakes he made, the lies he told, the truths about himself he refused to face either. He was a coward and it destroyed our mother's life and that of his lover and child. Do you really want to do that to Sabine? Because that's the way it starts—one lie, one misstep, one betrayal and then a thousand lies and cover-ups until it all comes crumbling down around you like a house of cards.'

Fraser gave a convulsive swallow, his eyes showing raw fear. 'I can't tell Sabine. It'll destroy her. She thinks I've never met Elodie before. She met her at a charity function and got a little star-struck by her. Next thing I know they're chatting online and, hey presto, she's invited her to be one of the bloody bridesmaids. I'm sure Elodie engineered it just to make trouble. I couldn't say I didn't want her in the wedding party because Sabine would have wondered why.' He turned away and scraped his hand through his hair. 'Can you imagine the scandal it will cause if it comes out now? What the press will make of it?'

'Why did you do it? Aren't you happy with Sabine?'

Fraser threw him a worldly glance. 'You've met Elodie. Why do you think I did it?'

Mack had no argument with his brother on finding Elodie Campbell stunningly beautiful. Any man with his fair share of testosterone would find her attractive. But there was something about her that didn't add up and he was determined to find out exactly what it was. It was as if she was acting a part, playing a role of femme fatale that didn't sit all that comfortably with her. He was prepared to accede that most public figures had another side to their personality, especially if they were representing a brand. They could be quite different in their private lives away from the spotlight. He was convinced the young woman he caught a glimpse of from the upstairs window was not the same woman who sparred with him a few minutes ago. It wasn't just about the hair and make-up and fancy clothes. Something about Elodie Campbell puzzled him and he would not rest until he figured her out. 'Just because you find a woman attractive doesn't mean you're entitled to sleep with her. Did she know you were in a committed relationship at the time?'

The dull flush on his brother's cheekbones darkened. 'No.'

'So you lied to her too.'

Fraser rolled his eyes and spun on his heels again. 'She would have slept with me anyway. She's a slut. Everyone knows that.'

Mack ground his teeth so hard he thought his molars would crack like his grandmother's heirloom porcelain china. How had his younger brother become such a misogynist? 'Careful, your double standard is showing. A slut is basically a woman living by a man's morals, so I would advise you not to use such an offensive term.'

'You would *advise*.' Fraser leaned on the word and made a scoffing noise in the back of his throat. 'It's all you ever do—tell me what I should or shouldn't do.'

Mack had had to step into a father role from the age of sixteen when their father committed suicide after his double life and the massive debts he'd built up were suddenly exposed. It had devastated their mother and Fraser, but Mack had had to set aside his own shock and grief and take control before any more damage was done. But even so, Fraser had subsequently acted out throughout his teens, skipping school, failing subjects he used to be star pupil in, dabbling in drugs and excessive alcohol. It had been a nightmare for Mack trying to keep his family together, to maintain some sense of normality when everything had been turned upside down. He'd had to put an end to his own career aspirations in order to run the estate.

Music had been his passion, his love, his everything and he'd had to give it up. He hadn't touched a piano since. It was as if a part of him had died along with his father. He'd had to work three jobs, sell off valuable heirloom items he wished he hadn't had to sell, beg and borrow huge amounts of money to cover the hair-raising debts his father had left behind. It had taken years of hard work and sacrifice to get the estate back in the black. 'Only because you seem incapable of getting your act together. I know it was rough on you when Dad died. It was rough on all of us, Mum in particular. But you're not fourteen any more, Fraser. You're a grown man about to get married. You owe it to Sabine to be straight with her.'

'It'll hurt her...'

Mack gave him a look. 'A pity you didn't think of that when you unzipped your—'

'Elodie started it. She came on to me.'

'And you had no choice? No moral compass to guide you? You just got down and dirty and forgot about everything but getting it off with a beautiful woman behind your fiancée's back.'

'You're such a hypocrite.' Fraser curled his lip. 'You've slept with dozens of women.'

'I'm not denying it, but I have never done so while

in love with someone else.' Mack had never been in love. Had in fact avoided any emotional entanglements that would require him to invest in a relationship longer than a week or two. He wondered if he was even capable of loving someone in that way. Love was supposed to be blind and in their mother's case it certainly had been. But when it came to that, he too had been blind about his father. Blindly devoted to his dad without realising his father was living a double life. Racking up gambling debts, keeping a mistress and child in another city for years, spending money he didn't have to fund his crazy lifestyle. In hindsight, Mack could recall each of his father's blatant lies. Lies that still hurt to this day. The fact that his dad had tricked him into thinking he was working hard for them for weeks at a time, missing important dates—birthdays, parent-teacher meetings, key sporting events—when the truth was he was with his other family.

The betrayal of trust had been life-changing for Mack. He no longer chose to be blind to a person's faults. He no longer possessed a pair of rose-coloured glasses. He went into relationships with his eyes wide open and got out of them before any damage was done. Trusting someone, loving someone made you blind to their faults, to their lies, to their cover-ups. He kept emotion out of his relationships. They were transactional and temporary and could be terminated without tears.

Fraser's expression was belligerent. 'I'm not going to sabotage my own wedding by confessing one little mistake to Sabine. And I'd appreciate it if you would keep Elodie Campbell under control as I asked you to.'

Mack had a feeling trying to control Elodie Campbell even for twenty-four seconds was going to be a challenge. But, hey, he liked a challenge and she was a rather beautiful and intriguing one.

But controlling his own red-hot attraction to her was going to be the kicker.

# CHAPTER THREE

ELSPETH WENT BACK to her room upstairs to phone Elodie without anyone listening in. It was no surprise to see another raft of text messages from her mother. She blew out a breath and quickly pinged off a text assuring her mother that she was fine and having a wonderful time. What was one more lie when she had told heaps so far? She then called her twin's number.

'What the hell happened between you and Fraser MacDiarmid?' she asked as soon as Elodie answered.

'Nothing.'

'It can't have been nothing. I just had him snarling in my ear downstairs, warning me to keep my mouth shut. I don't even know what it is I'm supposed to be keeping quiet about. The least you could have done is tell me. I feel like I'm on stage in a play in the West End, playing to a full house after memorising the wrong script.'

Elodie let out a sigh heavy enough to send a helicopter into a tailspin. 'I didn't tell you because I'm embarrassed about it.' She paused for a beat and continued, 'I had a one-night stand with him. I'm not even attracted to him but I'd just run into Lincoln and his latest squeeze in the same London bar... I don't know...

it made me a little crazy. I got chatting to Fraser and then I went back to his room. End of story.'

Elspeth knew her twin was a little reckless at times but picking up strangers in a bar was completely out of character. Yes, she was flirtatious and daring and outgoing but, as far as Elspeth knew, her sister wasn't a one-night-stand-with-a-stranger type of girl. But did she really know her twin as well as she thought? Elodie had always claimed she hadn't been in love with Lincoln Lancaster. That their whirlwind courtship had been out of balance from the start, for he'd been the one to insist on getting married when they had only known each other a couple of months. Why, then, would running into him with his latest lover upset Elodie so much? 'The least you could have done is tell me. I'm in over my head and I—'

'If I'd told you, you wouldn't have agreed to switch places,' Elodie said.

'Given the circumstances, why did you accept the role of bridesmaid in the first place? You said Sabine was only a passing acquaintance. You could have politely declined and—'

'I accepted before I realised who she was engaged to. Once I found out, it was too late to come up with an excuse not to accept the invitation. Besides, I figured it was a way to pay back Fraser for being such a sleaze.'

Elspeth suppressed a cold shudder. 'The sex between you was…consensual, wasn't it?'

'Yes, but he was a selfish lover and he didn't tell me he was engaged at the time. I would never have gone back to his room if I'd known that. I wanted to teach him a lesson and his delightfully friendly fiancée gave me the perfect way to do it.'

'But what about Sabine? Did you consider her in your plan for revenge?'

There was a weighted silence.

'Not at the time but since, yes.'

'Is that why you sent me instead of coming yourself? Your conscience got the better of you?' Elspeth asked.

'Partly, I guess, but I really did have a meeting here in London. I've only just finished it.'

'How did it go?'

'They want me to meet with them again tomorrow to discuss it further.'

A stone slab landed on the floor of Elspeth's stomach. '*Tomorrow?* But you're meant to be here first thing in the morning to switch places with me. In fact, shouldn't you be getting on a flight right now as you promised?'

'I can't be there. You'll have to keep up the act. It's only for another twenty-four hours. You've got this far without anyone guessing. Just keep doing what you're doing and everything will be sweet. Look—I've got to dash. I'm supposed to be meeting up with everyone from the meeting for drinks. Bye.'

Elspeth stared at the dead phone in her hand, her heart sinking in despair. Eek! Another twenty-four hours wearing her party-girl twin's shoes.

But what if she fell flat on her face?

Mack wondered if he needed his head examined for organising a private meeting with Elodie Campbell in the library. But the temptation to squirrel her away from the rest of the wedding party was too irresistible. Besides wanting to hear her side of her fling with his younger brother, he had a burning desire to understand more about her character. She was warm and friendly towards Sabine, acting as if butter wouldn't melt in her mouth, and yet, if it was true she'd slept with Fraser, what sort of friend of the bride did that make her? Fraser had admitted Elodie hadn't known he was engaged at the time of their brief encounter, but, still, agreeing to be Sabine's bridesmaid seemed a little inappropriate under the circumstances. What exactly was motivating Elodie to be here? She had a busy schedule taking her all over the world—it would have been easy enough to politely decline the invitation. And Sabine, being a sweet and generous-natured young woman, would have understood.

No, there was more to Elodie Campbell than he'd first thought. She was feisty and spirited when interacting with him and yet, every now and again he caught her chewing at her lower lip, looking uncertain and way out of her depth. And what about those blushes? He hadn't thought someone with the party-girl reputation Elodie had would blush so readily or so deeply. Or was that because she felt guilty about her fling with the groom of her friend?

But there was another reason Mack wanted time alone with her. He wanted to make sure she had no ulterior motive for being at his brother's wedding. Sabine had been a wonderful influence on Fraser over the last year or so and Mack was determined their wedding would go ahead. It had to. Apart from the money he had spent on the young couple's nuptials, Mack was worried that Fraser might spin out of control if Sabine called it quits. Sabine's wealthy businessman father had promoted Fraser high up in his company and given him extra privileges that would be taken away in a heartbeat if anything went awry with his beloved only daughter. Mack didn't want to think about Fraser losing his job, the career pathway that had been so stabilising for him.

Mack had to keep Elodie Campbell under control. He had to make sure the wedding went ahead without any dramas.

And one way to do that was to keep Elodie's attention focussed on himself instead of his brother.

And that, he decided, would be nothing if not entertaining.

Elspeth considered ignoring Mack's command to meet him in the library but curiosity got the better of her. And not just because the library of a centuries-old castle was to her one of the most exciting places in the world to visit. The enigmatic Mack MacDiarmid was even more exciting.

Dangerously so.

Elspeth found the library and was pleased he wasn't yet there. It gave her time to peruse the floor-to-ceiling shelves, to drool over some of the titles housed there. It was an archivist's dream to be surrounded by priceless editions that were hundreds of years old. There were journals and diaries from some of Mack's ancestors and she wished she had more time so she could read through them all. The room had a velvet-covered wing chair and a sofa in front of the windows that overlooked the dense woods behind the castle. A tall standard lamp was situated beside the wing chair, providing a perfect reading place, and she pictured herself curled up in it with one of the ancient books, with Highland snow falling softly and silently outside. She placed her clutch purse on one of the shelves and began to examine some of the titles. Her eyes nearly popped out of her head at some of the treasures housed on the shelves. Did Mack know the value of these books? Had they been archived and insured? She stared at row after row of priceless titles, her breath catching in wonder, her hands itching to examine them. But books as old as these needed special care. Cotton gloves for handling and a controlled-temperature environment to preserve them for generations to come.

The sound of the door clicking shut behind her made Elspeth spin round from the bookshelves. 'You have a lot of wonderful books. I can't believe what a treasure trove you've got here. Have they ever been valued or archived? Are they adequately insured?'

Mack stepped further into the room, his expression difficult to read. 'The most valuable were sold a few years ago.'

'But there must be others here that are worth a mint.' She gazed back up at the shelves and pointed. 'That one there—the leather-bound one I'm sure is a rare edition of *The Canterbury Tales*. A copy of it sold for several million pounds a while back. Could you get it down for me? And do you have a pair of cotton gloves?'

Mack took so long to answer, Elspeth turned round to look at him. 'Is something wrong?'

He stepped further into the light coming from the chandelier above. 'You have an interest in rare books?' His expression was still largely inscrutable but a piercing light in his gaze sent a tingling shiver skittering across her scalp.

Elspeth suddenly realised her gaffe. Her twin was a lingerie model who had chosen to leave school before she got her GCSEs in her quest to make a career out of modelling. There were numerous interviews Elodie had given about her struggle with dyslexia and how she had spent most of her childhood avoiding reading. 'Erm…yes, it's kind of a hobby of mine…' She turned away and gnawed at her lip, her heart racing so hard and fast she thought she might faint. She could feel her cheeks heating…so much for the controlled-temperature environment. At this rate, her cheeks would turn the precious books into ashes within minutes.

'What other hobbies do you have?'

Elspeth forced herself to face him again, painting a smile on her face, while her heart did somersaults in her chest. 'I draw. I dabble in watercolours.' At least those things were true. It was a talent she and her twin shared.

Mack came up to where she was standing, his eyes holding hers in an unwavering lock. 'Tell me something. Why did you accept the invitation to be Sabine's bridesmaid?'

The question blindsided her for a moment. She moistened her lips and averted her gaze, focussing it on the collar of his shirt. 'I like Sabine. She's a sweetheart.' That was also true, Elspeth decided. Sabine was a warm and friendly soul who deserved better than Mack's cheating younger brother, Fraser. She wished she could warn Sabine about the man she was marrying tomorrow but how could she do it without blowing her cover? Sabine would be hurt by not one but three betrayals—her fiancé's cheating, Elodie being the person he cheated with and Elspeth standing in for her twin as bridesmaid.

'Then why did you sleep with her fiancé, my younger brother?'

Elspeth swallowed. 'I—I don't wish to discuss—'

'We are not leaving this room until we have discussed it.' His tone had that determined edge that had so irritated her before.

Elspeth gave him a frosty look. 'You can hardly hold me prisoner.'

His grey-blue eyes darkened to gunmetal-grey. 'Don't tempt me.'

The air crackled with tension. A throbbing tension Elspeth could feel in her body. The low and deep secret tug of desire, the heightening of her senses, the flaring of her nostrils, the lowering of her lashes, the soft parting of her lips.

Mack's gaze became hooded and dipped to her mouth and lingered there for a heart-stopping moment. The tension in the air tightened another notch as if all the oxygen particles had been removed. Elspeth couldn't take her eyes off his lips, the sensual contour of them totally mesmerising. Was he going to kiss her? Her heart flip-flopped and she moistened her lips with a nervous dart of her tongue. She mustn't let herself get carried away but, oh, how amazing it would be to feel those firm lips against her own. She hadn't been kissed in a decade. She was a virgin who was nudging thirty with only one kiss under her belt.

One almost deadly kiss that had put her in hospital and sent her mother under the care of a therapist for over a year.

It was a timely reminder that Elspeth was way out of her depth. She might pretend to be sassy and in control but she was playing a role. She was shy and inexperienced Elspeth, not street-smart and ebullient Elodie.

Elspeth raised her chin a fraction. 'Right now, I'm tempted to slap your arrogant face.'

'Then maybe I should give you an even better reason to do so.' Mack took her by the upper arms in a gentle but firm hold, the erotic intent in his glittering gaze unmistakable.

'W-wait.' Elspeth placed her hands flat against his rock-hard chest. 'Have you been eating nuts?'

His brows came together in a deep frown. 'What?'

She licked her lips with another flick of her tongue. 'I can't allow you to kiss me if you've eaten nuts. I—I hate the taste. I find it nauseating.'

Mack measured her with his gaze for a long moment, his hands still on her upper arms. 'Do you want me to kiss you?'

*Gulp.* Elspeth blinked and she could feel scorching heat storming into her face. 'Erm… I—I thought *you* wanted to kiss me.'

His gaze dipped to her mouth for a nanosecond before reconnecting with her gaze. 'Now, there's a thought,' he drawled, his lips tilting in a smile that made her legs go weak. 'But I'm not sure it would be wise under the circumstances.' His hands fell away from her arms but he didn't move away.

'Because of the…the nut thing?'

'Are you allergic to them or just don't like the taste?'

Elspeth found herself confessing the truth. 'Erm… allergic. Badly. I can't even touch the same surface where nuts have been or use products that have almond oil in them.'

'That's tough. It must be hard to avoid them.'

'I'm used to it. I—I don't like to make too big a thing of it. It's not good for my image, you know?'

'You haven't thought of being the poster girl for peanut allergies? Using your profile to campaign for much-needed funding in allergy research—that sort of thing?'

Elspeth's cheeks felt as if they were on fire. At this rate, she could solve an energy crisis for a small nation. 'I like to use my influence in other ways. I don't like being reminded of my faulty immune system.'

He studied her for a lengthy moment. 'All nuts or just peanuts?'

'All nuts but peanuts are the worst.'

'I'm not a fan of them either.'

Her eyes widened. 'You're not?'

'I once inhaled one when I was a toddler and had to be rushed to hospital. I haven't eaten them since.'

She couldn't stop staring at his mouth, the shape of it captivating her. 'Oh…wow, I've heard that's pretty dangerous for little kids…'

'It is.'

He was still so close to her she could feel the warm waft of his breath against her face. Could see the flecks of grey in the blue of his eyes, reminding her of smooth stones at the bottom of a riverbed. Could feel her body responding to his proximity with soft little flickers of awareness, flutters of lust and need that bloomed inside her like an exotic flower under the searing rays of the sun. He slid a hand along the side of her face, his touch so mesmerising, so thrilling she was totally spellbound, trapped in a sensual stasis. She thought of stepping back away from his light touch but that was as far as it went—a thought. Not one muscle in her body agreed with acting on it.

'So, given that we've established I haven't consumed nuts, what harm is one little kiss going to do, hmm?' he said in a low rumbly voice, his eyes drifting to her mouth once more.

Elspeth disguised another gulp, her own gaze drinking in every contour of his mouth. 'So, you *do* want to kiss me?' She hadn't meant to sound quite so gobsmacked. Her twin probably kissed men all the time without a single qualm.

Mack's hand moved further back along her face until it was embedded in her hair, sending a shivery wave of pleasure across her scalp. 'I find myself incredibly tempted to do so.'

Elspeth stared at his mouth with her pulse skyrocketing. 'But…but *why*?' Her tone had taken gobsmacked to a whole new level.

He gave a soft breath of a laugh. 'Because for some reason I find you irresistibly attractive.'

What he found attractive was her version of Elodie, Elspeth quickly reminded herself. It had nothing to do with *her*. A sharp twinge of disappointment got her under the ribs. Would someone as suave and sophisticated as Mack MacDiarmid want to kiss the real Elspeth? Not flipping likely. 'That's very flattering but—'

'There's nothing about you having a nut allergy in any of the interviews you've given. Why is that?' Mack's tone had a probing edge that sent a wave of alarm through her.

'Yes, well, I didn't want to make a big issue out of it…or to have someone sabotage me just before an important shoot. Believe me, it's a jungle out there.' Elspeth was pleased with how she was handling the situation. Who knew she could think on her feet so well? She had clearly missed her calling as an improvisation actor.

His frown deepened. 'Another model would actually do that?'

'Who knows? It's very competitive out there on the runway. I decided long ago not to risk it.' She forced another smile on her lips and added, 'Erm…shouldn't we be getting back to the rest of the party?'

'What's the hurry?' His hand slid deeper into the cloud of her hair, sending more tingles over her scalp and a shiver skittering down her spine.

She was conscious of his strongly muscled thighs standing within inches of her own. Conscious of the citrus and wood notes of his aftershave. Conscious of how much she wanted him to kiss her. Conscious of the way his gaze kept tracking to her mouth. Her lips tingled in anticipation. Every inch of her skin tightening and twitching with awareness. 'They might be wondering what we're up to…'

His lazy smile did strange things to her heart rate. 'Maybe they think I'm making mad passionate love to you in the library.'

'Wh-why would they think that? I only met you an hour or so ago.'

'That's not stopped you before, or so I'm told.'

She moved out of his hold, wrapping her arms around her middle, her face hot as fire. 'You shouldn't believe everything you're told.'

'I don't.' Something in his tone made her turn back

to look at him. His expression was inscrutable except for that enigmatic smile curving his sensual lips.

'Why do I get the feeling you're playing with me like a cat does a mouse?'

Mack came back to stand in front of her. 'I'm fascinated by you.'

She disguised a nervous swallow. 'Wh-why?' She could safely say no one had ever been fascinated by her before.

He picked up a loose strand of her red-gold hair and wound it around his index finger. The slight tension on her scalp sent a delicious frisson through her body. The laser focus of his gaze sending her heart rate into the danger zone. But then, everything about Mack Mac-Diarmid spelled danger. She had never met a more potently attractive man. Never been so close to a man she could almost sense his body's primal reaction to her. A primal reaction that triggered a firestorm in her own female flesh. 'You're a mystery I want to solve.'

'I can assure you there's nothing mysterious about me.' Why couldn't she get her voice above a throaty whisper? Why couldn't she just step away from him and get the hell out of the library before she lost all control of her senses? She was hypnotised by his alluring presence, drugged by his touch, addicted to the sound of his voice, hungry for the crush of his sensual lips on hers.

'Ah, but that's where I disagree,' he said, slowly unwinding her hair from his finger. 'As soon as I saw you at the upstairs window earlier today, I sensed you were hiding something.'

Elspeth rapid-blinked and flicked her hair back behind her shoulders. 'Of course I was hiding something.

I was standing there in nothing but my wrap, for pity's sake.'

'You've been seen in much less by millions of people all over the world.'

She bit her lip for a nanosecond. 'Look—I really think we should get back to the rest of the bridal party. The rehearsal's about to start in a few minutes. It'll look odd if we're not there to play our role.'

'You're right.' Mack stepped back from her with a mercurial smile. 'We have both been assigned an important role to play this weekend, yes?' There was a cryptic quality to his tone that made her heart rate spike once more.

'Erm, yes…' Elspeth gave a nervous swallow. 'We have.'

But her job this weekend would be a whole lot easier if Mack MacDiarmid weren't so sharply intelligent and eagle-eyed observant.

Or so deliciously, knee-wobblingly attractive.

'What are your feelings towards my brother?'

Elspeth decided to be brutally honest. 'I don't think he's good enough for Sabine.'

A knot of tension flickered in his jaw and a hard light came into his eyes. 'So, you'd like to see the wedding called off? Is that what you're saying?'

Elspeth forced herself to hold his diamond-hard gaze. 'Do you think he's truly in love with her?'

His mouth twisted in a cynical manner. 'I'm not sure my brother understands the meaning of true love.'

'Do you?' The question was out before she could monitor her tongue.

Mack gave a harsh grunt of a laugh. 'I understand it,

I've seen it and the damage it can cause when it's unre-quited, but I haven't experienced it myself.'

'Nor have I.'

'Not even with your ex-fiancé?'

Elspeth mentally kicked herself for momentarily slipping out of character. But had Elodie actually loved Lincoln Lancaster? Their relationship had been hotly passionate from the get-go and Elspeth had felt a little envious that no one had ever looked at her the smoul-dering way Lincoln had looked at her twin. Elodie had claimed to love him right up until the day of the wed-ding. Then, as if a switch had been flipped, she'd in-sisted it was all a mistake, that she was too young to settle down, that Lincoln wasn't the right person for her, etc, etc. It had shocked everyone, Elspeth most of all because she had truly thought Elodie had found her soulmate only to watch her throw him aside as if he were a toy she was no longer interested in. 'I decided I was too young to settle down. I thought it better to call off the wedding rather than go through a costly divorce further down the track.'

'But did you love him?' His gaze was laser-pointer direct.

Elspeth raised her chin at a combative height. 'My feelings towards Lincoln Lancaster are none of your business.' She spun away but before she could move a step, his hand came down on her wrist, his fingers curl-ing around her slender bones in a gentle but firm hold.

'What about your feelings for my brother, Fraser? You cleverly avoided answering me before.'

Elspeth knew she should be brushing off his hand but, just for a moment, she let it stay exactly where it was. The warmth and tensile strength of his fingers on her wrist sent shivers racing up and down her spine and a spurt of liquid heat to her core. How could a man's touch be so magnetic? So intensely sensual? 'You want the honest truth?' she asked with a pointed look.

'If you can manage it, yes.' The cynical edge to his tone matched the glint in his eyes and both ramped up her ire.

Elspeth pulled her wrist out of his hold and rubbed at it as if it had been burned by his touch, which it had, come to think of it. A searing burn that travelled all the way to the core of her being, simmering there in secret. 'I dislike him intensely.'

'So you regret hooking up with him?'

Elspeth couldn't meet his gaze. 'Of course. It's put me in such an awkward position...' Wasn't that the truth? She chewed at her lower lip and added, 'I hate the thought of Sabine finding out but, again, I hate the thought of her marrying him tomorrow without knowing he cheated on her.' She returned her gaze to his. 'He should have told her well before this, so she could decide whether she wanted to continue their relationship or not. She thinks she's marrying a devoted and loyal partner but instead she's marrying a cheat and a liar.' Elspeth knew she was hardly one to criticise someone for lying when all she had done so far this weekend was do exactly that—lie and deceive people.

'So you believe in honesty in intimate relationships?'

Elspeth's gaze skittered away from his. 'As far as possible.'

'Meaning?'

She glanced back at him but his expression was inscrutable. 'I'd like to think if I was in a committed relationship with someone they would honour me by being truthful about their feelings. If they felt, for instance, their needs weren't being met in some way, wouldn't it be better to talk about it rather than have those needs met clandestinely with someone else?'

'I couldn't agree more.'

There was a silence that was so intense Elspeth was sure she heard a rose petal drop from the flower arrangement on the antique table in front of the window.

Then the silence was broken by the click-clacking sound of approaching footsteps and before Elspeth could put some distance between her and Mack, Sabine came in with a wide smile. 'Oh, here you two are. What on earth are you up to in here?' Her eyes twinkled like a fairy godmother on a matchmaking mission.

'I'm so sorry,' Elspeth said, moving away from Mack, conscious of the fiery heat pooling in her cheeks. 'Are we holding up the rehearsal?'

Sabine's blissfully happy smile was painful to witness. 'Only a little. I'm so glad you two are getting along so well.' She linked her arm through one of Elspeth's and added, 'It will make Fraser's and my wedding day all the more special, won't it, Mack?'

'Indeed it will,' Mack said with a stiff smile that didn't reach the full distance to his eyes. Then he reached for Elspeth's clutch purse off the bookshelf and held it out to her with an enigmatic look. 'You might not want to leave this behind.'

Elspeth was shocked to realise how distracted she had been by him that she had completely forgotten it. Her life depended on the EpiPens in that purse. 'Thank you.' She took her purse from him, only just resisting the urge to snatch it out of his hold. How could she have been so caught up in the moment she had compromised her own safety?

And not just her physical safety. She was beginning to realise Mack MacDiarmid was a threat to her emotional safety.

And sadly, there was no EpiPen for that.

# CHAPTER FOUR

ELSPETH MINGLED WITH the other wedding party guests, trying to make light conversation with one or two of them but all the while aware of Mack's watchful gaze. He seemed to be watching her every movement. Even when she wasn't facing him, she sensed his gaze on her. She had developed a sensitivity where he was concerned, an internal radar that tracked him as assiduously as he tracked her. What did he think she was going to do? Spill all to Sabine about her fiancé's perfidious behaviour? Elspeth was feeling more and more compromised by the situation her twin had placed her in. Elodie had the chutzpah to wing her way through just about any scenario but Elspeth did not.

Firstly, she hadn't had much of a social life over the years due to fears over her allergy, and secondly, she had zero experience in handling men like Mack Mac-Diarmid. But that didn't stop her being drawn to him as if by some wickedly mischievous magnetic force.

Once the rehearsal was over, the guests were led into one of the grand formal dining rooms for a lavish dinner. Elspeth saw from the beautifully calligraphed nametags on the table that she was seated next to Mack, opposite Fraser and Sabine. She was so nauseated by

Fraser's act of loving fiancé eagerly looking forward to his wedding day, she knew she wouldn't be able to eat the dinner even if she weren't worried about nut contamination.

But then, Elspeth knew she was equally guilty in her own game of charades, which unsettled her all the more. Every moment was filled with a sense of dread she would somehow forget she was pretending to be her twin. The fallout would be crucifying, mortifying and horrifying. But even more so, she hated the thought of upsetting the lovely Sabine. The bride-to-be had been nothing but warm and friendly towards her, and yes, perhaps Sabine was a little star-struck by Elodie's fame, but behind that Elspeth could see Sabine's genuine affection for her twin.

A wave of self-doubt washed over her. But she *wasn't* her twin. Was she doing a good enough job of being Elodie? Her twin would have been working the room, smiling at everyone with confidence, charming every man within her orbit. She wouldn't be standing to one side, wondering with a sinking feeling in her stomach how on earth she was going to get through the next couple of hours.

Mack came up beside her at the dining table and pulled out her chair with a smile. 'It seems we're destined to spend more and more time together this weekend.' His eyes contained a teasing glint.

Elspeth sent him a look that threatened to wither the whimsical floral arrangement on the table. 'I can assure you, the prospect doesn't thrill me one little bit.'

His smile tilted a little further and the glint in his gaze sharpened as if he was secretly relishing her sense of discomfiture. 'By the way—' he leaned down to speak close to the shell of her ear and a shiver tumbled down her spine '—I spoke to the chef and gave him strict instructions that your meal is not to be contaminated with nuts.'

Elspeth glanced up at him, her pulse still racing at his closeness. 'That was very...' she disguised a little gulp '...thoughtful of you.' And crazy of her not to have done so herself. How could she expect to sit through a formal dinner without eating a morsel without drawing attention to herself? And how could Mack have such a potent effect on her that he made her forget the one thing that had dominated every day of her life since she was two years old?

'He was totally unaware of your dietary needs,' Mack continued. 'Do you think you should've said something earlier to Sabine or the wedding planner so the caterers could be better prepared?'

'It was on my list of things to do but I got distracted by...other things...' Elspeth knew her reply sounded as unconvincing as it was for someone suffering a life-threatening allergy. But then, her twin didn't have an allergy and suddenly making a fuss about dietary requirements was only going to draw the sort of attention to herself she was hoping to avoid. The sort of attention Mack MacDiarmid was focussing on her now, as if he was trying to solve a perplexing puzzle. His brow was furrowed, his gaze slightly narrowed, his expression a landscape of deep concentration.

Sabine and Fraser came to their seats opposite and Elspeth couldn't help noticing the beads of perspiration beading across Fraser's forehead. He looked as if he had been imbibing a little heavily—his cheeks were ruddy and his eyes glassy and his movements a little uncoordinated—although it seemed he was doing all he could to disguise it. It occurred to her how different the two brothers were in temperament and behaviour. Mack was all about emotional regulation, steely control and steadiness. But his younger brother was wayward, reckless and self-indulgent with a lot less ability to control his impulses.

Elspeth couldn't help wondering what Sabine saw in Fraser, what qualities she was drawn to in him. Or had love planted a pair of rose-coloured glasses on her nose? One day those glasses would have to come off, and then what? Poor Sabine would have to face the truth about the man she married.

Sabine reached for Fraser's hand and smiled at him in a loving manner. 'Can you believe that this time tomorrow we'll be husband and wife?'

Fraser's answering smile was a little shaky around the edges. 'I can't wait, my love.' He picked up his champagne glass and raised it in a toast. 'To my beautiful bride-to-be, Sabine. My soulmate, the love of my life.'

Everyone chorused in. 'To Sabine.'

Elspeth wanted to vomit and, judging from the brief covert glance Mack shared with her, she wasn't the only one.

Later that night when the other guests had gone to bed, Mack stood in front of the windows of one of the smaller sitting rooms overlooking the loch. The moon cast long slim silver beams of light across the smooth glassy surface of the water. Such a tranquil scene to observe given the mental turmoil he currently was experiencing. He still couldn't make Elodie out and it deeply troubled him. Alarm bells were ringing in his head and he trusted his gut enough to know they were ringing for good reason.

But what was the reason?

Elodie Campbell apparently had a life-threatening nut allergy but had not notified the catering staff. There was no mention anywhere online of her having an allergy, only dyslexia, which was another red flag to him given her avid interest in his library. For someone who had struggled to read for most of her life, why then would rare books hold such appeal?

But it was the allergy that rang the biggest alarm bell. Why would she risk something like that? Caterers were trained to be able to handle specific food allergies— all she had to do was inform them. Was she really so concerned about her image that she would put her life in danger? And if she was such a risk-taker and the troublemaker the press and his younger brother made her out to be, why then hadn't she hinted at the one-night stand she'd had with Fraser over dinner? She'd had ample opportunity, not just at dinner but from the moment she'd arrived, and yet she looked as uncomfortable and on edge as Mack felt. Did she intend to sabotage the wedding at some point? Was that her goal, to wait for a moment when the impact of her revelation would be most explosive? Or were his brother's concerns more a reflection of his own guilt and nothing to do with Elodie, who had slept with him supposedly before knowing he was engaged?

Mack preferred to see Elodie as innocent, unknowingly caught up in a drama of his brother's making. But why was *he* so intent on trying to whitewash her reputation? He would be lying if he didn't admit he was attracted to her. Attracted to her in a way he hadn't been towards a woman in a long time, if ever. She was beguiling, bewitching, beautiful and at times completely befuddling, and yet he couldn't get her out of his mind. Her touch had stirred a sensual storm in his body. Every time she came within touching distance, he ached to be even closer. He had come close to kissing her in the library. Every cell in his body had throbbed with the desire to press his lips to her bee-stung ones, to see if they were as soft and responsive as they looked. And yet, she had acted so shocked when he told her he wanted to kiss her. As if she couldn't believe he could possibly be attracted to her. But what was so shocking about that? Men all over the world lusted after her, including his own brother. Surely it hadn't been false modesty on her part. She'd looked positively stunned by his confession. Besides, he'd sensed her attraction to him on more than one occasion. Was she acting coy and shy in order to ramp up the heat? If so, it was working a treat. He was hot for her, all right. Smoking hot.

The problem was—what was he going to do about it?

Under normal circumstances, Elspeth would have quite enjoyed the morning's preparations with the bride and the other bridesmaids under the expert ministrations of the hair and make-up team. She got a tiny glimpse of what her twin experienced in her life as a lingerie model. The pampering, the priming, the professional grooming had turned her into a stunning version of herself. Her skin glowed, her hair was expertly assembled in an up-do that highlighted her cheekbones and the slim length of her neck. The oyster silk bridesmaid dress was slim-fitting with shoestring shoulder straps, and the unusual mushroom colour worked surprisingly well with the smoky tones of her eyeshadow.

Sabine looked exquisite in a diaphanous white cloud of a designer off-the-shoulder dress, the cinched-in waist emphasising her womanly curves. The voluminous veil had a long train that made her look like a fairy-tale princess. Her face shone with happiness and her eyes with excitement. She glanced at the slim watch on her wrist—the borrowed item, from her grandmother. 'Right. It's time to go. I've made him wait long enough. Ready, girls?'

'We're ready,' the other bridesmaids chorused.

The wisteria walk where the ceremony was to be conducted was in full bloom, the scent intoxicating. Elspeth was aware of a creeping anxiety, no doubt triggered by the memories of her twin's ill-fated wedding day. Although her twin's ceremony had been in a church, a cathedral at that, with rows and rows of guests, the atmosphere was the same. The almost palpable sense of expectation from the gathered guests, the chamber music eerily playing exactly the same piece, the groom and groomsmen dressed magnificently in full Highland apparel, including kilts, waiting for the bride and her attendants to appear.

The bride was standing with her father behind a screen, waiting for the moment to come forward, once the bridesmaids had begun their progression.

Before she began to walk forward, Elspeth glanced back to see Sabine's father frowning as he talked to his daughter. It didn't seem like the sort of conversation a father and daughter should be having just moments from walking up the aisle. Why wasn't he smiling at his daughter with pride? Why was he looking so grave and serious? His hand was on her arm in a stalling gesture. His voice was pitched low but was still loud enough for Elspeth to hear her sister's name mentioned. A wave of panic flooded her being, a cold hand of dread gripped her insides and her knees began to knock together.

Sabine's expression suddenly folded and her gaze sought Elspeth's. 'Is it true?' she asked in a shocked tone. 'Oh, God, is it true you slept with Fraser?'

Elspeth opened and closed her mouth; her throat so dry she could barely get her voice to work. 'It's not what you think—'

Sabine thrust her beautiful bouquet towards one of the other bridesmaids and stalked towards Elspeth, the click-clacking of her heels on the flagstones as loud as gunshots. 'My dad assures me it *is* true. He overheard one of the groomsmen, Tim, ribbing Fraser about it when they were having a pre-ceremony whisky a few minutes ago. It was when Fraser was in London a few months back.' She narrowed her eyes to paper-thin slits. 'How *could* you? How could you be so crass as to agree to be my bridesmaid when you slept with my fiancé?' Her voice had become a screech, and there was a rumble of concern from the gathered guests on the other side of the screen.

Elspeth took a step backwards; worried Sabine might lash out at her. 'Sabine, please let me explain. It wasn't me... I mean, I—I didn't know he was engaged. He didn't tell me...we barely exchanged names before we...' she winced in embarrassment on behalf of her twin as well as herself and stumbled on '...hooked up. It meant nothing to either of us.'

'Well, it means something to *me*,' Sabine stormed back, eyes blazing. She turned to her father. 'Tell Fraser the wedding is off. I never want to see him again.' She turned back to Elspeth and added, 'And that applies to you too. I thought you were my friend but the whole time you've been acting, haven't you? You probably don't even like me.'

Elspeth had been acting but not the way Sabine thought. 'I—I really like you, Sabine. You deserve far better than Fraser. I'm sorry it happened this way but, believe me, I'm really not the problem here—the problem is Fraser's lack of fidelity. If it hadn't been with... with me, it could've been someone else.' It *had* been someone else, Elspeth desperately wanted to add but couldn't without betraying her twin. Was this what Elodie was hoping to avoid by sending Elspeth in her place? Had Elodie suspected something like this was going to happen? Sabine's father was a wealthy and savvy businessman and Sabine was his only child. No wonder he had informed Sabine of her fiancé's indiscretion before the marriage could take place.

Mack suddenly appeared and took Elspeth by the arm just as Fraser came rushing over, pleading with Sabine to listen to him. 'Sabine, my love. What are you doing? You know you're the only woman I love. Don't do this.'

Sabine let out a piercing wail and flung herself against her father's chest. 'Send him away. I never want to see him or that ghastly woman again.'

'Come with me,' Mack said, leading Elspeth away by the elbow.

She followed him in a numb silence, her stomach churning so much she could have made enough butter to supply Scotland's biggest shortbread factory. As much as Elspeth was glad Sabine wasn't going to marry Fraser, she hated that 'she' was to blame. How could her twin have put her in such a compromising situation? It was beyond embarrassing, not to mention laughably ironic. Elspeth, acting as her twin, was being portrayed as 'the other woman' when she had never had sex in her life.

Mack led her to his study on one of the upper floors well away from the central part of the castle. He closed the door once they were inside and let out a long breath, his expression difficult to read. 'Well, you achieved your aim. The wedding is off.' One ink-black eyebrow hooked upwards and he continued. 'It seems to be a habit of yours, calling off weddings at the last moment.'

'I—I'm not responsible for what just happened.' Elspeth tried to keep her voice steady but it was as shaky as her hands. She was still carrying her bridesmaid bouquet but, because her hands were trembling so much, petals were falling like confetti around her.

'Maybe not directly, but you said you didn't think he was good enough for Sabine. Does that mean you want him for yourself?' This time there was no mistaking his expression—it was dark and brooding.

Elspeth coughed out a startled cynical laugh. 'You must be joking.'

'I'm not.' The blunt edge to his tone sent a chill down her spine.

She turned away to put the bouquet down on his desk and chewed at the edge of her mouth. If only she could tell him the truth. If only Elodie had got here in time, she wouldn't be experiencing the most distressing episode of her entire life. Anaphylaxis was a piece of cake compared to this. She kept her back to Mack, her hands gripping the edge of his desk to steady her wobbly legs. 'I can assure you I have no interest whatsoever in your brother.'

Mack came up behind her and placed his hands on the tops of her shoulders. A thrill ran through her body and her heart picked up its pace. He turned her slowly to face him, his eyes locking on hers. 'Are you okay?'

'No, I'm not okay. Did you see how mad Sabine was? I thought she was going to slap me. I don't like the thought of her hating me so much. I really like her. She's a nice person and to have her wedding day ruined in such a way is just awful. Why did her father tell her just then, right before she was going to walk down the aisle? If only he had found out earlier then she wouldn't have had to go through such dreadful public humiliation.' Tears stung at the backs of her eyes and she furiously blinked them away and bit down on her lower lip.

One tear managed to escape and Mack blotted it away with the pad of his thumb. 'You really care about Sabine?'

'Of course. This was supposed to be the happiest day of her life and now it's completely ruined.'

Mack gave the tops of her shoulders a gentle squeeze. 'I want you to wait for me here. I'll get one of the servants to pack your things. I don't want this to blow up in the press. Hopefully, I can talk some sense into Sabine and—'

'Hang on a minute,' Elspeth cut across him and wriggled out of his hold, taking a couple of steps back. 'Are you saying you still want her to marry your brother, even though she's made her position perfectly clear?'

His jaw tightened like a clamp. 'Do you have any idea of how much this weekend cost?'

'So, it's about the money?' She rolled her eyes in disdain. 'What about what's right for Sabine? Your brother stuffed up and now it's time he faced up to the consequences.'

Mack let out a hefty sigh, one of his hands scraping through his hair, leaving it sexily tousled. 'It's not about the money.' His voice sounded weary, weighted. 'Fraser won't handle a breakup like this. Sabine has been good for him. She's been a positive influence on him over the last couple of years. He's been happier with her than I've seen him with anyone else in years, possibly ever.'

Elspeth folded her arms and sent him a cynical look. 'So happy, he hooked up with a woman he had never met before in London, without telling her he was already engaged. Yes, I can see how blissfully happy he must've been.'

Mack twisted his mouth. 'I'm sorry you've been caught up in the middle of this. He was wrong not to tell you his relationship status.' He moved to the other side of the room, his hand rubbing at the back of his neck as if trying to release a knot of tension. He let out another deep sigh. 'Fraser took our father's death hard. He was only fourteen—I was sixteen—and it threw him completely, as it did all of us.' He sent her a bleak glance. 'I tried to be a good role model for him but clearly that didn't work. He's reckless and impulsive and refuses to face up to responsibility. In many ways, he's very like our father, which is worrying.'

Elspeth frowned. 'How did your father die?'

'Suicide.' He swallowed deeply and continued. 'Our

mother found him. She had a nervous breakdown after that. She was never quite the same. She died five years later of cancer, which, of course, sent Fraser into another massive tailspin. But meeting Sabine a couple of years ago changed everything for him. He started to pull himself into line. He got a job with her father's company and he really applied himself. He gave up the wild partying, the party drugs. But now…' He shook his head and frowned as if he couldn't quite believe what had happened in the garden just minutes before.

'You think he'll go back to that lifestyle?'

Mack gave her a world-weary look. 'What do you think?'

'I don't know your brother well enough to speculate.' Elspeth's cheeks grew uncomfortably warm as she thought of how Mack must view her statement given 'she' had supposedly had a one-night stand with him. 'But I'm thinking Sabine's father isn't going to want him working for him.'

'Got it in one.'

Elspeth could only imagine the stress Mack must have gone through over the loss of his father and then the breakdown of his mother and subsequent acting out of his younger brother. And all while he was sixteen, only two years older than his brother. 'How did you cope with the loss of your father? I mean, it must have been so hard for you too.'

Mack's expression became masked and she realised then how he coped—by concealing his own struggles, his own deep distress. He was resilient, self-reliant, stoic. 'I grew up fast. I had to. There was no one else to take charge.'

'No grandparents?'

'My paternal grandparents died when I was four. Car crash. I can barely remember them now. Fraser can't remember them at all.'

'And your mother's parents?'

'My mother's mother died when she was thirteen. Breast cancer, the same cancer that got her. Her father died when I was ten. I have lots of fond memories of him. He was a good man, steady and reliable.'

'Like you.'

Mack shrugged one broad shoulder in a dismissive manner. 'Someone has to be steady in a crisis, which brings me back to the plan.'

'The plan?'

'The press are going to swarm around you like hornets, so you need to go to ground. Immediately.'

Elspeth gripped the back of an oak chair to steady her suddenly trembling legs. 'The press?'

'The paparazzi. One whiff of this and you'll be hounded for an exclusive tell-all interview. But I should warn you against giving one.'

Elspeth swallowed. The thought of the press hounding her, chasing her, thrusting microphones and cameras in her face terrified her. 'I would never do that.'

One dark eyebrow winged upwards. 'I'm afraid I can't afford to believe you, so I will be accompanying you until this blows over.'

Elspeth gawped at him. Had she heard him correctly? 'Accompanying me? Accompanying me where?'

'To a secret hideaway.'

'You're...*kidnapping* me?' Her eyes were so round they threatened to pop out of her head. Could this farce get any more ridiculous?

He gave a light laugh. 'Ever the drama queen. No,

I'm giving you a choice. You either come with me willingly or I leave you to face the destruction of your reputation and quite possibly your career.'

Elspeth's heart skipped a beat. Two beats. And then went into a wacky rhythm as if she were suffering some sort of serious cardiac condition. 'That sounds suspiciously like blackmail to me.'

'Think of it as a choice.'

She put her chin up and eyeballed him. 'Your way or the highway?'

His smile was indolent but his grey-blue gaze was steely with determination. 'I believe it's in your best interests to come with me.'

'For how long?'

'One night until the guests and the paps leave. But longer if necessary.'

'Longer? But what about my job? I can't just disappear without warning.' He wasn't to know she had already taken next week off work to have a look around Scotland to visit some of the villages her family's ancestors came from. And as to what engagements her twin had for the next few days, well, Elspeth needed to find a private room to call Elodie to tell her what was going on. Elodie would have to go into hiding too, until this scandal blew over. *If* it blew over.

'I'm sure you can take time off work but I'll reimburse you for any lost wages.'

No way did she want to face the paparazzi.

No way did she want to face the wrath of poor heartbroken Sabine.

And no way did she want to miss out on a night in hiding with Mack. Why shouldn't she go with him? It would be a perfect opportunity to see how the other half lived. This was her chance, maybe her only chance, to live a little dangerously. And it didn't get more deliciously dangerous than spending time with devilishly handsome Mack MacDiarmid.

'So now you're bribing me?'

'Is it working?'

Elspeth gave him the side eye. 'A little too well.'

# CHAPTER FIVE

MACK GAVE ONE of the most discreet of his household staff directions on packing up Elodie's things and transferring them to his car, along with food and drink for an overnight stay. He then tracked down his brother in his suite of rooms. Fraser was pacing the floor and swung to face Mack as he came in.

'You have to talk to Sabine, Mack. You have to convince her to change her mind. Her father's threatening to pull the plug on my career. I need to get her to reconsider, otherwise I'm doomed. That crazy Campbell bitch is behind this, I just know it. It's why she agreed to be bridesmaid.' He clenched his fists, his expression thunderous. 'She wanted this to happen. She planned it from the start.'

Mack was having trouble aligning his view of Elodie with that of his brother. It was as if they were talking about two different people. The Elodie he'd spent time with was feisty at times, yes, but underneath that was a warm and sweet person who seemed to care about others more than she did herself.

*Two different people...*

The thought got a little more traction in his mind. Those alarm bells had rung and rung and rung inside his head until he was almost deaf with the sound of them. Why hadn't he thought of it before? The answer was so obvious. What if he was dealing with two different people? Was it possible the young woman he had almost kissed in the library yesterday, the young woman he had convinced to go away with him overnight, was not the real Elodie Campbell? He whipped out his phone, pointedly ignoring his brother's continued ranting, and quickly did a search of press releases about Elodie Campbell's called-off wedding. His search proved fruitless until he typed in Lincoln Lancaster's name and then a couple of articles loaded, one with a picture. He stared at the grainy image of three bridesmaids gathered outside the church. One of them had her face slightly turned away but Mack would recognise that profile anywhere. The younger sister of Elodie Campbell was not just a younger sister but a twin. An identical twin.

'Are you listening to me?' Fraser said. 'I said I need you to talk to Sabine. Tell her she's making a terrible mistake.'

Mack put his phone in his jacket pocket. He decided to keep his new discovery to himself a little bit longer. He wanted to find out the reason for the switch, wanted to understand the motivations behind the decision to stand in for her twin. Wanted to know how far the beautiful little imposter was going to take this charade. 'I'm inclined to agree with Sabine. If she married you, it would be her making the terrible mistake.'

'How can you say that? I love her.'

'You don't love her. You love how she made you feel. She worshipped you, got her father to give you a great job, told you all the things your male ego wanted to hear. But you don't love her. If you did, you wouldn't have betrayed her.'

'It was Elodie Campbell's fault. I wouldn't have looked twice at her but she—'

'I'm tired of hearing how it's always everyone else's fault when you stuff up,' Mack said. 'I can't fix this for you, Fraser. This is your mess and for once I'm not going to untangle it for you.' He had been doing way too much enabling of his brother, he realised now. Stepping in when he should have stepped back. His fears over Fraser taking the path of their father were real fears but he couldn't spend his life babysitting his younger brother. The cancelled wedding was a huge wake-up call for Fraser and if Mack tried to intervene, it might lessen the impact. It was time for his brother to grow up and take responsibility for the mess he had made.

Besides, Mack had a little mess of his own to untangle.

While Mack went to see about the transfer of her luggage to his car, Elspeth took the opportunity to call her twin. 'Elodie? You'll never guess what happened.'

'I was about to call you. I just saw it on social media,' Elodie said. 'Whatever you do, don't say anything to the press. God, I don't need this right now.'

'But what about me?' Elspeth said. 'I'm still pretending to be you. How long do you think I can keep this up?'

'You can come home any time you like now the wedding's been called off. But you'll have to lie low, and, come to think of it, so will I.'

'Well, here's the thing—Mack MacDiarmid is insisting I go away with him overnight.'

There was a short silence.

'And you said yes?' Elodie's tone was incredulous.

'You're always telling me I need to be more adventurous, so that's what I'm going to do. Go with the flow.'

'But you're going as me, right?'

'Well, yes, because I can't exactly tell him I'm not you now, can I?' Elspeth couldn't imagine how she could ever reveal her true identity to Mack. Not after all the lies she had told. No, she would go away with Mack and enjoy the little adventure for what it was—a chance to live a little before she went back to her normal quiet life.

'No, I guess not but it's kind of tricky...' Elodie's tone contained a note of something Elspeth hadn't heard in it before.

'Tricky in what way?'

'What if the press see you together? I mean, while you're pretending to be me?'

Elspeth frowned. 'Hello? You're the one who insisted I stand in for you at a society wedding, remember? Heaps of photos have been taken all weekend, so—'

'Yes, but if you're having a one-night stand with Mack MacDiarmid, then—'

'I'm not having any such thing with him. He's just keen to keep me away from the press.'

'But you're seriously tempted.' Her twin stated it rather than posed it as a question.

Elspeth tried to ignore the little flutter of excitement in her belly. 'He's a very attractive man and, besides, you're always telling me I need to get out more. This is my chance to live a little.'

'But I can't be seen to be cavorting with Mack Mac-Diarmid right now,' Elodie insisted.

'Who's going to see you, I mean me?'

'Anyone with a camera phone, that's who. The media pay enormous sums for those photos these days and they often go viral. It could be very compromising for me.'

'Because of your financial backer?'

'That and...other things.'

'What other things?'

'Never mind. Just keep a low profile. And whatever you do, don't tell Mack who you really are. He might not take too kindly to having been hoodwinked by you.'

Elspeth quailed at the thought of revealing her true identity to Mack. While she sensed he had a good sense of humour, somehow she didn't think he would find her switching places with her twin all that amusing. Especially as it had brought about the cancellation of his brother's wedding, an event Mack had been determined would go ahead no matter what. 'Don't worry, I won't.'

A short time later, Mack helped Elspeth into a four-wheel-drive vehicle, and then drove, not out through the castle gates, as she was expecting, but deeper into the estate.

She glanced at him in confusion. 'Where are we going? Is there a back exit to the estate?'

Mack sent her an unreadable look. 'Not unless we climb over the Highlands on foot. There's an old crofter's hut up in the hills. We can hide out there overnight until the press leave. They won't find us there.'

'An old crofter's hut. Wow. That sounds kind of rustic.'

'It is.' He sent her another sideways glance. 'You won't find the lack of five-star accommodation off-putting?'

'No, it'll be like stepping back in time.' Not to mention right out of her comfort zone. But not because of the lack of creature comforts. Elspeth could barely believe she was agreeing to this—being spirited away to a secluded spot on the estate to be alone with Mack. To draw the attention away from her fluttering nerves she redirected the conversation. 'Did you speak to your brother? How's he handling things?'

He let out a deep sigh and adjusted the gears to drive over a deep pothole on the gravel road. She couldn't stop staring at his hands, so strong and competent on the gear stick and steering wheel as he negotiated the rough passage. No doubt they were just as competent moving over a woman's body. She suppressed a little shiver at the thought of his hands on her body. 'He's blaming you for everything.'

Elspeth bit down on her lower lip and glanced at the deep green forest on the left side of the car. 'And what about you? Do you blame me too?'

'Not at all.' There was something in his tone that made her glance at him but his expression was mask-like.

'You're not angry the wedding didn't go ahead? I mean, it must have cost a bomb to host it and all...'

His mouth twisted in a rueful manner. 'The money isn't the issue. I'm inclined to agree with you now that I've thought about it. Fraser isn't the right person for Sabine. He's not the right person for anyone and won't be until he does some serious work on himself.' He shifted the gears again and the car rocked from side to side as it went over another deep ridge. 'And he won't do the work if I keep stepping in and making things too easy for him.'

'I'm sure you've always done what you thought is best for your brother.'

Mack sent her a grim look. 'You're being way too generous. No, I've made plenty of mistakes with Fraser.' His knuckles turned white on the steering wheel and his jaw tightened. 'I sometimes wonder if our father hadn't died the way he did, would Fraser have turned out differently?' A shadow passed across his face like the scudding clouds across the sky.

Elspeth placed a gentle hand on his thigh, compelled to offer her support and comfort. 'You're a wonderful older brother, Mack. Anyone can see that. And don't forget you were only young yourself when your father died. And you lost your mother so soon after that. Sometimes people are the way they are, not so much because of circumstances but because of how they deal with the circumstances. And maybe that has more to do with personality than anything else.'

Mack placed his hand over the top of hers and gave it a gentle squeeze. Tingles raced up her arm like lightning, sending a wave of heat to her core. 'You're nothing like the press make you out to be. I was expecting a spoilt prima donna.'

Elspeth pulled her hand out from under his and laid it in her lap before she was tempted to let it explore further along his muscled thigh. 'I—I've encouraged a certain view of myself,' she said, recalling a conversation with her twin about building Elodie's brand. Smart, sassy, sophisticated, sexy—four words that certainly applied to her twin but not to her. 'But it's a public persona, it's not the real me.'

'As I've found out.' There was a cryptic quality to his tone that sent a shiver cartwheeling down her spine.

She chanced a glance at him but his expression was difficult to read, although she did happen to notice a twinkling light in his eyes.

They travelled a little way further before they came to a fast-running stream coursing across rocks. 'Hold on,' Mack said, shifting the gears again.

Elspeth gripped the edges of her seat and held her breath as Mack expertly guided the vehicle across the stream. 'You're really making sure no one can follow us, aren't you?'

He gave her a heart-stopping grin and gunned the engine up the steep slope on the other side. 'That's the idea, *m'eudail*.'

A few minutes later, Mack pulled up outside an old crofter's hut that was situated at the top of the rise with views across a deep valley. Elspeth was out of the vehicle before he could get to her door. She stood, taking in the spectacular view, the crisp cool air so fresh she could almost taste it. A wedge-tailed eagle freewheeled on the air currents above, the eerie sound of his call echoing across the valley. A stag deer raised its head in the distance, his giant antlers looking too heavy for him to carry. He returned to cropping the grass as if used to seeing Mack show up.

'Oh, my goodness, it's so beautiful…' Elspeth gasped in wonder. 'It's a wonder you can bear to live anywhere else…'

Mack stood behind her, his hands going to the tops of her shoulders in a touch as light as the air she was breathing but it still sent a delicious shock wave through her body. Just knowing his tall frame was so close to her made her heart race and her pulse pound.

He quoted in a broad Scots brogue. '"*My heart's in the Highlands, my heart is not here; My heart's in the Highlands, a-chasing the deer. Chasing the wild-deer, and following the roe. My heart's in the Highlands, wherever I go.*"'

Elspeth turned to look up at him with a smile. 'Robert Burns says it so well.' But inside, she was thinking of another Robert Burns quote that reminded her of the fine line she was walking. *'The best laid schemes o' mice an' men Gang aft agley. An'lea'e us nought but grief an' pain. For promis'd joy.'*

He gave an answering smile that made her heart flutter. 'I'm glad you like it here.' His voice was low and deep and rough.

'How could I not? It's the most stunning place I've ever been to.' Eek! Elspeth suddenly remembered all the stunning locations her twin had been to. Photos of Elodie were all over the Internet, posing beside spectacular views of mountains, beaches, rainforests—you name it, Elodie had been there. Would he pick up on her slip?

Mack's hands went to her hips, holding her within a hair's breadth from his powerful male body. 'But you've been to so many exotic locations for your work, have you not? This must hardly compare.' His gaze was unwavering and it made her heart beat all the harder and she could feel her cheeks heating up in spite of the cool Highland breeze.

'This is the sort of place I love the most,' Elspeth said, conscious of heat crawling over her face. 'It's so peaceful and timeless. If you look out there—' she pointed to the view across the valley '—there's nothing to anchor you to this century. We could be from any time in the past. Don't you find that amazing?'

Mack framed her face in his large hands, his gaze dipping to her mouth. 'What I find amazing is how I've resisted kissing you until now. Would you mind?'

Elspeth licked her lips with a nervous flick of her tongue. 'No... I mean yes, I want you to kiss me.'

His mouth came down to press against hers in a feather-light touchdown. He lifted his lips off hers and came down again, a little firmer this time as if driven by a pounding need for closer contact. The same pounding need that was barrelling through her own body. She gave a soft little whimper and linked her arms around his neck, opening her lips to the commanding probe of his tongue. Heat exploded inside her, molten heat that travelled to the centre of her womanhood, moistening and swelling tender tissues as primal need took over.

Mack groaned and angled his head for deeper access, one of his hands sliding into the thickness of her hair. 'I've wanted to do this from the moment I met you.' He growled against her lips.

Elspeth planted a series of short hot kisses to his lips. 'What took you so long?'

He smiled against her lips. 'You have no idea how much I wanted to kiss you in the library.'

She leaned against his masculine frame, her insides coiling with lust as she came into contact with the hardened ridge of his erection. 'What stopped you?'

Mack lifted his head a fraction and stroked a lazy finger across her lower lip. 'I wanted to get to know you better first.'

*You don't know me at all.*

Elspeth wished she could tell him the truth about her identity. It seemed wrong that he thought she was

Elodie. That he *thought* he was kissing Elodie. But the risks of confessing her true identity were too great. It would create an even bigger scandal, even more hurt for Sabine, who would feel betrayed all over again.

Elspeth traced a line around his sculptured lips. 'How well do you think you know me?' She couldn't get her voice above a thready whisper.

He took the end of her finger into his mouth, sucking on it gently, his gaze holding hers. A hot shiver raced like greased lightning down her back, heat smouldering in her core at the erotic intention in the caress. 'Well enough to know you want me as much as I want you.'

Elspeth suppressed a frisson of delight, her gaze locked on his by a force as old as time. 'I've never wanted anyone like I want you.'

He smiled a slow smile and cradled one side of her face in his hand. 'Same. So, what are we going to do about it?'

She licked her lips again, tasting the sexy salt of him, wanting him with an ache that throbbed like pain. 'I guess we could kiss again and see what happens.'

'Sounds like a good plan.' His mouth came back down to hers in a blistering kiss that made the hairs on her head stand up on tiptoe. His tongue entered her mouth in a brazen thrust that sent a hot dart of need to her feminine core. Her pulse picked up its pace, her blood thrumming with primal want, her mouth feeding off his as if it were her only lifeline.

He made a guttural sound and deepened the kiss, his tongue tangling with hers in a sexy tango that fuelled her desire even more. One of his hands went to the small of her back, pressing her closer to the potent heat of his male form. A delicious shudder went through her at the erotic contact, her body secretly preparing itself for his possession. Aching for his possession as if it had been waiting all these years for this exact moment.

Mack raised his head after a few breathless moments, his eyes glazed with lust. 'Let's take this indoors. I want our first time to be without mosquitoes and prickling heather.'

Our first time...

*My first time...*

Elspeth disguised a gulping swallow. 'Right...'

He captured her chin between his finger and thumb, his gaze suddenly searching. 'Is something wrong?'

How could she tell him it would be her first time without revealing her deception? If she confessed, he might pull the plug on their sensual encounter. How could she sabotage something she wanted so much? She was aching for him from head to foot, need pulsing inside every cell of her body. The need for him. *Only* him. He had awakened something in her and she couldn't bear to deny her body the satisfaction it craved. She schooled her features into a mask of confidence while inside her nerves were fluttering like frenzied moths. 'Nothing. It's just been a while since I... I got with a guy...' Her burning cheeks could have started a grass fire.

'You mean not since my brother?'

'Erm...can we not talk about that?'

'Sure.' Mack stroked a finger down the curve of her hot cheek. 'You don't need to be nervous. I'm nothing like my brother.'

*And I'm nothing like my sister.*

'I—I'm not nervous...'

He brushed her lips with his in a light as air kiss,

his taste delighting her all over again. 'I'm not going to rush you. We'll get unpacked and have a drink to relax first. It's been quite a day.'

Elspeth didn't know whether to be relieved or disappointed. She didn't need a drink—she needed him. Badly. 'Yes, it has.'

The crofter's hut was built on one level and made of local stone. While a little larger than some she had seen in books, it still had a quaint and timeless atmosphere. It was tastefully and respectfully renovated inside with a fireplace in the kitchen-cum-living-area as well as in the bedroom. And to her very great relief, there was even a small bathroom off the bedroom.

'Do you come up here often?' Elspeth asked, wondering how many women he had brought here for a private tryst.

Mack placed her bag on the floor near the bed. 'As often as I can when I'm home. It's my thinking space. I started to come up here after my father died. Like everything else on the estate, it was pretty run-down back then but over time I was able to fix things up.'

She perched on the edge of the bed, her hands clasped in her lap—a combination of nerves and an attempt at fighting the temptation to reach for him. 'You were named after him, weren't you? Sabine mentioned it when we were getting our hair and make-up done. But you don't get called Robert.'

'No.' He flicked a bit of imaginary dust off a side table. 'I was Robbie when I was a young child but everyone started calling me Mack during my early teens. It was assumed I'd go back to my father's name after his death but it never appealed to me. I stuck with Mack.'

'You wanted to distance yourself from him?'

He gave her a grim look. 'You don't get any more distant than death but that was his choice.'

Elspeth chewed her lower lip, wondering if he had ever dealt with the grief of losing his father in such a sudden and tragic way. He had had to step up and deal with the fallout from his father's death. He wouldn't have had time to process his own feelings, especially with his younger brother acting out and his mother needing so much emotional support. 'Maybe he didn't feel he had a choice at that point in his life. Things can seem so hopeless for a moment in time but even seconds later, things can look completely different. People talk about looking for the light at the end of the tunnel but life is not always a straight tunnel but more like a winding one. You can't see around the next bend but you have to hope that something good is waiting there for you. And if the good thing isn't around that bend, then you hope the next or the next will have it.'

Mack blew out a long sigh, his expression darkly shadowed. 'He lied to my face so many times. Blatant lies that I've gone over in my head ever since, wondering why he couldn't be honest. He ruined so many lives—my mother's, his lover's and their child's. Not to mention Fraser's. I can't help wondering if Fraser would have turned to drink and drugs if our father had just ended his marriage instead of his life. It was so unnecessary. We would have got over his affair, even my mother would have handled that, but it was the years and years of lies that hurt the most. And then his death. The finality of it, the fallout from it.' He shook his head, his eyes scrunched up as if in acute pain. 'Mum was never the same. I often wonder if my father thought of that when he…' He swallowed and continued in a ragged tone. 'I guess I have to be thankful it wasn't Fraser who found him, or Daisy, his little daughter.'

Elspeth's conscience was in agony, griping with agonising pain and guilt at all the lies she had told. How could she ever tell Mack who she really was? Lies had ruined his family, torn it apart in the most brutal way. He was still dealing with the fallout of his father's death by trying to keep his brother on the right path. He had lost both his parents within the space of a few short years and yet he had carried on stoically, doing all he could to save his ancestral home from being sold. But at what price to himself? Was that why he was a love-them-and-leave-them playboy? He didn't allow anyone under his guard. He didn't fall in love, in fact, believed himself incapable of it.

'Oh, Mack…' Elspeth rose from where she was perched on the end of the bed and went over to him, touching him on the forearm. 'I'm so sorry you had to deal with such dreadful heartache. But I admire you so much for staying strong for everyone else. For taking control when things were flung so wildly out of control.'

Mack lifted her chin with a gentle finger, his expression rueful. 'You're wasting yourself as a lingerie model, you know. You should be a counsellor.'

Elspeth shifted her gaze to study his firm chin where pinpricks of dark stubble were sprouting. 'Yes, well, it's amazing what skills you learn on the catwalk.' She painted a stiff smile on her face. 'You said something about a drink?'

'I'll bring in the supplies from the car. Make yourself comfortable.'

Elspeth let out a long breath once the door shut behind him. How could she ever be comfortable pretending to be someone else? She wanted to be with Mack as herself, not as her twin.

But how could she tell him she had lied to him from the moment she met him?

# CHAPTER SIX

MACK STOOD OUTSIDE the crofter's hut and took in a deep lungful of crisp Highland air. Somehow, unburdening himself to Elspeth had loosened the tight knot of pain deep inside his chest that had lain there for years. And yet, she was still intent on carrying on with her charade. How long did she think she could keep it going? While it was amusing to watch her valiantly act in her twin's persona, he found himself wanting her to confess, especially now they were alone. He wanted her to know he knew exactly who he was kissing. Who he was making love to. That it was increasingly difficult for her to stay in her twin's persona was more than obvious. But it had to be her decision to confess the twin-switch. How far was she prepared to run with it? That she had taken it this far showed a strong commitment to her twin, which was admirable, but what if there was some other motive? Or was he getting too cynical and jaded?

Mack came back to the hut with the box of supplies the housekeeper had organised for him. Elspeth was sitting on the small sofa in front of the fireplace, her legs curled beneath her. She had changed into casual clothes and her hair was loosened from the up-do and cascaded around her shoulders in a red-gold cloud. He wondered if he had ever seen a more beautiful woman. Or a more desirable one. She unfolded herself from the sofa, her graceful movements and slim figure reminding him of a ballerina. 'Do you want some help?'

Mack placed the box on the small kitchen table and began to take out the items. 'It's okay. I'm used to doing this.'

A shadow passed over her face and her small white teeth sank into her lower lip. 'Yes, well, no doubt you've brought dozens of women up here for a secret getaway.'

He placed the bottle of champagne on the table with a soft thud. 'Actually, you're the first person I've brought here.'

A look of astonishment came over her face. 'Really? But why? I mean, why me?'

*Good question.*

One Mack didn't have an answer for her other than she was the first woman he'd wanted to bring here to his private sanctuary. The first woman he felt would truly appreciate it in the way he did. The raw beauty of it, the isolation and starkness and untouched wildness speaking to his soul as no other place could. 'I wanted to get you away from the press and this seemed a good place. The best place. Only a handful of people know it even exists.'

Elspeth tucked a strand of her hair behind her ear, her cheeks a faint shade of pink. 'I guess I should feel honoured...' Her gaze fell away from his. 'Mack?' Her voice was tentatively soft.

'What's on your mind?'

'Nothing.' Her response was quick. Too quick. Her

gaze troubled, her teeth savaging her lip once more, her cheeks a darker shade of pink.

Mack placed a packet of oat crackers on the table next to the cheese and came over to her, taking her by the hands. 'Is there something you want to say to me?'

'Just…thank you for bringing me here. It's a beautiful place and I… I'm glad I don't have to face the press right now. I would've found it too distressing.'

Mack brushed a loose strand of her hair back from her face. 'But you're used to handling the press.'

She looked down at their joined hands. 'Yes, but this is different…everything about this…about us is different…'

He brought her chin up so her gaze met his once more. 'What's different about us?'

She moistened her lips with the tip of her tongue. 'I'm not really how I'm portrayed in the media. I want you to know that before we…go any further…'

Mack stroked her pink cheek with the broad pad of his thumb, his eyes locked on hers. 'There's another Robert Burns quote I like. *"O wad some Power the giftie gie us To see oursels as ithers see us! It wad frae mony a blunder free us, An' foolish notion."*'

She gave an effigy of a smile. 'So true…'

Mack lowered his mouth to hers in a soft kiss that made his lips tingle and buzz for more. Elspeth sighed against his lips and pressed herself closer, her hands going to the wall of his chest, her lips opening beneath the pressure of his. He wrapped his arms around her, bringing her as close to his aching body as he could. The slim contours of her body exciting him as no other woman had ever done. Need pummelled through him, a pounding, punishing need that drove every other thought out of his mind other than to possess her in order to quell this maddening ache of his flesh.

He kissed her deeply, thoroughly, delighting in the breathless murmurs of encouragement she gave. Her hands moved from his chest to wind around his neck and she stood on tiptoe, bringing her pelvis into blistering contact with his. Mack cupped the sweet curves of her bottom, holding her to his throbbing length, wondering if he had ever felt so aroused before. Something about her shy sensuality stirred his senses into a frenzy. Her body spoke to his in a language as old as the craggy peaks of the Highlands.

Mack placed one of his hands below her right breast, aching to feel the weight of the soft curve in his hand but not wanting to rush her.

Elspeth whispered her approval against his lips. 'Touch me.'

He needed no other encouragement. He gently peeled away her top and lowered the slim strap of her bra to access her breast. He drank in the sight of her before he brought his mouth to the creamy curve with its rosy peak. He caressed her with his lips and tongue, enjoying the sounds of her pleasure as much as he enjoyed the taste of her in his mouth. He moved to her other breast, uncovering it and caressing it with the same sensual focus. He finally raised his mouth off her soft flesh, looking into her lust-glazed eyes. 'I wanted you from the moment I met you.'

She stroked her hand down the length of his jaw. 'That soon?'

He smiled and ran his hands down the sides of her body to bring her hips flush against his. 'You sound surprised.'

'I am.'

Mack ran his hands through the silky thickness of her hair. 'I would have thought you'd be well used to men lusting over you by now.'

Something passed through her gaze like a faint ripple across a body of still water. Her gaze dipped to his mouth, her throat rising and falling over a swallow. 'Mack?'

He tilted her face upwards to meet his gaze. 'Yes?'

She swallowed again and stepped out of his hold, pulling her bra and loose-fitting top back into place. 'I need to tell you something...something about myself that you're not going to like.'

'Go on.'

She shifted her lips from side to side, then bit down on her lower one. She did it so often, he wondered if she was even conscious of it. 'I've been lying to you from the moment we met.'

'I know.'

She rapid-blinked. 'Pardon?'

Mack gave a lazy smile. 'I was wondering how long you were going to keep it up.'

Her expression was wary. 'Keep what up?'

'The act.'

She licked her lips, her mouth opening and closing. 'The...act?'

Mack came over to her and took her by the upper arms. 'You little goose. How long did you think you could pull it off? You're nothing like your twin apart from in looks.'

A host of emotions washed over her face—shock, relief, surprise, dismay, even a little anger. 'How did you know? *When* did you know?'

'Not until earlier today, although I had my suspicions from my first glimpse of you at the window when you first arrived at Crannochbrae.'

Elspeth pulled away from him and hugged her arms around her body again. 'Does anyone else know?'

'No.'

She began to pace the floor. 'No one can know, especially not Sabine. She's been hurt enough.' She stopped pacing and arched her head back to look at the ceiling and groaned. 'Argh, why did I allow myself to think I could do this? I knew I would stuff it up.'

'You didn't stuff it up,' Mack said. 'You convinced everyone.'

'Except you.'

He approached her again, stroking his hand down one of her slim arms. 'I'm the one who's spent the most time with you. I was drawn to you. You intrigued me.' He captured a handful of her hair and ran it through his fingertips and added, 'You were a beguiling mix of feisty and shy. The stuff I'd been told about you didn't add up, but it wasn't until I did a bit of research after the wedding was called off that I put all the pieces of the puzzle together.'

'What did you find? I asked Elodie to keep quiet about having a twin. I never wanted the fame she's sought since she was a kid. I hate being in the spotlight. I hate being compared to her and found lacking. I've had nightmares for years of people mistaking her for me and chasing me down the street. I dress simply, I never wear make-up or nail polish. I keep the lowest profile I can. I only did the switch because…well, I was a little tired of my boring life. And I genuinely wanted to help her.'

'There was one photo attached to an article about Lincoln Lancaster's aborted wedding. It wasn't a clear shot of you but I could see the likeness. Your name was there along with the other young women. I'm annoyed at myself for not guessing who you were sooner.'

'I'm glad you didn't.' She threw him a churlish glance. 'It might've caused an even bigger scandal if you'd outed me.'

Mack took her hands in his and gave them a gentle squeeze. 'Why did you do it?'

She gave a shuddering sigh. 'Elodie needed to be somewhere else for an important top-secret meeting. She convinced me to go in her place to the wedding, but she didn't tell me anything about her one-night stand with your brother. I was so shocked when he approached me and was no nasty towards me.'

'I'm sorry about his behaviour.'

'It's okay, I'm quite proud of how I managed it, to tell you the truth.' Elspeth frowned and continued, 'But as much as I wanted to put Fraser in his place, there was Sabine to consider. I know you wanted their wedding to go ahead but I was convinced it would be a disaster if it did.'

'You were right,' Mack said with a heavy sigh. 'Fraser has some serious growing up to do before he's ready to settle down with anyone.'

'There was another reason I agreed to step into my twin's shoes…' Her gaze came back to his. 'Because of my allergy, I've spent most of my life with my mother hovering anxiously over me in case I ingest a peanut. I only moved out of home a month ago and I'm twenty-eight years old. If I checked my phone right now I swear there will be fifty missed calls or texts from her.

I have to turn my phone off most of the time otherwise it drives me crazy. The last time I tried to have a weekend away, she turned up. I was so embarrassed having her fussing over me. I decided switching places with Elodie would be a chance to live a little. To experience things I've only ever dreamt about before.'

'What sort of things?'

Her gaze drifted to his mouth. 'The first and only time I was kissed when I was eighteen, I ended up in hospital with anaphylactic shock.'

It took a moment for Mack to realise the import of her confession. 'You mean you haven't been kissed until now?'

Elspeth gave a self-conscious grimace. 'I know, pathetic, right?'

He took her by the upper arms again. 'It's not pathetic. It's… I'm just gobsmacked that I'm the first person to…' He shook his head as another thought occurred to him. She was so inexperienced. He was the first person to kiss her in a decade. He was shocked and yet strangely touched. Honoured that she had allowed him to be the one to be the first. 'Does that mean you're—'

'A virgin? Yes. That's even more pathetic.'

Mack released her to score a hand through his hair. She was a virgin who had only been kissed once before. How could he think of having a fling with her now? He was used to sleeping with women who were at ease with casual relationships. Sleeping with a sweet, shy virgin was not in his game plan. 'No, it's not pathetic at all. But it changes everything between us.'

Elspeth looked at him in alarm. 'What do you mean?'

He waved a hand to encompass their intimate surroundings. 'We'll stay the night here because it'll soon be too dark to go back to the castle but we won't be sleeping together.'

'I see…' Her expression became masklike but he could sense the disappointment in her. The same disappointment he was experiencing. A bitter disappointment that was hard to swallow. 'Can I ask why?'

'For God's sake, Elspeth. You're a virgin and I'm a freaking playboy, that's why.'

She held his gaze with straight-shouldered pride. 'I hardly see how that's a problem. If anything, surely it would be an advantage? You know what to do and can help me.'

Mack rubbed a hand down his face, the sound of his palm raking across his stubble loud in the silence. 'It's not going to happen. I'm not the right person for you.'

'I'm not asking for a commitment, Mack. I just want to experience sex with someone I desire. It can be just the once. I just want to lose my virginity to someone who will treat me with respect. I know you will do that.'

Mack let out a swear word in Gaelic. 'I don't want to talk about it any more.' He stepped back to the table where he had left the box of food. 'We're going to have a drink and a light supper and go to bed. Alone.'

Her gaze drifted to the queen-sized bed through the open door of the bedroom off the living area. 'But there's only one bed.'

'I'll make do on the sofa.' His back began to ache at the thought. And not just his back but other parts of his anatomy that would have preferred sharing that bed with Elspeth. But how could he do such a thing? She was so innocent, so inexperienced and he had no right to be thinking of taking her in his arms. She was off limits. He had to be strong, in control of his desires, to be honourable and steadfast. He could do that, of course he could. He would have to.

'It won't be very comfortable for you. I'm not as tall—maybe I should sleep there instead.'

Mack shook his head. 'No. You have the bed. I insist.'

'But—'

'No arguments.' He injected his tone with a note of intractability, more for his own benefit than hers. He had to be strong. He had to ignore the chemistry that filled the crofter's hut with unbearable tension. He had to ignore the throbbing need in his body. He had to be out of his mind to even contemplate sleeping with her now he knew about her inexperience.

'Fine. We'll do it your way.' Elspeth swung away and stalked off to the bathroom, clicking the door shut behind her.

Mack let out a ragged sigh and stared at the bottle of champagne in his hand. He had never felt less like celebrating.

# CHAPTER SEVEN

ELSPETH STARED AT her reflection in the bathroom mirror, wishing she hadn't told Mack the truth. But how could she have slept with him as her sister? It would be taking the charade way too far. She hadn't been able to go any further without him knowing the truth. But now he knew who she was, he was pulling away. Was that because she wasn't enough on her own? That the layer of confidence she'd adopted while pretending to be her twin had been the allure—the only thing about her he had found irresistible? She wasn't enough as herself, but then, she never had been. She had always been lesser than her outgoing, talented twin. She had always compared herself to Elodie and felt she didn't measure up. Not just because of her allergy, which had limited her life so much, but because she lacked her twin's assertiveness, her audacity and energetic enthusiasm for adventure.

So where did that leave her now?

It left her feeling ashamed and alone and frustrated. Frustrated physically, because Mack's kiss had awoken her flesh and made her hungry for more of his touch. She lifted her fingers to her lips, tracing where his lips had pressed so firmly, so urgently. Her cheeks were still flushed, her body still throbbing with a low, deep, dragging ache.

Her hand fell away from her lips and she released a ragged sigh. How was she going to get a wink of sleep knowing he was only a few feet away, scrunched up on the sofa?

Elspeth came out of the bathroom after freshening up to find Mack had left the crofter's hut, presumably to give her some privacy. Unlike the castle, the walls here were thin, the rooms small, which would have made it the perfect love-tryst location.

*Love?*

She frowned at the word her brain had sourced at random. No, this wasn't love. This was lust. She was experiencing her first full-on body crush. Yes, there were lots of things about Mack besides his body she found enormously attractive. He had known who she was and had brought her up here to keep her away from the press. It was a kind and thoughtful gesture, but it didn't mean she had to fall in love with him because of it. No, she was attracted to him physically.

But then, who wouldn't be? He had drive and ambition in spades, a strong work ethic and he genuinely cared about doing the right thing by people. Which was why he was refusing to sleep with her. Was it because he was worried she would read more into the encounter than was warranted? That he had somehow assumed she would fall instantly in love with him and complicate things for him? She might be a little inexperienced in the ways of the world, but she wasn't a fool. She could handle a sensual encounter without losing her heart to him. One night with him would have been a perfect solution for her. A way of losing her virginity with a man she liked and respected and one who liked and respected her. Why wouldn't he accept the invitation? Was it because he didn't think she could handle a casual hook-up?

Elspeth sat on the sofa and cuddled a scatter cushion against her chest. She hadn't considered herself the casual-dating type. In spite of her sheltered background, she had quietly dreamed of one day finding the right person to settle down with and make a family. But the older she got, the more remote the possibility had become. Who would want her with her faulty immune system? What if she gave one of her children her allergy? There would be a lifetime of worry for her and her partner, not to mention her child. And then her mother would have double the worry. It was easier not to hanker after things other people took for granted. Easier to settle for less than to crave more and be disappointed. And wouldn't she be craving more than she could have by wanting more time with Mack? Wouldn't she be setting herself up for bitter disappointment? For Mack was not the settling-down type. He had stated it baldly—he was a hardened playboy. A man who moved from casual lover to casual lover without long-term commitment on the agenda.

The door opened behind her and Elspeth turned to see Mack coming in with some blocks of peat for the fire. The late summer twilight had brought with it a cool change, the wind was whistling outside in an eerie tone that sounded almost ghostly, ethereal.

'I think we might get a storm in a bit,' Mack said, bending down to attend to the fire.

Elspeth put the scatter cushion to one side and got

off the sofa to peer out of the nearest window. She suppressed a tiny shudder. Storm clouds were gathering, the sky so ominously broody it made the back of her neck prickle. 'It certainly looks a bit wild out there...'

Mack must have sensed something in her tone, for he turned from his kneeling position in front of the fire to look at her over his shoulder. 'You don't like storms?'

She grimaced and wrapped her arms across her middle. 'Not much.'

He closed the firebox and straightened, dusting off his hands on his jeans. 'This hut has withstood plenty of savage storms, so you'll be safe here.'

'What if I don't want to be safe?' She must have been playing her twin too long for the words just popped out as if she had oodles of natural confidence. She was taking a gamble, stepping way outside her comfort zone, terrified he would reject her hands down, but she wouldn't be able to forgive herself if she didn't make the most of this opportunity.

She was alone with him, totally alone and might never have the chance again.

Why shouldn't she be bold and brazen about what she wanted?

Mack rubbed a hand down his face. 'Elspeth. We've already had this conversation.'

'No, Mack. A conversation is where two people express their opinions and listen to each other, each taking on board what the other says.' Elspeth approached him, stopping within touching distance. 'You told me what you wanted without really listening to what I wanted.'

His eyes locked with hers. 'What do you want?'

Elspeth closed the distance between them, sliding

her hands up the hard wall of his chest. He sucked in a breath, his body jolting as if touched by a live wire. The same electricity that fired through her own acutely aware flesh. 'I think you know what I want. It's what you want too.'

Mack placed his hands on her hips and brought her flush against his hardened body. 'You don't strike me as the casual-lover type. And that's all I can be right now.'

Elspeth snaked her arms around his neck, tangling her fingers in his windswept hair. He smelt of the outdoors—fresh, wild, untamed. She lowered her gaze to his grimly set mouth. 'What if that was all I wanted right now? A casual lover?'

He tipped up her chin with one of his hands, his gaze searching. 'Are you sure about this? You might regret it in the morning.'

Elspeth leaned into his rock-hard body, her feminine flesh tingling with anticipation. 'I promise I won't regret it. I want to make love with you. I want it so much I can hardly believe I'm saying it. For all these years, I've ignored the needs of my body. It's like it's been asleep until I met you. Now, all I can think about is how it will feel to be in your arms.'

Mack framed her face in his hands, his gaze still locked on hers. 'You're making it so hard for me to resist you.' His voice was rough around the edges, his body against hers signalling the struggle he had to maintain control.

She smiled and stroked a finger down the length of his nose. 'Look who's talking. You've been making it impossible to resist you from the moment I met you.'

He gave a low deep groan and covered her mouth

with his in a passionate kiss that set her blood racing and her heart pumping. His arms came around her, holding her to his body as if he never wanted to let her go. His tongue slipped between her lips and she was lost to the overwhelming force of desire that swept through her like a fast-running tide. Her lips clung to his, her tongue tangling with his, her need matching his. A ferocious need that threatened to consume her.

Mack kissed his way from her mouth down the side of her neck, his lips and tongue teasing her sensitive flesh into a frenzy of want. She tilted her head to one side, shivering and gasping with delight as his tongue caressed the shell of her ear. 'Your skin is so soft…' he said in a husky voice that was like a caress all of its own. 'So soft and fragrant, I think I'm becoming addicted to it.'

'I think I'm developing my own addiction,' she said, stepping on tiptoe to press a kiss to his lips. 'I can't seem to get enough of your mouth.'

He made another guttural sound and deepened the kiss with a commanding thrust of his tongue, the sensations rioting through her body until she was quaking with need. The kiss went on and on, an exchange of passion that fired every nerve of her body into excitement. Warm humid heat pooled in her core, her lower spine trembled, her breasts tingled, her breathing became laboured.

He raised his mouth from hers, his own breathing heavy, and, kicking open the bedroom door with one foot, he led her to the bed. He ran his hands down the sides of her body, his touch light but electric. 'Are you sure about this? It's not too late to change your mind.'

Elspeth gripped the front of his shirt with both of

her hands, her lower body pressed tightly against his. 'I'm not changing my mind. I want you. And from what I can tell, you want me too.'

He gave a wry smile and grasped her hips once more. 'It's not like I can hide it.' He brought his mouth back to hers in a long drugging kiss, his tongue playing with hers in a sexy tango that made her blood sing through her veins. Heat bloomed between her thighs, hot damp primal heat that threatened to engulf her. He began to remove her clothes, slowly, gently, anointing her naked skin with his lips and tongue as he went. He left her in just her underwear, his gaze running over her hungrily. 'Your turn.'

Elspeth worked at his clothes but she was trembling so much with need it became almost beyond her capability. 'How do they make this look so darn easy in the movies?' she said, fumbling with his shirt buttons.

Mack smiled and finished the job for her, hauling the shirt to one side. His chest was broad and toned and lightly dusted with rough hair. He had a light tan and flat dark brown nipples. He kicked off his shoes and pulled off his socks and stood in just his jeans. 'Think you can manage the rest?'

Elspeth disguised a gulp and went for the fastener on his jeans. 'I'll give it a go.' Her fingers tingled as soon as she touched his hard, flat abdomen, heat racing up her arm like a live current. She lowered his zip and ran an exploratory finger across the tented bulge of his arousal. 'Wow, pretty impressive.'

He cupped one side of her face in his hand. 'Don't be nervous. I'll go slowly.'

His gentle tone made it hard for her to keep her emotions out of the situation. 'I'm not nervous. I want you.'

'I want you too.' He spoke the words against her lips, then kissed her deeply again. His hands lowered the straps of her bra, then he unclipped the fastener at the back and it fell away to the floor. He lifted his mouth off hers to gaze at her nakedness, his pupils flaring. 'You're so beautiful.'

'Small, you mean.'

'Beautiful.' He brought his mouth to her right breast, his lips soft and yet like fire on her flesh. His tongue traced around her nipple in a fiery pathway, making her shudder with delight. He took her nipple in his mouth and drew on it gently, the tingling sensation making her toes curl and her spine loosen. He moved to her other breast, exploring it in the same exquisite detail, sending shivers through her body.

His hand moved down to cup her most intimate flesh. The sensation of his warm palm against her, even through the barrier of lace, was nothing short of electrifying. She moved instinctively against his hand, yearning for more contact. He stroked a lazy finger down the seam of her body, a light, teasing touch that sent a shock wave through her. The come-and-play-with-me motion of his finger created a firestorm in her flesh and she groaned out loud.

'More…oh, please, more…'

Mack peeled away her knickers and she stepped out of them. She would have overbalanced if he hadn't had hold of her. His eyes were dark and lustrous with want and he drank his fill of her, his breathing rate escalating. 'I can't take my eyes off you.'

'As long as your hands are on me as well, I don't mind what you do with your eyes.' Elspeth pressed a hot kiss to his mouth, pushing herself against him, aching for him in a way she hadn't thought possible. A burning ache that heated her flesh to boiling point. He returned the kiss with a deep groan, his lips and tongue wreaking further havoc on her already dazzled senses.

She was impatient to touch him skin on skin and so, with a boldness she hadn't thought she possessed, she peeled his underwear from his lean hips. She touched him and was rewarded with a deep groan of pleasure that seemed to come right from the centre of his body. It emboldened her to be more daring. She stroked his powerful length, a vicarious thrill of pleasure passing through her own body at the feel of him under the pads of her fingers. He was velvet-wrapped steel, potent and yet strangely vulnerable. She wrapped her fingers around him and squeezed and he sucked in a harsh-sounding breath, a shudder of pleasure visibly rippling through him.

'You're a natural at this,' he said.

'I don't know about that… I'm just feeling my way here.'

'Feel away.'

Elspeth ran her thumb over the head of his erection where some pre-ejaculatory fluid had formed. 'You really do want me, don't you?' Her voice came out in breathless wonder.

'Like I said, I can't hide it.' He pressed her down on the bed, stopping only long enough before joining her to get a condom. He applied it with a complete lack of self-consciousness and she wondered if he had lost count of the times he had performed the task with other lovers. She was annoyed with herself for thinking about his life as a playboy. What did she care about any of that? He was here with her at this moment, not with anyone else. That was all that mattered.

He came down beside her on the bed and stroked his hand down from her waist to her thigh and back again. 'Are you still okay with this? We can stop at any point.'

Elspeth traced around his sculptured mouth with a slow-moving finger. 'I'm okay. I want this. I want you. This is what I believe is called enthusiastic consent.'

'I wouldn't settle for anything less.' His tone had a note of gravity in it that assured her of his nobleness all over again. Playboy he might be, but he wasn't the sort of man who felt entitled to a woman's body. He was respectful and considerate and Elspeth was glad beyond measure that he was going to be her first lover.

'I know that,' she said, running her finger across his fuller lower lip. 'That's why you're the perfect person to coach me.'

He captured her hand and pressed a kiss to the end of her finger, his gaze holding hers in an intimate lock that sent a frisson through her body. 'I don't want to hurt you.' His voice was low and husky.

'You won't.'

'Sometimes the first time can be painful for some women.'

'How many virgins have you slept with?'

'None.'

Elspeth raised her eyebrows. 'Really?'

He caressed the curve of her cheek with the back and forth movement of his thumb. 'You're the first.'

A thought suddenly occurred to her. 'Are *you* nervous?'

He grimaced, then squeezed her hand and planted another kiss on her fingertip. 'I'm nervous about you placing more significance on us making love than what's necessary.'

Elspeth gave him a playful punch on the arm, not all that surprised his muscles were as hard as stone. 'Will you stop trying to make me out as some sort of romance tragic who can't tell the difference between casual and committed sex? I have my feet planted firmly on the ground, although not right at this moment because I'm lying here with you—which feels amazing, by the way.' She ran her finger down his sternum to his belly button and back up again. 'I'm not going to beg you to marry me, Mack. After my twin's and Sabine's cancelled weddings, I'm starting to think weddings and me are a terrible combination.'

He gave a crooked smile and captured her hand once more, holding it against the throbbing heat of his body. 'So, we're clear on the rules, then there's nothing to stop me doing this.' He brought his mouth down to hers in a blisteringly hot kiss that made her skin tingle all over. He lifted his mouth from hers and continued, 'Or this.' He placed his lips on her breast, stroking his tongue around her nipple until her back arched off the bed.

Elspeth gasped and moved closer to the heat of his body, searching for him instinctively, aching for him with a primal ache that was uncontrollable. He moved down her body with a series of kisses that made her nerves twitch with need. He finally came to the heart of her femininity, the warm moist cave of her body that was preparing in secret for his possession. He brought his mouth to her folds, separating her with his tongue, his lips playing with her sensitised flesh, sending waves of tingling pleasure through her body.

Delicious tension began to build in her swollen tissues, tension that grew to a crescendo. A storm of sensation that threatened to erupt at any moment. His tongue flicked against her in a repetitive motion, fast and yet gentle flickers that triggered an explosion in her flesh. Her back arched, her legs stiffened, her toes curled as an orgasm rippled through her in giant waves. It went on and on, sending bright starbursts off behind her tightly closed eyes. Her body thrashed beneath the ministrations of his clever mouth, the sensations carrying her away to a place where all conscious thought was pushed aside.

Mack stroked the length of her thigh in the aftermath, his gaze warm and tender. 'It gets better.'

Elspeth let out a fluttering breath. 'You have to be joking. How could anything be better than that?'

He planted a soft kiss on her mouth, one of his hands cupping her breast. 'I'll show you.'

'I can hardly wait.'

He smiled a sexy smile that made her toes curl all over again. 'I won't make you wait too long.'

Elspeth kissed him back. 'You'd better not or I won't be answerable for the consequences.'

'Should I be afraid?' Mack gave her a teasing look, his eyes twinkling.

'Very.' She lifted her face for his kiss, losing herself in the sheer magic of the erotic choreography of their lips and tongue.

He moved over her, separating her legs with a gentle placement of his hand on her thigh, his strong body positioned so as not to crush her with his weight. She clasped him tightly to her, wanting more contact, wanting the closest contact of all. He nudged her entrance,

testing her readiness, his gentle sounds of encouragement helping her to relax. He slid in a small distance,
waiting for her to get used to him, one of his hands
softly stroking her face.

'Are you okay?' His eyes were dark, his tone gentle,
his touch magical.

'I'm fine. You feel…amazing…' She found herself whispering the words in wonder. Her body was
so ready for him, so hungry it welcomed him without
a twinge of discomfort.

'So do you.' He kissed her on the lips and went
a little deeper, his body thick and strong. He began
slowly thrusting, allowing her time to catch the rhythm
of his body within hers. Her flesh tightened around
him, accepting him, wanting him, needing him as
she needed air to breathe. The pleasurable sensations
began to build within her core, the tension ramping
up until she was desperate to fly free once more. But
she wasn't quite able to get there with just the movements of his body within her. She arched her spine,
needing more friction at the heart of her flesh but not
sure how to get it.

Mack slipped his hand down between their bodies,
touching her swollen tenderness with expert precision,
the coaxing movement of his fingers against her sending her into the stratosphere within a heartbeat. The orgasm rocked through her like a storm, tossing her about
in a sea of sensation that left no part of her unaffected.
Her body tingled from head to foot, all her nerves and
tissues in rapturous pleasure unlike anything she could
have ever imagined. The ripples continued in pulsing
waves that triggered his own release. Elspeth held him
as his body shuddered with the power of it, his final

deep thrusts sending another wave of pleasure through her. It shocked her a little to think she had given him such a thunderous release. She, who had had no experience of sex until now. She hadn't considered herself a sensual person at all and yet here she was lying in Mack's arms in the aftermath of a blissful encounter. Who knew her body could be so in tune with his?

Or maybe it was always like that for him. All of his lovers had a good time in his arms.

She was nothing special. How could she be? They were keeping their relationship casual.

But wouldn't it be wonderful to be his special someone? The person he chose to be with for longer than a night or two. Elspeth tried not to allow her mind to wander down that path…the path of happy ever after. But how could she not after experiencing such tenderness, such passion and excitement in his arms?

# CHAPTER EIGHT

MACK LEANED ON one elbow to look down at her, his other hand brushing the hair back from her forehead, momentarily lost for words. Her eyes were bright and luminous, her lips plump and swollen from his kisses, her slim legs still entwined with his. His body hummed with the aftershocks of pleasure—stunning, earth-shattering pleasure—that had taken him completely by surprise. The physical connection between them surpassed that of his other encounters but he wasn't too keen on examining why. It raised a red flag in his head. Questioning why this encounter was so unique was a no-go zone. It had to be. He only did casual relationships. He didn't commit. He didn't make promises. He didn't offer what he couldn't give.

Elspeth brought her hand up to his face, her palm soft as a cloud against his cheek. 'Thank you.' Her voice was barely above a whisper and contained a note of wonder.

Mack captured her hand and kissed each of her fingertips, his eyes holding hers. 'I should be the one thanking you.' He realised with a jolt how honoured he felt to be her first lover. Was that why their encounter had been so special? So off the charts in sensuality and connection?

'For what?'

'For choosing me to be your first lover.'

Her gaze lowered to his mouth for a moment, her cheeks going a faint shade of pink. 'I'm glad it was you. I can't imagine making love with anyone else.'

The bright red flag popped up in his head again. Mack was finding it hard to imagine making love with anyone else too. Who else would respond to him with such passionate intensity? With such sweet and trusting generosity? Her body had felt like an extension of his own, it worked with his in perfect tandem, producing a stunning eruption of pleasure from which he was yet to recover. He dropped a kiss to her mouth and then carefully eased away, making a business of disposing of the condom, when really what he wanted to dispose of were his wayward thoughts. Thoughts of offering her a relationship, a short-term fling where they could explore the passion that had flared between them from the moment they met. Would that be crossing a line? Taking things further than what was wise?

He wanted her.

She wanted him.

What else mattered for now?

Mack came back to where Elspeth was lying on the bed. He gazed down at her nakedness with fire burning with molten heat in his blood. He bent down on one knee, and placing his hands either side of her head, leaned over her to press a lingering kiss to her mouth. He lifted his mouth off hers. 'I should be offering you food but I keep wanting to kiss you.'

'I'm not hungry for food.' She touched one of her fingers against his lips. 'I'm hungry for you.'

He took her hand and gave it a gentle squeeze. 'El-

speth…' He took a deep breath, still trying to get his
head around what he was about to say. He didn't want
this to be a one-nighter like so many of his other casual encounters. The passion they had shared put it in
an entirely different category. But what could he offer
that wouldn't compromise his strict relationship rules?
He wasn't interested in settling down. He wasn't interested in anything permanent.

But he was interested in exploring more of the sensual energy that had erupted with such stunning force
between them.

Elspeth pulled her hand away and sat upright, covering her nakedness with the bed throw rug as if suddenly conscious of her lack of clothing. 'Is this the part
where you lecture me about how you only do casual
relationships? That what happened between us just now
is a one-off and won't be repeated?'

There was a long beat of silence. It was as if the
crofter's hut had taken a deep breath, not even a creak
of old timber or the rattle of a windowpane daring to
break the intense silence. Even the wild wind outside
seemed to have abated to a breathless, barely audible
whisper.

Mack sat on the bed beside her, reaching for one of
her hands. 'Hey.' He enveloped her small hand within
his, a little tingle of pleasure running through him at
the contact. 'Look at me.'

Elspeth turned her head to look at him, her teeth
momentarily sinking into her bottom lip. 'I know what
you're going to say…' There was a hint of bleak resignation in her tone that unexpectedly tugged on his
heartstrings.

He bumped up her chin with his index finger. 'Actually, I don't think you do.'

Her gaze shimmered and a look of puzzlement crept over her face. 'What are you going to say, then?'

Mack gave a slow smile and stroked a lazy finger down the slope of her cheek. 'I don't want this to be a one-off. I want you to come away with me for a few days. I have a villa in the South of France—we can have a short holiday together. By the time we get back, the press will have forgotten all about Fraser's wedding being cancelled. Then you can go back to your life, I can go back to mine.'

Her smooth brow furrowed and her eyes moved back and forth between his as if searching for something. 'Are you sure?'

Mack was sure of one thing and one thing only. He wanted her. 'I wouldn't ask you if I wasn't.'

A smile broke over her features and something in his chest flipped open. 'I would love to come.'

He gave her a smouldering look. 'We'll pack up in the morning. But for now, I have something to do.'

'I wonder what that could be.' Her tone was playful, her eyes bright and shining.

'Guess.' And he lowered his mouth to hers.

Elspeth woke during the night to find herself spooned by Mack's firm warm body, the coarse hair of his forearms tickling the sensitive skin underneath her breasts. It had been hours since they had made love for the second time, but her body was still humming with delicious aftershocks. Every time she thought of his powerful body entering her, a soft flutter passed through her lower body—a tiny, secretive frisson of remembered pleasure.

Mack let out a long, deep sigh and gathered her closer, her bottom coming into contact with the hard ridge of his growing erection. 'What are you doing awake at this hour?' His voice had a playfully gruff edge. He began to nuzzle the side of her face, the prickly regrowth on his jaw sending hot tingles down her spine.

Elspeth turned in his arms and slid one of her feet down his hair-roughened calf. 'I could ask the same of you.'

He rolled her beneath him, his gaze holding hers in a tender lock. 'It's too soon to make love again. I don't want you to get sore. You're new to this.'

'You have to stop treating me like I'm made of glass. I can handle anything you do to me.' A doubt popped up its head. *Anything?* Well, maybe not quite anything. The one thing she didn't want from him was a broken heart.

But she could keep her feelings out of this, after all, other people did.

Her twin did.

Why couldn't she?

Mack stroked his thumb over her lower lip in a fainéant movement. 'The last thing I want to do is hurt you.' His voice was low and gravel-rough, his expression etched in lines of concern.

Elspeth had a feeling he wasn't talking about physical hurt. 'I'm a big girl, Mack. I know how to take care of myself.'

He gave a lopsided smile and stroked her lower lip again. 'As long as we're both clear on the rules.'

She tiptoed her fingers all the way down his sternum and his taut and ripped-with-muscle abdomen. 'I think you need the rules for you, not for me.' She challenged him with her gaze and added, 'Am I right?' Her hand was poised just above the hot hard heat of his length.

He gave a shudder and groaned deep in his throat. 'There should be a rule against you looking so damn sexy first thing in the morning.'

She stroked her hand over his thickened erection. 'I'm sure you could resist me if you wanted to.'

His eyes darkened to gunmetal grey. 'I can't resist you. Not right now.' His mouth came down firmly on hers, sweeping her away on a tide of blissful longing, one she wondered if she would ever stop craving in spite of the rules.

It was late the following afternoon by the time they arrived at Mack's villa in the quaint medieval village of Lagrasse in the Occitanie region in the South of France. The villa was a large stone building that overlooked the River Orbieu and it had a wonderful view of the abbey that the village was subsequently built around.

Mack helped Elspeth out of the car. 'What do you think so far?' he asked.

Elspeth did a complete circle, taking in the breathtaking view. The warm summer late afternoon breeze caressed her face, the smell of flowers redolent in the air. 'It's gorgeous, Mack. I didn't even know this village existed before you brought me here. It's like stepping back in time.'

He looped an arm around her waist, leading her to the front door. 'It's reputed to be one of the most beautiful villages in the South of France. The wine from this region is spectacular.'

She playfully shoulder-bumped him. 'Did someone mention wine?'

He grinned and leaned down to plant a kiss on her lips. 'Am I corrupting you?'

Elspeth smiled back. 'Yes, but I'm enjoying every minute of it. How long have you had this place?'

'A couple of years now,' Mack said, and unlocked the door and turned off an alarm with a fob on the key-ring. 'I have a housekeeper who checks on things and a gardener-cum-maintenance-man. They see to things when I can't be here as much as I'd like.' He pushed the door open for her and waved her inside.

Elspeth stepped over the threshold and looked around in amazement. The villa was tastefully deco-rated in a French Provincial style with lots of white and grey and exposed woodwork. It didn't have the grand ostentatiousness of Mack's Scottish estate and she wondered if that was why he liked it. She turned to face him. 'How often do you come here?'

'Four or five times a year, often for only short vis-its, unfortunately. I have a lot of other business to see to at home.'

'Do you enjoy it? Your business interests, I mean?'

He closed the solid front door, his expression rueful. 'Not always. I inherited a lot of debt when my father died. I had no choice but to put my own career aspira-tions on hold and do what had to be done. It's taken a long time to get back in the black. Once you've stared down bankruptcy, it's hard to truly relax, no matter how much money you make. I have a lot of people de-pending on me.' He blew out a sigh and continued, 'And no doubt Fraser will be one of them now his dream job has been taken away.'

Elspeth placed a hand on his arm. 'I'm sorry things have been so difficult for you. You've given up so much for your family.'

He flicked her cheek with a gentle finger. 'Stop apologising. I'm happy enough.'

But was he? Did worldly possessions and plenty of money in the bank give him the fulfilment most people craved? He struck her as a loner, a man who stood apart from others. He kept his relationships short and casual. The only commitment he was prepared to make was to his career. A career he hadn't even chosen for himself but had inherited due to tragic circumstances.

'What did you want to do?' Elspeth asked after a moment. 'I mean, career wise?'

His smile was crooked. 'Nothing that would've made me anywhere near the money I've made. Come. Let me show you around before I bring in our luggage.'

Elspeth got the feeling he wasn't comfortable talking about that aspect of his life. The hopes and dreams he had left behind in order to protect his family's assets. It would have taken great courage and commitment to pull his family's finances out of the red. He had done it and done it brilliantly, but at what cost to himself?

After Mack gave her a quick tour of the villa, Elspeth wandered around on her own while he brought in their luggage. She was eager to explore all of the quaint rooms in more detail but even more eager to wander about the garden. She walked out of the kitchen door to a paved courtyard where pots of fresh herbs grew as well as a long row of purple lavender. Bees were busily taking the pollen from the lavender heads; numerous small birds were twittering in the trees and nearby shrubbery. It was easy to see why Mack loved coming here. The setting was so serene and restful, especially when the abbey's bells began to toll in the distance. She closed her eyes and listened to the rhythmic peels of the ancient bells, a mantle of peace settling over her.

Elspeth turned at the sound of a footfall to see Mack coming out of the villa carrying a bottle of champagne and two glasses. 'You really know the way to a girl's heart.' She could have bitten her tongue off for the vocal slip. He wasn't after her heart. He wanted no emotional commitment from her. All he wanted was a fling and she was fine with that because she had to be.

There was no other choice.

'When in France, do as the French do,' he said with a smile. He popped the cork and poured the bubbles into the two glasses and then handed her one. *'À votre santé.'* His perfect French accent almost made her swoon. Was there no end to this man's heart-stopping charms?

Elspeth returned the toast in French. *'À votre santé.'* The champagne was exquisite, the bubbles exploding in her mouth and tantalising her taste buds. She couldn't help thinking it was going to be hard to go back to drinking cheap sparkling wine once their fling was over. Her old life seemed so staid and boring and uneventful after just a couple of days in Mack MacDiarmid's company.

'What are you thinking?' Mack asked.

Elspeth gave him a self-conscious smile. 'I was thinking how hard it's going to be for me to go back to my boring life after this.'

A small frown pulled at his forehead. He put his champagne down. 'Why do you think your life is boring?'

She gave a one-shoulder shrug. 'Because it is. I work. I eat, I sleep. Alone.'

'You have friends though, don't you?'

'Yes, but I don't socialise much.' Elspeth plucked one of the lavender stalks off and twirled it beneath her nose.

'Because of your allergy?'

She glanced at him to find him watching her steadily. 'Not just because of that. My twin is the social butterfly, not me. I'm happy in my own company. As long as I have a good book, I'm content.'

Mack came closer and lifted her chin so her gaze met his. 'Have you always lived in Elodie's shadow?'

Elspeth let the lavender stalk drop to the ground. 'Mostly. She's way more outgoing than me. I can't compete so I don't bother trying.' She twisted her mouth and added, 'She's everything I'm not.'

Mack stroked her chin with the pad of his thumb. 'But you're you. And that's all you ever need to be.' He bent his head and lowered his mouth to hers in a kiss that stirred a deep longing in her flesh and in her heart. A longing for more than physical connection.

A forbidden longing.

He lifted his mouth off hers and stroked her chin once more. 'Have you ever switched places with her before?'

Elspeth put her champagne glass down, deciding that the delicious champagne was messing with her head and her heart. 'A few times when we were kids.' She gave a little half-laugh and continued, 'Our mother was never fooled but our father could never tell us apart. Not even when he lived with us.'

'Your parents are no longer together?'

'No. They divorced when we were five. We'd stopped being cute by then, so he decided to move on. He had a second family with another woman. A boy and a girl, neither of whom have allergies, for which he is mightily relieved.'

Mack frowned so deeply it formed a trench between his eyes. 'You think your allergy had something to do with your parents' divorcing?'

Elspeth wished she'd kept her wayward mouth shut. What was it with her? A mouthful or two of champagne and she was spilling all. Spilling things she had told no one, apart from her twin, before. 'It contributed, certainly. I had almost lost my life three or four times by then. My father doesn't handle stress too well.'

'It's not your fault he didn't have the maturity to handle a sick child. That's on him, not you.'

'I know but it can't have been easy, you know? My mum was a worrier at the best of times. My allergy diagnosis turned her into a nervous wreck. She has no life apart from me.' She grimaced and turned to pick up her champagne again, staring down at the vertical necklaces of bubbles rising. 'I sometimes feel like I ruined her life.'

His hands came down on the tops of her shoulders from behind. 'Don't say that. I'm sure she doesn't think that at all.' His voice was deep and low and husky.

Elspeth leaned back against him, drawn to him as an iron filing was drawn to a magnet. 'You have to stop giving me champagne.'

'Why?'

She turned in the circle of his arms and handed him her glass. 'Because I keep telling you things I've never told anyone else before.'

He put her glass to one side. 'Why is that a problem?'

Elspeth gave a rueful smile. 'Because we're practically strangers, that's why.'

He picked up a loose strand of her hair and tucked it behind her ear, his touch so gentle it made her heart tighten. 'You don't feel like a stranger to me.' His voice was still as rough as the pockmarked flagstones beneath their feet. 'And if it's any comfort to you, I've shared things with you I haven't shared with anyone else.'

Elspeth looked into his grey-blue eyes, struck by how dark and lustrous they were. 'Really?'

His smile was crooked. 'You have a strange effect on me, Elspeth Campbell.'

She moved closer, winding her arms around his neck so her lower body was flush with his. 'So I can tell. Thing is, what are we going to do about it?'

'This,' he said and covered her mouth with his.

Mack wondered if he would ever get tired of kissing her soft mouth. The sweet taste of her filled his senses, dazzled his senses into overload. He was supposed to be keeping her at arm's length but every time he was near her, he wanted her with an ever more pounding ache. It was like a fever in his blood—a virulent fever that had no other antidote but her.

Her body's response to him fuelled his desire. Making him burn, boil and blister with the need to get as close as humanly possible. He dragged his hungry mouth off hers only long enough to groan, 'I want you.'

'I want you too.' Her voice was whisper-soft, her beautiful blue eyes shining with desire. The same desire he could feel pummelling through his body. A desire that begged, pleaded, roared to be assuaged as soon as possible.

Mack couldn't wait for her to walk inside with him. He scooped her up in his arms and carried her indoors.

'What are you doing?' she squeaked. 'You'll do your back in.'

'I like holding you in my arms.'

'I like being held by you but that doesn't mean I can't walk on my own.'

'Indulge me. I've never carried a woman up three flights of stairs before. It'll be good for me.'

She laughed and linked her arms around his neck. 'Crazy man. You're a glutton for punishment.'

Glutton was right. Mack was hungry for her in a way he had not been for anyone else. It shocked him how much he wanted her. How could he have thought he could resist her? How could he have thought one night was going to quell the hot tight ache of his flesh? Why else had he brought her away to France? He wanted more time with her—time to explore the explosive chemistry that flared between them. The chemistry he had felt the first time he had been in the same room as her.

Was it her inexperience that had so impacted him? That she had gifted him herself in such a trusting way? How could he not be honoured and touched by her trust in him? How could he not be affected by their mutual desire? He couldn't explain the deep connection he felt with her. It was beyond anything he had experienced before.

And all he knew was, he wanted to experience it again. And again. With her.

Only with her.

# CHAPTER NINE

ELSPETH SENSED THE urgency in him all the way to his
bedroom. She could feel it in the bunched muscles of
his arms as he carried her, she could feel it in the blisteringly hot kisses he planted on her lips along the way,
she could feel it in the charged atmosphere. An electric charge that threatened to combust at any moment.
Her own body was on fire with need—a smouldering
simmering need that heated her inner core to boiling.

Mack shouldered open the master-suite door like
a hero from an old Hollywood movie. Her heart rate
spiked, her pulse leapt, her body burned. He laid her
on the bed and set to work on her clothes, only stopping long enough to help her with his.

Finally, they were both naked, their limbs tangled,
his mouth coming down on hers in a kiss that nearly
blew the top of her head off. His tongue slipped between
her lips with erotic purpose, sending a wave of raw lust
coursing powerfully through her body. Her back arched
in delight, her spine loosening vertebra by vertebra,
clawing need spiralling through every cell of her flesh.

'I can't get enough of you,' Mack said, bringing his
mouth to the sensitive skin of her neck. 'I want to kiss
you all over.'

'You only get to kiss me all over if I get to do the same to you. Deal?' Elspeth was constantly amazed at how brazen she was with him. Brazen and bold with no hint of the shyness that had plagued her most of her life. It was as if she was a completely different person when she was with him. A sensual, adventurous person who was not afraid of expressing her primal needs. But then, he was the only man who had ever made her aware of such needs. She had been asleep before she met him. Locked in a sensual coma that one kiss from him had rescued her from with such stunning impact she could never be the same again. She wouldn't be able to go back to being the quiet shy person she used to be. The person who had convinced herself she was satisfied with her lot in life. The person who had given up any hope of having a partner and family. The person who lived in the shadow of her outgoing twin and was resigned about doing so.

That girl was gone.

She had morphed into a woman with sensual needs that could no longer be ignored.

Mack MacDiarmid had changed her. He made her want things she had denied herself for so long. But there was no denying it now. Her need for him was shouting out from every corner of her body, every blood cell throbbed with it, every heartbeat carrying its primal message.

He captured her hand and pressed a warm kiss to the middle of her palm. His eyes held hers in an intimate lock that made her spine loosen even more. 'I don't want you to feel pressured to do anything you're not comfortable doing.'

'Here's the thing…' Elspeth tiptoed her fingers from

his lower lip to the base of his chin and back again. 'I'm completely comfortable with you. I want to pleasure you the way you pleasure me.'

His eyes glinted and he pressed another kiss to her palm, his lips making her skin tingle right the way to her core. 'Everything you do pleasures me.' He brought his mouth down to hers in a long kiss that simmered with passion. His tongue began a playful dance with hers, cajoling hers into a duel that made her insides coil tightly with lust. She stroked her hand down his lean jaw, her softer skin catching on his stubble. He groaned and deepened the kiss even further, his breathing becoming as heavy and laboured as hers.

Elspeth ran one of her hands down his muscled shoulders and the long length of his spine. Touching him was such a delight to her, a thrilling delight that filled her with excitement. His body was hard, toned, tanned and powerful and yet he was so gentle and careful with her.

Mack rolled over to his back, taking her with him so she was lying on top of him, her legs splayed either side of his pelvis. Her hair hung in long tresses, dangling over the hard wall of his chest. His hands held her by the hips, his eyes roving over her naked breasts and belly, his pupils flaring, his breathing going up another notch. 'I could look at you all day. Just like this.'

Elspeth leaned down to press a kiss to his mouth. 'I like looking at you too. But maybe later, because I have something I want to do first.' She wriggled down his body until her mouth was close to the potent length of him. He sucked in a harsh-sounding breath, his hands gripping the bedcovers either side of his body.

'Elspeth, you don't have to... Ahh...' The rest of his

sentence faded away as Elspeth got to work on him. She used her lips and tongue in ways she hadn't thought she'd ever have the courage or even the desire to do. But it was a form of worship to caress and pleasure him in such a raw and intimate way. She was rewarded by his deep gasping groans and hectic breathing. But before she could tip him over the edge, he grabbed her by the shoulders and pulled her off him.

'I want to be inside you.' His voice was husky with need. 'But I need a condom.' He gently eased her off him to access a condom from the bedside drawer. He put it on and she straddled him again. Seeing him so turgid with need ramped up her own excitement, her body craving his possession as an addict did a forbidden drug. 'This way you can control the depth,' he said, guiding himself into her entrance.

The sensation of him entering her this way took her breath away. Her body gripped him, her intimate muscles welcoming him, pleasure rippling through her as she began to move. He was right—she could control the depth and speed and it gave her shivers to rock with him in such an erotic way. She ached for more friction and discovered that with just a slight tilt of her body she could get it right where she needed it. The sensations trickled through her, slowly at first, then rising to a crescendo. Tension built in the most sensitive part of her, the surrounding nerves on high alert, waiting for the point of no return. And then it came with a rush of feeling that fanned out in pulsing waves from her core to the farther reaches of her body. She shook, she shuddered, she screamed with the cataclysmic force of it.

Within seconds, Mack followed with his own shuddering release. Watching him in his moment of bliss was both thrilling and deeply erotic. His face screwed up tightly in pleasure, he expelled a deep agonised groan, his body bucked and rocked and then finally relaxed.

Elspeth stayed where she was, perched on top of him, his body still encased in hers. She stroked his chest with her hands in slow-motion movements, watching as his breathing gradually slowed down. 'You look like you had a good time.'

He opened one eye and smiled a crooked smile. 'I did. Did you?'

She leaned down to kiss the tip of his strong nose. 'You know I did.'

He placed his hand at the back of her head and kept her mouth pressed to his. His kiss was slow and sensual, a kiss that sent shivers through her flesh and a flicker of hope to her heart. Could he be developing feelings other than lust for her? Their lovemaking was so physically passionate but there was another element to it that made her wonder if he felt an emotional connection as well.

Or was she fooling herself? Perhaps he made exquisite love to all his lovers. Perhaps they too were stunned by his touch, his kisses and his ability to give them mind-blowing pleasure. Was she being a silly little romantic fool to make more of their lovemaking than what was there? They desired each other, they had indulged that desire and he had made no promises that anything more lasting would come out of it.

But she couldn't help wanting more than a casual fling. Her feelings for him were growing by the second. They weren't something she could control. How could she have thought she could? They just were *there*. Feelings she had never expected to feel for someone so quickly but how could she resist Mack? He had stunned her from the moment she met him. Wasn't that why she had fought to stay in her twin's persona when in his presence? Because he spoke to *her* in a visceral way from day one. She was falling for him as an autumn leaf was programmed to fall from a tree. She couldn't stop it. It was like a force of nature, a primal thing that swept her up in a world of intense sensuality, one she never wanted to leave.

But how could she hope to stay with a man who didn't want anything more than a fling? A man who had never been in love and was convinced he would never fall in love?

Mack broke off the kiss and, after disposing of the condom, began to stroke his hands down her arms from shoulder to wrist, his touch gentle and yet electrifying. He lifted one of his hands to her face, stroking from below her ear to her chin and back again. He didn't say a word but his expression was cast in lines of contemplation, as if he was mulling over things in his mind. There was a small frown between his brows and a faraway look in his eyes.

Elspeth brushed her fingers through his hair in a tender caress. 'What are you thinking?'

He blinked a couple of times and gave a smile that didn't quite make the full distance to his eyes. 'Not much.' He gave her cheek another stroke and then placed his hand on the small of her back. 'I should feed you. Are you hungry?'

'A bit.'

He gently eased away from her and got off the bed, reaching for his underwear and trousers and stepping into them. Elspeth scrambled off the other side of the bed, suddenly feeling shy. 'I think I'll have a shower...'

Mack came over to her and lifted her chin with his index finger, his eyes searching hers. 'I'm glad you came here with me.'

'I'm glad you asked me.'

He smiled and dropped another kiss to her lips. 'I'll rustle us up some food. We can eat out on the terrace.'

'Sounds lovely.'

Elspeth made her way to the bathroom and stood under a refreshing shower, her thoughts tied up in knots. Every time Mack kissed her, every time he made love with her, every time he even looked at her, her heart leapt. Her twin could handle a fling, Elspeth could not. She didn't have the emotional software. It was like running the wrong operating system on a computer—it was incompatible with her nature. She didn't have the emotional armour to keep her feelings out of it. Was it because he was her first lover? Didn't they say no one ever forgot their first lover? Some couldn't forget because the experience wasn't pleasant, others because it was special, a once-in-a-lifetime event that signalled the beginning of sexual activity.

Making love that first time with Mack was unforgettable and each time since, even more so. His touch was imprinted on her flesh, she couldn't imagine wanting anyone else to touch her. She couldn't imagine wanting any other lips to kiss hers, any other arms to hold her close.

And that was a problem because Mack didn't hold his lovers close for long.

\* \* \*

Mack organised some food and drink but his mind was still replaying every moment of their recent lovemaking. He'd had plenty of lovers in the past and not one of them had made him feel the way Elspeth did. Her touch unlocked something inside him, opening up possibilities in his head he had never considered before. The possibility of having more than a short-term fling with her. Not anything too serious, of course. There was a boundary line in his head he had no intention of ever stepping over, not even for someone as adorable as Elspeth. But he did want more time with her. How could he have thought a few days would be enough? Normally it would be. He'd be ready to move on and wouldn't have a twinge of conscience about doing so.

The word 'love' wasn't totally foreign to him. He had loved his mother deeply, he had even loved his father, for all his faults. And he loved his brother and only wanted the best for him. He even loved his father's love child, his half-sister, Daisy. He had invested in her life, paying for her education and visiting her and her mother when he could. It was the least he could do after the devastation his father had caused in their lives.

But loving someone in a romantic sense had never been a possibility and he wasn't sure it ever could be. It hadn't even crossed his mind before now. He hadn't allowed it to. But something about Elspeth made him realise he had been short-changing himself in his relationships. He had always held part of himself back. He had engaged physically but not emotionally. Sex was just sex. It was a pleasant experience that had satisfied him physically but left him empty emotionally.

But not with Elspeth.

Something stirred in him every time he was with her. A soft flutter in his chest, like the hard-shelled pupa of a moth or butterfly slowly opening. He wanted more time with her. More time to explore the chemistry they shared but also more time to get to know her. Not to fall in love with her. That wasn't his game plan at all.

Elspeth came wandering into the kitchen with her hair still damp from her shower. Her face was completely bare of make-up and yet she looked as stunningly beautiful as ever. She was wearing a simple sleeveless dress that skimmed her body in all the right places, flowing out in a wide skirt around her ankles. Her feet were bare, which made her seem even more petite next to him. She carried over her shoulder a small bag that he assumed carried her EpiPens and her phone. He could only imagine the background worry she must deal with on a daily basis because of her allergy. He had been extra vigilant over preparing their supper, giving his housekeeper strict instructions to remove all nuts and nut products and to thoroughly clean all surfaces.

'Can I help?' she asked with a smile.

Mack leaned down to press a kiss to her mouth. 'You'll only distract me. Go and take the wine out to the terrace. I'll bring some supper out in a minute.'

She snaked her arms around his waist, her slim body pressing up against his sending fireworks through his blood. He hardened to stone, his need of her rising with every one of his heartbeats. 'I like distracting you.'

Mack liked it too, way too much. 'Wicked little minx.' He gathered her in his arms and lowered his mouth to hers in a deep kiss that made the hairs of the back of his neck stand up. He stroked one of his hands up and down the slender length of her spine, crushing her to him, relishing in the feel of her breasts pressed against his chest. Was there no end to this burning desire he had for her? He wanted her with a hunger that was relentless, all consuming, overwhelming.

She murmured sounds of encouragement and pressed even closer, one of her hands reaching up to play with his hair. Her touch sent shivers rolling down his spine, making him ache to possess her.

But he had to prove to himself he wasn't completely driven by raw desire. He had to prove to himself he could resist her because surely this craziness would soon burn itself out? It *always* did. The first flush of lust would soon fade to the point where he couldn't wait to get away. To move on to other more exciting pastures. He never wanted someone longer than a few days. He didn't want the complication of a long-term relationship. He didn't seek it, he didn't encourage it, he didn't allow it.

And yet…and yet…something kept tugging at him deep inside, a vague sense that he was somehow robbing himself by keeping things short and shallow. Mostly because it was impossible to be shallow with Elspeth. She was sweet and caring, with deep layers of intelligence he was only beginning to discover. She had deep insights about life in spite of her sheltered existence. A wise perspective on people and relationships that he admired.

Mack gave her bottom a playful pat and lifted his mouth off hers. 'Hold that thought. Supper first.'

Elspeth gave a mock pout. 'Spoilsport.'

Mack couldn't resist planting one more kiss to her

lips because her mouth was the most kissable he had ever come across. 'Off you go before I change my mind.'

She stroked a soft hand down the line of his jaw, her gaze suddenly uncomfortably direct. 'Does that ever happen? You changing your mind?'

Mack released her with a tight smile. 'Not often. And certainly not when emotions are involved.'

'Do you ever allow them to be involved?'

'No.'

She smiled back and picked up the tray off the bench that had a bottle of local wine and two glasses on it. 'That's what I thought.' But something about her tone made him wonder if she was disappointed with his answer.

## CHAPTER TEN

ELSPETH TOOK THE tray out to the terrace where the rising moon was casting a silvery glow across the landscape. An owl hooted its melancholy notes from a tree
nearby, frogs started a throbbing chorus from the pond
in the garden. The night air was sweet and fragrant
with the scent of jasmine and lavender and some other
exotic perfume she couldn't identify.

She placed the tray on the wrought-iron table setting and poured herself a glass of the crisp white wine.
She took it with her to the edge of the terrace, where a
stone balustrade separated the area from the tiered garden below. She took a sip of the wine, letting her tongue
savour the taste for a moment, but even top-shelf wine
couldn't remove the taste of Mack from her mouth. He
was proving every bit as addictive as the wine and she
wondered how she was going to deal with the end of
their fling. He hadn't put a definitive timeline on it.
They were here in the South of France for a few days.
Did that mean their fling would end once they returned
to the UK?

'Here we go.' Mack joined her on the terrace with
a tray with a wheel of camembert cheese and fruit,

as well as a fresh baguette. He put the tray down and handed her a side plate and a napkin. 'Help yourself.'

Elspeth was surprised to find she was starving and came back to the table to load up her plate. She sat down and waited for him to join her. He put a small portion of cheese and fruit on his own plate and poured himself half a glass of wine and took the seat opposite her. *Bon appetit.*

'Did you learn French at school?' she asked.

'Yes. But we also used to travel to France for summer holidays before my father died.' A shadow passed over his face and he continued, 'Those were happy times.' His lips twisted. 'After he died, it made me question everything about our lives. He always seemed happy enough with my mother and she was certainly happy with him. He was an involved father, or as much as he could be when he was home. He travelled a lot for business, or so he said.'

'What triggered the mental-health crisis that led to his suicide?'

Mack put his glass down on the table with a thud, his expression taut. 'My mother found out he had a mistress and a love child in another city. He'd been with her for five years. He juggled both families and his business all that time but, of course, it was never going to end well. He ran into money troubles, big troubles, and then it all came crashing down. His two lives collided.'

'Oh...how awful that must have been for your mum. But also for his lover. What happened to her and the child? They too must have been distraught when he died.'

Mack picked up his wine glass again and swirled the contents into a tiny whirlpool, his expression still set in shadowed lines. 'They were, especially Daisy, my half-sister. She was only four at the time. It was harrowing to see her and her mother at his funeral.' His throat moved up and down and he continued, 'I'll never forget the sound of them sobbing. It was so…so raw… My mother didn't want them there but I insisted.' His lips twisted again. 'I'm not sure I did the right thing by being so adamant about it. My mother was furious with me for months over it. But Daisy was just a little kid who had just lost her father. She needed closure. So did her mother, Clara.'

Elspeth leaned forward and reached for his free hand and gave it a gentle squeeze. 'It was so good of you to insist on them being there. Of course it would have been hard for your mother and you and Fraser. But you're right, Daisy and Clara needed to grieve too. But you were so young to have had that insight, especially when you were dealing with the shock of it all too. How on earth did you cope?'

He gave a loose-shouldered shrug. 'Someone had to cope. No one else was up to it.'

No wonder he locked his emotions away. No wonder he was strong and capable and self-reliant. He had to be. He had trained himself to stay in control at all times and in all circumstances. It made her admire him all the more to think he had put his own feelings to one side to consider the pain and suffering of others. He had searched for the higher ground in a difficult moral dilemma and he had stuck to his principles in spite of his own grief.

'Do you ever see them? Your half-sister and her mother?' she asked.

Mack put his wine glass down and gave a half-smile.

'I do, actually. Daisy's at university now, doing architecture. She's a bright girl. I'm really proud of all she has achieved.'

'She wasn't at Fraser's wedding?'

He shook his head, his smile disappearing, a frown taking its place. 'Sadly, no. Fraser has never shown any interest in being involved in Daisy's life.'

'But you've been a stalwart support to her and her mum all these years.' Elspeth posed it as a statement rather than a question because she was already certain of the answer. Mack would not have rejected them. He had too good a character to do something like that. It made her feelings for him blossom all the more. Feelings she had promised herself she would keep under control. But how could she stop feeling the way she did?

'Daisy and Clara are good people who had a bad thing happen to them. They had no idea my father had a double life. He'd kept us a secret from them just as he'd kept them a secret from us.' He gave a rough-edged sigh and added, 'I've lost count of the number of lies he must have told over the years. I thought I was close to him but sometimes I wonder if I knew him at all.'

'You can only know someone as well as they want you to know them,' Elspeth said. 'We all have parts of ourselves we would rather keep hidden.'

Mack gave another slanted smile and leaned forward to brush his fingers lightly over the back of her hand where it was resting on her knee. 'What parts of yourself do you like to keep hidden, hmm?' His grey-blue eyes meshed with hers with a steady intensity that made something slip sideways in her stomach.

One thing Elspeth was desperate to keep hidden

was her developing feelings for him. Deep feelings that had no place in a fling such as theirs. Not according to the rules—*his* rules. But her heart had no time for his rules, it was on its own journey. Every moment she spent with him made it harder to ignore the way she felt about him. He had all the qualities she most admired in a man: steadiness, loyalty, commitment to those he cared about, moral fortitude—the list went on. She gave a tight smile and moved her hand away. 'My twin is the one with stuff she likes to keep hidden. I thought I was closer to her than anyone but I had no idea she had a one-night stand with your brother. She isn't a one-night-stand type of girl. But apparently she ran into her ex-fiancé that night with his latest lover and it upset her. I'm not sure why it should have upset her so much. She was the one who jilted him. It seems a little inconsistent to be feeling jealous when he takes up with a new lover. After all, it's been seven years. He's probably had dozens of lovers by now.'

'Do you think she still has feelings for him?'

Elspeth shrugged one shoulder and picked up her wine glass. 'She says not but sometimes people lie to themselves more than other people, right?'

'They do indeed.' Mack leaned back in his chair and took a sip of his wine, his gaze still trained on her.

The night sounds from the garden provided a peaceful background soundtrack. Crickets had joined the croaking frogs and the tinkling of the water feature added to the peaceful ambience. She couldn't remember a time when she had felt so close to someone other than her twin. The intimacy she and Mack had shared had enveloped her in a bubble of bliss and contentment she was loath to let go. How was she going to cope when their fling came to an end? She wished she could spend the rest of her life like this—relaxing in his easy company, her body tingling with the memory of his magical touch. But Mack wasn't the happy-ever-after type. He was bruised by the betrayal of his father's double life. He was wary of long-term commitment, having seen the devastation of his mother when the truth about his father's mistress and love child had come out. It would have been a terrible shock to him, to see his beloved father in a completely different light. To lose his father in such tragic circumstances with so many issues left unresolved between them. But it didn't mean Mack had to shy away from finding true love himself. He would make such a wonderful life partner. He would be a kind and loving and supportive father to his children. Look at the way he supported and cared for his half-sister. It showed how deeply principled he was and Elspeth couldn't help admiring him for it.

'Mack?'

'Hmm?'

'You said you would have liked to pursue a different career other than take over your father's business interests. What was it you wanted to do?'

He put his wine glass down, his expression cast in shadowed lines. It seemed an age before he spoke, as if he was feeling compromised by talking about something he had let go a long time ago. 'I had dreams of becoming a professional musician.'

'What do you play?'

'The piano.'

'Do you still play? I didn't see a piano at Crannochbrae and there isn't one here.'

He gave a twisted smile. 'The one at Crannochbrae

was sold after my father died. I haven't bothered replacing it since. I haven't played in years.'

'Do you miss it?'

'Not any more.'

'But you did?'

Something flickered through his gaze—a flash of a memory, a lingering emotion, a hint of regret. 'For a while but I had to be practical. It's hard to make money as a professional musician. And I had to make money, lots of money, or my family's estate would have been lost.'

Elspeth wondered what else he had given up in order to keep his family's assets on track. He had sacrificed his dream and his youth to protect his family as well as his father's mistress and love child. She stood from her chair and came over to place her hand on his broad shoulder, looking deep into his eyes. 'I think you're amazing, Mack.' Her voice was as whisper-soft as the light breeze that teased the nearby shrubbery.

His hand came up to encircle her wrist, his fingers warm and strong. He tugged her down to his lap, his arms going around her. His eyes moved back and forth between each of hers for endless moments, his breath catching as if he saw something in her gaze that affected him deeply. One of his hands began to stroke from between her shoulder blades to the base of her spine—long, slow, languorous strokes that triggered a sensual storm in her body. His mouth drifted closer as if in slow motion. Her breath caught in anticipation, her hands going to his broad shoulders, her heart kicking up its pace. His lips brushed hers in a barely there kiss. A feather-light touch that sent a tingle through her lips and straight to her core. He placed his mouth against

hers again, firmer this time, his lips moving in a lei-
surely massaging motion that sent her pulse racing.

He lifted his mouth off hers, caught and held her
gaze for a pulsing beat—an erotic silent interval that
ramped up her need of him like a flame on dry tinder.
He didn't say a word. He simply framed her face with
his hands and kissed her again—a deep and passionate kiss that sent a shower of sparks down her spine.
His tongue tangled with hers in a sexy dance that made
her heart beat all the harder and faster.

Finally, he eased back to look at her, his own breathing heavy. 'I think you're pretty amazing too.' His
voice had a rusty edge, his gaze warm and tender. So
tender, she wondered if he was developing feelings for
her. Or was she fooling herself? Mistaking raw passion for something else?

Elspeth traced a line around his sculptured mouth
with her finger. 'Make love to me?'

He pressed a hot hard kiss to her mouth and stood,
taking her with him. 'With pleasure,' he said, and carried her indoors.

# CHAPTER ELEVEN

MACK HEARD A faint buzzing during the night and rolled over in bed to see Elspeth reaching for her phone. She checked the screen and gave a deep sigh and turned the phone off, placing it on the bedside table.

'Who was it?'

She turned to him with a rueful expression. 'My mother.'

He frowned, and propped himself up on one elbow. 'Doesn't she realise what time it is?'

She began to chew at her lower lip, her gaze drifting away from his. 'I didn't tell her I was in France. She thinks I'm in Scotland, doing a tour on my own.' She flopped down on the pillows and released another sigh. 'She texts or calls dozens of times a day or night. I'm so tired of it, I usually turn off my phone but I forgot when we went to bed.'

Mack trailed his fingers down the silky skin of her arm. 'She loves you and is probably worried about you.'

'I know but I can take care of myself. I'm not a little kid any more.'

'If you keep ignoring her calls and messages, she's going to worry even more. It's what mothers do—they worry.'

Elspeth turned her head on the pillow to look at him. 'What do you think I should do? Answer every one of them? I'd never get anything else done.'

Mack took her nearest hand and brought it up to his chest. 'Call her first. Let her know how you're doing. She's pursuing you because she's sensing you're pulling away. If you reach out to her instead it might re-balance things a bit. It's worth a try.'

'I guess...' She sounded doubtful.

Mack kissed each of her fingertips in turn, his gaze holding hers. 'Learning to let go is hard for some parents, especially when they've had good reason to worry in the past.'

'I know but I'm trying to live my own life now. She's spent the last twenty-six years fussing over me like I'm going to drop dead in front of her. I need to know who I am without her. I need autonomy but she won't let me go.'

Mack could only imagine the terror for a parent having a child with a life-threatening allergy. His mother had told him of her fear the day he inhaled a peanut that went down to his lung. He had only been a toddler and had only the slightest memory of it but she had never forgotten it and every time she had spoken of it, he had sensed the raw unmitigated fear she had experienced that day. But Elspeth's mother had had many such harrowing days. Days when she would have been terrified that the anaphylaxis would take away her beloved child. 'I really don't know how parents cope with the stress of bringing up kids even without a life-threatening allergy. It seems like such a lot of hard work.'

Elspeth looked at him with her clear blue gaze. 'Don't you want to be a father one day?'

It wasn't the first time he'd been asked the question but it was the first time he paused for a moment over his answer. He had always ruled out having a family, figuring he'd been responsible for two already. But now, he allowed the thought some space in his mind... picturing what it would be like to hold a baby, his own baby, in his arms. A baby conceived out of love.

And there was that tricky word again—love. The word he avoided, the concept, the emotion he shied away from because it had already done enough damage in his life. Loving had led to hurt, to loss, to bitter disappointment. To scars that never quite healed.

'Mack?' Elspeth's soft voice broke through his moment of reflection.

He gave her hand a playful squeeze. 'Not right now.'

'But maybe one day?'

He shrugged. 'Who knows? What about you? Is becoming a mother important to you?'

A shadow passed over her features and she focussed her gaze on their joined hands. 'I'd be worried about a baby inheriting my allergy.'

'There's no guarantee it would, though.'

She gave a tight smile that was sad at the corners. 'And no guarantee it wouldn't. The genetic lottery being what it is.'

'There are worse things to have than a peanut allergy, surely?'

Elspeth turned on her side to face him. 'Twins?'

He stroked a finger down the cute slope of her nose. 'Was it hard being a twin?'

'No, not really. I adore my sister but while we might look exactly the same, we're completely different in personality.' She paused for a beat before adding, 'I found it hard to keep up with her, especially with Mum being so overprotective of me all the time. In some ways, Elodie got shoved aside. I guess that's why she always craved the spotlight because she certainly didn't get much attention from Mum. But then, Elodie got to do heaps of stuff I never could. Going to school, parties, playdates, that sort of thing. I lost confidence, became shy and introverted. My world shrank while hers expanded.'

Mack gently tucked a strand of her hair behind her ear. 'You have no reason to lack confidence. You're an accomplished young woman in your own right. And beautiful and sexy too.'

She gave a rueful grimace. 'I'm not sure I'm going to be so confident when I next have a lover.'

A sharp pain in his gut caught Mack off guard. But of course she would have another lover one day in the not too distant future. He might be her first but he wouldn't be her last. Not unless he changed the rules… The rules he had never thought of changing before.

He forced a smile and leaned down to press a light kiss to her lips. 'Go back to sleep. I have something special planned for the next few days.'

Her eyes lit up. 'What?'

'That's for me to know and for you to find out.'

Elspeth snuggled closer, her legs tangling with his. 'I'm not sure I'll be able to get back to sleep now you've got me all excited.'

*Right back at you, sweetheart.*

Mack wrapped his arms around her and for the next half an hour or so sleep was the last thing on his mind.

Over the next few days, Elspeth enjoyed discovering more about the village of Lagrasse. They went on walking tours of the village, picnics by the river and explored the Corbières wine region—the largest wine-producing region of France.

On the last day before they were due to go back home, Mack took her on a tour of the Abbey Sainte-Marie, informing her of its history and other interesting details about its construction.

'The construction of the abbey was given the go-ahead by Charlemagne in 783,' he said, walking hand in hand with her. 'The village developed later and is known for both the abbey and its bridges. The abbey was active from the eighth century until the French Revolution, when many monasteries were destroyed. After one hundred and fifty years of neglect, a restoration programme was established and what we see today is the result.'

'It's certainly magnificent,' Elspeth said, looking around her in wonder and awe.

Mack's arm went around her waist, drawing her close. 'I hope I'm not boring you with the history lesson?'

She smiled up at him. 'Me? Bored? You must be joking. I'm loving every minute.' She was loving every minute of being with him. He could be talking gibberish and she would still be loving it. But that was the trouble…she was loving not just the sound of his voice, not just the protection of his arm around her waist, not just the way he looked at her, not just the way he made love to her, but him.

She loved *him*.

The realisation was like a lightning flash, momentarily blinding her. How could she be so foolish as to fall in love with a man who had no interest in falling in love with anyone, much less her? And how could it be possible to fall in love with a man she had only met a handful of days ago? Was it even possible? Or had she let the romantic setting get to her?

Elspeth took a step forward but almost stumbled and Mack's arm quickly tightened around her waist. 'Are you okay?' he asked with a look of concern.

She forced a smile and touched a hand to her warm face. 'I'm fine. But perhaps a little thirsty.'

'Come on.' He led her to the nearest exit. 'Let's get a drink and something to eat.'

A short time later they were seated in one of the cafés in the central square of the village. The square was surrounded by beautiful houses, their facades dating back centuries and adding to the old-world charm of the village. Elspeth sipped at a glass of mineral water and Mack had coffee while they waited for their food to arrive. She was conscious of his gaze resting on her, his expression still etched in lines of concern.

'Feeling any better?'

Elspeth put her glass down and smiled. 'I'm perfectly fine. I've enjoyed everything you've shown me. I wish we had another day or two to see more.'

There was a small silence.

'We could extend our stay,' Mack said, picking up his coffee cup and cradling it in his cupped palm. 'I can take a bit more time off work. A day or two at least. How about you?'

Elspeth ran the tip of her tongue over her lips. 'Are you sure you can spare the time? I guess I could ask for another day or two off work. But aren't you worried about your brother? Have you heard how he's doing?'

He put his cup down again. 'He called me this morning when you were in the shower. Sabine's father has decided to keep him on after all.'

Elspeth frowned. 'Really? But how does Sabine feel about that? Won't she feel her father is being disloyal to her?'

Mack shrugged one broad shoulder. 'Sabine's father is like a lot of hard-nosed businessmen—they don't let emotions get in the way of a good business decision. He's been impressed with Fraser's work. That would be his deciding factor in keeping him on, not whether or not it upsets Sabine.'

Elspeth reached for the last of her mineral water. 'I wonder if he's hoping they'll get back together again. But unfaithfulness is a tough thing to forgive.'

'Yes. And trust hard to build up again.'

Their food arrived at that point and the conversation switched to other things. But Elspeth had only taken a couple of bites of her salad when she felt a tingling in her mouth, then, within a second or two, her tongue began to swell along with her throat. Panic gripped at her chest, her breathing becoming laboured, her heart rate escalating, a sweat breaking out on her body. She dropped her fork with a clatter and looked around for her bag. 'Quick. I need my EpiPen.'

Mack was out of his chair so fast it fell over backwards with a noisy clatter. He rushed around to get her bag off the floor, quickly searching for the EpiPen and then handing it to her. 'Can you do it or do you want me to do it for you?' His voice was calm but she could see the worry in his gaze.

'I can do it...' She grabbed the EpiPen and jabbed herself in the thigh and within seconds her heart began to race and a wave of intense anxiety washed over her as the epinephrine raised her blood pressure and opened her airways. And then, she stopped thinking as the effect of the drug clouded her mind and rendered her body useless…

With one hand on her shoulder, Mack whipped out his phone and called for an ambulance. He could barely get his voice to work to give clear instructions to the emergency service personnel. His heart was hammering, a cold sweat breaking out over his body. He couldn't lose her. He couldn't let her die. She had to live. She had to survive. The panic built in his chest until he could scarcely inflate his lungs. He bent down and lowered her into the recovery position, gently soothing her, trying to keep the raging panic out of his voice. 'They're on their way. Stay with me, that's a good girl. You're doing fine.'

*Please let her be doing fine*, he prayed, to a God he hadn't prayed to since he was a kid.

Within a short time an ambulance came wailing into the village square and Elspeth was loaded in, with Mack accompanying her. The plan was to take her to the emergency department of the hospital in the nearby town of Carcassonne. The paramedics monitored her, giving her oxygen and another shot of epinephrine when her vital signs deteriorated.

The wailing of the ambulance siren rang inside Mack's head, ramping up his panic to an unbearable level. What if she didn't make it? What if there wasn't a doctor there who knew what to do? She looked so pale and sweaty, almost lifeless. His gut tied itself into hard knots—knots that twisted and turned until his stomach burned with pain. A pain that crept higher, higher,

higher until it wrapped an iron band around his heart.
How could he lose her? It couldn't be possible. It must
*not* be possible. He had never felt so powerfulness, so
out of control, so bereft at the thought of her not making it. It reminded him of the day his father died, that
terrible day he could never quite erase from his memory. The piercing screams of his mother, the ambulance
siren wailing up the driveway—a pointless arrival for
there was nothing anyone could do by that stage. Mack
had watched them wheel his father out on a stretcher.
He hadn't even been able to say goodbye. The words
had been locked in his throat, so he'd swallowed them,
shoving them deep inside him, along with his feelings.
He had learned that day his feelings were of no use in a
crisis. He had to be strong and in control to get everyone else through the worst time of their lives.

This was another one of those times.

They finally got to the hospital and Mack had to step
out of the way as they took her inside. He gave what
information he could to the admission staff, relieved
he spoke fluent French. Doubly relieved when the doctor came out and said Elspeth was going to be fine but
they were going to admit her overnight for observation.

'I want to stay with her,' he insisted. The words
echoed in his head for the next few minutes until he
was allowed entry to her room.

*I want to stay with her. I want to stay with her. I
want to stay with her.*

Elspeth came out of her drug-induced stupor to see
Mack sitting by her bedside. His features were haggard
and his hair looked as if his hands had been through
it many times, for it was sticking up every which way.

'The doctor said you insisted on staying overnight with me but you don't have to.'

'I'm not leaving you and that's final.' His tone was so strident, even if she'd had the energy to argue with him, she wouldn't have bothered. But in her weakened state, she was secretly glad he was going to be with her. Having anaphylaxis at any time was terrifying but having it while in a foreign country even more so. She was just grateful Mack had acted so swiftly and not gone into a panic himself as her father used to do.

She lay back on the pillows and closed her eyes, exhausted from the drama and fear, her body still recovering from the dose of epinephrine. But also painfully embarrassed at how things had turned out. She should have double-checked the menu but her French wasn't anywhere near as fluent as Mack's. There must have been nut contamination in her salad or in the dressing.

'Mack?'

His hand gave hers a gentle squeeze. 'I'm here, *m'eudail*. Try to rest now.'

'I'm sorry…'

'It's not your fault. If it's anyone's it's mine. I should've ordered for you. I didn't think.' His tone was ragged around the edges and full of self-recrimination.

Elspeth tried to open her eyes to look at him but overwhelming tiredness got the better of her. She gave a wobbly sigh and drifted off…

## CHAPTER TWELVE

Mack brought her limp hand up to his mouth, pressing his lips to her fingers. His chest was tight as a drum, his lungs too cramped to draw in a decent breath. He blamed himself for not being vigilant enough. Elspeth had a life-threatening allergy and seeing her like that, struggling to breathe, was confronting. Not just confronting but terrifying. What if it had happened when they were out of reach of a hospital? What if she hadn't brought her EpiPens with her? Over the last few days, he'd almost forgotten about her allergy. He'd been so caught up with spending time with her, making love to her, knowing their fling was coming to an end, as all his flings did.

But seeing her so ill had shaken him to the core. Making him realise he didn't want their fling to end like all the others.

*I want to stay with her.*

He had grown close to her in a way he hadn't expected, closer than anyone else he had ever met. Not just physically close but forming a deep connection that opened his heart to possibilities he had never considered before—possibilities he had never wanted to consider. He had never asked anyone to live with him

before. That had always been a step too far. It reeked
too much of commitment and he didn't do commitment.

Almost losing her had shocked him into realising
he had developed feelings for her. The sort of feelings that he had never felt for anyone else. He wasn't
ready to call it love, the sort of love that romantics went
on about. But he cared deeply for her. Why else had
he panicked as he'd never panicked before seeing her
struggling for air? He couldn't imagine not seeing her
again. He had already extended their fling another day
or two. What would it hurt to extend it a little longer? A
little longer than he had ever done before? It would be a
practical solution, a convenient arrangement that would
give them a little more time to enjoy each other's company. How much longer was not something he could
answer with any definitiveness, which was unusual
for him. But he didn't put too much significance on
that. He was not going to let things get out of control.

Mack shuffled his chair closer to Elspeth's bedside
and gently stroked her hair back from her forehead.
Her face was pale, her features relaxed in sleep, and his
heart squeezed as if it were in a cruel vice. His throat
thickened, unfamiliar emotions rising in his chest.
'I'm not going anywhere,' he said in a rough whisper.
'You're stuck with me for a while longer.'

Elspeth woke a couple of times during the night when
the nurse on duty came in to do a set of obs. And every
time, she saw Mack sitting beside her bed, wide awake
with his concerned gaze on her. Once the nurse left,
Elspeth turned to him. 'Have you had any sleep at all?'

'No.'

She ran her gaze over his weary features. His eyes were darkly shadowed, his jaw was heavily peppered with regrowth, his skin looked paler than normal and there were fine lines around his mouth she had never noticed before. 'You look terrible.'

'Thank you.' His tone was dry.

She plucked at the starched white sheet covering her. 'I bet I don't look too crash hot either.'

He grasped her hand and kissed her bent knuckles, his eyes meshing with hers. 'You look as beautiful as ever.'

Her heart swelled at the tenderness in his gaze. 'Thanks for staying with me. It's usually my mum who sits there hour after hour.'

He suddenly frowned. 'I should have thought to call her. And your sister. Do you want me to do it now or—?'

'No, I'm quite safe with you and I don't want to stress them.'

'Will you tell them once we get back home?'

'Maybe.'

'I can see why your mother panics,' Mack said, stroking her hand. 'You scared the hell out of me.' He swallowed deeply and added in a husky tone, 'I'm not going to be game enough to let you out of my sight after this.'

Elspeth gave a lopsided smile. 'You're going to have to though, soon, aren't you?' She looked back down at the sheet she was toying with. 'We're having a fling, not a long-term relationship. Those were the rules. Your rules.'

There was a pulsing silence.

'What if I wanted to tweak the rules?'

She looked at him in shock. 'What do you mean?'

He grasped her hand even more firmly as if worried she would pull away. 'I don't want our fling to end just yet. I want to continue seeing you.'

Elspeth ran her tongue over her suddenly dry lips. He wanted to extend their fling? 'What time frame were you thinking?' For there would be a time frame, of that she was sure. He would not be offering her a for-ever relationship, a full-time commitment such as marriage. It was probably silly of her to expect it given they had only known each other such a short time. But a part of her longed for such a commitment from him anyway. For she knew how she felt, she was sure of her love for him. The trouble was knowing for sure if love was behind his offer, or simple lust. The health scare he had witnessed had created a sense of urgency and drama, which had probably coloured if not downright influenced his decision to extend their fling. Dramatic circumstances experienced by a couple often had that effect—made them draw closer together for a time—but it didn't always last, not unless deep and lasting love underpinned it.

And how could she be sure it did?

'We can take it a day at a time,' Mack said. 'Just enjoy each other's company as we've been doing.'

Elspeth was trying to figure out how such an arrangement would work in reality. He was based in Scotland, she in England. She had a job she adored, a flat she had not long rented. A year-long lease she had only just signed. How would her mother cope if she moved out of London? Judging by the number of missed calls and text messages she'd received from her, Elspeth doubted her mother would ever agree to her moving to Scotland. And could she even be sure she would get a position in another library, especially at such short notice? What exactly did Mack expect of her? 'I don't know, Mack...' She softened it with a smile. 'We live in different parts of the UK. I don't want to quit my job or—'

'I'm not asking you to quit, just ask for a transfer,' he said. 'We'll figure the details out later but, for now, I want you to get well and at least consider moving in with me for a few weeks when we get back home.'

Her eyebrows shot up. 'Move in with you?'

'Why are you so surprised? It makes sense to co-habit for the sake of convenience. It's way more practical than trying to conduct a long-distance relationship.'

But whose convenience was he talking about? It certainly wouldn't be convenient for her, not unless he was willing to commit his whole heart to her. 'I'm not sure I'm ready for such a big step...' she began. Not unless she was sure his feelings for her were the same as hers for him. 'You're probably only asking because of what happened. It scared you and you think you need to take care of me, but you don't. I can take care of myself.'

'Why don't you think about it for the rest of the day?' he suggested. 'We don't fly home until tomorrow. You can decide then.' He rose from the chair and pressed a kiss to her forehead, sweeping her hair back in a tender gesture as he straightened. 'I'm going to let you sleep while I head back and have a shower and a shave. You should be ready for discharge by the time I get back.'

'Okay.' She sank back against the pillows with a sigh. 'I'll think about it.'

Mack walked out of the hospital with a spring in his step. The convenience of having her move in with him was his primary motivation for asking her. And he was confident Elspeth would agree once she'd had time to consider it. She was young and inexperienced, so it was a big step for her, but he didn't want their fling to end any time soon and he was sure neither did she.

He stopped off to buy her a gift on the way back to the villa to lift her spirits. Her health scare had obviously deeply unsettled her, as it had him. His gut still churned as he recalled the harrowing moment at the café when she went into anaphylaxis. Her life could have ended then and there and *that* didn't bear thinking about. He couldn't imagine losing her. She had only been in his life such a short time—a matter of days—and yet he had developed feelings for her that he had not experienced for anyone else before. They were so unfamiliar to him he didn't know how to describe them.

All he knew was, he wanted her with him for much longer than a casual fling.

The jeweller's assistant showed Mack a diamond and sapphire ensemble of pendant, earrings and an engagement ring. He hadn't asked to be shown an engagement ring and wondered why the woman had brought one out. *Sheesh.* The French were such romantics. He glanced at the ring with its winking solitaire diamond and deep blue sapphires and then back at the middle-aged woman serving him. 'I won't need the ring, just the pendant and earrings.'

The older woman raised her brows over twinkly raisin-dark eyes. 'No? Maybe *monsieur* will come back for it another time?'

Mack gave a stiff smile. *'C'est impossible.'*

* * *

Elspeth came back to the villa with Mack later that day. He was attentive and solicitous with only marginally less fussing over her than her mother would do. He helped get her comfortable on a lounger on a shady section of the terrace and then brought her out a refreshing cup of tea and a plate of fresh fruit.

'Here you go.' He set it down next to her. 'Is there anything else I can get you?'

'No. This is lovely, thanks.'

He reached for something inside his white chinos' pocket. 'I bought you a little gift.' He handed her a rectangular dark blue velvet jewellery case. 'I hope you like them.'

Elspeth took the box with bated breath. The box was too large to be a ring box and she was annoyed with herself for even hoping a ring could be in there. She prised open the lid to find a beautiful diamond and sapphire pendant and matching droplet earrings. They were stunningly beautiful, quite easily the most gorgeous she had ever seen. She didn't dare think about how much they had cost. Her twin was used to wearing ridiculously expensive jewellery, but Elspeth was not and wondered if she ever could. 'Oh, my goodness... Oh, Mack, you shouldn't have. I can't accept these. They're too much.'

'Don't be ridiculous. I want you to have them. Consider them a "get well" gift.'

Elspeth glanced up at him as a thought occurred to her. An uncomfortable thought that triggered a tiny flicker of anger. 'Are you sure they're not a bribe?'

He gave a sudden frown. 'A bribe? What do you mean?'

She closed the lid of the box with a little snap and handed it back to him. 'I know what you're doing. You want me to move in with you and this is a way to convince me. But I don't want gifts.'

'What do you want?' His voice had a raw edge to it, but his expression was shuttered. And he ignored the box in her outstretched hand.

Elspeth put the box on the table next to the lounger, and then swung her legs over so she was in a sitting position. 'I want more than expensive jewellery. I want to know how you feel about me.'

'I told you how I feel about you. I enjoy your company. I like being with you. I care about you.'

Elspeth rose from the lounger to put some distance between them. 'You barely know me, Mack. We only met a handful of days ago. And for part of that I was pretending to be my twin. How can you be sure you care about me, the real me?'

Mack stood and came over to her, taking both of her hands in his. 'I know the real you. That's who I've developed feelings for—you, only you.'

'Are you saying you're in love with me?'

There was a beat or two of silence. Too long a silence. A heartbreaking silence that told her all she needed to know.

'I'm saying I'd like our fling to continue for as long as we both enjoy each other's company.' His expression remained inscrutable but she sensed a carefully restrained tension in him.

'I know how silly this is going to sound but I can't accept your offer,' Elspeth said, pulling her hands out of his. 'I want more than a let's-see-how-it-goes relationship. I want more than someone to enjoy my company. I want more than someone to care about me. I want the sort of love that most people aspire to. But you've ruled that sort of love out. The love that binds two people together for a lifetime.'

He sent one of his hands through his hair in an agitated manner. 'Isn't it a little too early to be talking about marriage?'

She gave him a challenging look. 'Would there ever be a time when you'd be agreeable to talk about it? You said you never wanted to settle down. You've already ruled out the possibility, so how can I wait in hope that you might one day change your mind?'

He walked over to the edge of the terrace, standing with his back towards her, his gaze focussed on the view of the abbey in the distance. 'Marriage is not something I'm willing to discuss, now or in the future.' He turned to face her, his face set in intractable lines. 'I'm offering you a relationship for the time being. That's all.'

'I'm flattered by your offer but you'll have to forgive me for declining it,' Elspeth said. 'If our feelings aren't the same for each other, what would be the point? We'd be wasting each other's time and, quite frankly, I feel I've wasted enough years of my life already. I need to take charge of my own destiny and not wait around hoping good things will come my way. I have to go out and find those good things. And one of those good things I most desire is to be loved for me. As I am, allergy and all.'

His dark eyebrows shot together. 'You surely don't think I'm holding back on marriage because of your allergy? For God's sake, Elspeth, didn't you see how worried I was about you? You almost gave me a heart attack collapsing like that. The thought of losing you is what triggered me into asking you to come and live with me. I want to take care of you.'

She slowly shook her head at him. 'If I allowed you to do that, I would be simply exchanging you for my mother. I'm not your responsibility, Mack. I want to be much more than a liability you feel pressured to take on out of guilt. I want to be your equal, your partner in life, not a temporary interest that has no possibility of a long-term future.'

He muttered a curse word not quite under his breath. 'So where do we go from here? You want out? Now?'

Elspeth gave a deep sigh. 'I think it's for the best, don't you? Why prolong something that's going to end anyway? You were only attracted to me because I was playing the role of my twin. That's what first got your attention but that's not who I am. I don't wear designer clothes and exotic perfume and sky-high heels. I'm not a party girl who can work a room. I'm a shy and introverted homebody who doesn't belong in your world. If we continued our fling, you'd soon get tired of me, I'm sure. I'd rather we part now as friends.'

'Friends?' His top lip curled, his eyes flashed, his jaw tightened. 'I don't need you as a friend.'

'The thing is, Mack, you don't need anyone, not in an emotional sense. You won't allow yourself to.'

'What do you feel for me?' The question blindsided her for a moment, especially when it was delivered in such a blunt tone with zero expression on his face. He was like a robot, an emotionless robot programmed to issue commands but with no capacity to feel.

Elspeth knotted her hands in front of her body, wary of revealing too much of her feelings for him when there was no possibility of them ever being returned. 'I've enjoyed being with you. You've taught me so much, not just about sex but life in general. I enjoyed this time here in Lagrasse, in spite of my health scare. I will always look back on our time together with… with fondness.'

His top lip went up again. 'Fondness?' His tone was cynical. 'Is that all? And yet, here you are practically begging me to get down on bended knee and offer you a marriage proposal.'

A streak of anger rippled down her spine. 'What you offered me was a proposition, one that's probably not unlike the one your father offered to his mistress. I suspect he kept her going for years with false promises, fanning her hopes with each little gift when he visited, making her think that one day, her dream would finally be fulfilled, that they would live happily ever after. But it didn't happen, did it? He was unable to love either her or your mother the way they wanted to be loved.'

'Please do not bring my father into this discussion.' His words came out through thinned lips, his tone embittered, his gaze diamond hard.

'We both have father wounds, Mack,' Elspeth said, softly, realising it with a flash of insight. 'We were both let down by our fathers, betrayed, rejected and abandoned by them. But that doesn't mean we have to live our lives frightened of others betraying, rejecting or abandoning us. We have to be courageous enough to ask for what we want, to not be afraid to embrace it when it happens to come our way. To not short-change ourselves in the fear of losing the one thing we crave above all else—love.'

Mack strode back to the balustrade of the terrace,

his hands gripping the stone with white-knuckled force. His back was rigid with tension, his shoulders hunched forward as he fought for control. 'All right.' He turned back to face her, his face still devoid of emotion. 'I'll change our flights for this evening. There's no point staying another night when you're so keen to leave.'

'You don't have to do that, Mack. One more night won't—'

'On the contrary, I do have to do it. I'll book your flight for London. I'll fly to Edinburgh. We won't have to see each other again after today.'

He turned and walked down the steps leading into the garden, disappearing from sight before she could think of a single thing to say. But what could she say that hadn't already been said? Wasn't it easier, less painful this way? A clean cut was better than a long drawn-out goodbye.

There was next to no conversation between them on the way to the airport later that day, but there was a surfeit of tension. Elspeth could feel it pulsing between them in the air in invisible waves.

As they were waiting for their flights to be called to the gate, Elspeth looked up at him. 'Mack? Please don't let us end this way.'

His expression was set in tight lines, his mouth a thin line. 'It was your choice to end it. Not mine.'

'You're being unfair. I don't want to end it with any bad feelings between us. The least we could do is part on good terms.'

'All right, then.' He offered her his hand in a formal handshake. 'Goodbye. I hope you have a pleasant flight.' It was the sort of thing he might say to a stranger he had just met, or a business associate he had nothing in common with other than work. Not the sort of farewell one would say to one's lover, a lover who had shared his bed, his body. He was her first lover. Her first love. Her only love.

Elspeth slipped her hand into his and tried to ignore the tingle his touch evoked in her flesh and the arrow of pain in her heart that this was the last time she would feel his touch. A wave of grief swept over her, making tears sting at the backs of her eyes and a lump rise in her throat. 'Goodbye, Mack. Thank you for everything you've done for me. I really enjoyed getting to know you.'

He was still holding her hand, his gaze shuttered. 'You've got your new EpiPens with you?'

She patted her tote bag with her free hand. 'Yes.'

His gaze drifted to her mouth, his throat rising and falling over a tight swallow. 'Right, well then, I'd better let you go. Your flight is due to board any second now.'

Elspeth pulled her hand out of his and forced a smile. 'Right. Don't want to miss it.'

He seemed to hesitate for a long moment, just staring at her without speaking. But then, he took her by the upper arms and pulled her close and planted a brief but firm kiss to her lips. 'Stay safe, *m'eudail.*' His voice had lost its brisk impersonality and instead was deep and husky.

'I will.' Elspeth turned to join her departure-lounge queue but when she glanced over her shoulder, Mack was gone.

Mack strode down the concourse of the airport to his own departure gate willing himself not to look back.

He never looked back when he left a fling. And that was all his relationship with Elspeth was, wasn't it? A fling. A fling that hadn't gone the way he'd wanted and that stuck in his craw in a way he didn't like. He was usually the one who decided when a relationship was going to end. He liked the sense of control it gave him to have the power to pull the plug when it suited him. He didn't like surprises and Elspeth rejecting his offer to move in with him was an unpleasant surprise. A shock, a gut-wrenching disappointment that he couldn't explain other than it had thwarted his plans. He had envisaged a few weeks, possibly months of being together, enjoying the passion that had fired between them. He wasn't the settling-down type, marriage was not and never had been in his plans. He had no wish to commit to one person for the rest of his life. His mother had done that and it had all but destroyed her to find the object of her love had betrayed her in the most despicable way. Love had destroyed his mother as it had Clara and to a lesser degree Daisy, his half-sister. It had certainly contributed to the wayward behaviour of his brother, which had continued to this day. Loving someone gave them the power to hurt you, to wound you, to destroy you.

And he was not going to allow anyone to do that to him.

Ever.

# CHAPTER THIRTEEN

ELSPETH HAD ONLY been home a matter of hours when Elodie turned up. She breezed in with her usual whirlwind restless energy and plonked herself down on the squishy sofa, curling her slim legs beneath her. 'It was all for nothing,' she said without preamble. 'The financial backers pulled out. I'm back where I started unless I can find someone else to fund my label. And that's hardly likely now everyone knows I'm the one who caused Fraser MacDiarmid's wedding to be cancelled.'

'I'm so sorry,' Elspeth said, curling up next to her. 'But things kind of backfired for me too.'

Elodie made a *poor you* moue with her mouth. 'So, your little fling with the Laird of Crannochbrae came to an end?'

Elspeth picked up one of the scatter cushions and began to toy with the ribbed hem. 'I ended it, actually.'

'Why?'

'Because for the first part of our time together, he thought I was you. I wasn't convinced he liked me for me.'

'You mean he found out you were you and not me? What, did you tell him? You promised me you wouldn't.'

'He guessed before I told him.'

'Did anyone else guess?'

'No, only him.'

'Smart guy.'

'Yes, very. I think he suspected something right from the start even though I was doing my level best to be you.'

Elodie gave a tinkly bell laugh. 'I would have loved to be a fly on the wall, especially when Fraser saw you.'

Elspeth gave a mock glower. 'I'm not sure I've quite forgiven you for not telling me about him.'

'Sorry about that but I just wanted to forget it ever happened.'

'Having met him, I can understand that. But Mack is nothing like him. He's so rock steady and hard-working and he's sacrificed so much for his family.'

'So why did you end it with him if you liked him so much?'

'Because I wanted more.'

'More as in what?'

'More as in love.'

Elodie leaned forward, her expression incredulous. 'Are you saying you're in love with him?'

Elspeth tossed the cushion to one side. 'I know it probably sounds ridiculous, but I think I fell in love with him more or less straight away.'

Elodie bounced off the sofa as if there were an ejector button beneath her. 'For pity's sake, Els, you can't possibly fall in love that quickly. You're a little star-struck by him, that's all. You have so little experience with men, no wonder you fancy yourself in love with him. I was like that with Lincoln. He was so charming and suave it blew me away but look how that ended.'

'I might not have as much experience as you do,

but I know what I feel. He wanted me to move in with him. That would have meant me quitting my job and uprooting my life to live with him in Scotland. How would Mum cope with that?'

'You have to stop worrying about Mum. It's your life and you have to live it the way you want.'

'I know and what I want is someone to love me. To be brave enough to at least be open to the possibility. Mack doesn't want to settle down, and he's ruled out the possibility of ever falling in love.'

'It doesn't mean he won't fall in love,' Elodie said. 'The more those hardened playboys protest, the harder they fall.' She plonked back down on the sofa. 'I'm glad you're back, though. I was dreading someone taking a picture of you with Mack and people thinking it was me.'

Elspeth frowned. 'Why were you so worried about that?'

Elodie shrugged. 'My reputation is already shot to pieces. I don't need any more scandals attached to my name.' She blew out a long breath and added, 'But thanks for stepping in for me at the wedding. I'm sure you did a great job of being me.'

'Too good a job, it seems.' Elspeth sighed.

Mack filled his days with work, trying to distract himself from the emptiness he was feeling. He didn't want to admit how much he missed Elspeth. He hadn't realised how much he enjoyed her company until she was no longer in his life.

*No longer in his life...*

How those words tortured him in his darkest moments. It had been her choice to leave. He had offered her a relationship and she had chosen not to take it. That was her privilege—he didn't want anyone to stay with him out of a sense of duty.

But why *did* he want her to stay with him? The sex was great, better than great. Amazing, the best he had ever had. The physical connection with her had shown him something about himself he hadn't realised before. He'd had sex with his previous partners but he had *made love* with Elspeth. Her inexperience had been part of it, but he suspected there was more to it than that. She gave of herself so trustingly and he had worshipped her body, treating it with such reverence, which had made their lovemaking rise to a different level—a level of awareness, of sensual feeling that transcended the physical. He missed the physical connection, but he missed even more the companionship, the conversation and emotional connection he had with her.

*Emotional?*

Mack mulled over the word, allowing it a little more space in his brain than he normally would. He was so used to dismissing emotions, masking them, denying them, eradicating them, that it was strange to give his mind permission to examine how he actually felt. He had blunted his feelings for years. Bludgeoned and smothered them in order to survive the aftermath of his father's death. He hadn't had time to grieve, he'd had to spring into action and help everyone else with their process of grieving. His mother, his brother, his father's mistress and his half-sister.

But what about him?

Elspeth had mentioned something about them both having a father wound. Mack had dismissed it at the time as psychobabble, yet another trendy term that had no relevance to him. But he realised now that his father's death had left its mark—a deep scar on his heart that had practically shut it down for fear of more hurt. He had forgotten how to access his emotions. He could barely recognise the feelings other people took for granted. There were so many feelings he had buried and he had been too scared to dig down to find them.

Being back at Crannochbrae reminded him of himself. A fortress, secure against the elements, strong and capable of withstanding the harshest weather and yet the rooms inside were just rooms, tastefully decorated and functional but without heart. He was like the suit of armour in the foyer—cold, hard and empty.

Mack wandered into what used to be the music room, which, for years now, was a sitting room filled with sofas and whatnot tables and priceless artwork and so on but lacking the one thing that had once set it apart. It had been a long time since his fingers had touched a piano keyboard.

Too long.

Maybe it was time to do something about that.

Elspeth was on a lunch break from work in a local café when she looked up to see Sabine standing next to her table. She put her coffee cup down with a tiny clatter. 'Sabine? How are you?'

Sabine gripped the top of the chair opposite Elspeth's. 'I wanted to see you.'

But who exactly did Sabine want to see? Her or Elodie? Had anyone told her of the switch? Had Mack?

'Please, sit down. Can I get you a coffee or something?'

'Maybe later.' Sabine pulled out the chair and sat,

her gaze fixed on Elspeth's. 'I can see the difference now but back at Crannochbrae it was impossible.'

'Did Mack tell you who I really was?'

'No, Elodie called me yesterday and apologised for everything.'

'Oh, I'm so glad. I know she never intended for you to get hurt. And nor did I. I was aghast when I found out about—'

Sabine held up her hand like a stop sign. 'Please don't mention Fraser's name. I'm still furious with my father for keeping him on in the business.'

'That must be awful for you.'

She sighed and put her phone on the table, two of her fingers doing a slow little tap dance on the glittery cover. 'I'm kind of used to it, to be honest.' She stopped tapping her fingers and met Elspeth's gaze. 'Dad isn't the sensitive type. I thought Fraser was nothing like him, but I was wrong. Dad's had numerous affairs and my mother always turns a blind eye. I'm ashamed of how blind I was to Fraser's faults, but I liked how he needed me. I made him feel good and that made me feel good. But true love is a two-way thing, right? One person can't be doing all the emotional work. It has to be balanced.'

'I couldn't agree more,' Elspeth said. 'I'm so sorry for deceiving you. As soon as I met you I liked you. And when I met Fraser, I was worried you were going to be unhappy in the long run.'

Sabine gave a twisted smile. 'I'll be all right. Plenty more fish in the sea and all that. But how about you? It can't have been pleasant being slut-shamed by the press when you were completely innocent.'

'Yes, well, Mack made sure I was out of the firing line for a few days.'

There was a little silence.

Sabine's eyes began to twinkle. 'So, how was that?'

Elspeth could feel her cheeks heating enough to froth the milk for a cappuccino. 'It was…actually, I'd rather not talk about it. I'm sorry.' Tears stung at the backs of her eyes and a thickness in her throat made it hard to breathe. She could barely think of those few days with Mack without breaking down. She missed him so much. Her body ached for him. Her life seemed so empty and lonely without him in it. Was he missing her? Or had he moved on already by now? Going back to his playboy lifestyle as easily as taking his next breath.

Sabine reached for her hand across the table and gave it a supportive squeeze. 'I thought you two had a special connection. Are you going to see him again?'

Elspeth shook her head. 'I don't think it's wise. We want different things out of life.'

Sabine leaned back in her chair, her expression thoughtful. 'I don't know… Mack seemed really drawn to you.'

Elspeth gave her a wry look. 'That's because I was pretending to be Elodie.'

Sabine frowned. 'But he knew you had switched places. He was the only one who guessed. Elodie told me when she called me yesterday.'

'Yes, but he's only interested in a short-term fling. I want the fairy tale.'

Sabine sighed and picked up the cardboard menu that was propped up against the salt and pepper shakers on the table. 'Don't we all?'

\* \* \*

Mack spent the next three weeks travelling as he saw to various business interests. The evenings he spent alone in his hotel room. He wasn't in the mood for socialising, he had no interest in pursuing a hook-up. His gut churned at the thought of sleeping with anyone other than Elspeth. How had he been satisfied with such impersonal hook-ups all these years? It made him feel ashamed of himself, that he had settled for such shallow encounters when he could have enjoyed a deeper connection.

A connection he still missed.

He got back home to Crannochbrae to find the piano he had ordered had been delivered and tuned. He sat down at the shiny black instrument and stretched his fingers out in front of him. Years had passed since he had played. Too many years. Could he even do it now? He had memorised whole sonatas in the past, pages and pages of music filed away in his brain. Could he access those notes now or had the years wiped them away?

He took a deep breath and placed his fingers on the keys. He began playing Debussy's 'Clair de Lune', the hauntingly beautiful cadences filling the music room, unlocking something in his chest. He continued to play, losing himself in the moment…or was he finding himself? The music spoke to him on a cellular level. It was part of who he used to be and yet he had not allowed it any room in his life for years. He hadn't realised how much he had missed it until now, when he was playing again.

And that was not the only thing he missed.

His body throbbed with a persistent ache for the feel of Elspeth's arms around him. He longed to see her clear blue eyes looking into his. He longed to feel her soft mouth crushed beneath his, her body welcoming him with such enthusiasm and sweet trust it made his heart contract even more than the music he was playing.

*His heart...*

His fingers paused on the keys, the press of his last notes giving an eerie echo in the music room. Since when had his heart been involved in his casual relationships? Never, not until Elspeth. She had opened him to the possibility of feeling something for someone other than lust. He realised with a jolt that the emptiness he was feeling was because he loved her. He was unfamiliar with the emotion in this context. Of course, he had loved his parents and still loved his brother, and Clara and Daisy also had a special place in his affections and always would.

But no one had captured his heart like sweet, shy Elspeth. She had unlocked his frozen heart, making him need her far more than physically. He needed her emotionally. He needed to be with her, to share his life with her, all the ups and downs and trials and triumphs that, up until this point, he had been experiencing alone. Without her, he was an empty music room without a piano. A suit of armour without a body.

But he was no longer willing to be a cold, hard, empty suit of armour. He was a living breathing man with a beating heart—a heart that beat for a young woman who was perfect for him in every way. He couldn't let another day pass without seeing her. Without telling her how he felt, how he had felt from almost the moment he'd met her. He had sensed she was his other half. The one person who could encourage him to be the person he was meant to be.

* * *

Elspeth was walking home from work with her head bowed down against the driving wind and rain. She had forgotten to bring an umbrella and the cold needles of rain were pricking her face like tiny darts of ice.

A tall figure appeared in front of her and she looked up to see Mack carrying a large umbrella. Shock swept through her. She had never expected to see him again. She blinked a couple of times to make sure she hadn't conjured him up out of desperation. But no, it really was him. Her heart leapt, her pulse raced, her hopes sprouted baby wings. 'Mack?' She couldn't keep the surprise out of her voice, couldn't stop the hammering of her heart, the ballooning of her hopes.

He placed the umbrella over her head. 'May I escort you home?' His deep mellifluous voice with its gorgeous Scottish accent almost made her swoon on the spot. How she had missed him! But why was he here in London? She knew he occasionally came down for business, but her place of work was a long way from the business district he worked in. Had he made a special trip to see her? But why?

'Oh, thanks. I didn't realise it was going to rain.' Elspeth fell into step beside him, her heart beating harder than the rain pattering down on the skin of the umbrella above them. 'What brings you to London? Business?'

He stopped walking and held her in place under the shelter of the umbrella with a gentle hand on her arm. 'I came to see you.'

Elspeth looked up into his grey-blue eyes and those baby wings of hope in her chest began to flutter. 'Why?'

Mack gave a crooked smile. 'Because I can't live

another day without seeing your beautiful face. I've missed you, *m'eudail*. Ever since we parted in France, I've been moping around like a wounded bear. I can't believe it's taken me this long to realise I love you.'

Elspeth gaped at him in shock. 'Did you say *love*?' She was dreaming…surely she was dreaming. The rain must have soaked through to her brain and turned it to mush.

He brought her closer, somehow juggling the umbrella above their heads while the rain cascaded down around them, hitting the footpath in loud plops and splatters. 'I love you with every fibre of my being. You are the one person, the only person who has opened my heart to love. You were right, I was too afraid to harbour the possibility of loving someone. I was too afraid of being vulnerable, of one day losing that love. But loving someone always comes with a risk. But I'm prepared to take that risk now, but only with you.'

'Oh, Mack, I can't believe you're here and saying the words I longed so much to hear,' she said, wrapping her arms around him and squeezing him so tightly he grunted. She looked up at him under the shadow of the umbrella. 'I love you too. So much it hurts to be away from you. I've missed you every second we've been apart.'

Mack stroked her face with his free hand. 'I never want to be parted from you again. I know it's a big ask for you to move to Crannochbrae with me. We can commute back and forth so you can keep working in London. I'll buy us a house here. I'll do whatever you want but please say you'll be my wife.'

'Your wife?' Her eyes went out on stalks. 'You're asking me to marry you?'

He smiled so widely it transformed his features. 'Forgive me for not going down on bended knee, but right now there's a river of water running over my feet.'

She glanced down and realised they were standing in a puddle, but she had barely noticed. 'Wow, so there is.'

'How far away is your flat?'

'Just a couple more streets.'

'Good, let's go there so I can do this properly.'

They ran along the footpath, their footsteps splashing as they went. Finally, they came to Elspeth's front door and she quickly unlocked it and they went inside. Mack placed the soaking umbrella in the umbrella stand and smiled. 'Now, where was I?'

'You were about to propose to me on bended knee.'

'Oh, yes, that's right.' He took her hand and then went down on one knee in front of her, his eyes holding hers. He took a familiar-looking velvet box out of his jacket pocket and, deftly flipping it open with one finger, handed her the diamond and sapphire pendant and earrings, but this time, there was a gorgeous engagement ring as well. 'My darling Elspeth, would you do me the very great honour of becoming my wife?'

Elspeth stared at the ring for a long moment, her heart pitter-pattering like the drumming rain outside. 'Oh, Mack…' She dragged him up so he was standing in front of her. 'Of course I will. I love you and want to be with you for ever.'

'Thank goodness for that.' He took the ring out of the box and then, setting the box to one side, slipped the ring on her left hand. She wasn't a bit surprised to find it a perfect fit. 'There. I should have given that to you the first time. I had to fly back to France to get it.'

Elspeth grinned at him. 'Couldn't you have got it posted?'

His eyes were twinkling as bright as the diamond on her hand. 'I wanted to tell the lady who sold me the ensemble she was right. She must have sensed my love for you even before I realised it myself.' He lowered his mouth to hers in a long and loving kiss that sent her senses spinning. She hadn't thought it possible to feel so happy, so overjoyed, so blessed. He finally broke the kiss after some breathless minutes and gazed down at her with adoration shining in his gaze.

'You are everything I could ever want in a life partner. I can't believe I'm so lucky to have found you. And I'm ashamed that I almost lost you out of my stubbornness to admit how much I loved you. I didn't even recognise my own feelings. How stupid is that? When you had that episode of anaphylaxis, I was so terrified of losing you, but I didn't recognise that as love. I insulted you by offering you an extended fling. And you were right to call me out on it. I've wasted so much time not opening up to how I really felt. Time we could have spent planning our wedding.'

Elspeth linked her arms around his neck, gazing up at him in rapture. 'I can't wait to marry you. I didn't realise how much I wanted the fairy tale until I met you. I've spent most of my life hiding away, missing out on the things other people take for granted. But meeting you changed all that and I found I couldn't go back to being happy with my old life. I'd outgrown it. You have made me outgrow it.'

He hugged her close, his expression full of love. 'I'm so glad we found each other. I can't imagine how lonely my life would be without you. You've taught me so much. I'm even playing the piano again.'

'Really?'

'Yes, really. And it was like finding a part of myself I'd lost a long time ago. You gave it back to me, my darling. You taught me how to be whole again.'

Elspeth stroked the lean length of his jaw. 'You taught me things too. I took on board what you said about handling my mother. I now check in with her first thing each day and last thing at night and guess what? She's improved out of sight, and, not only that, she's started seeing someone. She hasn't had a partner since the divorce because she's always been so preoccupied with taking care of me.'

He smiled. 'I'm glad for her and for you. I'm looking forward to meeting her. Do you think she'll approve of your choice of husband?'

'I'm sure she will,' Elspeth said. 'And Elodie will too. I just hope she finds the same happiness one day.'

'That's one of the things I adore about you,' Mack said. 'You're always thinking about others. The way you worried about Sabine at the wedding, for instance. I was so touched by that.'

'I ran into her a few weeks back,' Elspeth said. 'She turned up at my regular lunch spot close to the library. She was lovely about everything. She seems to be coping quite well without Fraser in her life. How is he doing, by the way?'

'Surprisingly well,' Mack said. 'He's enjoying his career and seems determined to turn his life around. I hope you can find it in yourself to forgive him for everything that happened between him and Elodie. I know he can be a bit of a jerk but, this time, I think he's genuinely trying to work on himself. Losing Sabine has made him grow up at long last.'

'Do you think he really loved her?'

Mack shrugged. 'Who knows? But it's too late. Sabine has moved on.'

Elspeth raised her eyebrows. 'Really? You mean she's found someone else? She didn't say anything when we met but, then again, that was weeks ago. I haven't been in touch since.'

'She's dating an old school friend, apparently he was her first boyfriend. It looks serious.'

Elspeth smiled. 'They do say you never forget your first love.'

Mack gathered her close and brought his mouth down to just above hers. 'Especially when they are as unforgettable and adorable as you.' He brushed her lips with a soft kiss and added, 'I think this occasion calls for a bit more Robert Burns, don't you?'

'What did you have in mind?'

His smile was warm and full of devotion as he quoted, *'"But to see her was to love her. Love but her, and love for ever".'* And then his mouth captured hers in a kiss that swept her away on a cloud of happiness.

\* \* \* \* \*

# COMING SOON!

We really hope you enjoyed reading this book.
If you're looking for more romance, be sure to
head to the shops when new books are
available on

# Thursday 14th October

To see which titles are coming soon, please visit

**millsandboon.co.uk/nextmonth**

# MILLS & BOON

## Coming next month

### UNWRAPPED BY HER ITALIAN BOSS
Michelle Smart

'I know how important this maiden voyage is, so I'll give it my best shot.'

What choice did Meredith have? Accept the last-minute secondment or lose her job. Those were the only choices. If she lost her job, what would happen to her? She'd be forced to return to England while she sought another job. Forced to live in the bleak, unhappy home of her childhood. All the joy and light she'd experienced these past three years would be gone and she'd return to grey.

'What role do you play in it all?' she asked into the silence.

He raised a thick black eyebrow.

'Are you part of Cannavaro Travel?' she queried. 'Sorry, my mind went blank when we were introduced.'

The other eyebrow rose.

A tiny dart of amusement at his expression—it was definitely the expression of someone outragedly thinking, *How can you not know who I am?*—cut through Merry's guilt and anguish. The guilt came from having spent two months praying for the forthcoming trip home to be cancelled. The anguish came from her having to be the one to do it, and with just two days' notice. The early Christmas dinner her sister-in-law had spent weeks and weeks planning had all been for nothing.

The only good thing she had to hold on to was that she hadn't clobbered an actual guest with the Christmas tree, although, judging by the cut of his suit, Cheekbones was on a huge salary, so must be high up in Cannavaro Travel, and all the signs were that he had an ego to match that salary.

She relaxed her chest with an exhale. 'Your role?' she asked again.

Dark blue eyes glittered. Tingles laced her spine and spread through her skin.

Cheekbones folded his hands together on the table. 'My role...? Think of me as the boss.'

His deep, musical accent set more tingles off in her. Crossing her legs, thankful that she'd come to her senses before mouthing off about being forced into a temporary job she'd rather eat fetid fruit than do, Merry made a mark in her notebook. 'I report to you?'

'*Si.*'

'Are you going on the train ride?'

Strong nostrils flared with distaste. 'It is no "train ride", lady.'

'You know what I mean.' She laughed. She couldn't help it. Something about his presence unnerved her. Greek god looks clashing with a glacial demeanour, warmed up again by the sexiest Italian accent she'd ever heard.

'I know what you mean and, *si*, I will be on the voyage.'

Unnerved further by the swoop of her belly at this, she made another nonsense mark in her book before looking back up at him and smiling ruefully. 'In that case, I should confess that I didn't catch your name. I'm Merry,' she added, so he wouldn't have any excuse to keep addressing her as 'lady'.

His fingers drummed on the table. 'I know your name, lady. *I* pay attention.'

For some unfathomable reason, this tickled her. 'Well done. Go to the top of the class. And your name?'

'Giovanni Cannavaro.'

All the blood in Merry's head pooled down to her feet in one strong gush.

*Continue reading*
UNWRAPPED BY HER ITALIAN BOSS
Michelle Smart

*Available next month*
www.millsandboon.co.uk

 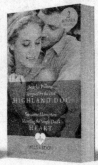 

# JOIN US ON SOCIAL MEDIA!

Stay up to date with our latest releases, author news and gossip, special offers and discounts, and all the behind-the-scenes action from Mills & Boon...

 millsandboon

 millsandboonuk

 millsandboon

*It might just be true love...*